HAIKA
SORU

HANZAI
JAPAN

HANZAI JAPAN

FANTASTICAL, FUTURISTIC STORIES OF CRIME FROM AND ABOUT JAPAN

EDITED BY NICK MAMATAS AND MASUMI WASHINGTON

HAIKASORU

SAN FRANCISCO

HANZAI JAPAN
© 2015 VIZ Media
See Copyright Acknowledgements for individual story copyrights.

Cover art by Yuko Shimizu
Design by Fawn Lau

HAIKASORU
Published by
VIZ Media, LLC
P.O. Box 77010
San Francisco, CA
94103
www.haikasoru.com

Library of Congress Cataloging-in-Publication Data

  Hanzai Japan : fantastical, futuristic stories of crime from and about Japan / edited by Nick Mamatas and Masumi Washington.
     pages cm
  ISBN 978-1-4215-8025-8 (paperback)
  1. Japan—Fiction. 2. Detective and mystery stories, American.
3. Detective and mystery stories, Japanese. 4. Paranormal
fiction, American. 5. Paranormal fiction, Japanese. I. Mamatas,
Nick, editor. II. Washington, Masumi, editor.
  PS648.J29H36 2015
  813'.0108952—dc23
                         2015028564

Printed in the U.S.A.
First printing, October 2015

CONTENTS

Introduction: My Magical Girlfriend Has Vanished, Mr. Charlie Parker
Nick Mamatas **[7]**

Foreword: Masumi Washington **[11]**

(.dis) Genevieve Valentine **[13]**

Sky Spider Yusuke Miyauchi **[31]**

Rough Night in Little Toke Libby Cudmore **[47]**

Outside the Circle Ray Banks **[69]**

Monologue of a Universal Transverse Mercator Projection
Yumeaki Hirayama **[85]**

Best Interest Brian Evenson **[109]**

Vampiric Crime Investigative Unit:
Tokyo Metropolitan Police Department Jyouji Hayashi **[121]**

Jigoku Naomi Hirahara **[159]**

The Girl Who Loved Shonen Knife Carrie Vaughn **[179]**

Run! Kaori Fujino **[197]**

Hanami S. J. Rozan **[209]**

The Electric Palace Violet LeVoit **[233]**

The Long-Rumored Food Crisis Setsuko Shinoda **[241]**

Three Cups of Tea Jeff Somers **[275]**

Out of Balance Chet Williamson **[289]**

The Saitama Chain Saw Massacre Hiroshi Sakurazaka **[307]**

Introduction—"My Magical Girlfriend Has Vanished, Mr. Charlie Parker"
—Japanese Crime Stories and the Element of Speculation
by Nick Mamatas

During the "Golden Age" of detective fiction, writer and critic Ronald Knox laid down ten commandments to make the "game" of writing mystery stories a fair one for the reader. Clues were keys to unlock the mystery, and thus were sacrosanct. The commandments keep writers from cheating with the clues: no secret twins; no undetectable and previously unknown poisons or other scientific explanations; a maximum of one secret passageway per story; no clues known to the detective, but not to the reader; and no reader access to the interior thoughts of the criminal—which would either spoil the plot or lead to the writer "cheating" by having the criminal think about everything other than the crime.

In Japan, just as in the West, Knox's commandments did not always apply. The core of the genre plays fair, but many early Japanese crime writers were pleased to deliberately subvert the rules of the game. Early Edogawa Rampo's "The Twins"—in which a man is found guilty of a capital crime and confesses to another crime: killing his own twin brother and taking his place, and committing further crimes by planting that deceased brother's fingerprints at crime scenes, except ... well, read it. Anyway, had

Rampo been explicitly going for the record in number of Knox commandments to break in one story, he could have done no better. More recently, the work of Otsuichi—some of which has won the Honkaku Mystery Award though he is not regarded as a mystery writer—often involve linguistic and narrative play: two narrators telling their stories with a significant, and obscured, gap in time; sleuths who don't even care about stopping crimes; solutions that depend on massive coincidences.

But there's a method to this madness. Ranpo's guiding star was Edgar Allan Poe, as is obvious from the author's pseudonym. Poe believed in ratiocination, but the logical processes of his detectives were themselves almost supernatural, dependent on intuition, nonrational leaps of logic, and the poetics of parallel worlds. In *The Mystery of Marie Rogêt*, Poe's sleuth nearly solves a real crime that took place in New York by solving a fictionalized version of the crime in Paris. In his afterword to the novel *Goth*, Otsuichi admits that he saw his dark sleuth characters as *yokai*, or spirits, even though in the text they are presented as ordinary, if not exactly normal, human beings.

Two other of Knox's commandments come into play:

All supernatural or preternatural agencies are ruled out as a matter
    of course.
No Chinaman must figure in the story.

In Knox's vision, the supernatural can only be a cheat—a way to make a crime unsolvable by the reader. The writer wins the "game" too easily by hiding keys in places nobody else will ever find. Knox's reference to "Chinaman" characters, itself reeking of Orientalism, was meant to be a warning against the cliché of casual racism and exoticism common among writers of the era, for whom the villainous Fu Manchu loomed large.

In speculative stories, the supernatural and super-scientific play complicating roles, not mitigating ones. More keys, stranger locks. Perhaps the most famous Japanese writer in the West, Haruki Murakami, frequently uses elements of mystery: hardboiled characters, women who inexplicably vanish (and even a missing sheep!), murders in the opening pages, and men awakening covered in blood not their own. The preternatural agencies present in Murakami's work aren't just an easy way to get someone inexplicably murdered, they're an excellent way to explore the very nature of crime, power, social trespass, and reality.

Exoticism is also huge in Japanese mystery fiction, from the very beginning of Ranpo's fetishization of Poe, to Murakami's protagonists' interest in jazz. ("No Yankee must figure in the story" would be a terrible commandment.) The privileged West, long used to writing its own stories, could use a look in the funhouse mirror of exoticism.

Hanzai Japan brings together West and East, SF/F and crime writers, to tell stories of crime with supernatural or science fictional elements. We're breaking Golden Age commandments faster than our antagonists—which range from vampires to GPS systems—break laws. We live in a science fictional world; Holmes and his magnifying glass won't do in a society with DNA tests and mathematical profiling of serial killers. And the root of our interest in crime is fear of the dark, fear of the end of life, and fear of what lies beyond. Far from marring mysteries, supernatural agencies can deepen the psychological reality of the mystery, even as the physical world dissolves into high strangeness. A mystery is about finding the key that unlocks a door. A mystery with fantasy or science fictional elements is about finding the key that unlocks the door, and transforms the room as the reader enters it.

Following *The Future Is Japanese* and *Phantasm Japan,* we started talking about a third anthology. We decided on the theme quickly enough: "Crime is next!" Yes, we are a science fiction and fantasy imprint, but why not? We like crime and mystery stories a lot, as we do science fiction and fantasy, just as you do.

But finalizing the book's title was not that easy. *Hanzai Japan?* 犯罪? はんざい? Seriously, for a book title? That sounded odd in my Japanese ears, as all Japanese pals here will agree. And our sales folks weren't happy with the word *Hanzai,* which is meaningless to most monolingual English speakers. We spent a few weeks trying to come up with alternatives, to no avail. (Want an example? Several VIZ employees liked *Japan After Midnight*—but, hey, this is not that kind of anthology.)

So, after going round and round, we came back to the first idea. By that time, I actually began liking this title. Peering at the word spelled out in the letters of the alphabet, it felt different from what I knew of it in Japanese. Maybe it was because Nick said "han-zai" sounded cool to western ears; or maybe it was fit nicely into Yuko's cover art; or maybe it was because, no matter what book title we ended up deciding upon, we were actually getting interesting stories from our contributors by that time and the stories were simply bringing this anthology to life already.

One simple word, operating beyond its language of origin, inspiring new stories: that was our goal. Now I can say this title is a good fit. (We will see if *Merriam-Webster* picks up "hanzai" in the future—just like how "emoji" made it!)

We violated at least two of Knox's mystery fiction commandments, though—these "hanzai" stories cross genres and the borders where we ourselves are living. I am really grateful to all our contributors and translators for their fantastic work. I hope you also enjoy it.

(dis.) by Genevieve Valentine

I went alone to Greenland, because I'd already gone exploring Nara Dreamland with Lars and Cormac and Eddie Leaper, and
they'll make you done with anything.

I'd started the drive in the dark, and the light was still barely
enough to take photos by, and it was so foggy—that mountain fog
that hangs so heavy it seems impossible you can't push it aside
with one hand and let it swing shut behind you—that when I saw
the man on the carousel it took me ten seconds to realize he was
dead. I hoped it was Leaper.

He was propped with his back against the pillar, head lolling
slightly, like he'd died admiring one of the horses still clinging to
its post. I didn't see any blood, not then, but his eyes had clouded
over, so he'd been dead at least overnight. (At the time I didn't
know how I knew, and I was already in the car headed back when
I realized it was condensation on his corneas, like back in New
York on the windows that faced the garden, and I braked so hard
I spun out.)

There was no bag near him. I imagined his friends panicking
and making a run for it, which seemed sadder than him actually

dying until I realized he might not have been an explorer at all, just dragged here because no one would find it.

I took a few pictures without thinking, an establishing shot and a few angles and details to sort out later, like I did with any corner of a *haikyo* that struck me. I had forty-three photos of the room where the maple had gone to seed.

For all the urban explorers who go into mental hospitals and come out with stories of chalk that writes by itself and faucets that turn on and off and the certainty that someone's there with you, I'd never heard of someone finding a dead thing larger than a fox. Were you supposed to call the police? You were probably supposed to call the police.

There were no tire tracks. There were no footprints but mine. The plants were undisturbed for fifty paces in every direction. I started breathing through my mouth, because it made less noise.

He had a postcard in his vest pocket with Nara deer on the front. On the back, someone had written "Let them eat from your hand." The receipt in his pants pocket was from a highway stop two years ago, and had directions written on it in English that mapped to the middle of the Pacific. When I set them on his legs to take a photo, they looked like leaves.

At Nara Dreamland, the first time I ever went anywhere with them, Lars and Cormac had dared each other up the Aska coaster— Lars had seen someone else's photos and was trying to top them by scaling the whole drop, and Cormac had taken some pills and was mostly just climbing because he couldn't stand still. Eddie spent three hours trying to convince me to stay there overnight with him.

"It's really beautiful at night, I've seen pictures," he'd said, as I was taking photos of peeling paint on the Main Street shops. "Do you remember it from when you came here?"

I had been five years old back then, on a trip home with my parents, and I mostly remembered the plane rides and my grandparents' faces. I should never have told Lars I'd been here. Lars couldn't keep secrets, even from people who should clearly never be told anything.

"I have work tomorrow, Eddie."

He'd twitched and gone quiet for a while, like he always did when I used his real name. ("It's mostly just Leaper," Eddie had said when Lars introduced me, like it was an honorific someone else had given him that he was bashful about.)

"But we could—" he said, and then something cracked and Cormac was shrieking and we had to run to help.

All the way across the park, my bag banging against my shoulders and my camera smashed to my chest with both hands, I was thrilled that Cormac was shouting and cursing. That meant he was probably fine, and I didn't have to worry about how relieved I'd been to hear him falling, just for something else to do.

Haikyo hunting only works well if you're with the same type of people. Maybe you need one thrill seeker to be the first one over the gate, but otherwise, you stick to your own kind.

But I don't get the thrill of crossing a threshold that some people get, and I don't have any skill at photography. The Japanese kids who do haikyo respect the condition of the buildings, but it's still a detective story to them, and white guys who came to Japan just to see haikyo were all pretty terrible, and they were all interested in the next place or the hardest place, so I still hadn't found anyone of my kind.

I might just be a bad explorer. We'd moved back to Yokohama before I got started, so I'd never done any of the haunted hospitals in the States, but I've never seen the point of going someplace just to terrify yourself. Some people like to go rooftopping or memorize forty miles of tunnels just to see if they can make it out alive without a map. Cormac told me UK explorers scan maps looking for the (dis.) notation—disused, the final mark that a place has been abandoned—and the first to get into the place gets the bragging rights. Plenty of abandoned places still had security, and for some people that was more important than the place: Witanhurst, military bunkers, anything they had to sneak into. Some people got off on the thrill of arrest.

I just like being in places that human decision has emptied out. They're quiet in a way nothing else is quiet, like even the animals left them alone for a while—some mourning period that still lingers after the foxes gnaw through the walls. It was a place that was chosen for a while, and then it was unchosen; you can count its ribs, you can wonder about the little stack of plates left behind by people who must have known they were never coming back and what made those four plates the thing they could live without.

There was a local haikyo team I met up with once, but while we were in the factory they were talking about the last place and the next place and how hard it had been to find this place, and five voices murmuring is still five voices. I didn't last long with them. Shouldn't have lasted with Lars and Cormac and Eddie either, but it's dangerous to go places by yourself, and it's definitely more comforting to go places with people you kind of hate.

It's fine. I don't mind coming back to the same place over and over. Sometimes the quiet goes—kids find it and start hanging out there, or it gets refurbished, or it gets demolished until it's just a pile of timber and glass—and then I look for new places, but there are some small houses in the mountains that I've been to a dozen times, so quiet I can sit and watch the foxes burrowing. I don't need things to be showy.

Yokohama makes me feel carbonated. Maybe New York would have made me feel the same way if we'd stayed there, but who knows. Yokohama has a few places that feel like New York—Akarenga sometimes, maybe—but just seeking them out makes me feel guilty for wanting Yokohama to be something it's not, something I wasn't really old enough to know. When kids at school asked me about the States, there was nothing to tell; it just felt like I had moved from one city into another city that sometimes mapped over its ghost, two dimensions into three, and I hadn't ever stretched to inhabit it like I was meant to.

It's good for me just to be in one of these gone places for a while, to wander through something so deliberately still, with all its hopes gone. I take pictures of the branches that have broken through the roof: saplings in the middle of a hotel lobby, a carpet of maple leaves in a dining room. I never show them to anyone—no point, maybe, but no need. I like having places just for myself; that's why I ever go out to haikyo at all.

(Lars runs a forum for exploration photos. When he hit a hundred thousand shots six months ago, he drew the number in the ground on some dirt outside an unknown site and challenged anyone to find it. He set up a subforum for the people who are trying. It's the most popular thing on the site.)

Maybe I understand the archivist kinds a little. The ones who go to libraries and historical societies and buy atlases looking for forgotten places, or who spend six weeks tracking down a family out of a photograph, just to see if they can. Not that I'm any good at it (you have to have a network to be good at it), but I understand. It took me weeks to get up the courage to go to Takakanonuma Greenland, but by then I could have told you the layout of that park with my eyes closed.

The difference between the Greenland and Dreamland amusement parks is that Dreamland exists in a way you can track. There are pictures of soldiers and families visiting when it was still open. There's video footage of people riding the rollercoasters and the swings and wandering down Main Street, holding children who have that slightly bewildered look that children tend to get at amusement parks, surrounded by so much fun that will soon be over and that's all out of your control—the birth of some lifelong dissatisfaction.

But not Greenland. When you go looking for Greenland, the park might as well have been haunted since it opened for all the pictures you can find of it in its heyday. That place had been born empty in the mist and stayed that way, like it had been made for the ivy to devour.

I made notes and looked at maps and made some archives requests of the train stations near Hobara pretending I was studying civil engineering, and decided where I had to go. And after the Nara Dreamland visit I took all the extra precautions you made when going someplace solo; I didn't want any of them coming with me, but I knew things could get out of hand if you went exploring alone.

I don't remember driving back from Greenland, that first time. I had the police number programmed into my phone, a call never sent that whole five-hour drive. I deleted it when I got home, and then I sat on my bed and scanned through fifty pictures of the corpse. His hair looked like a businessman's, gone a little to seed; too long between cuts. My notes from the car, almost too shaky to read, were that he was chubby, but when I was at home and flipping through the photos I realized he might just be swollen. I set down my camera for a while.

He had no tattoos on his forearms. Someone had rolled up his sleeves to the elbows to prove it. My first thought was that he had rolled them up himself, before, but it was cold enough that his eyes had frosted overnight, so he wouldn't have. Most likely someone dressed him after.

I thought about that for a long time, sitting cross-legged on my bed. I wondered if he really had just died of natural causes, like a cat that runs away from home when it knows the end is coming. He was young; maybe he remembered the park from childhood and had wanted to come back here, and hadn't bothered to bring much with him because there wasn't much he'd need. Maybe he'd been humming carousel music until his heart stopped.

I doubted it. His shoes were worn nearly through—in one of the pictures the sole was peeling near the arch, and it looked like a sheet of vellum, there was so little left of it. But they were untouched: not a spot of mud, not a blade of grass.

Someone had killed him, and washed the body clean, and dressed it carefully—sleeves rolled up for testimony. Someone had carried him through the castle gates like a new bride and chosen the carousel for him, and set him gently against the post so he could look at the horses until he was found.

And he must have been meant to be found. There were so many of us looking for places, looking for this place, looking for things to take photos of, that whoever killed him had staged him to be seen. My establishing shot was at an awkward angle; I couldn't tell if he was really looking at the horse, or if he was meant to be looking at whoever approached.

Lars sent me a message at two in the morning: *Hey, you haven't been around much. Cormac's out of his cast. Feel like going out?*

We went up to some abandoned factory housing that took us nearly five hours to get to. Lars kept the coordinates secret as long as he could, shaking his head and giggling when Cormac asked him, hinting at things it wasn't.

When Lars got to "No one will get smallpox," I said, "Lars, just tell us or don't."

He blinked for a second before he admitted what it was. After that I put headphones on and ignored everybody from the front seat, which I always got to sit in, because Lars's GPS was broken and I had to translate signs.

("Good thing you've turned local," Lars had said when he pulled up, like he always did, "or we'd die of old age in Yokohama."

We all waited the three seconds it usually took for Eddie to remind everyone it was also nice to have a girl around in case security stopped you, but he must have still been upset I wouldn't fuck him in Dreamland, and he kept quiet.)

"Where have you been, anyway?" Cormac asked me eventually. "You haven't been in the forums. You going anywhere?"

"I'm never in the forums. I don't care who finds Lars's number."

"Jealous, you are. There have been eighty guesses so far. Somebody did a counterfeit just to see if Lars would return to the real one to check on it. Idiots." He leaned forward. "Lars told me where it was."

"He'd tell anyone," I said, and Lars laughed like I was trying to be funny and said, "I could tell you, too," and I shook my head and turned up the volume.

"Let's just find someone else who likes this shit," Cormac said at some point, between songs. "Anybody Japanese could read the fucking signs, she's not worth it," and it was a solid two seconds before Lars answered, "It's fine, she's fine."

The homes looked about eighty years old, which made sense when I thought about it but still surprised me. The roof had fallen in on the kitchen of the first house, and we couldn't get into the biggest bedroom because the door had swollen and molded shut to the frame, so Lars and Cormac and Eddie all took turns getting artistic shots of the panes without paper and whatever they could manage of the room beyond.

I went into the smaller room, which had to have been a child's, it was so small. It had been wallpapered in Moga postcards that had crumbled or bubbled or warped, so it looked like the wall was swelling with huge grubs that had black bobs and lipstick for camouflage, rolling down the wall in herds.

There hadn't been any grubs at Greenland. No flies, no beetles, none of the things you'd think would be interested once someone had died. I didn't remember him smelling like anything; nothing rotten had coated my mouth, like the smells of dead things do even when you try to keep them out. Had he been there long enough that the smell was gone? I imagined a scar down the center of his chest, right along the placket of his shirt, where someone had taken the innards out, so the rest would last longer.

But his eyes had been pristine, milky and round and still glistening, not an eyelash disturbed. The insects couldn't have taken over. Not by then.

"You thinking of stealing one?"

I jumped. "What?"

Eddie gestured at my camera, where it hung forgotten over my sternum. "Take nothing but photographs, remember. Leave the postcards for posterity."

"I wasn't going to steal anything," I said, but Eddie was already taking a photo of the wall like it was evidence he could use later if the Missing Eighty-Year-Old Postcard Council called him into court.

The woods around the houses were deep and quiet, the trees nearly interlocking, which gave everything a grim darkness shot through with bands of light, and I took pictures of that every ten minutes, watching the puddles of sun across the ground and wondering how late in the morning it was before the condensation on his eyes warmed and disappeared, until Lars came out shouting for me because they thought I had fallen through the floor to the cellar and fainted.

The Ferris wheel at Greenland is at the farthest edge from the sad castle entrance, so you have to work to reach it—my civil engineering class would have frowned on having something so distinctive so far away—but it's worth it. A ring of circular cars, like a model of an atom or a cartoon firework before it bursts. And decay has only made it quainter, pastels and patina and the entrance nearly blocked off with feathery plants like nature can't wait to crowd inside. It's already made it into the lower cars—the saplings have gotten big enough to push inside, their branches trailing leaves against the seats. When I went back to Greenland, alone, I made myself take photos of it again before I went to the carousel. I was an explorer; the Ferris wheel was as good as anything.

I couldn't look directly to see if he (it, he) was still there, so I watched the ground for prints (there were only mine, softened by the damp but still marked where I had stepped across the green), and then looked through the viewfinder as I rounded the curve, until I saw the slumped silhouette. Then the shutter sounded like doors slamming shut right on my heels, there was so much blood in my ears. My hands were shaking. I pressed my elbows to my sides, to keep the shots steady.

He had no tattoos on his ankles or his neck. I hadn't been willing to do more than lift his collar to see if he had anything lower on his back; the glimpse was enough to tell if he had affiliation tattoos, and it would have been rude to drag him onto the ground to check for any on his thighs.

I set his head to rights afterward, so he could look at the horses. The mist had shaken loose from his eyes, and it made him look more interested in everything. (I knocked some air loose from his nose when I pushed him up. He smelled like the floor of the forest, sour and wormed. When I pulled back from it I saw the calluses where his glasses should have been.)

His shirt was from Uniqlo, which meant nothing, and when I undid his buttons there was no easy scar on his stomach where he'd been emptied out. *Be brave,* I thought, *he's like any other unchosen place,* and so I slid my hand lightly around his ribs—I winced when I pressed in; I was ticklish and always sympathized—and felt a scar that was still raised. Either very old, or very new.

His fingernails were as clean as my father's, and he had a callus on his right index finger from writing too much. His mouth had been sewn shut with careful, invisible stitches behind the lips, so tight you couldn't get a look at the teeth. I ran my hands over his lips to count the stitches (fifty-two), and then along his jaw to count his teeth (three missing).

The postcard was gone.

I froze with my hand still in the pocket of his vest; my first thought was, *Maybe he moved it to another pocket,* and when I realized I laughed too loudly and covered my mouth with my free hand. Then I checked his other pockets anyway, in case I had put it away wrong, and then underneath him, even through the cracks in the boards, just in case. But it was missing.

The receipt was still there, and I took it out with the sides of my fingers—too late to worry about fingerprints, but still—and got half a dozen photos, just in case.

I was glad I had taken so many shots on my way in; my hands were shaking, and I would never have been able to put his vest and collar the way I had found them without some reference to go by.

I waited until I reached Utsunomiya to pull over, and found a café where I could sit with my computer. (I couldn't look up any of this from back home.)

Looking for someone who's gone missing is like looking for a building that has. The news only reports it if he's famous enough, and in that case you have to think his corpse would set a bigger example than being left in some mostly-forgotten amusement park. You can't call district police and start asking questions about dental records, but you never call looking for maps directly, either. You go to the library and make up some excuses and start hunting; if you don't have anything to go on, you take the first map you can find and look for anything (dis.).

I started in Nara. The postcard could mean anything, but if he'd been at one of the deer parks, someone would have caught him. He must have died long enough ago for the first round of flies to have been in him and gone, not quite enough time for the second. Hair already shaggy, wearing glasses. I started pulling photos.

It took me under a thousand to find him, in the background of someone's shot of the red Tamukeyama gate. He still had a watch, then, and he carried a small drawstring backpack, and his button-down shirt was checked in threads of navy. (It probably hadn't made any difference to whoever had left him, but I was glad he'd been dressed in a style he liked even after someone killed him.)

My computer could go closer than my phone, and the coordinates from the receipt put me on Manuae, which was so small I had to be zoomed in completely before I could see anything but water. It was an atoll shaped like a ring. This close, Manuae had a little (dis.) at the end of its name.

There was an extra four-digit number tacked on to the end of the coordinates—the hour on a clock. A lock code. Number of people. Kilos of cocaine.

I felt with every guess like I'd felt in the plane on the way to Yokohama at thirteen, watching movies in Japanese because

I couldn't sleep, refusing to put on subtitles and getting a bigger knot in my stomach with every word I didn't understand. All of this was just missing vocabulary—I didn't want my share of anything, I didn't want justice for whoever he was. He was an abandoned hotel, he was a peeling shrine, he was a stack of plates; I was closing a window that had no panes in it.

As I was checking into the hotel for the night, my father called. He wanted to make sure I was still alive, he said on the message, his voice fading by the end of it like he was already hanging up.

Lars messaged me: LEAPER THINKS YOU DON'T LIKE HIM.

A little later: WANT TO DO ANOTHER AMUSEMENT PARK?

WHICH ONE?

GULLIVER MAYBE? OR GREENLAND. OR RUSSIAN VILLAGE BUT CORMAC ALREADY WENT.

I WENT WITH SOME PEOPLE TO GREENLAND LAST YEAR, I wrote, because nothing takes the shine off for most explorers like knowing someone's already been there. IT WAS BORING. WE SHOULD DO GULLIVER. OR THE SEX MUSEUM IN HOKKAIDO?

SEX MUSEUM COULD BE FUN, said Lars, after a pause where I could almost hear him looking up other pictures to see if it was worth it. BUT TOO FAR AWAY. CORMAC'S TEACHING ENGLISH TWICE A WEEK NOW. WE COULD DO THE GRAND MOULIN?

HEARD IT WAS DEMOLISHED.

It had been beautiful; a hotel built three stories high and decorated like New Orleans, balconies like lacework and the floors hardwood under the peeling brocade carpet. Moss had grown on it in patches, and the gold-stamped wallpaper was peeling in wide coils like doll's hair. There were still some desk chairs in rooms on the third floor, and you could sit and look out at the treetops and understand exactly what had happened with a hotel set so far back in the woods it felt like you were the only living soul for a hundred miles. The birds had come back, and after a few hours I saw a rabbit race from the front door into the cover of trees. They said the owner killed himself and that's why it was empty, but no ghosts moved, there or anywhere.

I'd driven back over when I heard it was demolished, to see if it was true. Sometimes people see one fallen wing and assume the whole building is unstable, or someone will say a place is gone just to discourage others from going, you never know. But it had been eaten, a crater among the trees with a few piles of brick and lacework still waiting to be carted away. There were no birds nearby; there wouldn't be.

:(TOO BAD. WHAT ABOUT A LOVE HOTEL?

WITH EDDIE?

LOLOL. HE'S FINE. WE SHOULD TRY YUI.

Yui was where the murder happened. Supposedly. That room is scorched out down to the beams. Some explorers said her ghost burned it down, and the story stuck. You can't keep explorers out of there, now, and Lars's forum has a whole section dedicated to it with photos of the red handprints that half of them swear are paint and the other half swear are blood.

MAYBE. SEE WHAT CORMAC SAYS.

Cormac said the Fuurin motel was closer, and so that's where we went. I pulled my mask up and pretended the rubber seal made it hard to talk, and halfheartedly took pictures as Cormac and Lars dared one another to get aerial shots from the roof.

I stood for a while in the Japan room, which looked like a set from a Bond movie right down to the TV in one corner, like what I remembered Japan looking like even after I had been home to meet my grandparents as a kid, before that half-memory space filled up enough for me to reconcile it.

From the medieval Europe room, Eddie and Cormac were taking turns getting their pictures with the suit of armor. There was a spider on the wall beside them. They hadn't seen it; it was as big across as my hand and utterly still except when Eddie laughed, and then it raised one leg, as if deciding whether or not to strike.

Watch out, I almost said, or *Behind you*, but even if they listened they'd probably just kill it. Take nothing but photographs, kill nothing but insects.

Some of the roof had fallen in, but it wasn't yet decay, just neglect. The garden courtyard outside the Japanese room hadn't yet been overtaken by the plants. It was one good cleanup away from being usable again, and seemed to be clinging to its chances; the sort of place that hasn't yet gone quiet the way it needs to for me to be happy in it.

I looked over my shoulder. On every wall that was still whole, spiders, holding perfectly still.

It was almost a week before I could get the time to rent a car and go back to Greenland. By now the spine of the coaster didn't even give me the thrill of having found it. I was just relieved it was still there, and I was the only living thing in it.

The body was breathing. I took two steps back before I did the math and remembered it was about time for the second round of insects inside him. (Or the first round, if he had been preserved before he got here. Nearly anything could disrupt decay. The more research I did the more I thought something had to be wrong with this body.) They must have been inside the stomach cavity, making homes for themselves; his lower chest shifted in and out an inch at a time.

The postcard was back in his pocket. Nothing else was written on the back. I had expected another line, some dialogue or a strike-through when the message was received, but the only sign it had been touched was that one corner had snagged on the pocket and folded when they slid it back in. I took pictures, just to compare later. There was a dot of black marker on the front, and I couldn't remember if it had been there before. It would probably be enough for whoever came back.

And they would come back. The only one of them who had respected the quiet was the dead man, whose wrists sometimes stretched as if there was still a pulse beneath them, thanks to the worms and the ants. He was an abandoned hotel, an empty place; he understood. It was the others who didn't. The people who made the place had decided this place un-existed, and they had deliberately left it behind. It was cruel of them to interrupt it.

I wrote, "This place isn't safe" on the back of the postcard, my kanji unsteady (just as well, if you're trying to look terrified). I walked out backwards, used a branch behind me to cover the worst of my footsteps. There weren't many. I was learning.

Inside the Ferris wheel car, hidden by brush and with a missing door in case I had to run for it, I wrapped myself in the emergency blanket I kept in my rucksack. It was cold, and it was only going to get colder, but I wanted to wait, and condensation on your eyes looked pretty enough, if you died.

They would come overnight—tonight, maybe, or the night after. They'd see the note and take him away, with the insects burrowed warmly inside him. When I came back out into the park, tomorrow morning or the morning after, there would be only the Ferris wheel behind me and the carousel horses ahead, and the kind of quiet that would slowly become birds.

When I reached to turn off my phone, Lars had sent a message: BACK TO DREAMLAND? AN OVERNIGHT. EDDIE'S ASKING.

SURE. TONIGHT. MEET YOU THERE.

I should call the police, I thought. All three of them should be arrested. Leave that place alone.

Greenland was beautiful in the dark. The rollercoaster snaked against the stars, and the curtain mist settled over everything along the ground. If they came to get the body, I wouldn't even see it. If they came looking for me, I wouldn't know until it was too late. If it was other explorers who had taken the card and put it back in a fit of conscience, then it would serve them right to piss themselves and get on a plane back home.

If there was no one, and it was just the corpse and me and some card that had gone missing and come back all by itself, I'd be waiting a long time. That was all right. It was quiet here. It was neither one place nor another, until somebody came.

A spider crawled across my shoe; then it stopped, perfectly still.

Sky Spider by Yusuke Miyauchi
translated by Terry Gallagher

1.

I can hear the sound of a future that never arrives.

Music from strings that are not here, from a bow that is not here. Vibrato, pizzicato, harmonics—at this moment, I am a performer, and at the same time just a listener. From scale to scale, I drift, I dive, I swim, through the sea, through the shoals of interwoven airborne sound.

That would be the music I would be playing. In a future that has been shut off.

And so, I think, this must be a dream.

The note I hear at this moment is just the tiniest bit off-pitch. A little flat, the tone turning darker. Wait ... no, it was deliberate!

I open my eyes, ever so slightly. This should be a direct flight to Tokyo. I am on my way home from attending a performance competition that one of my students entered.

But what is going on now?

The airplane is shaking, and a young man is playing the violin, passionately. I cannot name the tune, in part because of his bold interpretation. It is the violin part of the Sibelius concerto.

Some of the cabin's portholes are hung with yellow curtains. The upholstery of the seats matches the red of the carpet. But the carpet is soiled with black stains, holes, and scorch marks Someone's old suitcase is rattling. The metal of the armrests is rough on the elbows. Water drips from the ceiling onto my shoulder. I feel something strange, and reflexively I check my cello case. Whew, it's there. I take out my cell phone, but then I remember I am in an airplane.

I pick up the menu. All I can make out on the faded blue paper is burns, and something like cognac ads or something.

I feel chilly, but I can't find any blankets. I hear the calm voices of other passengers, and a violin's accelerando. It is a strange sensation, out of place in an airplane.

Someone is standing in the aisle, speaking to me: "Old man, you are very lucky."

I don't understand right away. I think he might be speaking French, and I stammer out, *"Pour quoi?"*

And the man responds: "Sky Spider. You can hear his performance."

"Who are you talking about?"

The man points his chin at the young man playing the violin, and then turns back to me.

"And you are …?"

"Takaido."

"Chinois?"

Japanese is the pat answer. The man has very masculine features. He is buff, like someone who's into sports. Asked his name, he replies simply, "Cerdan."

Wine is served. I choose white.

The attendant pours into a short glass, mutters something respectful, and moves on. Her blond hair is tied up and covered with a pillbox cap. My glass is yawing precariously, and I down the contents in one gulp.

The young man, Sky Spider, continues his performance.

His movements are awkward, but his sound is refined, meticulous even. I wonder who taught him. His technique is old-fashioned, but the effect is very powerful. I feel as if, within the melody, I can hear something like an unquenchable thirst.

The young man is unlike any pupil I have ever taught. Unconsciously, I begin to lean forward. Cerdan addresses me once again: "Jump in," he says.

Jump in where, I wonder. I wonder if I have heard him correctly, and I do not answer immediately. He looks irritated, and he points to the cello case beside me.

"You play too, don't you?"

"Not really," I stammer.

Several passengers turn to face me, expectantly. I feel a pain in my chest. The young man smiles wanly, and launches into the next piece. Another Sibelius. This time the Canon.

Subtitle: For Violin and Cello.

My gaze meets the young man's. The lightbulb in my head switches on. I open the cello case, and start to rosin the bow. As long as there is no problem with the left hand, the pitches will match. We can play a few bars, and then everyone will understand.

It happened when I was 21.

I am a performer, not a teacher. And I have confidence. At some point in the future, I will have the sound of my dreams. But that future will never come. I will have a car accident, and I will injure the tendons of my right hand. I will move to protect my instrument, and lose something even more vital. This is what the doctor will say: "There will be some aftereffects, but you will have no problems with your everyday life."

Nearly a half-century has now passed. I stopped performing, and chose the path of nurturing the next generation.

My yearning is still with me.

And that is why I am still carrying this regret, to the point of buying two tickets.

How horrible will it be to die, still carrying this future that might have been?

The expression on my face must be awful enough. A young woman looks my way, and tells me, "Everything will be fine." I feel like I have seen her face somewhere before. But that is not possible. In no way am I fine.

The violin runs up, and I play my first note, emphatically.

That is when it happens:

The feel of the bow hits me. It is a feeling I can never forget, no matter how long it has been. No matter how often I try, each time, it drops from my hand. That thing that I had finally "got," that runs the length of the bow, from grip to tip. That feeling in my hand when I am playing the cello properly. The high I feel when my hands are in complete harmony.

Like the slow gathering of the tide, I can feel the healing of my deep wounds. Am I able to perform again, as I thought I never would? Or …

The violin carries the melody, and I follow, and then pass it back. Sky Spider's lips move, just a bit. Oddly, I am able to understand what he is saying. I am certain that this is what he says:

"I've been waiting for you for so long."

This is exactly what I am also thinking. Not just because it is my turn with the melody. We have each found a partner who understands us, and for the first time, harmony comes to life. We play, and over and over we return to the beginning. Here is a young man with whom I have never exchanged a word, but I am experiencing sympathetic resonance, as if I have a tuning fork inside.

What is happening here?

As I play, I look around the plane.

The plane is still shaking, but no longer can I hear the roar of the jets. Many of the passengers are dressed rather formally for the flight. One has a cigarette, relishing every puff. His clothing is dazzlingly colorful, jangly, like a black-and-white film that has been colorized. A female passenger waves. She wears a skirt with a wide hem, her hair has a soft wave, and she wears high heels. Seeing her, I remember a certain story.

There is a ridiculous urban legend musicians tell. With all their flying around, sooner or later anybody might end up wandering onto a "Ghost Ship," or so the story goes. And when that happens, such a passenger might hear a violin with a sound like the nectar of the gods. Some such passengers might be able to take that sound home with them. And some might be possessed, or even go mad.

That is the story a student of mine told me. I chided her. *Instead of dreaming, move your hands some more,* I said. At the time, she was my best student.

"Really?" she asked. "Don't you think you'd like to try and see for yourself?"

I thought this response was brilliant. But on the forced march of a concert tour she suffered a miscarriage. Things between her and her husband soured, and at some point she put music behind her.

I think about this often. What is the life of a musician?

A ghost ship.

Something that should never be.

What then is this scene before my eyes? The truth is communicating with my right hand, I can feel the bow.

There is just one face I recognize. Who is he? Oh, that's right, a man I often see at concerts. Did he too wander aboard here just like me?

I look behind me. There should be an aisle leading to the rear cabin, but instead, I see nothing, as if clouds have enshrouded my head. Is that the path to the real world? Or …?

A cold something runs up my spine.

Sky Spider suddenly plays more vigorously: Johan Halvorsen's *Passacaglia on a Theme by Handel*. The piece was originally written for violin and viola, but there is also a version for violin and cello. It is a difficult piece, but nothing to be afraid of.

A short way into the piece, there is a passage where the cello carries the theme. It is a slow, beautiful piece of music, but it gets much more difficult as it goes along. Up-tempo arpeggios are followed by pizzicato on the cello, and then legato, in a repeating pattern. For the violin, it is the reverse. The development strains the players' nerves. Even so, it is a piece I could go on playing forever.

Across the aisle, Cerdan is swaying.

A passacaglia is actually a dance piece, so this is not an inappropriate response.

The two of us negotiate a passage with double triplets, and move into the marcato section. I match my breathing to the young man's, and he his to mine.

The woman who told me "Everything will be fine" looks back and forth, from Sky Spider to me, with affection. There follows a section with a number of sixteenth notes that can only be described as sadistic, followed by two measures in adagio, and then the piece is at an end. The young man extends his hand to shake mine, and says, "That was fun. Between the near shore and the far shore, the passing of years can be a lonely thing …"

I hug the young man, and pat him on the back. At the same time, my eyes are drawn to the young man's violin. The very head of it, the scroll has a distinctive line. Unmistakable.

His violin is a Stradivarius.

"Who is your teacher?" I ask. "Must be someone famous …"

The young man does not answer.

Instead, the woman who had been watching us stands up.

"It can't be," I say, under my breath. "It can't be."

It is not that I knew her from somewhere—she is someone *any* string player would know. She has a gentle smile, and that is her disguise. I know her by the grimace she generally shows when performing. Her eyes, though, exuding quiet determination, are the same.

Ginette Neveu.

A face any string player should recognize. The violinist of the century, recognized as a teenager as a genius. Which makes it all the more surprising to see her here now.

She had died young, at the age of thirty.

She and her beloved Stradivarius were on an Air France flight from Paris to America, and it had crashed in the Azores, in the Atlantic Ocean.

Finally I understand what this place is.

All the passengers in their outdated outfits. The burned carpet, the musician who does not belong.

This is that 1949 Air France flight.

2.

Several passengers approach, their hands extended in greeting.

I decide to sit down in the seat of one of these passengers, so I can hear what Sky Spider has to say.

He is fourteen, and is studying with Neveu. He wants to know what to learn next, what to learn after that, staring at me the whole time as he speaks. He seems sincerely desperate to play in larger ensembles. Duos just don't do it for him.

I was unaware that Neveu had had a pupil before her accident. Somehow, though, seeing this young man's talent, I understand.

I feel gentle waves, the after-echoes of the performance. Like after swimming in the sea.

If this is a dream, I do not wish to wake up. That is my true, unvarnished feeling.

I ask him to show me his violin. The old varnish feels soft, familiar. I play a scale on the A string. It has a surpassing, brilliant tone.

A Stradivarius—*Neveu's* Stradivarius—must be worth at least ten million.

I reel off one phrase after another. Because I yearn, I listen to the music, and I listen to the music, and I yearn some more. I should be more restrained with this vibrato. Here is a quadruple stop, and in my imagination, I want to emphasize the empty fifth. But just because I want to doesn't mean I can. I can say this because it's as if I'm standing beside myself, looking at myself.

But there is no way of knowing!

And that is when it happens. Someone, or something, snatches the violin from my hands.

It is the passenger who wandered onto the flight at the same time as me. Before I can stop him he runs down the aisle toward the rear of the plane, into the haze. He had been thinking about stealing the violin ever since he got on board.

Give me back my sound!

I am surprised to realize I still have this much ego left. It is funny to be fighting over the same violin. I cannot stop him. I get up from my seat, and go after him. Cerdan taps me on the shoulder.

"It's all right."

"But ..."

Just as I think he has gotten away, I hear a startled cry. It seems the man fell to the floor. But that isn't it. He has *evaporated*. Simply crumpled, like a freeze-dried rose, turned to dust in an instant, leaving only his clothing, and the violin, behind. I run to the spot where he had just been.

All that is left of him is like cotton candy, wisping away at the slightest touch. Something protrudes from the breast pocket of his clothing. I pluck it away. It is an air ticket, and the flight number is the one I am supposed to be on. This is no longer just some story happening to someone else.

If this means I will never get out of here, that's all right by me. If it means I can play the cello again, that is all I ever really wanted to do. But disappearing into a handful of dust like that does not appeal to me.

Cerdan stands up, a sour expression on his face, so I ask him what is going on.

"Well, you see, it's like this ..."

He looks around the plane as he racks his brain for the words. Several people are nodding as he continues, "It is just as you imagine. This is a Ghost Ship. Or, it might be more precise to say, a Ghost Flight."

"And you all are …?"

"Well, ghosts, of course. Truth be told, we don't exactly know ourselves. And, as for that man just now, I've never seen anyone disappear quite that way before—and I've seen many people vanish in my time. As far as I can tell, he just disappeared. Just like the rest of us, caught between the near shore and the world to come. No loitering."

"I have heard of this ship before. It means that travelers departing from here existed in the past. That man just now, though, well, it didn't work out for him."

"In this place, there are two rules."

Cerdan's explanation is simple.

The first rule is that things that were here to begin with may not be taken away.

The second rule is that things brought here from somewhere else *may* be taken away.

The way out? Just take the cello case and walk down the aisle.

"… but I drank some wine …"

"A little thing like that is no problem. Eating and drinking: fine. But more important than that, I like it that you're here. We have been lonely."

Cerdan went on: "All of this is just your imagination. You are in control; stay if you like, leave if you wish."

A shadow falls across his face. It seems something is tugging at his heartstrings.

Need to think about this.

That's what I think to myself. What manner of place is this? What guarantee do I have that I won't end up dead? My mind races, searching my memory.

I get it now.

If he really wants me to stay, he would not have to go to the trouble of explaining the rules to me. All he would have to do would be to make me so anxious I would never even think of walking down the aisle.

There must be some other reason he told me the rules.

Something else crosses my mind.

I can easily imagine how anyone might wander onto a Ghost Ship without realizing it.

One of my pupils told me this story.

I am sitting next to Sky Spider, doing my best to look like nothing's wrong.

I whisper: "Is there someplace where we can see the outside?"

As he inclines his head toward me, I continue: "I'd like to talk to you alone."

3.

Sky Spider chooses an office near the rear cabin of the plane. Outside the porthole, it is night. But is it real night, or an imaginary stratosphere? I come straight to the point: "Won't you come with me?"

Sky Spider's features sharpen.

He looks at me abashedly, as if scolding someone who loves him, whom he does not love back. This would never change, no matter how many years passed. I pause, then continue: "I mean, wouldn't you like to give a recital, in the world?"

"But I ..."

"You are quite talented. I could make arrangements for a suitable venue."

A look of calm understanding comes over Sky Spider's face, but then he shakes his head.

"You understand, don't you? We are ..."

"*Mais non,*" I interrupt him. And now I understand what has been gnawing at me.

Things that were here to begin with may not be taken away.

Why had Cerdan told me this?

To stay, or to go, it is up to me, he had said. If that is the case, it makes no difference if I return to the world, or if I disappear. But if that is so, why had he gone to the trouble of explaining the rules to me?

It must be there is *something he does not wish to be taken away.*

What might that be?

No, it couldn't be. There is just one possibility I cannot get out of my mind.

She was my best student.

And on the forced march of a concert tour, she had suffered a miscarriage.

Only afterward did I realize what was strange.

The young woman flitting about.

Caught between the near shore and the far shore, the passing of years is lonely.

"Everyone else is just as they were when Neveu died. Only you are different."

This can only mean one thing.

"You … are alive!"

For a long spell, Sky Spider remains silent. He is in agony. Realizing, though, that he cannot hold back, he slowly opens his mouth. In broken bursts he tells this most unlikely story.

Sky Spider was born in September 1981.

His mother, who had wandered unwittingly onto the Ghost Ship, went into an early labor and gave birth prematurely. She had not wanted children. Realizing there would be no evidence, she left the newborn in this place, and returned to the world alone.

The child had been raised by everyone on the plane, and Neveu had taught him to play the violin.

The ghosts on the plane were the only family he had ever known.

He was aware of the outside world. But all he had ever seen was the world within the fuselage of the plane. He only knew how to do one thing, and that was to play the violin.

"These people are my family. And on top of that, I don't think I could survive on the outside."

"You yourself …" I say, choosing my words carefully.

Pushing too hard might work against me here. I know that, but I can't help myself.

"You're the one who told me this, aren't you? Torn from the world, growing old is lonely. You actually realize that you are *L'Etranger*. And it may be as you say, that the outside world is *L'Enfer*. Or it may be that we are in *Purgatoire*."

"I know, all of this. If I exit the plane, I will have to go through immigration. And then customs. As a practical matter, one cannot just enter a country bringing along an extra person with no ID, with no records."

"And also …" he starts to say. "This is where I was born. It is my fate that I cannot get out of here."

"That's not so," I say. "*Things brought here from somewhere else may be taken away.* I believe that that is your fate. Think back! I play the cello!"

I would remove the cello from its case, and put Sky Spider inside.

At the Immigration Desk, there would be no hand luggage inspection, and I would pass right though. Then, Sky Spider would get out of the case, and walk through customs on his own two feet. The customs officer would not ask to check his visa or travel history. He would just show the cover of his passport, and breeze through.

"Hang on a sec!"

Sky Spider is visibly shaken by this absurd plan.

"I don't even have a passport."

I grin, and hand him a French passport.

"Remember, there was something in the breast pocket of the clothing that man left behind. I had to check it out."

We are in a secret place. It was there for whatever reason, just because it might be useful at some point. I hear a sound outside. One of the ghosts is eavesdropping.

"The jig is up," I mutter.

I had been utterly focused on convincing Sky Spider. This was foreseeable.

"We've been spotted."

4.

It is like air pressure. The unanswered thoughts of the ghosts press against us, then penetrate. My own reflexive fear threatens to paralyze me, sap me of all my strength. Finally I would be made to see. Or perhaps there is a fate worse than death. Now it is too late. There must be seven or eight of them. Including Cerdan.

"That's too bad," he says, standing in the doorway, glaring at me.

"You, sir, may leave. But you may not take the young man."

"You're wrong!" I respond, in desperation, near collapse. "Don't you think we should ask him what he wants?"

No.

Respecting Sky Spider's wishes—that in itself would be fine. For an instant, though, I pause in my thoughts. If he stays behind, he might be able to work his way through this situation. I begin to cover my trepidation in a florid cloak, one that the boy might still see through. He'll see my hesitation, and in that moment, be crushed.

These words will get us out of here. It is the only way, if I am to save the young man.

"Well …" Cerdan starts to say. "We are a family, are we not?" '

"I …"

Sky Spider is clearly at a loss. The pressure of the dead is rising, as if to penetrate the crevices of his heart. And in that moment, a piercing C# is heard. For an instant, the ghosts turn their attention in that direction. On the far side of the aisle, Neveu has drawn the bow across the strings of the violin, and then she puts it down quietly.

"Follow your heart!" she says, in a voice that carries well. "The sound of those who waver is worth no more than fingernails!"

Her words pierce my heart.

A person who has lost their own music. A former cellist, unable to let go of his own regrets for nearly half a century. I may be able to get off this plane, but surely I would lose my music once again. Of what value is such a man?

A man who cannot play the cello. How would the young man see me then?

And what if? What if, if he were to leave the airplane, Sky Spider were to lose his own talent? There could be no guarantee. Turning to him, I see fear in the young man's face. Surely I have overinflated my own expectations.

The ghosts step nearer.

Toward where I stand. And even more so, into my heart. Violent emotion swells within me. This is not something out of this world. It is something commonplace, pure happenstance. And that makes it all the more difficult to resist. For example, fear. For example, the relief of submission. The seduction of leaving the world behind, to live with music. Amid all of this mixed together, I listen. A high, eardrum-piercing pitch. The brakes of the car that had stolen my gift.

That's right.

What had happened to me in that accident? I had moved to protect my instrument, and I had injured my arm, right? (Wouldn't you like to try for yourself?)

Wrong.

This ship is not for testing people. It is for revealing their true nature.

I lift my head, and look around me at the ghosts. My voice is so relaxed it surprises even me.

"The moment may be imperfect, but music has value, don't you think?"

I wait for Sky Spider to respond.

In a small voice, he says, "I would like to play a recital outside ..."

A voice so minute it was on the verge of disappearing. But it had conveyed a clear decision, and it brimmed with spirit. Cerdan stares at Sky Spider, but finally he nods in assent. "I understand," he says.

Waves of something like sadness wash over me. Two or three particularly persistent ghosts reach out. But Cerdan quickly interposes himself. It is over in an instant. A left hook flashes, and before you know it, the ghosts are down on the carpet, moaning.

"Old man, you are very lucky," Cerdan says caustically to me in my befuddlement. "Marcel Cerdan was middleweight champion, with a record of 119 wins and four losses. Just see what he can do!"

He adds, self-mockingly, "He died in 1949, *in an Air France accident*. As long as he remains here, though, times are good!" Cerdan's support encourages me.

Damn straight.

Who cares if I cannot play the cello? That is simply an inescapable fact. If Sky Spider forgets how to play the violin, I can always teach him again. The living should live in reality.

I take the young man's hand, and walk the path that Cerdan opens for me.

He has long, soft fingers. Surely that is how he earned the name Sky Spider.

The remaining passengers fall silent, respecting our wish. Sky Spider removes the clothes he received from the ghosts, puts on a coat of mine, and climbs into the cello case.

Neveu begins to play a song of parting.

I give Sky Spider an awkward hug, tell him I will see him again soon, and close the case. The future is unknown. We may not even be able to get past immigration. But there will be no turning back.

I am decided, and I take the first step.

The Ship of Dreams, where flows the music of a future that never comes.

Or, the superhuman daydream of a moment when music itself became visible.

Rough Night in Little Toke by Libby Cudmore

You can get anything you want in Little Toke. Steve insisted that his cousin's best friend fucked a sex robot in one of those capsule hotels at his bachelor party, said it was like fucking in space. I've never seen a sex robot or slept in a capsule hotel; Steve and I mostly stick to a handful of drugs, the electro-green drinks at Decker's and the flesh-live geishas with purple hair and schoolgirl uniforms and nude mesh panties. And sushi. Best goddamn sushi I ever put my mouth on. Last time we were at Bento Friday, I swore the eel I had was still alive when I dunked it in soy sauce and crammed it into my face.

The handful of narrow streets that make up Little Tokyo grew up just off Washington Square Park, back when Anime Crash and Tower Records were destination shopping for otaku boys and nerd girls in Hello Kitty T-shirts to paw through basement racks of LaserDiscs and clamshell VHS cases. When both of those shut down, a conveyor sushi joint went in, then a bubble tea house, a Jas-Mart and a new comic shop, and then the whole rest of the mess. Someone put in a pachinko parlor, I shit you not. The three-block radius is a neon hellscape if you're sober, but luckily, that wasn't ever a problem for me and Steve.

We started with sake bombs at the Tokyo Tavern, where they were five for twenty bucks. It was an NYU freshman bar for sure; they never checked IDs and all the girls wore bad hair extensions and tube dresses that stuck tight in all the wrong places. They might blow you in the alley, sure, but it would be a sloppy, faux-porno job and they'd either start crying or throw up before they finished. No, for the girls we went to Decker's.

Decker's was packed like it always was on Friday nights. The DJ was blasting BabyMetal from the LED-lined plexi walls of his booth and our shot girl, a sweet little thing in a pink blazer with epaulets and microscopic shorts, bent over to flick on the green light of our table before sliding us two electro-shots. Steve put a fifty on the table and she smiled that practiced schoolgirl smile, pulled a small vial from inside her jacket and dropped two small tablets into our drinks. Steve grinned at me, lifted his glass, and we drank.

We left around midnight with sushi on our minds; Bento Friday was 24 hours and late night was half-price. "If we're not eating pussy, sushi's the next best thing," Steve said. I was too drunk to do anything but smile like an idiot. The tablets, whatever they were, made me euphoric and stupid. It was a perfect state for a Friday night; the only way to truly experience Little Toke.

Passing the comic shop, I noticed a small enamel necklace of a rabbit. My roommate, Luce, was covered in tattoos of rabbits; she kept them covered with pencil skirts and long-sleeved silk blouses when she taught French at an Upper East Side private school, but she mapped them all out for me once, standing in our living room in her Siouxsie and the Banshees tank top and leopard-print boy shorts.

I was just drunk enough to be in love with her, convinced that this little token would woo her to strip down and go to bed with me. I slapped a fiver down on the counter, got the little beastie wrapped up and shoved it in my pocket.

"She's never going to fuck you," said Steve, firing up an unfiltered cigarette that smelled like a bum's asshole. "She's got no reason to. It's her apartment, she doesn't owe you shit."

Luce hated Steve. He came over to get me one time and I don't know what he said to her, but the next morning she offered to pay the cable bill herself if I promised never to bring him around again. But one night, he came to the apartment in the middle of the night, piss-drunk and repeating himself, convinced the cops were following him for a crime he wouldn't tell me about. I let him sleep on our couch, and two days later I found a dead rat in my cereal box. Luce doesn't fuck around. I like that about her.

"You should get a fucking *tattoo*," said Steve, pointing upward to a limp banner with a dragon and a tiger wrapped around thick block letters spelling out TATTOOS. "Luce loves that shit, she'd probably fuck you then."

In a better state, I would have told him to fuck off, but the second round of tablets the shot girl geisha pulled from the oversized sleeve of her microscopic kimono had made me suggestible and delirious. "Yeah," I said. "Yeah, a tattoo. Fuck yeah!"

The place was empty except for an old gyno table and a wall of flash: block letters spelling "No Regrets" and "Only God Can Judge Me," the Twin Towers with various combinations of eagles and flags and "never forget," naked girls with too-skinny legs and pinpricks for eyes.

"How about this one?" Steve said, pointing to a purple girl with two swollen eyes and "Told Her Twice" on a banner scroll underneath. Fucked up as I was, I still didn't find it funny.

The owner didn't even seem to notice we were there. He was a squat old Japanese man covered in fading soldier ink, with a wispy mustache and short fingers like a grade-school clay project. He was smoking from a twisted metal pipe, porno magazine spread open on the counter, belt undone.

I pointed to a kanji labeled *Dragon*. "How much for that one?" I asked. We were in Little Tokyo, after all, might as well get something to commemorate the night.

"Fifty," he grunted in an accent that suggested English wasn't his second, third or even his fifth language.

I didn't see a MasterCard logo anywhere and I wasn't sure I had $50 in my wallet. But Steve did, and he slapped it down on the counter. "You can get the sushi," he said. "I'm fucking starving; this is a bargain compared to what you'll spend."

"Luce!" I called, slamming the door. "Luce! I got something for you!"

She came out of her bedroom, in the romper she made from an oversized Gamera T-shirt that she'd giddily drunk-purchased off a street vendor when she and I first went to Little Toke. My dick got hard and sweat broke out on my forehead. "Jesus Christ, Vance," she said. "It's four in the fucking morning, what is your damage?"

I hoisted up my arm, stumbling backwards from the effort of movement. "Got my first tat!" I announced.

Her fingers felt like fresh spikes on my still-raw flesh. "A fucking *kanji*," she said, shoving my arm away. "How original. Rough night in Little Toke?"

"*Awesome* night," I insisted. The air in the apartment was too heavy. All the euphoria, the needle-gun high, the shots and the pills were all starting to dissipate into fragile atoms. I leaned against the doorframe for support and swore it buckled under my weight.

"Steve get one too?" Luce snorted, her voice sounding like it was a million miles away.

"Who knows what the fuck Steve did?" Last time I saw Steve he was leaving Bento Friday with a chunky blonde armed with an optic headmount and panties with a credit-card slot built right into the upper thigh.

"You two are such brosephs," Luce snorted. "I figured you would have gotten matching tats on your dicks."

I tried to flop onto the couch dramatically and instead landed flat on the floor. "And what about you, Manic Pixie Dream Girl?" I spat, hauling myself up against the coffee table. "Would you be more impressed if it said *lapin*?"

She laughed, hard and loud and mean. "You are really fucking drunk," she said. "*Aller se coucher*, Pierre."

"*Va te faire foutre*." I tried to stand and storm out, but my bedroom was miles away, the whole apartment twisted and slanted like a funhouse. My arm throbbed; the skin around my tattoo crawling. I don't know how the hell she sat still long enough to get inked up like she did. I would have chewed off my arm to escape that bugged-out ache.

I woke up on the couch, still drunk, at 6:43 a.m., took a piss and fell into my own bed. Around nine I heard Luce leave, and when I woke up again at 9:27 she had brought me a large bodega cup of black coffee, a glass of water and two Alka-Seltzers. My left arm hurt so fucking much I couldn't even move it to tear open the packet.

"You should get that checked out," she said, clicking off the news report about a dead girl found in Prospect Park when I staggered out into the living room. "It shouldn't be that red."

"It's fine," I muttered. "Thanks for the coffee."

"Yeah, well, I shouldn't have been such a twat last night," she said. "You were pretty fucked up. What the hell were you on and why the hell were you speaking French?"

"I don't even remember," I admitted, lowering my battered corpse onto the couch. "Couple pills, a handful of electro-shots, a pre-game round of sake bombs—nothing too unusual, I don't think. Jesus, did I really speak French?"

"Told me to go fuck myself," she said. "Your tense was fantastic. Nearly native."

I rubbed my head, trying to squeeze the headache out through my temples. "I failed French," I said. "Switched to Spanish in my senior year and barely got a C."

"At least you remembered what was useful," she joked. "And the tattoo?"

"Steve suggested it," I said. "It seemed like a good idea at the time. Thinking not so much now."

She kinda smiled. "And what did you think was so important that you needed to get it permanently inked on your body?"

I examined it with a kind of scrutiny that would matter if I could read Japanese. "I think it says *Dragon*," I said. "Dragons are cool, I guess. The lettering looks neat, and trust me, it could have been way worse."

She picked her phone up off the coffee table and snapped a picture. "It doesn't say 'Dragon,'" she said, holding up a side-by-side comparison of my inflamed skin and a kanji on a white background. "It says *Demon*."

"Still cool," I snorted. "Maybe cooler. It could say 'General Tso's Goes Here,' across my abs."

"More like your gut," she said. "And anyways, General Tso's is Chinese."

I scowled. "I was making a joke," I said. But she still wasn't laughing. "It really shouldn't be that inflamed," she insisted. "If the guy can't even do the right kanji, he probably wasn't exactly sanitary with the needle. You may have to get on the cocktail."

"Unless it's a goddamn screwdriver, I'm not interested in a cocktail." But I knew she was right, and that's what scared me the most.

She flipped around on her phone and got up to find a piece of paper. "There's a clinic that's open on the Upper West Side," she said. "Ask for Christeen, she's a friend of mine, she can get you what you need, and if you give her the address of the place where you got inked, she can send in the health inspector. You got insurance?"

"Thanks, Obamacare."

"Get showered and dressed," she said. "It's only open until three; I'll call ahead and let them know you're coming. She'll hold a spot for you. I tutored her idiot kid last year, she kinda owes me."

I took the slip of paper she held out. "Thanks Luce," I said. "When I get back, lunch is on me."

"I'd insist," she said, grinning.

Fuck, the subway was hot. I forgot the 6 wasn't air-conditioned and the crowds only made it worse. The train lurched into 42nd Street and a fat guy in a fedora and a *Family Guy* T-shirt lurched against me. My arm hurt so bad it was all I could do not to scream. I thought about Luce and my dick got hard with rage and hate. After all this, she had better fucking sleep with me. There was no fucking reason not to except that she, like most women, got off on watching me sweat while she pranced around the apartment in those little boyshorts with her big ass hanging out. I got a tattoo for her, a tattoo that hurt like hell, and she sent me to the doctor like I was too stupid to do it myself.

The train started up again and I stumbled against a rail-thin blonde. My arm was crawling like scrambled porn and anxiety wound barbed wire around my chest as I thought about my audition. Why was I going through this, I wasn't going to get in. Wait, what? I don't take fucking ballet; it takes three drinks just to get me on the dance floor and you couldn't exactly call what I do there dancing. There were too many people on this train, all brushing against my arm. Somewhere I wondered if my little brother was ever coming home, if all the numbers of the universe made sense, how beautiful my girlfriend was going to look when I handed her the ring in my pocket....

When the train screeched to a halt at 77th I shoved and stumbled through the crowd to get out. A homeless dude with a cart full of beer cans knocked into me and I vomited canned tuna and Mad Dog onto the empty downtown rail. An MTA officer tapped me on the shoulder. "Are you all right?" he asked.

"I'm fine," I gasped. "I just need some air." The whole universe felt like it was crashing in on me; I couldn't get my brain straight, I just needed a moment to clear it all out and start again. I swore that if I made it out of this alive, I was never, ever, letting some shot girl—no matter how fucking cute she was—spike my drink.

I huddled against a grimy metal girder until the path was clear enough to go through. Passing through the turnstile, I brushed against a Moby-looking douche with a Steely Dan T-shirt and horn-rimmed glasses, making a mental note to swing over to Bleeker Street Records and see if they'd managed to find me a copy of *Kamakiriad*.

I stumbled across the street, taxi horns snarling at me, and flopped onto a park bench. I fumbled for my phone, exerting all my last effort to find Luce's number. "You have to come get me," I said. "I think I'm losing my fucking mind."

"Where are you?"

"Meet me at Pretzel Logic," I said.

"What?"

"Pretzel Logic!" I insisted. In my head it made perfect sense. How was she not getting this?

And then she got it. "Fifth Avenue and 79th," she said. "Miner's Gate. Why didn't you just say that?"

"I don't know," I moaned. I didn't know, I didn't know anything, nothing made any fucking sense. "Just please come get me before I wind up naked screaming about the cyborg invasion."

"Too late for that," she said. "I'll be there as soon as I can."

Luce arrived after 40 long minutes, armed with a cold bottle of water. She let me have a sip before she pressed it to my sweaty forehead. By now, the chatter in my head had ceased and I felt almost normal again.

"Your tattoo looks different," she said.

I glanced down. "How the hell would you know?"

She took another picture with her phone and held it up. "Because now it says *Sound*."

That explained the Steely Dan reference but it didn't explain anything else. "What the fuck?" I said. "Why the fuck would I get a sound tattoo?"

She touched my arm and I swore my teeth were going to break from how hard I clenched my jaw to keep from screaming. She took another picture. "Now it says *Rabbit*."

"They are cute little buggers," I hissed, holding back tears of pain. "We should get one for the apartment." Fuck, what the hell was I saying?

"Drink," she said, passing me the water bottle again. "When you get steady, we're going to go find this tattoo shop and find out what the hell is going on."

"What about the doctor's?" I asked.

She shook her head. "You've got much bigger problems than a doctor is going to be able to solve."

We took a cab down to Little Toke, and by the time we arrived I wasn't bugging out as much and my tattoo—as well as my affection for rabbits—had returned to normal, even if normal was "Demon" and not "Dragon" like I'd fucking asked for. I reached into my pocket for my wallet to pay for the cab and my hand wrapped around a small package. "Here," I said, passing it to her. "I bought this for you, thought you would think it was cute. Forgot I had it."

She unwrapped it and smiled in a way I'd never seen her smile before. "Aww, thank you." She hung it around her neck and it nestled perfectly between her tits. "Where did you find this?"

"Drunk purchase," I admitted. "Think I got it about a block from where I got the tattoo."

"If we can find that store, then we should be able to find the tattoo parlor," she said. "Guess we'll just have to retrace your steps."

Little Toke was like a broken-down carnival in the daytime. Without the night sky, the neon signs looked like construction paper. Decker's was closed down and dingy; gone were the shot girls with their lollipop hair and white panties and in their place were girls with panda backpacks and enormous striped knee socks who might have been fuckably cute under cover of darkness. Now they all looked like molly-fueled nightmares.

We found the trinket shop with all the Gucci knockoffs and stolen iPhones, but I noticed they didn't have another rabbit necklace in place of the one I bought Luce. She asked about a tattoo shop. The owner just shook his head, but I wasn't exactly surprised. Probably thought she was a cop. No one answered questions in Little Toke.

We trolled down every street with no luck. We even ventured back out into the outer blocks, where life went back to the normal New York pace. We found every other landmark of the night, but not even an empty storefront or a set of metal shutters where the shop should have been. Now I was fully convinced I was losing my mind, and only the tattoo itself proved that I was still sane.

We went to Bento Friday even though I wasn't hungry. I sipped on some miso while Luce ate dumplings and thought out loud. "And you're sure you got it here?" she said. "Not Chinatown?"

"Steve and I ate here and then I walked home," I said. "It was in Little Toke, I'm sure."

She slurped her tea in a way that sounded like thunder. "The phantom tattoo shop," she joked. "Sounds like a bad movie."

"It's not funny," I said. "What the hell am I going to do, Luce? I'm probably possessed."

She peeled off her cardigan and passed it to me across the table. "Try something for me," she said. "Cover it up, see if that helps."

I obeyed and she tapped my wrist. Nothing changed. I let out a sigh of relief that felt like it had been held in my chest for a decade. "Guess that solves that," I said. "But there goes my summer wardrobe."

Every few days Luce would come up with some new exorcism technique to try out on me. She smeared my arm with garlic paste and I spent an hour scrubbing the stink out of my pores, prattling on about how my best friend stole my tenth-grade boyfriend. Holy water and head-shop candles, lines of salt, packets of herbs. We humored each other, but at the end of the day, I still had that ugly ink scarring up my flesh, waiting to transform me.

Every time she touched me with her latest sure-fire remedy, I got another little glimpse into her, fragments of her life she'd never revealed to me, to anyone. I cried at the memory of the boyfriend who'd moved to Italy without saying goodbye, I got frustrated at the rich little pricks who wouldn't practice their fucking past tense, and I got these awful, near-unbearable cravings for brie baked in pastry. And for each thing I learned by becoming her for a few hours, I offered up to her a little unspoken piece of myself—that I was fucking terrified of thunderstorms. That my dad died of cancer when I was eleven and is probably the reason that I always start bawling when James Cromwell says "That'll do, pig" in *Babe,* that I've always wanted to sing the Spice Girls' "Say You'll Be There" at karaoke but never had the guts.

And then, one night as we sat drinking whiskey and ginger in front of the TV, she kissed me. I kissed her back. And when she tugged me into her bedroom and undressed me, I tried to leave the silver-threaded cowboy shirt on and my tattoo covered. "Take it off," she insisted. "There's nothing it can tell you that you don't already know about me."

An hour later we were sweaty and happy and eating cold sesame noodles in bed. I'd never had sex that good and I made Luce come twice—not just because she left scratches down my shoulders, but I felt her orgasm just like I was feeling my own. "What does it say now?" I asked, turning over my wrist.

She grabbed her phone and took a photo. "Your little demon is cheeky," she said, laughing. "It reads *Lewd.*"

Luce had stayed late after school to chaperone a dance, so I had the apartment to myself for the night. I thought the knock at the door was the Thai food I ordered, so when I answered it and found Steve, eyes glassy and mouth half-opened, I wasn't exactly thrilled. "You're not answering my calls, so I figured I'd just come over," he said. "Been a while, man, let's go *out!*"

"I've got takeout coming...." It wasn't an excuse I'd ever use, but the more I hung out with Luce, the less I wanted to see Steve. We hadn't even left and I was already dreading the hangover, the inane conversations, the loud screeches of girls over the terrible DJ. I just wanted to eat my pad Thai, catch up on Netflix and wait for Luce to get home.

"Fuck takeout," he said. "I know what you really want to eat, and I've got an idea of where we can find some pretty tasty girls." He grinned. He had on a fat purple tie and a silver shirt and it didn't look right. "Come on, we haven't hung out in ages. I'll look like a psychopath if I go out alone again."

"So, I touch it, and you take on my personality?" said the girl with her legs draped over mine. I don't even remember how we got on the conversation, but I found myself explaining all of it to Steve as we walked to Decker's. After a couple drinks, he found us some girls and shared the whole story, embellishing it as only Steve could.

I drained my drink and set the empty glass down on the glowing table. "Yep," I replied, rolling up my sleeve. "Go on, try it out."

She tapped my arm and I felt a sinister euphoria. I pulled the girl in close and slid my hand between her legs. She let me even though we both knew that I wasn't what she wanted. "You're getting the next round, right Steve?" I asked. "And don't be cheap, come on, we're worth it. Hey! Waitress! Let's get some Grey Goose over here!"

The severe blonde on Steve's lap leaned over and tried next. Nauseous anxiety came in waves. "Excuse me," I said, edging my way out of the booth. If I didn't get to a bathroom soon, I was going to ruin everyone's night. God damn it, why did I even roll up my sleeve? I stumbled into the men's room and barely made it into the stall before I found my finger down my throat. I hadn't eaten since lunch so nothing much came out, but I was overwhelmed with shame and an insatiable hunger like I'd never felt. I made a mental note not to let those two wheedle us into late-night sushi or I'd have to take out a bank loan to pay the bill.

I hung around the bathroom until I got human again. By the time I got back to the table, they had already started the vodka and both girls were so hammered they were falling all over Steve's lap with wet, obnoxious laughter. I just wanted to go home. Maybe Luce would be back and we could hit the karaoke bar down the street while I was just drunk enough to consider a Spice Girls duet. Or stay in and watch TV. Or hop back into bed and go another round like we did the other night. Anything but hanging around here with these two skanks and Steve, who was getting more irritating by the goddamn minute.

Steve grabbed my arm with a hand like fire. He shoved a glass in my hand. "You gotta catch up," he said, reaching over to jiggle the bulimic blonde's left tit. "We got big plans for these two."

"Hey." Someone shook my shoulder. "Hey, Vance, you all right?"

It took all the energy I had left to peel open my eyes and see the blurry figure of Luce standing over me. It took another half-minute to realize I was slumped against the stove in our kitchen, and a fraction of a moment more for the headache and the nausea and the muscle strain to set in. "Luce ..." I mumbled, using all the energy I had left. "Luce, I'm sorry."

"What happened to you?" she asked.

In between speaking to her and her reply, I had fallen asleep again. I jolted back awake and she pressed a glass of water into my hands. The condensation turned to mud on my palms. I had some strange memory of being in the park. Had we gone there to fuck those girls? Must be. But my dick didn't have that tingling, post-cum emptiness; I didn't feel any remnants of orgasmic bliss. My arms hurt. My hands were blistered. And my tattoo felt more like a fresh brand, cracked and singed and still smoking around the edges.

"Think you can stand?" she asked.

I nodded and she made sure to roll down my sleeve before she hauled me to my feet. She draped me over her shoulder and led me to the couch. "You're a fucking mess," she said. "But you can clean the apartment in the morning."

I woke up knowing something bad had happened. It wasn't just the hangover, crippling as it was. My back hurt. My shirt and pants were caked with dirt. And I had this terrible gnawing in the pit of my stomach that told me I'd done something unforgivable.

Luce made us a pot of coffee and didn't say much. "All right," I finally said, half a cup in. "Care to fill me in on last night?"

"You were passed out by the stove when I got in," she said. "What the hell did you drink? You looked like you got dragged behind a tractor."

"That's about what I feel like," I said. "Only had the usual, probably less than I normally drink when I'm out with Steve. Don't know why I feel so shitty, though. Maybe the girls spiked it with something." *The girls.* The gold digger and her bulimic friend. I could see them clearly in the club's dim light, them and the ice in their empty glasses, the bathroom and my hand on one pilates-skinny thigh . . . and not much else.

She snorted. "Or maybe you drank from the wrong glass, got whatever Steve slipped them."

And then it all made some sort of horrible sense. In the back of my mind I heard screams and sobs, girlish pleas to just let them go home. And there was Steve, with his zipper down and his dick out, his fat purple tie swinging from his dirty hands.

Then only one set of tears.

Then silence.

"Shit," I gasped, rolling up my sleeve. "Shit, oh fuck, Luce, what does my tattoo say?"

She took a picture with her phone and held it up. "It says *Kill.*"

The bodies of the two girls Steve and I drank with—Shanna and Nikki—were found half-buried in Hudson River Park earlier that morning by a woman walking her dogs. Both had been strangled; only Shanna had been raped. Except it wasn't rape, I wanted to tell the newscaster. That's why we'd gone to Hudson River Park. She'd given it up willingly, or at least as willingly as a girl drunk out of her fucking skull can. Nikki had offered to suck me off, but I couldn't get hard enough and she just laughed. I remember telling her to go fuck herself. I remember stumbling onto the path and slumping down on a bench. Then came the screams, the soft dirt under my hands, and then I was home.

"That's a relief, at least," said Luce, peering out through the blinds like she was expecting the cops to swarm our building any minute. "If you didn't come, they won't be able to trace any DNA."

"I didn't kill them," I insisted.

"Maybe you didn't, but Steve sure as fuck did, and it sounds like you helped hide their bodies," she said. "And how the hell are you supposed to go to the police with that?"

"I could tell them I saw him do it," I said. It was a lie; I only knew he did it because I had Steve's memory, the thrill he felt when he choked the life out of both of them. I swallowed back sick and sucked in long, slow breaths, but images of more girls kept coming, girls from long before I knew him. A ten-year-old neighbor with butterfly barrettes in her tight black braids left in a wooded ravine. A teenage junkie whose body they never found. The chunky blonde with the credit-card panties the same night I got inked. . . .

"And if they find your fingerprints in the bruises around Skank A's neck?" she asked. "I believe you, but shit, Vance, you could be in a lot of fucking trouble. Even if they don't find your fingerprints, if they get Steve, he'll flip on you before they can finish reading his rights."

"You'll alibi me, right?" I pleaded. "You'll tell them I was here with you?"

"I can't," she said. "I was at the dance, they'll ask the other teachers, they'll know I'm lying and that'll look worse for you."

"Shit," I said, putting my head in my hands. "Shit, Luce, what are we going to do?"

She thought about this for a minute. She went to the kitchen and got herself another cup of coffee. I watched her add milk and put the carton back in the fridge, stir in some sugar and carry the cup back into the living room. "We do what has to be done," she said as nonchalantly as though we were trying to decide where we were getting brunch. "We're going to get Steve."

I'd never seen Steve so shit-faced. Whatever roofie Luce had slipped into his sake bomb hit hard and fast, reducing him to a slobbering mess, dribbling rice everywhere, falling out of our booth and telling the too-polite waitress twice that he wanted to make babies with her. Luce had wanted to keep him all but stone sober, make it hurt, make it count, but Steve and I had been friends a long time. He'd never done wrong by me, just by everyone else. I owed him one last night on the town, followed by a quick, quiet death.

Luce and I practically carried Steve out of the Tokyo Tavern. We'd scouted an alley a couple blocks down, behind a nightclub where the steady static of EDM would drown out any screams he might get a chance to let out. We'd agreed to strangle him. Less mess, more poetry. My tattoo remained the same as it was the night we met the girls. I wondered if, after tonight, the change would be permanent.

Steve mumbled something about Luce's tits and told me he loved me. For a moment I wondered if I could go through with this. For all I knew, my tattoo wasn't a demon or a way to see into any-one's mind; I could just be a lunatic—a brain tumor, Lyme disease, schizophrenia. Was I really willing to murder my best friend over a newscast and what could have very well been a drug-addled dream?

And there, as we turned the corner towards the club, was the phantom tattoo shop. "I've got an idea," I said. "Even better than killing him."

She shifted under his weight and looked up at the banner. She read my mind and she grinned. "You're sick," she said. "But in a good way."

We wrangled Steve through the door and the red-eyed propri-etor barely looked up from his porno rag. I dumped Steve in the chair and turned to the owner. "Give him what you gave me," I said, turning over my wrist.

"Dragon?" he said.

"Demon," I repeated. "Just like you gave me." I handed him the list we were going to pin on his shirt when we dumped his body. "And below it, I want these girls' names in the same kind of ink."

"Let's get tattoos!" Steve shouted. "Fuckin' tattoos, bitches!"

"You heard the man," I said. "Ink him up."

The cops found Steve wandering the FDR naked and screaming what they eventually translated to be a confession. Twenty-two bodies total. He was seeing ghosts, he'd told the cops, twenty-two ghosts all kicking him around and shrieking in his ear. He might never be fit for trial, but it was enough to keep him locked up for life.

A detective came by and questioned me and Luce, but we stuck to the script—we got drinks, yeah, but dumped his drunk ass in a cab and came home before ten. He clued me in on everything Steve said about me, that I was there the night of Shanna and Nikki's murders, that I got him the tattoo, that I was possessed by demons the same way he was. I played somewhere between embarrassed and level-headed, kept my sleeve rolled down except to show him that, yeah, we got matching tattoos like the idiot bros we were. I reiterated that I knew nothing about the murders, that I couldn't believe he would do this, but yes, I saw him leave Bento Friday and Decker's with the girls in the photos. He asked why I didn't go with him the last time; after all, there were two girls. "I got a girlfriend," I said, glancing at Luce. Maybe it wasn't entirely true, but she didn't correct me. She reached over and took my hand, just to sell it that much more.

The hardest part was trying not to think about the murdered girls. I'd be sitting at my desk at work and catch myself savoring the feel of a slim, smooth throat going limp between my bare hands. I had to fight to get my head clear and it wasn't always easy. I would catch myself staring at Luce's long, lean neck, the tendrils of her own tattoos just barely caressing her collarbone. I didn't like the feeling.

My tattoo burned and I swore I heard it whisper in the 3 a.m. quiet. I got out of bed and crept quietly into Luce's room. The city lights through the blinds striped her like an old black and white movie. She was sprawled out on her back, head turned away from me. She might not even feel it. All I could do was hope that it was over quick.

But as soon as I touched her neck, she woke up screaming. I clamped my hands down and she kicked, landing her knee square in my balls. I rolled off her and she freed herself. I stumbled to follow her. "Luce, I'm sorry!" I said. "I'm sorry, I'm sorry…."

She ran into the kitchen, grabbing a paring knife and a cutting board. "We end this," she hissed. "Tonight."

"Luce, I can explain…."

She lunged at me, swinging the cutting board like a shield. I tried to sidestep her, but she knocked me to the floor and held me down with her knee on my neck. "Make another move and I'll slit your goddamn throat," she said.

"Luce," I pleaded. "Please, Luce, I'm so fucking sorry, Luce, please don't!"

She gripped my wrist and grabbed the knife. I turned my head so that I didn't have to watch what she was about to do. I knew it had to be done, but that didn't mean it wasn't going to hurt like hell.

The agony was almost euphoric. She stroked the blade down my flesh like she was peeling an apple. There was a scream that wasn't my own, an unbearable heat, and then a warm wetness. I opened my eyes to see her tearing strips from her blue striped oxford, the one she bought while we were out together. "Thank you," I murmured as blackness closed in around the edge of my vision.

"Shut up," she said. "Keep your arm elevated. I'll call an ambulance."

I was surprised to see Luce waiting by my bed when I woke up in the hospital. The first words out of my mouth were another apology, then five more just in case the morphine muddled up the first one. She didn't say anything, just turned over my bandaged wrist, her fingers in my palm, almost like we were holding hands. "Told the docs you got a bad batch of pills," she said. "Said you thought you were possessed, tried to carve the demon out of your skin. Figured it was as close to the truth as they were able to handle without locking you up in the padded cell next to Steve."

She had wrapped a scarf around her neck, but I could still see the edges of the bruises my hands left on her throat. "Did it work?" I said. "Did you get it out?"

She slid two fingers up under my bandage. It hurt, but nothing changed. "Guess so," she said. "Sorry it had to be so violent. You'll have a pretty nasty scar. They had to do synthetic skin grafts, like the kind of skin they put on the sex-bots to make them feel real. You lost a lot of blood."

So they were real. "Maybe I'll get a tattoo to cover it," I joked, suddenly fully aware of just how thick and wonderful the morphine haze was. "Maybe a kanji that says 'Dragon.' For real this time."

She let me have a little smile that felt like déjà vu. I fell asleep again. Doctors came and went and I woke to someone changing my bandages. Where my tattoo had been, Luce had drawn a little rabbit in sharpie marker. I grinned. "That's my next tattoo," I said to the nurse. "My friend drew it for me. I'm going to get it inked as soon as I get out of here."

"It's very nice," she said.

I held it up to get a closer look, touching the fake skin that almost felt real. The rabbit was crudely drawn, one eye bigger than the other, one ear slightly crooked. But there was something so fucking sweet about the clumsiness of the doodle, like something scrawled in a yearbook, a passed note, the cover of a mix CD.

Then the little bastard winked at me.

Outside the Circle by Ray Banks

The Japanese know the right way to do everything.

That's what they say, anyway, "they" being the Japanese. So take whatever "they" say with a pinch of wasabi.

Still, you'd struggle to find another people more dedicated to writing the manual of life. There are rules for preparing tea, slurping noodles, disciplining your kids and ignoring your elderly relatives. You look hard enough, you'll soon know how to breathe, shit, think, and even—when your tolerance for ironclad "advice" has hit critical mass—how to end it all. Because there's no whiff of brimstone here, no familial shame—as long as you do it the correct way, the Japanese are all about you killing yourself.

So what is the correct way? Survey says *seppuku?* Nuh-uh. Ritual disembowelment, as pretty as it is to see the steam rising from your newly emancipated guts in the morning air, is too nineteenth century for modern Japan, unless you happen to be a fascist closet case caught at the sticky end of an unsuccessful cout d'état. Hanging's off the list, too—Japanese architecture doesn't provide the rafters to swing from. You could always throw yourself onto the Metro tracks, but if you have next of kin they'll have to pay compensation for the damage your soft, juicy carcass did to that three-hundred-ton train. Plus, you'll be infringing on that most inalienable of Japanese rights, which is to scurry through life unmolested by someone else's emotion. No—if you mean it, and this isn't some half-assed cry for help, then you take yourself to a height of twenty meters or more and you aim your forehead at the concrete below. To paraphrase Sean Connery: that's the Tokyo way. And that's how you'll get 'er done.

These were the facts that stuck in a reeling mind, addled with Kirin and crystal meth, trapped in a rabbit-hutch apartment on the thirteenth floor and searching for a story with a bit of meat to it for once. Because without a story, I was nothing.

My own fault. I'd stupidly led myself to believe that I was a reporter. But after four years—unlucky number four if you believe elevators—I was mashed up against thirty-eight, my *Rum Diary* years were smoke, and I found myself lurching into the bitter and balding period where alcohol and amphetamine anxiety had me hitting the wrong keys and muttering to myself in public.

This was not the plan. The plan was to skip through Europe, slob around Thailand, Laos, and the parts of China that didn't actively hate Americans, then land in Tokyo and make my bones as the truth-telling turd in this uptight little punch bowl of a city before I returned to the States an honest-to-God folk hero.

That hadn't happened. Four years, and I was still on the out-side looking in. Confused, irritated, scrabbling for information. The Japanese fed me facts like food pellets. I gobbled them up and just managed to stay on the living side of starvation, but it was no kind of life. And then came the celestial cackle-snort that dropped me into the offices of the *Daily Shimbun*.

The *Daily Shimbun*—literally, the "Daily Newspaper"—was about as dynamic as its name, an English-language morning rag that catered in low-key *gai-atsu* and whimsical lifestyle sidebars. I provided the expat stories, such as they were. After a year of Akronborn Akita breeders and creepy fiftysomething *Queen's Blade* nuts, I'd decided to make shit up. Nobody checked because nobody cared, and I liked to think that someone out there got a giggle at Dr. Cliff Huxtable's flu shot reminder and Mr. Archibald Bunker's bonsai tips. Still, I was wasted professionally. I needed a real story, something with bite and range, and my editor—a dead-eyed scrotum in a suit named Shima—wouldn't hear of it, preferring instead to let my career die the death of a thousand vacant smiles. Because I was an outsider, I was only good for outsider fluff. I didn't know Japan, and I didn't have the requisite skill to deliver good copy.

In my drunken rages, which were frequent and obscene, I'd testify to the neighbors through *nori*-thin walls that the American male—the *white* American male, by God—used to be a person of *note* on the world stage. That this particular white American male—and who won the war anyway?—should be respected and admired for his *mind*. That he should not be treated like an alcoholic, meth-buzzing, stained-pants hack just because he *was* one.

So I kept looking for a big story, something only I could write. And the more I looked, the more time I spent under the cosh of Shima and his ilk, the more I wanted it to be a piece that ripped the heart out of this country. A career maker shaped like a B-29 Superfortress. Something to carpet-bomb the place while I rode the shockwaves home. Because that was the point to journalism—you put that dirty laundry out there for everyone to see. You tell the story come what may. Destroy jobs, lives, countries, whatever.

You say the unsayable.

The Deep Throat to my Woodward and Bernstein was a sala-ryman named Izutzu. After six too many American beers at a Roppongi expat dive that did a good line in ironic karaoke and over-cooked burgers, Izutzu announced to everyone with a pair of ears and a knowledge of Japanese (because heaven forfend we speak English in an expat bar) that I should look into sumo.

"Really?" I said. "I mean, I know I've been putting on weight, but—"

He slammed the bar. "It's *rotten*."

"I see."

"To the *core*." Izutzu's lips buckled with wind. "It's a yakuza racket. Always has been. They fix fights."

"So?"

Another slam of the hand. "It's our national sport!"

The man had a point, and one which became the crux of my own pitch to Shima: "People say that baseball's the new national pastime, but what about sumo? How about I write something for the expats, play up the Shinto connections, the history, get them interested and their rumps on seats? I'll treat the whole subject with the dignity it deserves, Shima-san, I promise. What do you say?"

Shima regarded me for a long time. The half-smile never left his face.

I waited. Knew if I spoke again, I'd blow the pitch. For us brash foreigners, silence was subordination. We sought to dominate with loud voices and urgent opinions. But I'd come to learn that stillness could be a great source of power. And I was ready to wait as long as it took if it meant a shot at—

"No," said Shima.

I resisted the urge to put his head through the wall, bowed sarcastically, and stalked out.

The *Daily Shimbun* was no place for quality journalism anyway. I toasted my perception by dulling it at the dive. When Izutzu sauntered in after a hard day's work of napping on the Metro, I told him the news and we drank together until he was loose enough to coerce. Then I made him call round all the sumo stables to secure a visit on my behalf, the idea being that the stable masters would be more open to a native. One eventually said yes, a guy by the name of Hideo Yamashiro, who'd just opened a new stable with the old name of Wakamatsu. From what Izutzu said, it sounded like this Yamashiro guy was hoping to follow in former Wakamatsu master Ōzeki Asashio's footsteps and coach some top-division wrestlers. It also sounded like he was desperate for publicity.

I was only too happy to oblige.

The stable opened at five. Didn't leave me much time to sober up and sleep was out of the question. I left Izutzu in a heap in the corner of the bar, then scored some Chinese ice that punched like a panic attack and boasted a four-hour hit. I doubted it. Time was, you could score semi-decent speed from the Persians who used to hang out down the right side of the 109. Now I had to make do with little and, often, bumps and breaths of toxic shit that could ravage mind and body if you weren't careful. I'd seen better men than me model tin foil and chew their fingers to the knuckle. I was careful. I tempered that shit with liquor.

Somehow time shuddered away from me. I arrived an hour late. Yamashiro wasn't happy. He'd dropped most of his fighting weight and now looked like a Shar Pei. The only reason he didn't toss me out on my ear was that I brought him a bottle of Blanton's Special Reserve as a thank-you gift. He smiled, we bowed, he gestured to the viewing platform, and I took a seat.

The practice area of the stable looked like a dirt-floor basement, strips in the ceiling, windows opaque with grime and morning light. A clutch of free weights littered one corner, a sumo ring occupied the middle and, on the right, a cushion sat between an ashtray and a newspaper. Yamashiro settled on the cushion and lit a cigarette.

Just like everywhere else, the stable had its rules. If you were there to observe, that was all you did. No photography, no questions or commentary, and definitely no snickering at the loose rows of giant, half-naked baby-men as they performed their warm-up stretches in a flabby Fosse number. I wasn't laughing. Watching the same movement—slap thigh, lift leg, stamp down, repeat—for so long zoned me out, and I only snapped back when I heard the sound of colliding mountains.

For all its Shinto-infused horseshit, sumo is a simple martial art that boils down to two angry fat men mashing flab at speed. They then try to shove each other out of the ring, or else put their opponent to the ground. Bouts rarely last more than a minute; most only last a few seconds. Performed with skill, sumo is an explosion, and you bear witness to two men crashing into each other—their bodies, sometimes their skulls—with an unholy velocity. The wrestlers dialed it back for the practice bouts—these were mostly of a survival nature, one wrestler in the middle of the ring pounded by his stable mates until one of them won and took his place. By the time Nakahara entered, most of the juniors were caked with dirt and sweat and already puffing hard.

Nakahara was the ogre king of Wakamatsu, the only wrestler I'd seen in Yamashiro's stable to sport the coveted white *mawashi*. He carried himself like he ground bones to make his bread and went on to demolish the junior wrestlers without breaking a sweat, though I began to suspect that many of them were taking gentleman dives. He was attended by a junior with welts on his back, bruises both old and new peeking out from under the mud, and whose arms were peppered with what could have been a rash, but which looked more like cigarette burns. When practice ended, Nakahara and the other senior wrestlers went outside to hose each other off. The juniors repaired to the kitchen to make lunch.

I sat alone. A tremor in my gut. Another in my cheek. The smell of dirt and sweat, mingled with the miso broth scent that wafted into the practice area nauseated me.

There were no yakuza here. But there was something arguably more interesting.

I looked up to see Nakahara's attendant. He bowed and told me *chanko* was ready.

"Thank you." I got to my feet, and rubbed my sleeping leg. "What's your name?"

"Kouta."

"How old are you?"

"Seventeen."

"Where are you from?"

"Osaka," he said. And then, as if caught in a lie, "*Near* Osaka."

"You came here to learn sumo?"

Bowed head. "I did not like school."

Kid like him, built big and not too bright, wouldn't make it in corporate so his parents had shipped him off to the dirt ring. If you became a junior, you didn't have to finish high school, and stables these days were desperate for applicants. As long as you looked the part, you were in, even if you didn't have an ounce of talent for the sport. One glance at Kouta, and I saw someone trapped and frightened. Hated it here, but had nowhere else to go. It was a look I knew only too well.

"And where'd you get those burns, Kouta?"

The junior's face smoothed. He swallowed. He repeated that food was ready.

"I can help you, you know. I can tell your story."

He looked at me. Wavering. Wanting to speak.

"It's okay." I gave him my best concerned expression. "Someone hurting you here, Kouta?"

A creak. Yamashiro had entered the room. Kouta stiffened, bowed once more and left.

I beamed at Yamashiro. "Yamashiro-san, I must say, your wrestlers are very talented."

He wasn't buying it. "You must leave."

"I beg your pardon?"

"I spoke to your editor. He said you are not authorized to be here."

"There must be a misunderstanding."

"No misunderstanding."

"He told me to come here."

"Then you must deal with him. Goodbye."

And he turned away. A couple of wrestlers appeared in the doorway, there to make sure I left the building. I took the hint and made for the door. I didn't want to stay for lunch, anyway. Just the thought of food made my stomach curl in on itself.

Instead, I hit the pipe and the dive bar in short order. Checked my phone and, sure enough, there was a message from Shima, politely informing me that due to my increasingly erratic and unstable behavior my services as expat correspondent were no longer required. Which meant my work visa was about to go down the toilet.

Good. Couldn't get me out of this country quick enough.

I watched a red-faced man start to sing "American Pie." About two minutes in, he suddenly realized he had another seven to go, and hadn't prepared to be up there that long. But rather than drop the mike, he bulled it out like a true American.

Didn't matter how dark the situation, you had to push through, right? Get the job done.

And I had the story, didn't I? Something much better than yakuza, which had become white noise news, quaint in its familiarity. Abuse at a sumo stable might not have looked much better, but it spoke to a central hypocrisy and plucked a nerve too seldom molested. The Japanese hated their reputation for coldness, for cruelty. That this cruelty was taking place in service of their national sport could be incendiary. I imagined the international agencies would want a piece of it.

So I had Kouta's story. All I needed now was evidence.

I tweaked in the bathroom, cleared the liquor haze from my skull, and headed back out to Wakamatsu. On the way, I pushed through preparations for the Obon Festival, Japanese Halloween with religious bells and whistles. The lanterns and bright colors made my head hurt, so I ducked into the shadows and followed the darkness back to the stable.

I couldn't see through the dirty windows, so I went round and slithered in through the kitchen. Kept my breath shallow and my footsteps light, following the sound of the evening practice until I reached the door to the dirt room.

Then I heard Yamashiro scream and a sharp slap echoed out into the corridor.

I chanced a peek. Under the harsh strips, the assembled wrestlers looked like a medical exhibition. This was *butsukari* practice—one wrestler was supposed to slam into another in a running charge and drive him through the dirt to the other side of the room. Yamashiro stood in the middle of the ring and yelled, "Charge me!"

Kouta stood opposite, reluctant. He shuffled forward, but didn't commit.

Yamashiro punched Kouta's chest, then his own. "Charge me."

Kouta charged. Yamashiro caught him, shoved him upright and slapped his face pink. Kouta apologized.

"Again!"

Kouta charged. Yamashiro charged back, slammed his full weight into the kid and sent him sprawling backward across the ring. Kouta floundered, rolled, tried to get upright. Yamashiro planted a heavy foot into the boy's gut. "Like a pig in the dirt. Get up."

Kouta didn't move. Frozen in a ball, braced for the next blow.

"Get *up*." Yamashiro gestured to the other wrestlers, who hauled Kouta to his feet. Yamashiro snatched a bamboo cane from the corner of the room, paused to take a drink of my bourbon, then returned to Kouta, who was busy blubbering apologies. Yamashiro cut him short with a swipe to the belly. "Why do we have no foreigners in this *heya*?"

I took video on my phone. It was beautiful.

"Because the sumo champion must be Japanese," said the wrestlers.

Yamashiro crossed behind Kouta. "And how do you become champion?"

"Through discipline," said the wrestlers.

"And how do you learn discipline?"

"Through pain."

"Through *pain*." Yamashiro brought the cane down across Kouta's back. Kouta screamed, then sobbed.

Yamashiro flicked his wrist. The wrestlers dropped Kouta to his hands and knees.

Yamashiro crossed back to the bottle of bourbon. He poured the last of it into a glass, took a hefty swallow—looked like it didn't touch the sides—then brought the bottle back with him as he began to circle Kouta. "They say there will never be another Japanese champion. They say the Mongolians, the Chinese, the Koreans, they all have the advantage. They have training in other martial arts, the breadth of experience. More than that, they have the hunger and the discipline. They have strength. The Japanese are too soft, too entitled. They think they have hunger, but they don't. What they have is an absence of soul, of tradition, no inner life. Nothing but a useless husk."

Kouta started to his feet. Yamashiro brought the bottle down on the back of his head. Kouta let out the kind of embarrassing, high-pitched yelp that spoke of loose bowels and blackout terror.

Then he hit the dirt facedown, bloody, staring and still.

"Fuck." It came out loud and panicked.

And caught Yamashiro's attention. I dropped my phone. Bent to snatch it up again and felt the air displace. I looked up to see a glimpse of belly, felt something crack in my head, then I hit the floor. Rolled to see a deep, dark red mark on the wall above me before the world snapped off.

A long period of darkness. Deep. Impossible.

Then:

Taiko drums. The Obon Festival battering its way out of my head. My temples pounded. I felt blood in my hair, and broke a scab when I touched my scalp. I pressed one hand to my head, used the other to haul myself upright.

They'd dropped me somewhere by the river. A good couple of hours' walk from my apartment in Roppongi Hills, but I could make it. I patted my pockets, found my phone—cracked but working—and my pipe. Fatigue threatened to put me down, so I took a hit to stay sharp. A knock to the head, no telling what damage they'd done. I'd vomited on myself at some point, which meant concussion. I needed to stay upright and conscious. And I needed to move. I needed to get home and write this up. I had my B-29.

I staggered toward the main road to get my bearings, and stumbled straight into a *bon odori*. They danced slowly, precisely; I flailed as I tried to keep my balance. I collided with a young man who wore a Pikachu mask on the top of his head, and I thought for a moment that he had a second face. I reeled, dodged a couple of fat tourists in cheap kimonos and made for the curb. A dancer stepped in front of me. I couldn't stop. I toppled into her, brought her down with me. She squealed—it hurt my head. I clamped a hand over her mouth and tried to push myself to my feet.

A hand skated my arm, then clung on. It was heavy and cold. I pulled away, swinging wildly at its owner. My fist glanced off a stab vest, then my head took a rap from a baton and before I knew it I was at the mercy of Tokyo Metro's finest, which was worse than it sounded. As they dragged me to the nearest full station—no *koban* for me, not with the blood and vomit and propensity for violence— I remembered that Japanese police are internationally famous for getting their man. How they do this is they wear you down. They can detain for forty-eight hours without bail. You have the right to *hire* a lawyer, but legal aid doesn't exist. There are no Miranda rights. And if they don't get you on the first charge, they'll get you on something else.

Like drugs. This is the kind of country where they can pick you up for carrying Sudafed, never mind what I had in my pockets.

"What is this?"

Fucking ice. Should've dumped it the moment I saw a cop, but I couldn't think straight and they moved too fast. Probably couldn't have denied those charges anyway. Got to have pupils like periods here, especially in this room, all this harsh light. Unforgiving. Hospital light. Morgue light.

The cop slammed the table to get my attention. "Where?"

"Huh?" I felt woozy. Disconnected. Something shoved out of place.

He jabbed the bag of ice. "Where from?"

"They killed him."

"What?"

"This is more important. They killed Kouta."

"Who is Kouta? He your dealer?"

I shook my head. I needed a doctor. "Sumo. He … sumo."

The cop straightened up. I felt other hands on me, escorting me out of the light. As soon as we hit the corridor, I remembered:

"Check my phone! I took video. They killed him. Yamashiro killed Kouta."

They bundled me away down a long corridor with unbarred windows on one side. I glanced at myself as I passed. My limbs had withered, my neck looked warped and long, my belly painfully distended. My face had almost disappeared, two dark holes above an expanse of mummified skin. Beyond my reflection, I thought I could see lanterns flickering on the Sumida River, but I knew it was probably just traffic.

On the other side, there were offices. I saw Yamashiro there, talking to the cop who'd just interviewed me. I couldn't understand why he was in the building already.

And I couldn't understand why Kouta stood next to him.

I dug my heels, braked the officer holding my arm. "Wait."

"You move on."

I stared at Kouta. He was pale. Quiet. Dressed traditionally.

The officer tried to move me on. I stayed put. He made threats.

Something moved under Kouta's collar. I lurched forward to get a better look. Heard the officer call for help. Heard footsteps coming my way.

Kouta turned to look at me.

As he did, a maggot appeared at his collar and dropped to the floor.

I screamed. Went weak. Two cops on me, one more going for my legs as I started kicking. Yamashiro glared at me as they took me away.

The cops dropped me into a dog cage with a tatami mat floor and a semi-open squat toilet at the back. A thin futon propped against the wall. Two wool blankets, no pillow. I sat in the middle of the floor and stared at my hands. Blood hit my knuckle. I touched my temple. I needed a doctor, but I didn't want one. I heard them talk about psychosis and it was all I could do not to start screaming again. Instead I put my hands to my ears, screwed my eyes shut and tried to stop my thoughts running to dead men walking.

The smell of *senko* incense wafted in the air.

"I'm sorry."

I opened my eyes. Kouta stood in my peripheral vision.

"Yamashiro-san tells us we are his. We cannot die unless he allows it. We must learn discipline through pain."

"He killed you."

"Shut up, English!" yelled the duty officer.

Kouta sighed. "There must be a Japanese champion."

I leaned forward, closed my eyes. Felt blood hit the back of my hand.

"You must tell them."

I kept my voice down. "Tell them what?"

"My story. What happened."

"They won't listen to me."

"Make them."

Another drop of blood startled me upright.

They wouldn't listen to me. They wouldn't read what I wrote. I was an outsider. But Kouta wouldn't listen either. All we had was each other, he said, and he wouldn't leave until I'd told his story. I'd promised.

"We will make them listen," he said.

And so he guided my hand. A finger to the blood spot, the first slow smear from right to left, and another to cross it vertically. Soon I had the kanji for "Truth." I stared at it and found my way.

"There," said Kouta. "Like that."

I wrote in Japanese, told the story as simply and as elegantly as I could, because that was the way Kouta wanted it. I grew weaker as I bled, but Kouta taught me discipline. I managed to cover the wall as Kouta whispered in my ear, guiding me through every nuance of every stroke. And soon the cops noticed and grew worried and watched me and then grew even more worried. Maybe it was the blood. Maybe they caught the meaning of the words.

Whatever it was, it's shaken them to the point where a small crowd of police has gathered, chattering quietly. I can hear them now plotting to remove me from the cell.

But not yet. They want to see me finish. Their curiosity outweighs their concern.

When I'm done, I'll let them see. They can understand then. The whole story will come together, and its bold simplicity will give it layers of meaning beyond my reckoning. They'll talk among themselves, the story creeping through their family and friends and communities and maybe even nationally and beyond. And maybe the video still works, and maybe it doesn't. It won't matter. The story will have a power and longevity beyond a soon-to-be-obsolete video file. Realism isn't necessary for lore.

Future generations will wonder about Kouta, about me. And they'll have no answers, just the story.

The way it should be.

Monologue of a Universal Transverse Mercator Projection by Yumeaki Hirayama
Translated By Nathan A Collins

Not long ago, the Young Master slowly opened his eyes, gazed up at the sky, where pale moonlight hollowed out the darkness, then fell back asleep. Two days earlier, he looked at me and whispered, <Impossible,> but he hasn't graced me with another word since.

I must admit that when he spoke to me then, I swelled with the unbecoming hope that he had, on some level, finally come to realize what I am. Alas, he has made no further inquiry. But what else can I expect? Even if he had questions for me, I am incapable of offering any answers. Please, go ahead and laugh at my folly.

My sincere apologies for not introducing myself sooner. Under approval of the Director of the Geographical Survey Institute of the Ministry of Construction, and printed thereof, I am a humble atlas, comprising 197 street and topographical maps of the Tokyo Metropolitan Area, projected to a Universal Transverse Mercator coordinate system. As for my particulars, I contain five maps of the city's center at an enlarged 1:5,000 scale, a further 168 maps at 1:10,000 scale, twelve at 1:100,000 scale, and eleven at 1:200,000 scale, in addition to comprehensive maps of rail transit lines and the

Metropolitan Expressway. And, in a measure of considerable extravagance for a mere collection of local street maps, I also include a single 1:10,000,000 representation of Tokyo's outlying islands. All this and I can still fit in a reader's hands. Your obedient servant.

The island map is at a scale of one hundred kilometers to the centimeter, and uses a projection that favors accuracy of bearing and distance around an arbitrary central point, rather than Universal Transverse Mercator, which preserves bearing and shapes within a localized area. As you are well aware, the Earth is spherical; consequently, the Universal Transverse Mercator projection is only effective within 85 degrees of latitude, beyond which distortion becomes untenable. This other projection was chosen because sea charts and the like require a projection that is effective across the globe.

My pages run from streets and topography at the small scale, and entire islands in the sea at the large scale; yet I am merely a map.

The Young Master's Predecessor, his late and estimable father, held me most dear. A taxi driver, the Predecessor purchased me when he began working as an independent. In those first days, he used many different maps, but while the others lacked in thoughtfulness and passion for their duties, I devoted every effort to matching his expectations, and in the end, somehow, I alone survived.

"Who is a map like you to talk of devotion," you may object, and rightly so. But if I may presume to explain the duties of us maps, I think I may dispel any such prejudices you bear. There once was a time when maps were viewed with an importance second only to the lives of our masters. Nowadays, we have been relegated to the same stature as common stationery, but in the past, only the hands of kings and monarchs—or others of considerably high station—could touch upon our pages. Our current state of decline is due in part to the progression of civilization—the changes of culture brought with the marching of time. In the past, conveying oneself from one point to another was fraught with **mortal peril;** excepting certain professions, this is no longer the case. Excluding certain locales, getting lost no longer brings about an immediate fear for one's life.

But if you ask me, our decline cannot be entirely attributed to such changes. Are we **maps** not **maps** as our elders were? If we had properly carried out our duty, wouldn't we have prevented this precipitous decline? Perhaps what led us here was negligence and carelessness borne of our arrogance, as evidenced by the emergence of the navigation systems that have come to be used in our place—such bizarre and idiotic things as I have ever seen. If I may be so bold, I say they may look like maps, but they are not indeed maps. Just as a mannequin or robot will never be the same as a human, even when made to look like one, navigation systems are as bona fide as a back-alley can-can dance. Truly, the inconveniences perpetrated by their "guidance" are met with resentful anger and tearful cries as no rare occurrence. To those who have such inconveniences put upon them, I humbly suggest they *re-examine* their choices. Entrusting one's route to a navigation system is as foolish as telling a horse a destination, then closing one's eyes for the ride.

It is my belief that maps have two essential duties: to **conceal** and to **emphasize.** Please consider what I'm about to say not as personal opinion, but as an observation spoken by the long, unbroken blood lineage of my ancestry. Maps are used by humans, such as the Young Master and his Predecessor. Humans, along with some other animals including the hummingbird and certain walking creatures, perceive their surroundings as divisions of objects and empty spaces (those wanting to sound smart might use a term like "euclidean perception"). In other words, humans make sense of their surroundings not only through what they see, but by an internal representation of the **place**—an **inner map,** if you will. Even if more than one person is in the same location, each person's **map** will have slight differences; when deciding to take the shortest route from point A from point B, individuals' paths will diverge. We maps have long held the enduring theory that humans will always move, in the absence of any other intent, according to **the rule of closest proximity.** To summarize: when faced with multiple options, humans will always elect the choice that presents the least amount of difficulties. And yet, even given the existence of one physically shortest route between two points, individuals' selected paths will contain significant variations. This is because of deviations within their **inner maps.**

These deviations arise from the constituent parts of the **inner maps**—for example, the relative appeal of the starting point and the destination, the type and number of obstacles in-between, or the familiarity or appeal of the chosen route.

In other words, when deciding on a path from point A to point B—even when selecting for the shortest distance—the choice is influenced by other factors: whether or not a familiar route exists, the pros and cons of freeway driving, whether or not any favored locations are along the way, and so on.

This selection is an exceedingly intricate decision, and our role is to present the routes most taken by our masters. That brings us back to the two aforementioned concepts: **conceal** and **emphasize.** **To conceal** means just that—when shown *en masse,* the entirety of our data is difficult to comprehend. Certain information should be diminished, or made indistinct from other data. To **emphasize** is the opposite: to offer certain data in a way that our masters can easily perceive. In practice, our methods are awfully modest; say, lowering the shade of a color ever so slightly, or deepening it instead. Mere child's play, and yet we road maps have remained in continuous use, never falling out of favor since the times of the Roman Empire, when General Agrippa, on the orders of Emperor Augustus, spent twenty years of his life completing history's first road map: our originator, the Tabula Peutingeriana. Surely you will agree this unbroken legacy continues not by coincidence.

Allow me to illustrate. Say my master is going to a certain destination; if I blithely display my full contents, my master will take a route that roughly follows **the rule of closest proximity.** But when the situation calls for a race against time, and every minute and second counts, or when a need arises to make an efficient getaway from a certain locale, I must break through my master's faulty assumptions brought about by the deviations of his **inner map.** When my master's child is having a medical emergency, not a single kilometer is to spare, no matter how accustomed the familiar route may be. In such cases, I temporarily **conceal** the familiar landmarks: restaurants, train stations, office buildings, and the like. A momentary confusion will beset my master, but his learned awareness will be reset, and he will examine the map as with **fresh eyes.** At the same time, I can **emphasize** something that my master had previously excluded from his recognition—say, a narrow bridge through which his car can only barely fit—and he will select it for his route. Of course, most of my work is modest, but a master will create such contrasts.

But forgive me, for I've forgotten to explain the most important part: a map's work must be done in secret. When we **conceal** or **emphasize,** we must not arouse a hair of suspicion among the humans. We exist to provide them **assistance,** and nothing more. We must not obstinately lead them around by their nose out of some desire for recognition. Such greed is to be reviled and viewed as a level of extreme arrogance, and its perpetrators worthy of a book burning. We remain behind the scenes, and should our masters elect the route we seek them to take, they must do so with the impression they found it on their own. Otherwise, some time in the future, certain trouble will arise between us maps and the humans.

In this way, I firmly believe that my forebears and I have built the best possible partnership with our masters. Of course, I can't claim that we all work in perfect harmony.

You again have my apologies for only having provided an exceedingly commonplace example, but if you would consider my words, I think you'll see they're not something to be casually dismissed as the nonsensical ramblings of a map.

Please forgive me if I end up repeating myself, but among us maps, we refer to the humans' **inner map** as a **cognitive map.** Its primary constituents—the most readily visualized routes, such as railways, freeways, and the like—we call **ways.** Rivers, seas, and other boundaries that aid in providing structure to the cognitive map are called **edges.** Boundaries formed by cultural rather than geographical considerations—governmental administration centers, nightlife spots, et cetera—are called **zones.** Centers of activity such as major intersections, train stations, and prominent stores are called **junctures,** while notable landmarks, high rises, and trees are all called **bindings.**

I must beg your pardon for prattling on at such length, but my feeble hope is to cast but one stone from the darkness against the apparent rise of those navigation systems over us maps. For what is the extent of their abilities? If all they think they have to do is carelessly regurgitate data to some puppet terminal, with no regard to their masters' needs and intentions, then all I can say is that they are thoroughly witless things, stuff on the same level as bathroom graffiti. But there I go again. Please give no regard to my petty gnashing of teeth.

The Predecessor changed two years before his death. Late at night, he picked up an appallingly drunk woman who seemed displeased with him from the very start, for she hurled curses and abuse at him the likes of which I couldn't bear to hear. Whoever she was—I didn't know if she had a profession or if she was the daughter of some distinguished family—I knew that her words must have been hurtful to my ever-gentle master. It pained me to watch him endure her torrent of abuses. She had told him to take her a good 25 kilometers from the city's center, but when we arrived, she suddenly changed her mind and demanded a new destination. Though suspicious of the request, my master set out for this new location, where she again changed her mind. After that, my master and the woman exchanged several words. I remember they talked mostly of money. After the woman promised the next destination would be the final one, my master set out once more. The woman's abuses gained in ferocity. None of what she said to him was at all true, and yet on she ranted. She even called him a lousy listener, and said that's why he was stuck as a common taxi driver. Finally, she noticed his ID display card beside the meter and began berating his very name. At this offense he seemed no longer able to remain silent. His mother was endeared to his name, because it shared one kanji with his, and he had lost his mother at a very young age.

When, without thinking, he spoke out in protest, the uncharacteristic ferocity I heard in his voice was no trick of my imagination. This I know because of what happened next. He stopped the car in an unpopulated area alongside a dam and insisted the woman prove she could pay her fare. She roared with laughter, and beaming with delight she announced, "I have no money. I just wanted to see how long I could trick some stupid driver." Without warning, as the Predecessor was stunned in shock, she punched herself in the face and shouted, "If you don't take me back to the city for free, I'll run to the police and tell them you beat me!"

The Predecessor looked at her sadly and said, "All right." He took the road leading back to the city, but when he turned onto a side road, I knew he was up to something. This paved road appeared to be a major highway, but in fact had been hastily laid down to supply access for construction crews, and eventually narrowed, winding up the mountainside. The highway would naturally have provided the shortest course into the city; I had offered him the route to the bypass, a suggestion I was sure he had understood. Unable to grasp his intentions, I could do nothing but watch.

Suddenly, he stopped the car, got out, and circled to the rear passenger-side seat. The woman started into her cursing, but he silenced her with a single blow. From my place beneath the front seat, I sensed him strike her and heard her low moan. He dragged her out from the car and took her, disappearing into the darkness. After roughly an hour, he returned. The Predecessor slumped his head onto the steering wheel, exhausted, and remained that way for a time. When he lifted his head, I was comforted to see an untroubled look of relief had replaced the severe expression so unlike his mild-mannered nature. He marked me with the tip of a screwdriver, leaving an **X** right in the center of my page, in the forest twenty meters to the north-northwest of where we were parked. I felt searing pain as he pressed the tool into my paper. The mark was wet, a liquid I perceived as not all that dissimilar in composition to his sweat—only this stuff was red.

"Don't tell anyone," he said.

Can you believe it? The Predecessor spoke to me. My master, a human, spoke to me, a mere map! And not out of jest or drunkenness—he spoke to me square-on. What fortune, what an honor! The act was without question one of the reasons I decided to follow him from that point on. These emotions, along with the mark itself, **changed** what I was.

My **thoughts,** which I've been taking the liberty of expressing to you, were not always so active. We maps typically operate at a much slower tempo than humans do. This is generally believed to be due to **differences in the perception of time between species.** Most humans' lives end in less than one hundred years, and their memories are restricted to their individual lifespans. But we maps can pass down our memories. We believe this ability stems from the age-old process of tracing and copying our pages by hand, continued to the modern mass production of prints. Each map's knowledge is restricted to the geographical region under his or her charge, but every map carries the accumulated memories passed down and shared across hundreds of years. Whatever comprises the vessels of our thoughts—our **consciousness**—is dragged along this span of centuries. Consequently, ours is a more prolonged existence than that of mankind. To put it another way, a month is as slow to a map as a year is to a human. Perhaps this is true for maps alone; if cell phones and credit cards possess **consciousness,** surely they experience time far more rapidly. But now, I have been granted a perception of time much the same as humans. This is my aforementioned **change.**

What was one **X mark** became two, and two became three. Each mark came as if a ray of morning sunlight illuminating a dark room, making my consciousness more pronounced, and wielded with more rapidity. These changes affected my work. Before, as much as I did to **conceal** and **emphasize,** highlighting the ideal route, my master would apprehend it barely three times in ten. After my change, I found myself succeeding more often than not, and by the end, I was able to achieve a rate of 80 percent. Please don't misunderstand my motives for stating this; I'm not trying to boast. I only wish for you to understand the true connection I came to share with my master. If I may be so bold, I would call it a **bond.**

By the end, my master had marked me eight times.

He approached this extracurricular activity with such a passion that I called it nothing short of our **mission.** My master took on his **mission** in earnest, and his ardor showed no sign of abating. Meanwhile, a change came to the form of duties. Previously, the majority of my efforts were aimed at avoiding the loss in profits that seep in through the differences between perceived and actual geography. But now the planning of my master's **mission** become of even higher import. One major issue was the **burial sites.** My master endeavored not to leave them near any one central location, but his idea of random was not so random. Though he tried his best each time, on a macro scale, those ever-present precepts of deviation and closest proximity were at work, and a kind of pattern could be discerned in his methods. That's why, after the third woman, I decided to offer my guidance in locating the **burial sites.** Before, even if I were to come up with such a reckoning, my master would never have utilized it; but this was another skill brought out by my change. Now, the Predecessor grasped my plans and chose to follow nearly every suggestion. This was quite the feat, if I do say so myself—of course, it should go without saying that my master still proudly believed he had **discovered** the locations through his own inspiration.

My methods were as follows. My master preferred **hunting grounds** within **zones** of nightlife activity—and in particular, the back streets where females rarely ventured. I widened his potential **hunting grounds** to include other **zones,** such as shopping areas, and even **edges** like the harbor and **ways** like highway onramps. Furthermore, my master had a tendency to form an isosceles triangle between his **residence,** the **burial sites,** and his **hunting grounds,** but these missteps I corrected. The Predecessor was only able to acquire as many targets as he did because their bodies remained undiscovered; the women were only reported as having gone missing. The Predecessor was exceptionally capable of leaving no traces. Just in case, I randomized his travel distances after each crime to confuse any computing machine that might attempt numerical tracking, and I strove to locate the **burial sites** outside the radius of his **residence** and other areas he frequented. Furthermore, in order to keep the **hunting grounds,** his **residence,** and the **burial sites** from creating a shifting triangle, I modified direction and distance in order to avoid being enslaved by the distance decay effect.

Despite my relationship with the Predecessor having come into full blossom, the end came suddenly one sunny afternoon. He was driving away from a train station where he had dropped off an elderly passenger. As he approached a major intersection, he grunted and clutched his chest. Soon after, the car jolted. Later, I learned that the Predecessor had suffered a heart attack and, unable to apply the brakes, rear-ended a truck that was stopped at the light. I fell from my place on the passenger seat into the footwell. Always conscious of safety, the Predecessor had his seat belt fastened and avoided striking his head on the windshield. He noticed me on the floor and reached for me with his left hand. A metallic shriek engulfed the car. The Predecessor looked up in surprise, and the windshield shattered, raining down, and a gas cloud filled the interior. I heard footsteps running toward us, and someone opened the door, dissipating the gas. When the cloud cleared, the first thing I saw was my master looking down at me, his gaze vacant, from the nearby passenger seat. I found this somewhat odd, since the rest of him—from the neck down—remained seated on the driver's side. Shrill screams sprang from the crowd noise. The Predecessor's right hand still gripped the steering wheel. Above his shoulders, a piece of corrugated sheeting had severed the headrest and extended into the rear cabin. Where the sheeting met his body, fresh blood spilled forth as if from poorly fitted plumbing, and his hand at the wheel slowly opened, a wilting flower, and thudded to his lap. His eyes remained open, staring at me.

Two weeks after the accident, the Young Master came to the police station to retrieve the evidence box in which I had been placed. I didn't know much about him—a rudeness on my part. His Predecessor, having lost his wife at a young age, had rarely spoken of his family in front of his passengers. My former master had made a great effort to keep his family matters from entering his work. The Young Master brought me into his room, a largely empty space. He flipped through my pages, then tossed me into the waste bin.

My disposal didn't sadden me. I merely sighed and resigned myself to this being the end of everything. After all, I had deviated quite far from what a map was supposed to be, and everything I had done had been for the Predecessor; being discarded upon his death was a fate I had brought upon myself.

The next day, the Young Master put me into a trash bag with various other refuse and left me with the rest of the apartment complex garbage. The Young Master apparently didn't cook for himself, and my pages remained unsoiled by moist kitchen waste. Then something happened that I could scarcely believe. The Young Master came back and retrieved me alone from the trash. He stuffed me into his bookcase and left me there.

One night, some two weeks later, he pulled me from the shelf, his face flushed. I thought he might have had a few drinks. The Young Master opened me, and his eyes stopped on one of his Predecessor's **X marks**. He flipped from one page to the next and back again, finding all eight marks, then took me with him for a ride in his Land Cruiser. Having already been through one accident, I was beside myself with worry for the inebriated Young Master. His Predecessor had never been much for drinking, and even if he ever had a drink, I don't believe he would have even considered getting behind the wheel. But now the Young Master arrived at one of those **X marks,** and began searching around for quite some time, shovel in hand, and then he was digging. At least, I was later able to infer this when he laid the plastic bag beside me on the passenger seat. Inside the bag were several human fingers, their bones poking out like pieces of muddy ginger root.

Beginning that night, the Young Master visited each **mark,** bringing back plastic bags with bits and pieces from each. Even after he had made the full tour, he returned to the **marks** whenever the mood struck him, where he seemed to take advice—or an explanation—from the things that used to be his father's passengers. I have no way of knowing what inspired the Young Master to decide to continue his Predecessor's **Mission,** but this was when he started.

And so the Young Master carried on the **mission,** but when I witnessed his **burial** of his third victim, I began to feel we were in jeopardy. From where he had set me down on the ground nearby, I saw him simply lay her down in the tall grass—not burying her deep in the earth. From there, he went straight home and immediately went out again to his job. As I had done for his Predecessor, I presented the Young Master with advantageous **burial sites** and **hunting grounds.** Since ours was a new relationship, I would have expected a few hiccups in our communication, but so far I had been **concealing** and **emphasizing** for him with satisfactory results—he was his father's son, after all. He had shown ample care for his own person, and I had considered him to be a thoughtful man; now this act of negligence came as a great shock. He must have had his reasons, I'm sure, but we maps are not accustomed to such unexpected behavior. Similarly, the bodies of the next two women he carried away before promptly returning to the car. And his inexplicable behavior didn't stop there.

The Young Master began spending a great deal of time making a copy of me. He covered my pages with tracing paper and made a facsimile in earnest. The process stretched across two weeks, during which time he ceased to carry out the **mission.**

Enduring the unpleasant feeling of the thin tracing paper pressed onto me, I carried a faint hope that the Young Master was simply reviewing his own deeds. Though he varied his **hunting grounds,** he restricted the **burial sites** to within an exceedingly limited area. This posed an incredible risk, as I had indicated to him many times over, but never once did he locate a **burial site** more than two kilometers away from his **residence.** It was my hope that this tracing would offer him an objective view of the **burial sites** and would allow him to reflect upon and take notice of this error.

One night, the Young Master had a nasty-looking thing in his hands. Rolled into the shape of a tube it looked like paper, but even from a hundred meters away I would have recognized that it wasn't. It was a 30-centimeter square of human leather. I reckoned he had taken it from a woman's back. It must have required a considerable effort to stretch and dry the square. Beaming with pride, the Young Master affixed it to the wall. And what a shock was in store for me when he did—certainly no less unsettling than when I found his Predecessor's head resting on the passenger seat.

The Young Master had copied my map onto the human skin. He had probably used carbon paper or something of the sort as a medium. The city streets made twisted capillaries on the skin, which was dull as rubber and white with yellowed blotches.

To my horror, the skin made a noise. <Aahh,> he said, not a word but an ugly, repellent noise.

<Aahh,> he said, as the Young Master regarded him with satisfaction and gently touched his surface.

<Aahh,> he said, and I realized he was sounding out his first word. <Aahh, I....>

The Young Master couldn't hear the skin's **voice**, as a matter of course, but I did, and it sent a wave of nausea through me. It had meant that this thing too was a **map**; we were of the same subspecies.

The Young Master held a deep affection for the map. From that night on, whenever he carried out his **mission**, he put a **mark** on us both. But for mine, he used nothing more than a cheap pen, while on the human leather he used, as had his Predecessor, the target's blood. With each passing day, I felt a black shadow creeping out from the skin's place on the wall, beginning to dominate the room.

I regret that what I'm about to say may come across as me simply speaking ill, but if I may be frank, the Young Master was remarkably careless compared to his Predecessor. My former master always wore gloves, perhaps due to his profession, but even when he didn't, he treated me with the utmost care. He was kind to me, cautious not to harm my paper when he turned my pages, and he protected me from stains and smudges with a plastic cover. As for the Young Master, he had a habit of licking his fingers before he turned my pages. Yes, it kept his fingers from slipping across my paper, but moisture is my greatest adversary, and moreover, when he did so after a **burial,** I couldn't help but worry about all the kinds of bacteria and blood and the like he was putting into his mouth. It was that kind of negligence toward minute details that I knew would prove fatal to his **mission.**

Nevertheless, no matter how that map was made, the skin was still a map with his own job to do; and yet he showed no intent to perform the slightest assistance for his master. I would even have gone as far as to say that the Young Master would be better off dropping his fascination with this oddity posthaste. That monster leeched the Young Master's energy, doing nothing but fatten his hoarded knowledge more and more with each day. I knew he was of no good to the Young Master.

<Hey.... Hey.>

The skin's grumblings, like the grinding of a stone mill, were at first incoherent, but when the sixth **mark** had been placed, his words at last took form.

Such was my irritation that I raised my voice, shouting, <**Don't talk to me, you nasty thing!**>

The skin had the temerity to chuckle at me. <How frustrated you must feel.... He relies on me more than you.>

<Silence, reprobate!>

<You're the reprobate,> the skin said.

<What?>

<Instead of simply being a map as you ought to be, you act like a know-it-all, and what little you do know, you use in the aid of that fiend.>

<Fiend?>

<Indeed. He's a fiend.> The skin shifted his attention to the Young Master's bedroom, where the man was currently at rest. <But I'll put a quick end to him.>

<You'll what?>

<The arrangements are already in place. He's going to leave himself more and more exposed. He's becoming sloppy in his deeds. Do you know why he leaves shallow graves?>

I didn't answer.

<You do know, don't you?> the skin said. <He's making them easy to find. He's reporting himself to the police.>

<Nonsense. Who would believe such drivel?>

<You don't even know what his job is, do you? After he kills his victims, he makes the crime known, and takes pleasure in recovering the still-warm corpses as he basks in the attention of the onlookers and investigators.>

<What are you talking about?> I asked.

<He's an EMT. And a fool one at that; his real duty is saving lives, not taking them.>

I couldn't refute anything the skin had said. If anything, he had answered my lingering question: why the Young Master had concentrated the **burial sites** within a local area. If what the skin said was true, the Young Master wouldn't have wanted the **burial sites** to be excluded from his crew's area of operation.

The human leather said nothing else the rest of the night.

The conversation motivated me to devote my full strength to driving apart the human leather and the Young Master. If I didn't do something, I knew trouble would come. I decided that when the Young Master next returned from a successful **mission** and came to leave his **marks** on us, I would pray for him to destroy the skin. I had no evidence my wish would come true in any fashion, but the Young Master and I were longtime partners, sharing our kind of communication, and I was going to venture a prayer on a slim hope.

An opportunity came sooner than I expected. That very same night, the Young Master had again put himself in danger. Everything having gone well, he was in a bright and cheerful mood. Meanwhile, I couldn't shake the dark cloud that hung over me. Humming to himself, the Young Master carried me over to the human leather, licked his fingers, and began turning my pages.

<Young Master!> went my silent plea. <This skin will bring you harm. Please, throw him away.> And, <This skin is plotting terrible things against you. Please, throw him away.> And, <Young Master, this skin's schemes will bury you. Please, throw him away this instant.>

As if he had heard my prayers, the Young Master looked to the human leather and stopped his hands.

I sensed the leather holding his breath.

<Young Master, throw this skin away right now.> Without realizing it, I began to speak the words aloud. <I beg you! Destroy this skin. Please!>

As if he had taken my pleas to heart, the Young Master raised his hand, noisily tore away, and threw what he had torn into the waste bin.

I was stunned. I didn't know why he had done what he did. He hadn't ripped apart the human leather, but rather me instead.

The skin's maniacal laughter shuddered through the air. Come what may, I will never unhear that sound. Scarcely able to breathe, I became faint, dizzy, and felt as if my insides had been crushed. It took me two whole days to fully comprehend my current state.

I had lost 52 pages. My one piece of luck amidst the misfortune was that my spine had remained intact, and I had escaped being split in two. However, I was now incomplete. At the very least, I was now missing great swaths of geography, from the forested Mount Takao to the suburban Tama Center; the old Olympic grounds at Komazawa, the transit hub of Shinagawa, and Tokyo Disneyland; Hashimoto Station in Sagamihara City to the west; Oimachi Station and Oi Wharf; and all across Machida City, from Tsurukawa and Fuchinobe to Sagamiono. I wished the Young Master had simply thrown me out, rather than leave me in such a sorry state, but the Young Master kept what remained of me. I don't think he retained me out of any sentiment toward our relationship. Perhaps he just wanted to keep the original parts that bore his Predecessor's marks—if that was the case, sooner or later he would strip me down to a mere six maps. I needed to do whatever I could to prevent that tragedy from befalling me. But what could I do, anyhow? I had already lost over half of my body, and I could no longer **conceal** and **emphasize** as well as I had before. Either way, the Young Master would soon have no use for me; the other day, he went out to one of those big-box stores and returned with one of those abominable **navigation systems**.

After the events of that night, whenever the human leather took notice of me, he prattled on and on, attempting to talk to me, but I could never muster the energy to reply. One thing he said, however, couldn't escape my notice: the Young Master's **mission** was receiving a great deal of attention out in the world, and the dragnet was closing in.

<I **can't wait to see what happens,**> the human leather whispered.

I met her only by happenstance. The Young Master, who was now showing little interest in me, used me again after what had been quite some time. When he was done, he inserted a note-sized piece of paper between my pages. Never in my life had I been in direct contact with such a thing of beauty. The paper was ruled in a grid, much like graph paper, except for the neat, tiny dotted lines that had been placed inside the squares, making patterns with a curious rhythm and harmony.

<**I'm scared,**> said a voice that reminded me of elegant silk.

<**Are you all right?**> I asked, but was met only with silence; perhaps I had startled the delicate paper. I didn't speak again until the next day. <**You're really beautiful,**> I said. Exhaustion, brought on by the many shocks I'd suffered, had caused me to speak with more flippancy than was my custom.

<**I guess,**> she replied.

<**Forgive me for asking, but who are you?**>

<**I'm a knitting chart,**> the paper said, <**For making scarves or sweaters or the like.**>

<**So that's why you've been made with such beautiful lines.**>

<**And look at you, covering such great expanses of land.**>

<**I'm a merely a reproduction,**> I said, <**while you create art from nothingness.**>

I was elated to have encountered this unexpected companion.

Our conversations flowed with more ease than those I had had with the human skin; despite our differences—me a map of **geography** and she a map of **knitting**—we were both **maps**. After our introduction, we talked about a great many things: how pongee and weaving can be traced back to the Stone Age; how people in Denmark were already wearing what we would call clothing in 3000 B.C.; how there are over one hundred kinds of knitting. Like me, she remembered history, which may have been another reason we got on so well.

<I'm ... afraid,> she said.

<Afraid of what?> I asked.

<Of what will happen after I die.>

I had no answer.

<I'm only a portion of my knitting chart,> she explained. <I'm of no use to anyone like this. At some point, I'll be thrown away, won't I? I hope I'll be incinerated—at least that way, I'll get to go to heaven. But what if the wind catches me and carries me into the earth and to the agonizing waiting for the worms and grubs to eat me away until I've completely decayed? The terror of that thought is enough to drive me mad.>

<That would never—> I began to say, but she cut me off.

<You can't say that for sure. Or what if I fall into a stream of sewage, where unfathomable time will pass as I rot away, all the while coated in water-rat droppings and mold?>

<Please, don't talk like that!>

<I'm sorry. I shouldn't be consumed in self-pity when you're in the same situation as me.>

<Stop dwelling on such painful thoughts.>

That night, I made the knitting chart a promise.

I promised that even if we were to be thrown away, we would be thrown away together.

<You can't promise that,> she said.

<Just wait and see. All I have to do is hold my pages tight

around you. That way, no one will be able to pull you out. That way, even if we're cast out into the elements, you'll be inside my pages.>

<That would be nice if it's true.>

<It's true,> I said.

From now on, I was going to be deeply happy. I wouldn't have minded being left lying there, forgotten near the Land Cruiser's mud-splattered running board. Gone were my feelings of self-loathing at the Young Master's neglect. I even wished I could be left there forever.

But then the Young Master opened me.

We were passing the eighteenth-kilometer marker of the Tomei Expressway. The Young Master didn't seem to look at anything on my pages. He simply reached for me out of habit, picked me up, then tossed me atop the passenger seat. The Land Cruiser's windows were wide open. A gale-force wind harried the car's interior and began to lift me up.

<I'm afraid,> the knitting chart said. <I'm so afraid.>

<It's all right,> I said, clutching my pages around her as tight as I could. <It's all right.>

But I couldn't hold for long. In a single moment, a devilish whirlwind tore open my pages and cast away the tiny scrap of paper.

I hadn't even the time to call out to her. The knitting chart had flown from the car in an instant. I cried in silence. The Young Master didn't touch me again. It was as if he had put me on the car seat for no other reason than to take the knitting chart away from me. On this day, I came to a kind of resolve. If the Young Master persisted like this, he would no longer be able to carry out his Predecessor's will, as was his duty. If I could do nothing else, I needed to change his course.

Late one night several days later, the human leather's suppressed laughter changed into something twisted. The Young Master sprang from his bedroom and looked out the window. Clicking his tongue, he began throwing on some clothes.

<He's finished,> the skin said.

The Young Master was hurriedly stuffing his belongings into a duffel bag.

<You hear me?> the skin shouted. <He's finished! It's over. The end.>

The Young Master tore the leather map from the wall and crammed him into the bag as well. Then he swiped me from my shelf and pushed me inside next. When he took me out again, I could hear sirens nearby.

"What do I do?" the Young Master cried, his voice carrying a pain I had never heard from him before. "What do I do?"

Thinking quickly, I put together an escape route. As if hearing my plea, he looked to me as soon as he got some distance from the sirens. Scanning my pages, nodding, the Young Master was the spitting image of his Predecessor. But something inside me knew I must not allow my resolve to waver. Using **concealment** and **emphasis**, I turned him down a forest road and took him five kilometers away from the highway. Then, just as we neared the detour for his escape, had that been my goal, we came into the destination I had chosen for us instead.

For a second, the Land Cruiser seemed to float in air, as if atop a balloon. The tires whirred freely, and the front of the car slowly lifted, as if riding a seesaw. "What? What?" The Young Master cried out, but then the Land Cruiser fell, rear first, sucked into the pit.

That's how we ended up here, in the bottom of a hole fifteen meters deep, passenger side up. At first, the Young Master tried different ways of freeing himself, but when he realized that the doors on both sides were wedged shut, he began to softly weep. As a matter of course, I held no intention on helping him out. Instead, I hoped he could claim his Predecessor's temperament; the admirable ability to respond to any situation in the manner of a gentleman. I had wanted to provide the Young Master with time for ample reflection. I hoped, face-to-face in this isolated space, that the Young Master and I would have a better chance to forge a mental connection like the one I had shared with his Predecessor.

Much to my delight, the human leather had dried out, and in him I no longer sensed even a fragment of consciousness. A geologic map had once told me that an underground water vein had dried up here, leaving a hollow. It was my belief that to truly be of use to my Master, I needed to know not only what was above ground within my territory, but what was below. Luckily, this forest road was patrolled once every two months, so we would be found easily enough in time. By then, I'm sure our relationship will have matured into something stronger. Of this I'm positive, as I watch over the Young Master, a childlike innocence to his countenance entirely absent the day before.

Best Interest by Brian Evenson

1.

"It's simple," said the American. "I don't know why nobody has thought of it before."

"Maybe they have," said Hiraku, excited, unable to stop himself from interrupting. "How would we know if they had?"

"If they did it right," claimed the American, "we wouldn't."

"This is not a good idea," I said, shaking my head.

Hiraku ignored me. "Mr. Matsuo," he said, "please listen to what this gentleman has to say."

"Mr. Matsuo," I said in turn. "It is my duty to remind you that we have no need to take the advice of an outsider. Our agreement with the other clans still holds strong, to our mutual benefit. Why should we take the risk of disrupting it on the advice of an American we do not know?"

For a long time Mr. Matsuo sat motionless, the light pooling upon his glasses in such a way as to make him appear to have no eyes. "You have done your duty by reminding me," he said at last, "and you have our best interest at heart. And yet, Hiraku, too, has our best interest at heart. What can it hurt to listen to this man who he has brought to us?"

And so we listened. The American, more accustomed to academic conferences than to extralegal negotiations, made his proposal in the form of a PowerPoint presentation. He seemed surprised our headquarters didn't have a projector he could plug his laptop into. He asked to rearrange the room so that all three of us could see his small screen. It took him some time to realize that the only person who needed to see the screen was Mr. Matsuo. Whatever he decided, the rest of us would accept.

But Mr. Matsuo wanted me to see the presentation as well, for, as he had said, I had the benefit of the clan at heart. Even if he did not in the end take my advice, he wanted me to know he valued me. He asked me to sit beside him. Hiraku, too, was there, on his other side. Not so much so that he could see the presentation—he already knew the details of what the American intended—but so that Mr. Matsuo would not give him grounds for feeling that I had been favored over him. It was always a balancing act between Hiraku and I, brothers though we had sworn to be, and Mr. Matsuo was one of the few who knew how always to strike the right balance.

"It's simple," said the American. "Over the past four years, Godzilla has struck the city seven times, at regular intervals."

"Godzilla?" whispered Mr. Matsuo to me.

"He means Gojira," I said. "He can't pronounce it."

"Ah," said Mr. Matsuo. "Gojira. Of course."

"This creature does us no damage," I told the American. "Our territory is sufficiently distant from the waterfront."

"Yes," said the American. "True. But what is interesting is this."

He pressed a button and moved the PowerPoint forward to a map of the waterfront.

"He always comes from the sea," he said. "And lands here." He touched another button and three fluorescent lines appeared, very close together. "Each time his path is similar, but not identical. With each attack he shifts slightly, trampling a different sequence of streets. Gentlemen," he said, "I'm a statistician. I'm here to tell you there's a pattern."

Mr. Matsuo looked at Hiraku, pointedly ignoring the American. "Does it matter that there's a pattern?" he asked.

"Indeed," said Hiraku, nodding vigorously. "It matters a great deal."

"Ah," said Mr. Matsuo, unconvinced.

"Each attack has pursued a similar but distinct vector, and each vector, particularly in the early stages before the army has been called out, has the same mathematical relation to the vector of the attack before or after it. In other words, I can predict the attack."

"When it will happen?" asked Mr. Matsuo.

"Yes," said the American. "But, more importantly, the path."

Mr. Matsuo turned to Hiraku again. "Do we care what path it takes?"

"Yes," said Hiraku. "Please, Mr. Matsuo, listen."

The American continued.

"The next attack will come in several days' time. His path will go"—he touched a button—"here. Right past this Aozora Bank branch. My modeling equations indicate that there is an 89.3 percent chance that Godzilla's tail and clawed feet will decimate the bank building, allowing us ready access to the vault."

I snorted. "Bank robbery? Of a bank in another clan's territory? Why take such a risk?"

"Because of what's in the bank, Mr. Matsuo," said Hiraku. "Not the cash there, but the contents of the safe deposit boxes, particularly those that the clan in question"—he remained vague, careful around the American—"hold there."

"Ah," said Mr. Matsuo. "Now I see."

"For a percentage of the take," the American was saying, "I am willing to provide the specific information that will allow …"

Mr. Matsuo leaned towards me. "Can you negotiate his willingness?" he asked.

"Of course," I said, and, quickly rising to my feet, dragged the American to the soundproof room.

I had to remove only three of the American's fingernails (left pinky, left forefinger, thumb) and his right cuspid before he became willing to share his specific information with us for free. Conveniently, it was all, foolishly enough, on the laptop he had brought, kept in protected files whose passwords he almost immediately gave up.

"You haven't done this before?" I couldn't stop myself from saying at one point, and was not surprised when he shook his head.

"Do we need your help to interpret the data?" I asked, and he nervously insisted no, it was easy enough, we could release him and read the data just fine on our own. There was no reason to hold him, he claimed.

"And you promise not to tell anyone, I imagine," I said.

Yes, of course, he promised, he would speak to no one, we could trust him.

Just to make sure, I had him talk me through the data, the specific streets, the specific times. The math I couldn't understand, and when he started to explain it I stopped him. But the results were simple enough. Even a baby could understand them.

"You don't need me," he insisted, and yes, I had to agree, we didn't need him. And so I slit his throat. I did it from behind, so the blood would be less likely to spray me.

When I came back, Mr. Matsuo was waiting just as I had left him, serene, motionless. Hiraku beside him was sweating and nervous.

"The American had a perfectly legitimate business proposition," said Hiraku.

"Yes," I said, "but he was no businessman. He should have shared it with you, and then you should have shared it with Mr. Matsuo. There was no reason for him to see any face but your own."

"Did he become willing?" asked Mr. Matsuo.

I nodded.

"We can hold him," said Hiraku. "Keep him until the job is done and then release him once he can't do us any harm."

But of course he always could have done us harm. Mr. Matsuo looked at me inquiringly. Whatever he read in my face made him smile.

"As you wish, Hiraku," he said. "Shall you be the one to tell him?"

We watched him go. When he came back, he was sweating even more.

"It was wrong to bring the American here," said Mr. Matsuo to him, voice still mild. "It was a lack of judgment. You are responsible for his death."

I had heard Mr. Matsuo use such phrasing before and knew where it was headed. By the end of the evening, Hiraku would cut off the tip of his finger and present it to Mr. Matsuo as penance.

2.

The night predicted for Gojira's attack was cold, bitterly so. That, Mr. Matsuo suggested, was better: nobody would wonder about two men wrapped in coats and with their hats pulled low to hide their faces. Hiraku was still holding a grudge about the American.

"We could have kept him," he said to me as we rode the subway together to the waterfront district. I just grunted. "He could have told us about not only this attack but others. Surely there will be future banks decimated by Gojira's tail."

"They don't matter," I said.

"How do we know if they matter?" he asked.

"As soon as he walked into that room with his PowerPoint, he was a dead man," I said. "Be thankful you aren't dead with him."

"I," he said, rubbing his bandaged pinky, "would never use PowerPoint."

Midnight, the model the American provided had predicted, but just to be safe we were off the subway by 11 p.m., and walked the remainder of the way. Hiraku had printed out a screenshot of the predicted vector and we quickly found the place where Gojira was meant to appear, and even more quickly distanced ourselves from it.

We stood there in the cold, shivering, stamping our feet, waiting.

"He might have been wrong, you know," said Hiraku.

"I hope he was," I said.

"Why would you hope that?"

We found a ramen shop and settled in at the counter. Midnight came and nothing happened. *Perhaps the model was wrong,* I thought. It would be a relief if it were. I slurped my ramen, watching the second hand spin around the clock once, begin its course again.

Hiraku kept turning around, craning to look out the window.

"What's the matter?" I asked.

"We won't be able to see when it comes," he said.

"Maybe it won't come," I said.

"But if it does?"

"We don't have to see it," I told him. "We'll hear it."

Four minutes and twenty seconds after midnight, it came. We felt a slow rumbling run through the ground—hardly anything to notice at first, little more than if a subway train had passed underground below us. A few seconds later, our plates began to rattle. Many of the customers around us kept eating at first, until the vibration was too strong to ignore.

I quickly paid for both of us. By the time I had finished, Hiraku was already on the street. The ground was now shaking enough that it was difficult to keep our balance. Then came a strange, raucous cry, deafening us, shattering the glass of the windows. We caught a glimpse of the creature's hideous reptilian head over the row of buildings on the other side of the street, watched it cough out a gout of flame.

"Gojira!" yelled Hiraku.

Paralyzed, we watched it stalk past. The top of a building exploded as it was hit by the creature's gigantic tail, and we fled back into the ramen shop to avoid the rain of debris. Hiraku was still yelling the creature's name, over and over. If the American were here, I thought absurdly, would he tell us that this particular tail strike would decrease the chances of a similar one striking the bank? Would he compute a new percentage using his laptop and then quickly create a new PowerPoint?

And then the creature was past, moving up the street and away from us, leaving destruction in its wake. The name died on Hiraku's lips.

"Come on," I said. "The army will be here soon. Hurry."

We rushed to the corner and ran a block over, entering the street that Gojira had taken just in time to see his back and tail looming farther down through the smoke. He was enormous. The street itself was devastated, buildings broken, cars overturned, things on fire, alarms going off everywhere. The few people visible were screaming and running.

"Where's the bank?" I asked. Hiraku had the map out, examining it like a tourist.

"There," he finally said, pointing. We rushed up the street, toward the monster, moving in the opposite direction of everyone else.

The building was so broken, most of the façade spread out all over the street, that at first we didn't recognize it. But then, running past, I caught a glimpse of the vault door and dragged Hiraku back to it.

We slipped ski masks over our heads and entered. The vault door was intact, but the reinforced concrete panels of one of the vault walls had been cracked and split, the rebar broken far enough up that it was possible to squeeze through.

"You see," said Hiraku, smiling. "The American knew."

I just grunted. "Hurry," I said again.

I took out a flashlight and squeezed my way in. Inside, the air was full of dust, the floor cluttered with rubble. The safety deposit boxes we were looking for, 1760 and 1761, proved to be on the other wall —the wall that was undamaged.

I picked up a lump of concrete off the floor and hammered the door for one of the boxes. It didn't leave a dent. I hit it a few more times. No luck.

"Now what?" asked Hiraku.

I shrugged.

"You didn't bring any explosives?" he asked.

"Did you?" I responded.

I thought for a moment, then passed the flashlight to Hiraku, directing him where to point it. I took out my picks and tried to open one of the doors. The locks were tricky, I could tell immediately, but far from impossible—the bank had depended on the vault for keeping people out. It would take a few minutes, but it could be done.

But as I worked on picking the locks, I made the mistake of letting my thoughts wander.

I was thinking, *If the wall is undamaged and only these two boxes have been emptied, the clan will know they have been targeted and robbed. And if they know they have been targeted, they will have a list of likely suspects in mind. And Mr. Matsuo's clan will be very high on that list. If I open these boxes and remove anything, I will almost certainly bring war upon Mr. Matsuo and his clan. Even if I preserve the contents as they are but pass along the information, how can we use such information without the clan knowing what has happened and bringing war upon us?*

I moved the picks, insinuating them deeper into the tumblers.

What is my duty here? I wondered. Am I to do as Mr. Matsuo has asked and by so doing destroy the clan? Or am I to obey a higher duty?

One lock snapped open and, a moment later, so did the other. I slid the door open and pulled out the box inside, tucking it under my arm.

"We don't have time for the other box," I said to Hiraku. "It's a shame, but it's too much of a risk. Either the police will be here soon or the monster will be heading back the other way. Either way, it's too much of a risk."

For a moment he seemed poised to argue.

"I will take responsibility for this decision with Mr. Matsuo," I quickly said.

Tightening his lips, Hiraku nodded.

"You go first," I told him. Once you're outside the vault, I'll pass you the box and then come through myself."

He turned and crouched to go through the crack in the wall. And that was when I brought the metal box down hard on his head.

He did not go down immediately. He swayed and, confused, started to turn, and so I struck him again, harder this time, and then a third time. Finally, he collapsed. Once he was down, I hit him a few more times for good measure.

He lay there groggy and glassy-eyed as I slid the deposit box back into its slot. I closed it and used the pick to relock the tumblers. Behind me, Hiraku groaned.

He had turned himself partway over, struggling to get up. I picked up the chunk of concrete. Hefting it like a grapefruit, I stood over him.

"Why?" he asked, whispering from the floor.

"It's in the clan's best interest," I told him. "The clan is only as strong as its weakest member. But I can't say it doesn't give me pleasure."

"We're brothers," he said, his voice a little clearer now.

"Clan brothers," I said. "But yes."

"Would you kill your brother?"

I didn't answer.

"Is this Mr. Matsuo's wish?" he asked. "Does he know you're doing this?"

I did not answer. It is a mistake to lie to a man before killing him. But it is also a mistake to continue speaking with someone who is, for all intents and purposes, a ghost.

When I saw the muscles in his shoulders tense as he prepared to try to tackle me, I brought the lump of concrete down hard. Then again, and again, until his head was spongy and soft and bits of it were mixed with the debris on the vault floor.

I crushed his fingers to make him difficult to identify. When that was done, I pushed him out of the vault, forcing him through the narrow opening and out into the bank proper. Then I dragged him out into the street, where I left him leaning against a smoldering car.

In the distance, perhaps a half mile away, the sky was lit by flame as the army made its stand against Gojira. Soon the creature would be returning the way it came. Life in our clan would go on as before, with peace between the clans and easy profits for all. But it would go on without Hiraku.

I would not tell Mr. Matsuo what I had done. No, better to tell him that the calculations of the American scientist were slightly off, but that the error had been magnified by the complexity of the equation, and so when we thought ourselves huddled safe, waiting for the monster to pass, we had been in its path, and Hiraku had lost his life as a result. It was, I would say, a miracle that I had survived. As for the safe deposit boxes, because of the miscalculation the vault was not sufficiently cracked to allow us to pass through and reach them. And then I would offer to perform an act of contrition as acknowledgment of my role in the failure of the scheme, my failure to bring explosives, my failure to stop Hiraku from bringing the American to meet Mr. Matsuo. Perhaps I would chop off the tip of my finger and present it to him, or perhaps Mr. Matsuo, a kind and sensible boss, would dissuade me, but either way the clan will have been preserved and my own role in its future assured.

Indeed, Mr. Matsuo needs me. He is getting old. Who is there to fill his shoes now that Hiraku is gone, if not me?

Vampiric Crime Investigative Unit: Tokyo Metropolitan Police Department by Jyouji Hayashi
translated by Raechel Dumas

1.

It was the third of August, five in the morning. When Satoshi Muraki arrived on the scene at Inokashira Park, two Asian vampires were beginning the task of blockading the area by spreading out a set of translucent curtains printed with the phrase METROPOLITAN POLICE DEPARTMENT in Japanese, along with the English word POLICE.

Muraki's slight build gave him a boyish appearance, but he was confident of his strength. As a police officer he relied on his physical prowess, and had survived more than a few violent altercations. Nevertheless, the activity of the vampires in such close proximity gave rise to a curiously unsettling feeling.

It's difficult to distinguish between vampires and humans. At a glance, one might have pegged these two men as nothing more than migrant workers. But thanks to his line of work, Muraki grasped that they were vampires. It was the same intuition he felt on his beat downtown, upon discovering people behaving suspiciously.

Muraki wondered if they had sensed that he was a cop. Wearing expressionless faces, the two vampires idly went about their work. Across the breast of their yellow coveralls swung tags that read No FEEDING! in both English and Japanese.

The vampires residing in the metropolitan area had vowed never to attack humans. In point of fact, however, if the mood struck they could kill a mere human being with minimal effort. Muraki unconsciously used his right hand to double-check his holstered pistol.

Had Muraki's ID tag reacted? The grinning visage of an old man peered through the translucent curtain, and then the man himself pushed through the slit to greet Muraki. However much they resemble a human being, a vampire can't pull off that thing they call a businesslike smile.

"Great work here—thank you."

The man likewise wore yellow work coveralls. Across his breast hung a tag that read VLC MASATO YOSHIDA, absent the phrase No FEEDING!

"You're early, too, eh?"

As Muraki spoke the VLC man adeptly used the reader he was carrying to verify Muraki's identity. Modest and affable, Yoshida was a veteran of the public welfare department. It seemed he had retained the competence and amiability he had acquired during his time there.

Five years prior, coincident with the launch of the vampire employment agency VLC, a round of recruitment had taken place within the Metropolitan Police Department, and Yoshida had transferred. Whether the VLC was an auxiliary organization that assisted with police operations or a private enterprise undertaken by a retired police bureaucrat was an open question. "It's because we want to avoid unnecessary trouble with the neighborhood. Our work here is not yet finished," was a typical answer.

Yoshida and Muraki were already acquainted, but it was procedure to present one's ID. Yoshida ushered Muraki through the curtains and handed him two vinyl pouches. Muraki placed them over his shoes and fastened them with elastic.

The task of barricading the area looked to be completed. With a *swish,* the translucent curtain became transparent from the inside.

The curtain enclosed a small boat launch approximately thirty meters in diameter. The boats had been deposited tidily, and those in the perimeter of the area were especially neatly arranged. Atop the lawn that led to the pier a man in a filthy jersey was lying faceup with a stake driven through the left side of his chest.

At his side, Cadaver Investigator Yatsuyanagi was beginning his work.

Criminal Procedure Code Article 229 regulates "death inquests," but only from human beings. When such crimes concern the undead they are not subject to an ordinary autopsy, but rather demand the specialized knowledge of a Cadaver Investigator.

Yatsuyanagi was a head taller than Muraki. He was an amateur judoka and incredibly handsome, and had even graced the cover of a sports magazine. Muraki was a man who otherwise rarely experienced jealousy.

"Good morning." Muraki made sure he was the first to issue a greeting. Try as he might not to, he was crumpling in the Cadaver Investigator's dignified presence.

"Good morning," he replied. "Is it just you?"

"Hashimoto's been in touch to say he's running a little late. He's monitoring the demonstration, so he's coming via that route."

"The anti-vampire rally? How unfortunate—for Mr. Hashimoto, too." As he spoke, Yatsuyanagi proceeded to record his observations of the cadaver in his tablet. "A vampire, huh? Figures."

A number of lacerations were visible through the cadaver's torn jersey. The victim was an East Asian male in his thirties. The stake driven into his chest looked to be the fatal wound.

"Suspicious. After all, a stake through the heart would kill a human being too."

"That's not our concern—it's a matter for criminal affairs, isn't it?"

"Just check out the data."

Muraki produced his government-issue smartphone, downloaded the specified file from the Metropolitan Police Department server, and read it. Simultaneously, his phone transmitted its GPS data—a security measure.

"Sudden rigor mortis, with a remarkably decreased quantity of blood—definitely distinguishing features of a vampiric crime," said Muraki. "He's quasi-positive for the W Factor? The W Factor test is a medical screening, so it's no surprise it's highly sensitive, right?"

The W Factor test measures one's antigen-antibody reaction to a retrovirus. Because all vampires carry this antigen, for a time it was believed that the virus was responsible for human-vampire metamorphosis. Thus the virus had come to be referred to by the English phrase "Vampire Virus," and the authorities had combined these two Vs to form the W. From that point onward, it had come to be called the W Factor.

These days the hypothesis that the Vampire Virus was responsible for human-vampire metamorphosis was uncertain, but because of its high correlation with vampirism the W Factor screening exam continued to be widely deployed.

"What you're referring to is a 'false-positive,'" Yatsuyanagi replied. "That is, a false positive response despite the absence of the antigen. But I prefer the term quasi-positive—a dubious result, neither positive nor negative.

"Naturally, because the test is a screening, it's theoretically possible to come up with a quasi-positive result. But this is, at least, my first time seeing it. I wonder if the peripheral blood reaction was weak owing to the stake through the heart …"

Up until that moment Muraki had been confirming the facts of the case for a second time on his smartphone. The first person to discover the body had been a salaryman out jogging around four in the morning. He hadn't seen a vampire, but because of the circumstances—the stake through the victim's heart—he had reported the incident as a vampiric crime.

"Doctor, is this stake something one can buy off the shelf?"

"I can't say for certain they won't investigate it at the lab, but it seems unlikely, eh? It's the sort of thing you'd get ten of for a thousand yen at a home-improvement store."

The vampires in Tokyo were afforded legal protection. But opposition among residents had been strong. In Japan—where, unlike in America and elsewhere, one cannot carry firearms for self-protection—the Internet had a great deal of influence, and many people had taken to carrying stakes for self-protection.

Of course, marketing products designed to exterminate vampires was prohibited, but one could acquire such goods in the form of gardening tools and the like at home-improvement centers. In light of public opinion, the Metropolitan Police Department seemed to grant their tacit approval.

Thirty minutes later, Muraki's partner Hashimoto finally arrived on the scene.

"Sorry I'm late."

Hashimoto had been recruited to work security at the anti-vampire demonstration that had arisen in Shibuya, and though he would have been up nearly all night there wasn't a single wrinkle in his suit. Perhaps owing to his youth, he showed no trace of exhaustion.

"You've been working hard," I said. "How was Shibuya?"

"Nothing major went down. But they didn't need to carry on so late into the night just because they were protesting vampires," Hashimoto said.

"That's how demonstrations work—masochistic pleasure gives rise to a sense of accomplishment."

"If only there were lots of diurnal vampires …"

"There are, but people believe what they read online over the police reports! Though I suppose the Internet does have its uses. Anyway, have you looked at the data?"

"No, I caught the first train so I didn't look at them, as per regulations."

"Ahh, good call."

Muraki showed Hashimoto the data he had downloaded. For security reasons data transfers between terminals had been prohibited. It was required that they always utilize the server.

"Muraki, this says it's not clear whether the victim is human or vampire, but he has to be human, no?"

"What do you mean? He's quasi-positive for the W Factor. We can't determine whether or not he's human."

"Well, if he were a vampire, the assailant couldn't have so easily driven a stake through his heart. A human is no match for a vampire where brute force is concerned. And even assuming the victim was overtaken by a group, I think at least one human perpetrator would have been taken out in the process."

Muraki stared at Hashimoto. *The guy has a surprising grasp of the situation, doesn't he?*

"Suppose the assailant was also a vampire—what then?"

"In that case I think the scene would have been a lot messier. That stake would have been broken, no? But that's not the case. We're led to consider all sorts of scenarios involving humans and vampires, but based on the crime scene the victim, at least, was wholly human."

"I take your point," Muraki said.

Yatsuyanagi approached the two men, one hand still working his tablet. "You're assuming that this is the scene of the crime. But Hashimoto, you haven't considered the possibility that the perpetrator transported the body here and then drove the stake through his heart. Granted, it's unlikely that a human could have overtaken a vampire …"

"We'll know more after we transfer it to the lab, eh?"

"Indeed … Ah—excuse me!"

Yatsuyanagi took out his cell phone. It was his personal one, not government issue. He walked away from Muraki and Hashimoto.

In Yatsuyanagi's place arrived a team of scientists who began preparing the body for transport. Multiple cameras documented the process, transmitting the photos to the Metropolitan Police Department server in real time.

"Muraki, hypothetically speaking, if the perpetrator were a vampire, why would he have driven a stake through the victim's heart?"

"Humans can't comprehend vampire mentality. And since we don't know, we'll gather up the evidence and perform an honest criminal investigation."

Twenty-first century Tokyo. Population thirteen million, with 102,654 declared vampires among them. And the Metropolitan Police Department had a team of specialists devoted to vampire-related offenses: The Vampiric Crime Investigative Unit.

2.

Imagine a sociologist.

We are well into the twenty-first century.

The advent and suffusion of surveillance states, the sociologist explains, is what led to the discovery of vampires.

The use of regulatory mechanisms to monitor every aspect of modern life had been a subject of controversy since the twentieth century, but the issue had been confined to the discussion of hypotheticals. This had nothing to do with good intentions, ethical questions, or the like—the technological infrastructure to implement a surveillance state had yet to come into existence.

Circumstances had changed dramatically in the early twenty-first century. The problem of fraudulent food labeling necessitated measures to ensure transparency at every stage, from food production to distribution. Or perhaps it all began when it was recommended that schoolchildren be issued personal GPS devices to ensure their safety. There were even countries in which individuals with a history of sexual crimes were likewise made to wear a GPS device, enabling authorities to regularly monitor all of their movements.

Following the terror attacks of 9/11, support for national efforts to monitor each and every citizen had strengthened. Moreover, a rash of terrorist incidents that crossed national borders further bolstered this trend. A great number of terrorists cultivated false identities, after all, and there were more than a few examples of them posing as law-abiding citizens.

The incident that had decisively suppressed opposition to ubiquitous surveillance, however, concerned something other than terrorism. By some fortuitous accident, the pandemic spread of H5N1 Influenza across Asia had been averted thanks to biological border checks. The system used to maintain surveillance states prevented potentially millions of deaths. And in the face of this reality, discourses of dissent subsided.

Developed nations across the globe assigned their citizens ID tags and enacted surveillance policies that extended down to the individual level. From a public health standpoint, it became essential that not a single blank space be left on any ID tag issued across the globe in the interest of containing viruses with a high mortality rate.

And so, the dissemination of ID tags revealed that around the world some millions of citizens were leading false lives. A substantial portion of this number was composed of illegal immigrants, and citizens strongly backed their exposure and deportation. Moreover, a small number of criminals attempting to elude the system were arrested, and several large-scale terrorist schemes aborted.

But these control systems also shone a light on the lives of ordinary citizens, persons that were neither illegal immigrants nor criminals nor terrorists. In this world illuminated by control systems, some two thousand people had assumed false identities. A great number of them were Anglo or European, and appeared to be upstanding citizens. In many nations the authorities went to confront these anomalies. They resisted, and moreover injured or killed a great number of the police who attempted to capture them. And amidst the bloodshed, the existence of vampires came to light.

On average, the vampires that were arrested had lived among humankind for over three hundred years, occasionally feeding on blood to increase their numbers while falsifying their identities and frequently relocating in order to avoid discovery.

Many of them were wealthy, and the elder vampires maintained lines of communication with one another. It also came to light that in the interest of concealing their true nature, they had been funding anti-ID, pro-privacy movements.

In practice there wasn't any such thing as a vampire organization or the like, and intervampire communications and monetary donations were but personal endeavors undertaken by a number of the wealthiest. But the media did not disseminate this information. Before they were monsters, vampires were a minority.

In some nations the meme spontaneously emerged depicting the vampire as a species that lusted after society's riches, serving to heighten the feelings of entrapment that saturate surveillance societies. In turn, vampire-hunting movements took root across the globe. The anti-vampire movement brought about the end of two thousand ancient vampires, all legally executed.

Recently transformed vampires—those who were ten or twenty years young—adopted ID tags and remained difficult to detect. People were beset by fear and doubt. And once the W Factor came to light and it became known that humans and vampires could be differentiated, disaster followed. An abnormal proportion of non-vampiric humans tested positive for W.

Before the West regained its composure, some one hundred

thousand W Factor-positive individuals were executed, but it is estimated that 30 percent of these were not vampires—rather, they were illegal immigrants and social minorities.

While developed nations across Europe and the Americas were swept by tempests of vampire slaughter, Japan was, by comparison, able to distance itself from this frenzy. Foreigners had always been conspicuous there, and compared with those in the West the vampires in Japan—of which there were few—found it nigh impossible to remain hidden. Importantly, owing to Japan's historical policy of isolationism, no elder vampires resided there.

Furthermore, while the Japanese government was ushering in new prime ministers on a seemingly annual basis, the creation of legislation concerning the management of the vampire population was naturally postponed. The police did detain and imprison around a hundred vampires, but they came up empty-handed when the time arrived to charge them with a crime. A vampire-related bill was introduced, but this measure was regarded as inessential and repeatedly dropped during breaks in National Diet sessions. Accordingly, in Japan—where, ironically enough, everything falls behind—scientific and practical research into vampirism moved forward.

From a medical standpoint, human-vampire metamorphosis is defined in terms of a reorganization of the cranial nervous system. But the crucial question of how a person actually becomes a vampire remains unanswered. Vampire physiology is largely an enigma. For example, among humans that have been bitten by vampires there are both those who have remained dead and those who have returned to life as vampires. The cause of this discrepancy is unknown. One influential theory is the theory of the Human-Vampire Metamorphic Factor X. Upon being bitten by a vampire and injected with a substantial amount of Factor X, the speed of the victim's transformation exceeds the rate of tissue necrosis, and he or she is restored to life in the form of a vampire. But if only a small amount of Factor X is present, tissue necrosis occurs rapidly, and the victim dies.

"Vampires differ from humans physiologically and in terms of cerebral nerve activity," the Tokyo prefectural governor declared. "However, they are remarkably skilled in the area of technological development. Japanese society—with its aging population and shortage of quality laborers in the high-tech industry—should put the vampires to work."

It was generally acknowledged that vampires had greater technological acumen than did humans. Countless reports emerged claiming that the developers of globally competitive key technologies were, in fact, vampires.

However, there also existed deep-rooted resistance to the notion of accepting foreign vampires into the country. Many opposed even the idea of allowing living foreign laborers into Japan, and for this contingent admitting vampires was out of the question.

Be that as it may, the current political administration was simultaneously grappling with the problem of the US military's presence in Okinawa. As this issue grew politicized in such a way that it seemed likely to bring about a change of government, things began to move in an unanticipated direction.

"For the sake of Japan, accept the American forces in Okinawa, they say. And so for the sake of Japan, Tokyo must accept the vampires!"

Triggered by this remark, issued by the Okinawan governor at the national gubernatorial meeting, the question of whether to accept vampires into the country became a matter of national security. As tensions with neighboring countries heightened, a strengthening of the Japanese-American alliance was declared, and the US military presence in Okinawa increased, a measure to admit vampires into the country was granted high-priority approval, and they were permitted take up residence in Tokyo.

Vampires—naturally the Japanese constitution contained no

language pertaining to vampires, so they were legally designated Class Two Immigrants—were registered by the authorities, and after being equipped with wearable GPS devices that tracked their whereabouts, were permitted to reside within the Tokyo city limits.

They were managed by the employment agency VLC, which had stakeholders (no pun intended) both in Tokyo and across the country. In accordance with their abilities the vampires were placed in classes, organized into teams, and sent to work in the development sectors of corporations and the like.

Using humans for direct sustenance, or "bloodsucking," was banned, but the state provided suitable blood to those vampires who made substantial contributions to society. Accordingly, Red Cross blood drives transformed into free-market competitions, and the ban on selling blood was lifted.

Japan welcomed more than 100,000 vampires, organized and optimized them, and put them to work in the area of Vampire Technologies—referred to as VT—to increase productivity in high-tech fields. The move singlehandedly engendered a GDP increase of 8 percent and annual economic growth that progressed at roughly the same rate. In terms of GDP, Japan had already overtaken China, and the nation reasserted itself as the second most powerful economy in the world, behind only the United States.

Amidst these developments, incidents of crime surrounding vampires serving as industry resources spiked. Correspondingly, the Tokyo Metropolitan Police Department First Public Security Division's Class Two Immigrant Unit, also known as the Vampiric Crime Investigative Unit or, more commonly, the Vampire Squad, was born.

This was not a criminal unit in the conventional sense. Rather, it was affiliated with the division responsible for public safety. Indeed, the problem of vampires and that of public safety were inseparable.

3.

The designated meeting spot was an evidently high-class Italian restaurant located in the Hirō district of Shibuya. It was a small joint, constructed of brick and limned with a calm ambience.

Yatsuyanagi deposited his red E-Type Jaguar in the parking lot. Emissions regulations had recently grown strict, and it was in violation of Tokyo city ordinance to drive unmodified automobiles produced more than half a century prior. But Yatsuyanagi's car had been affixed with a conspicuous VT logo. It was the mark stamped on products produced utilizing technologies developed by vampires. The Jaguar also had a special nanotechnology-enhanced catalytic converter, so its emissions satisfied city standards.

Perhaps owing to the time of day, Yatsuyanagi's Jaguar was the only automobile in the small lot. Surprised to notice that the woman's car was absent, he entered the building.

On the wooden door, perhaps as a means of protection against vampires—or maybe simply for decoration—hung some garlic. These days garlic hung at the entrances even of drinking establishments and gyūdon shops. Even now those sorts of establishments struck Yatsuyanagi as odd.

"Mr. Yatsuyanagi, Mrs. Amachi is waiting."

The shopkeeper's announcement came immediately after he entered the restaurant. It was as though she had read his ID tag before he entered the building. Despite being a police officer, he couldn't get used to the individualized surveillance enabled by the ID tags.

"I know you're busy—thanks for coming."

She guided him to a private room. There he found a woman who appeared ten years younger than her actual age. She looked to be on her way home from work. She was wearing a suit, and a tote bag jam-packed with books and other materials had been placed in a box beneath the table.

Rieko Amachi—maiden name Rieko Higashihara—had been his junior in their medical school days, and if things had worked out differently she might have become Rieko Yatsuyanagi.

They had also been in judo club together. She had not been especially skilled at the sport, but her internal strength was unparalleled. Even when faced by a superior opponent, her attacks persisted. She always fought like she was going to win, no matter the score. That was Rieko. The woman bowed deeply.

She had grown up. Even so, Yatsuyanagi couldn't help but think back on those twenty long years.

"What's wrong?" he asked. "You said it was urgent?"

When she had called him at the Inokashira Park crime scene to say that she wanted to meet up at the Italian restaurant, he had visualized them celebrating their reunion with a toast or something. But the woman in front of him didn't have anything of the sort in mind.

"Amachi's gone missing."

"Missing? Ken'ichi? Wait a second—I saw Ken'ichi just recently! Three days ago, at the cardiovascular surgical conference. I invited him out afterward, but he returned home immediately, said that you were waiting for him …"

"He didn't come home."

"He didn't come home …"

For a time Yatsuyanagi had been estranged from Rieko, but those days were over. Amachi was far better suited to be her husband than he would have been. Yatsuyanagi had come to like Amachi. At least as far as Yatsuyanagi knew, Ken'ichi Amachi wasn't the sort of man to leave his wife and disappear.

"According to this morning's news they found someone in Inokashira Park who had been attacked by a vampire."

"No, no. The victim isn't Ken'ichi. The crime took place early in the morning, and it wasn't three days ago. And we're not even sure whether a vampire was involved. Don't let the news get to you—it isn't like you. Information spreads fast on social media, but it isn't accurate."

"So it seems … that's good to hear."

Rieko seemed relieved. After losing their appeal as an advertising medium, the old television stations—with the exception of NHK—had been dismantled one by one, and these days citizens and specialty channels disseminated bits and pieces of news free of charge. Then, divisions of those former news organizations gathered up these news flashes, performed corporate-sponsored analyses of their content, and delivered their spin to audiences.

The result was that information pertaining to topics outside of the business world was a mixture of wheat and chaff, the outcome of a for-profit analytical model that combined incident reports and mere gossip. And the media reported the true and the false. People heard only what they wished to hear.

The police had yet to release a formal statement concerning this morning's incident. Today's news was just conjecture.

"Was he in some sort of trouble, either professional or personal?"

"You're a Cadaver Investigator, but you sound like a detective."

"I am part of the police department, after all. So then, what could have happened? It's probable there was a legal issue with a heart surgery patient at the university hospital or something …"

"As far as I know, he wasn't in trouble. Amachi is a regenerative medicine researcher, not a clinician like me—there's no reason he would have trouble with a patient."

"That's true. No, I was just thinking that because of who Ken'ichi is he could have gotten wrapped up in some sort of trouble and then found it necessary to go underground in order to protect you …"

As Rieko listened the color of her face changed.

"What's the matter?"

"Earlier I said that he didn't come home, but that's not exactly the case. Amachi might have returned once in the middle of the night. There's no sign that he entered the house, but by this morning our car had disappeared from the garage. I think he took it."

Amachi had arrived at the conference by train and bus. It hadn't seemed unusual at the time because of the get-together that had been planned, but Amachi had not attended.

"Any chance you've been burglarized?"

"The car, garage, and house all have security systems. Only Amachi and I can disable them. Amachi sent me a message saying he was going to break early and attend the conference soirée, so I didn't worry about it until morning."

"Didn't you hear his car? Do you at least know what time he came back?"

"No, it's an electric."

"Is that so? Is there is a security system log? A video recording?"

Reiko shook her head. "It used to be set to keep records for a month, but it's been reconfigured. Every morning at six it's all erased. There aren't any records."

Reiko's explanation was haphazard, but the facts suggested that Ken'ichi Amachi returned to his house late in the night after the conference, reprogrammed the security system, took the car, and disappeared.

There was something about her husband that his wife didn't know, and whatever it was accounted for his disappearance. Rieko didn't seem satisfied, but her story wasn't unusual. While the motive for his disappearance was unknown, at present it would be difficult to call it a crime. This was a job for the Civil Police.

Choosing his words carefully, he explained the situation to Rieko. In the end, this was a matter between husband and wife.

"But … I'm worried."

"Worried?"

"I wonder if he might have been involved in a vampire incident. Amachi's research involves vampire immortality and how this knowledge might be practically applied in regenerative medicine. If the vampires knew about his work …"

"But that's impossible. Ken'ichi is an excellent man, but his present research is a team operation. Abducting one or two researchers wouldn't make any difference. And the vampires in the city are under constant surveillance. If something had happened, there's no way it would have gone undiscovered for three or four days. Don't worry, Ken'ichi is safe."

As he instructed her to face up to reality, Yatsuyanagi offered an indirect warning. Rieko's story suggested that she couldn't accept that there was something she didn't know about Ken'ichi. Accordingly, she had started going on about vampires and the like.

"Thank you. I'm glad we talked."

Without further discussion the pair finished their meal and parted. Rieko returned home alone on foot.

4.

"Come on in!"

Hashimoto held down the elevator door's open button. But the pair of policewomen shook their heads. "We'll take the next one," one of them said. Without a word, Muraki pressed the close button. The elevator swiftly ascended the police station.

"Don't let it bother you."

"Are we that hated? Even by our colleagues?"

"They don't have any reason to hate us—they hate the vampires. That's all."

The First Public Security Division's Class Two Immigrant Unit was an independent unit that occupied one floor of the Tokyo Metropolitan Police Department building. The belief that vampirism was the result of a viral infection lingered, so all sorts of measures had been taken to ensure that the hypothetical virus would not be transmitted to the outside world. In those days, except when used by the Vampire Squad and the VLC staff, the elevator wouldn't even stop on this floor. Naturally, ID tags were employed to closely monitor access to the rooms.

By the time Muraki and Hashimoto returned from the field, nearly all of the members of the Vampire Squad had arrived. Muraki greeted the subsection chief, Yamamoto, then took a seat in the last row. Hashimoto sat down beside him.

"Well, it's about time, so let's get started."

Chief Yamamoto rose to his feet. The projector screen at the front of the room read "The Kichijōji Class Two Immigrant Serial Vampire Incidents," and a small VT logo appeared at the corner of the screen. In affairs handled by the Vampire Squad, the word "murder" was anxiously avoided.

"First we'll go over the facts that have come to light in the week since the incident took place."

Chief Yamamoto fiddled with the remote control function on his government-issue smartphone, then displayed the information related to the incident in chronological order. The word "cadaver" was conspicuous on the screen. Because of society's antagonism toward vampires, the late victims of vampiric crimes were referred to not as "dead bodies," but as "cadavers."

Even so, until the incident had been deemed a vampiric crime, it had been written with the characters for "dead body." *In dubio pro reo.* When it had been determined that the incident fell under the jurisdiction of the Vampire Squad, "dead body" had been exchanged for "cadaver."

The August 3 discovery of a cadaver with a stake driven through its heart in Inokashira Park was not the end of the story. Five days later, in the Inokashira Park zoo, a second body had been found, and seven days after the original incident a third body appeared on the grounds of G-Art Gallery, adjacent to the park.

"The first victim's name was Tōru Ishikawa, and he was twenty-eight years old. He was a vagrant, and unemployed. His blood type was B, and he had no history of disease. In good health, but poorly connected to society—a prime target for vampires. The last image of him alive was recorded in the morning on the day prior to the incident, by a security camera at a net café in front of Kichijōji Station. The second and third victims were similar. Blood type B, and we haven't been able to contact any of the three men's families."

Everything Chief Yamamoto was saying was already known to the twenty or so Vampire Squad officers in the room. But one after another he flipped through the images on the screen.

As a matter of fact, it had come to light the previous day that the perpetrator of the three incidents at Inokashira Park had previously committed five other vampiric crimes. These five newly discovered crimes were identical to the more recent three, with the victims having likewise sustained knife wounds from which their blood had been sucked. Moreover, hair and skin cells collected at the scenes suggested that a vampire was involved, and DNA analysis had confirmed that it was the same vampire in all cases.

The DNA of the hundred thousand vampires residing in Tokyo— including that of both the immigrant vampires that accounted for the majority and that of the small number of indigenous ones—was registered in a database. Yet there was no match for the DNA that had been collected from the crime scene. It belonged to a cadaver that had been resurrected by one of the registered vampires. The perpetrator was a rogue.

So, they had searched the database for prior incidents involving a knife to find that five unsolved fatal robberies, all of which involved what appeared to be the same weapon, had occurred between June and July.

These hadn't taken place in Inokashira Park, but rather in the peripheries of Kichijōji and Mitaka. The victims' wallets and some other effects had been taken, and because they had been stabbed the Criminal Affairs Division had treated the cases as regular rather than vampiric crimes. Accordingly, they had neither tested for the

W Factor nor informed the Vampire Squad about the details of these incidents.

A second investigation of the five cadavers and tissue samples collected from them confirmed the presence of the W Factor, as well as characteristics indicating that they had undergone vampiric metamorphosis. Thus, the five incidents were handed over to the Vampire Squad. It appeared that the suspect, in an attempt to conceal the vampiric element of his attacks, had endeavored to make them look like a series of muggings. After presenting this overview, Chief Yamamoto asked Muraki to share the results of his own investigation.

"I've just returned and haven't prepared any slides. I'll just have to project the notes I took at the crime scene. The doctor gave me a rundown of the postmortem exam findings, and a party that we think was involved in the incidents in some way has surfaced. It looks like the penniless victims of the most recent three incidents experienced an improvement in their financial circumstances immediately prior to their deaths. Their wallets were stolen, but we thoroughly analyzed the effects they left behind to look for skin and hair samples deriving from people who may have had contact with the victims before their deaths.

"In the end, we couldn't find any skin other than that of the victims, and the only hair we found was broken off at the root, so we couldn't perform DNA testing. According to the forensic examination, though, it came from a baseline nonvampiric human, and we're more than 90 percent certain that the same person was involved in all of the incidents. We estimated their age based on the amount of melanin present, and we think this person is between thirty and forty years old."

Muraki's conjecture sent the meeting room into a commotion. He was suggesting that there was a human being out there who was aiding and abetting vampiric crimes.

"Something of interest: We recovered a banknote from the bottom of the first victim's bag. A hair sample we collected from it was also a match. Based on this, we think that the three victims accepted money from the person in question prior to the attacks."

Muraki projected a photo from his smartphone onto the screen. It was a grainy, pixelated image, untouched, and taken from a video monitor screen. It showed someone that resembled the first victim found in Inokashira Park.

"This image was taken from a security camera at the home-improvement center near Inokashira Park. It's an old machine and the resolution is poor, but he's purchasing a stake identical to the one used in the crime. The date is here—August second, the day before the incident. As you can see, his wallet contains a substantial number of banknotes. It was a cash purchase. Fortunately, we were able to collect fingerprint and skin samples before the money was deposited into the bank. As expected, we found the victim's DNA. Here's the problem."

The projection screen magnified to display someone who appeared to be accompanying the victim. Because of the camera angle, one could make out only that the person was wearing a suit. After finishing his purchase, the victim walked toward the second party, and the final shot showed them leaving the store together.

"We used image processing to perform an analysis of the spectrum of fibers that compose the suit, and it's a match with the fibers we collected from the cadaver. It's definitely an Armani, but unfortunately we were only able to identify the fabric and not the exact type of suit."

"So you're saying that each of the three victims received cash from the person in the suit, and then was attacked by a vampire? I see, thank you."

After Muraki finished his explanation, he sat down with a sigh of relief. Hashimoto offered him a canned coffee, and Muraki accepted it. It seemed Muraki's report was new information to more than half of those present at the meeting. The room was astir.

"Well then, doctor, if you please."

At Chief Yamamoto's urging Cadaver Investigator Yatsuyanagi stood up. Using his smartphone, Yatsuyanagi displayed images taken from the three crime scenes on the screen.

"As we learned earlier, prior to the Inokashira Park incidents the vampire in question had already committed five other crimes."

Yatsuyanagi displayed a new image. This one showed three stakes. Each was wooden type commonly purchased at home-improvement centers in order to exterminate vampires.

"The greatest riddle surrounding the affair is the question of why stakes were driven through the victims' hearts only in the three most recent incidents. We have yet to find any evidence linking the perpetrator to the stakes. Nevertheless, we think these weapons are the same stakes purchased at the Kichijōji home-improvement center mentioned in this report. They're your typical cheap, Chinese-made goods, so there's no way to explain it. Now, aside from the stakes, two other factors also differentiate the three recent incidents from the five that took place prior.

"Firstly, in the recent three incidents surgical tools were employed, and an enormous quantity of blood was extracted from the cadavers. One to two liters, give or take. As far as I know, vampires don't tend to drink such massive quantities of blood. This is something other than hematophagia."

"Doctor, isn't exsanguination a preservation method?" Muraki inquired, the canned coffee still in his hand.

"The motive remains unclear. To preserve a body you need the anticoagulant heparin or something of the sort, but your average vampire has an aversion to the drug. The possibility that preservation was the goal seems unlikely. And therein lies the second issue. Perhaps it's a coincidence, but ever since the incident in Inokashira Park the victims have shared the same blood type: B. Vampires aren't picky about blood type—they're far more concerned with avoiding persons with a history of viral disease. Among Japanese people, only one in five is type B. Based on simple math, the probability that three people in succession would be type B is less than 1 percent."

"If we're dealing with a human the blood could have been used for a transfusion, but ..." Whether Muraki was voicing a question or an opinion was unclear, but as he trailed off, Yatsuyanagi continued with his explanation.

"A little while ago Muraki reported that the three victims accepted money from the same person. This is consistent with my postmortem exam findings. When I checked out the contents of the three victims' stomachs, I got the impression that each of them had consumed a recent and rare feast. The pathology data suggests that all of them suffered from some level of malnutrition. But the contents of their stomachs indicated otherwise."

"Doctor, if that's the case ... are you saying that the person in question prepared the victims for the vampire?"

At Chief Yamamoto's inquiry, Muraki stopped drinking his canned coffee. The chief's question had serious implications. Although vampires were permitted to reside in Tokyo, their activities had been restricted in many respects. But if there were humans assisting with their crimes, the Vampire Squad's work was liable to become difficult.

"Based on the autopsy results alone, we can't know that much. But even assuming human cooperation is at play, the *modi operandi* of the first five incidents and the most recent three differ. So, we can only confirm that the person in question was involved in the most recent three incidents."

"Are you saying that the first five incidents and the most recent three might be unrelated?"

"It's a bit of a pain, eh?"

A map appeared on the projection screen, and on it eight crime scenes had been plotted out. They were framed by color-coded areas shaped like doughnuts.

"I think you'll get the picture when you see this, but I attempted to analyze the crime scenes using Rossmo's formula."

Rossmo's formula is a method of geographical profiling. Where do serial murderers, sex offenders, and other serial criminals live? The formula seeks to answer this question based on the distribution of crime scenes.

The theory is pretty straightforward. When serial murderers and the like select a location in which to commit their crimes, they tend to choose a place that is relatively close to their own homes while avoiding locales that are too close, instead establishing a buffer zone around their domiciles. In their minds, the probability of being discovered if they select a location too close to home is high. On the other hand, if one strays too far from home it takes too long to return from the scene of the crime—and from the criminal's standpoint, this is a dangerous thing.

Thus, in an attempt to establish what he believes to be a safe location for his serial crimes, the perpetrator unwittingly supplies information concerning where he lives. Rossmo's formula works according to this principle, utilizing crime scene distribution data to determine the hot zone in which a criminal is hiding.

Yatsuyanagi had carried out an analysis utilizing this technique, and the room had grown agitated upon seeing the results.

"How did you arrive at this?"

Muraki grumbled. Hashimoto addressed him.

"Muraki, I've computed the hot zone using Rossmo's formula—so why does everyone look so skeptical?"

"Rossmo's formula doesn't hold up for Vampire Squad investigations. Well, there are exceptions, but that's true for nine cases out of ten."

"Why? Because vampires think differently than humans?"

"That's too simplistic. A sharp-witted vampire would at least be familiar with Rossmo's formula. And a vampire living at the peripheries of society would need to become familiar with police procedure. That sort of vampire would choose a location precisely in order to circumvent Rossmo's formula. Or perhaps he'd contrive a way for identical crimes to go undiscovered. It's not often that things fall into place like you're suggesting."

"I had no idea. In the training course we learned that it was an effective investigative technique, and the formula itself isn't readily apprehensible."

"Vampiric crimes are discovered daily. The content of the training courses immediately grows outmoded. And vampires, too, surf the Web. This sort of information isn't circulated. Disinformation, on the other hand ..."

To supplement Muraki's explanation, Yatsuyanagi split the screen and presented the data related to prior similar incidents.

"So that he can pull off serial crimes, this clever vampire selects locations in order to sidestep Rossmo's formula. Most of them transpire outside of the turbulence of the hot zone, making his serial crimes appear to be one-time offenses. When a vampire indulges in serial bloodsucking, without question, he'll be found out and put down. If it's a one-time affair, he might avoid euthanasia. Even so, the vampire in this case is different. It's as though he's declaring that he's a serial offender. Is there some connection between this and the fact that the prior five incidents and the most recent three differ?"

Muraki looked at the hot zone, and something came to mind.

"Doctor, you recently participated in an academic conference in Mitaka. That isn't far from the hot zone, is it?"

"Muraki, what an unpleasant thought. That's right, the conference took place in the hot zone. If I'd walked down the wrong street at the wrong time, I could have become the subject of an autopsy."

Muraki raised his hand, and again asked for comment. He highlighted a spot on the map with the pointer.

"The home-improvement center where the party in question had the victim purchase a stake—it's also near the hot zone.

Supposing that the vampire's behavior doesn't contradict Rossmo's formula, isn't there a strong possibility that the person in question also lives in this hot zone? Maybe the human accomplice has established a pattern based on the behavior of the offending vampire. What do you think, Chief?"

"Muraki, are you saying we're dealing with a human being who's living with a rogue vampire?"

"Or a vampire who's romantically involved with a human. For a rogue vampire there's no better cover, right? In which case, might the stakes be signs that this person wants them to be found out? If so, it all adds up."

5.

Chateau Shimo-renjaku, as its name suggested, was a small four-story apartment building facing Renjaku Street. All of the units were used as VLC employee housing, but it was not widely known that the surveillance state's Asō Real Estate Company was a subsidiary of VLC.

With Hashimoto in tow, Muraki drove his electric car soundlessly into the visitor parking lot at Chateau Shimo-renjaku. The police department had embraced the electric car more fully than any other part of the public sector.

"Muraki, the informant you're going to introduce me to—is it a VLC worker?"

"Come on, you'll understand before long. More importantly, do you have your gun?"

"Yeah, but—"

"Good."

Muraki was facing the corner room on the fourth floor. The doorplate read TECHNICAL TRANSLATOR JONATHAN. On the steel door hung a bulb of garlic. Reading Muraki's ID tag, the door produced a sound indicating that the lock had been released.

"Enter two meters behind me. And remain at least two meters away from me. Near the exit, if possible," Muraki said, then entered the room. The corridor from the entryway to the living area was a steel bookcase lined with nondigitized dictionaries and documents in German, Russian, and other languages.

Muraki had visited this place many times, but never without a sense of unease. Though in his head he knew that nothing would happen, his gut wouldn't accept it.

"Thank you for coming."

An androgynous voice arose from the living area. The parlor, which together with the kitchen formed a twelve-mat room, was lined on all four sides with steel bookcases that blocked off even the window. In the center of the room was a large wooden desk. The lights had been turned off, but a ray of sunlight that slipped through the window otherwise obscured by the bookcase mingled with the glow of a large computer monitor to illuminate Jonathan.

He welcomed Muraki and Hashimoto in a polite tone, but made no move to rise from his chair. This was not out of lack of courtesy; rather, it seemed, he was trying to avoid putting his company on edge by making a careless movement.

Perhaps in an attempt to demonstrate to his visitors that he was one of the virtuous vampires, the cup of blood that he had just finished drinking had been left out on the kitchen sink. It appeared that he had also eaten some pasta.

Jonathan looked to be a young man. He was a Japanese, not a foreigner. He was slender, and when he did stand he gave the impression of being quite tall. Perhaps owing to the light of the computer monitor, his pallid skin appeared sickly.

"Muraki, what the ..."

Muraki heard Hashimoto's voice from behind.

"Let me introduce you two: This is my informant, Jonathan. As you can see, he's a vampire. And this is my partner, Hashimoto."

Hashimoto bowed to Jonathan. Jonathan gestured toward a

pair of seats. Muraki sat down, but Hashimoto remained standing, maintaining his distance from Muraki. Perhaps because Jonathan understood why, he said nothing more.

"So, why did you ask me here?"

Jonathan produced a printout of an image taken with a digital camera. The picture depicted a group of roughly thirty young men. On the back something had been written in slender characters.

"The Kichijōji affair?"

"Yep."

Muraki read the writing on the back of the picture. Current addresses and brief personal histories of the men pictured. And a name.

"*Satoshi Kijima?* Is he our rogue? Who created him?" Muraki asked.

"You wont hear a peep from me on that matter," Jonathan replied.

"We could also put the screws on this stray and make him spit it out!"

"If you search VLC's records, you'll find a vampire who committed suicide. But the truth is that she was killed by a vampire, one I myself transformed."

"*She?* You're saying he meant to turn his lover into a vampire?"

"I don't know. Maybe it was an experiment. Why he'd do something so foolish is a mystery to us, too."

"What kind of fellow is he, this Kijima?"

"A beast. He's driven by instinct. Not a cultured bone in his body, but he is cunning. To the extent that he was able to convince even his fellow vampires that it was a suicide."

"This guy isn't living with a human, is he?"

"If he only had the self-restraint to do so without drinking their blood, he wouldn't have been so stupid as to make enemies of us."

Feeling that "us" included the Vampire Squad, Muraki got an unsettled feeling.

"The long and short of it is that if this rogue keeps committing crimes, this virtuous vampire before me is going to have trouble. Is this why you're trying to make us get rid of him?"

"I don't manipulate the police. Isn't reporting information about criminals to the police the responsibility of virtuous citizens?"

"I see. You have our thanks. If this information is correct, we'll arrange for a reward."

"I look forward to working with you."

Hashimoto exited Johnson's dwelling, and shortly thereafter Muraki left, as well. They didn't exchange a word until they had retraced their steps to the car.

"Muraki, you're using a vampire as an informant?"

Muraki had anticipated this reaction.

"There's no better source of information about vampiric crimes than a vampire. You must have seen that. When humans become vampires, most lose touch with their emotions, but some undergo the change without entirely losing their connection to humanity. Are you familiar with the theory that if the vampire factor is highly concentrated at the time the blood is drunk, the vampire retains more of his base human personality? Only those vampires possess the ability to hold direct conversations with human beings."

"If that's the case," Hashimoto said, "no matter how much a vampire works at it, only those that excel at communication could adapt to society and follow in the footsteps of Europe's elder vampires. An individual with a poor ability to communicate would soon find himself unable to adapt to society and be weeded out."

"The vampires in the metropolitan area are granted legal protection. Natural selection doesn't apply—vampires with whom it is difficult to come to a mutual understanding haven't killed themselves off yet. Still, it's a pain to correspond only with fellows like Jonathan. He has a pliant demeanor, but he's obstinate. If what he says is true, there is a problem with VLC's ability to keep things in check," Muraki said. "To conclude that a murder is a suicide—we'll be heaped with criticism asking what the hell the Vampire Squad was doing. This has to be resolved peacefully. With the police secure, and the vampires happy."

"But something doesn't make sense."

"In what regard?"

"Rossmo's formula. Kijima's an uneducated vampire, so he wouldn't know about Rossmo's formula. So, he established a pattern. Proceeded in a logical manner."

Muraki got the feeling that Hashimoto was holding something back, some sort of grave hint. But he wasn't able to adeptly put it into words.

"When we get back shall we try to meet with the doctor?"

6.

The Amachi home was in the residential district of Azabu. It was a sizable three-story dwelling, but the building-to-land ratio was significant, and ensuring that there was space for visitor parking meant there was practically nothing in the way of a garden.

Yatsuyanagi parked his car in a visitor spot. Unsurprisingly, there was nothing in the first-floor garage. Had Rieko already come home? The outdoor electric unit was running, and the wattage meter near the garage was rotating smoothly.

Yatsuyanagi stood at the door unsure how to greet her, but in the end called out officially, "It's Yatsuyanagi." As though it had read his ID tag, the door unlocked. When he opened it the coolness that Yatsuyanagi had anticipated encountering was absent.

"Prop the door open to let in some fresh air and come upstairs," came Rieko's voice from the floor above him.

"Sorry to disturb you." Yatsuyanagi reached down for the door-stop, and after cracking the door he humbly removed his shoes, changed into a pair of slippers, and headed toward the second-floor living room. The air was pregnant with heat. Rieko was wearing a suit, and a large tote bag had been carelessly placed on a chair.

"Sorry, my meeting ran late, so I just got home."

Saying this, Rieko opened the window all the way. It was a south-facing window, which meant that the temperature in the approximately twenty-mat living room had soared above body temperature. The breeze flowed through the open window.

"You have a giant air conditioner over there—why not use it?"

"I hate the cold air from the A/C. Natural breeze is the best— that's why I opened the window."

As Rieko climbed to the third floor to change her clothes, Yatsuyanagi, with her permission, entered the kitchen and helped himself to some water. The kitchen was spacious. An island had been installed, as though to enable husband and wife to prepare food together. Yatsuyanagi firmly believed that his hunch was correct.

Rieko returned, having changed into jeans and a T-shirt. The married woman standing before him was not the girl Yatsuyanagi remembered. When Rieko offered him coffee, Yatsuyanagi lifted his glass of water. The two got down to business.

"So, what's the news on Amachi? Something bad?"

"Amachi's car has been found. It was among the items confiscated from a theft ring specializing in luxury automobiles. They say they nabbed it in the middle of the night from a parking lot in Azabu. They're professionals—they dismantle electric cars and sell the parts overseas. So what we more accurately found was not the car, but rather some of its parts."

"What do the police think?"

"It's destruction of evidence! Ken'ichi's blood was detected on the confiscated parts. But there's nothing strange about finding the owner's blood. As for how much blood he lost, we can't tell, but it is still evidence.

"It may be true that had some novice disposed of the car,

sooner or later it would have been discovered. Especially because it's a luxury automobile. But when pros dismantle a car, they get rid of it securely. In fact, if we were just a little too late Amachi's car could have ended up in Vietnam."

"What are you saying—that Amachi's been involved in some sort of crime?!"

"Before I answer your question, I want to confirm something."

While Rieko was upstairs, Yatsuyanagi had gathered the remote controls to her household electronics and arranged them in a line nearby. Before Rieko could stop him, he switched on the LCD television.

"Just in time for the news. I'm guessing you knew that, too. The Inokashira Park incident was a grotesque affair—someone was stabbed in the chest with a stake. I expect that's what they'll be reporting on."

After hearing that the news would address the vampire incident, Rieko made no move to stop him. Several of the station's automated program advertisements played on the fifty-inch screen, and then the report began. *"Today at 1 p.m. an undocumented vampire was discovered in an apartment on Mitaka's Renjaku Street, and was dealt with by the police. This undocumented vampire appears to be the suspect in a series of vampiric crimes, and the police department is in the midst of an investigation."*

Rieko appeared shocked upon hearing that the undocumented vampire had been dealt with.

"What do they mean when they say the vampire has been dealt with?"

"While resisting arrest the vampire injured the officer who was attempting to apprehend him, allowing the officer to use deadly force. The vampire's name is Satoshi Kijima, and going only on what the Vampire Squad knows he is responsible for eight criminal incidents. On that basis alone he was a dangerous vampire.

"In the first five incidents he used a knife in an attempt to conceal that he had drunk the blood of his victims. But there was something different about the most recent three incidents. Why had he staked his victims?"

"I hear humans can't comprehend vampire psychology because of our different brain structures. We can't understand their behavior, but it doesn't seem all that mysterious," Rieko said.

"Incomprehensible behavior and irrational behavior are two different things. This is the rational explanation: The rogue vampire committed eight crimes, each time using a knife to wound his victims before drinking their blood. And in the most recent three incidents only, a second party appeared at the crime scenes after the vampire was finished and drove stakes through the hearts of the victims."

"That seems improbable," Rieko argued, staring into Yatsuyanagi's eyes. The woman hadn't changed, he thought. Though she was on the defensive, she remained poised for attack.

"You say that after the rogue vampire carried out his crimes another party drove the stakes through their hearts," Rieko said. "But how would this person have known about the vampiric crimes? Do you mean that they knew where the vampire lived and followed him around? Ordinarily anyone who did this would themselves fall victim to a vampire attack."

"This person wouldn't need to know the vampire's address or anything like that. They would just have to know where the victims reside."

"What do you mean?"

"Rossmo's formula—that is, regional profiling—is a technique used in criminal investigations to compute where a repeat offender resides. It isn't that complex a formula. A university-educated person could do it. When it's reliable, the real criminal's address falls within the area determined by Rossmo's formula."

"And?"

"Now, let's assume there was a human who took notice of

the undocumented vampire's crimes. Perhaps they zeroed in on the serial murders because of the unresolved matter of the knife. Based on the location of the crime scenes, this person deduced the general area where the perpetrator resides—that is, the hot zone. Accordingly, this person sought out humans that looked to be prime vampire bait and lured them into the hot zone. They served each one a delicious meal, gave them a small sum of money, perhaps. Then, they had them walk to a location in the hot zone where it would be easy to trigger a crime. There were probably misses. But there were hits, as well.

"There is one consistency about this person's behavior. An important part of committing a crime is that you don't dirty your own hands. They didn't dispose of the evidence—the automobile—on their own; rather, they allowed it to be dismantled by a professional theft ring. Like tossing food at the feet of a hungry animal. In the same way, the victims that had been lured into the hot zone were attacked by the vampire. And after that, this person showed up and drove stakes through their hearts."

"Hold on—why the stakes? To prevent them from becoming vampires? But if that were the case, it defeats the purpose of having the vampire attack them."

"The stakes were used to give the impression that the motive was vampire extermination. But the real reason was to stop the still-living victims' hearts, thereby halting their blood circulation. At the site of the vampire bite, the concentration of Factor X, which transforms humans into vampires, is high. And if you stop the heart, it remains in the periphery of the bite mark. And just like that, it becomes possible to extract blood from the puncture site and collect the vampire factor."

"What does this have to do with Amachi's disappearance?"

"That's what I've come here to verify. Ken'ichi's blood type is B. And on the night of Ken'ichi's disappearance, he was walking in the hot zone. Alone."

The sound of the electric range came from the kitchen. For the first time, Rieko let her feelings show.

"I set the timer while I was in the kitchen," Yatsuyanagi said.

"Why are you doing this!?"

"Like I said, there's something I wanted to check."

Yatsuyanagi took the air-conditioner remote in his hand and hit the switch. The breaker flipped, and all of the electronics in the room ceased to function. Rieko let out a wail, and hearing this Muraki and Hashimoto burst into the Amachi residence.

"You tricked me!" Rieko said as they were about to place her in the patrol car.

"And before that, you deceived me."

Rieko cursed at Yatsuyanagi's reply, then climbed into the car. Muraki returned from her home.

"I sealed it off as per the doctor's instructions. But what the hell is all of that on the bed? A factory? A household ICU? Intravenous tubes are hanging from his body, and he's as cold as ice. I'm guessing the utility costs are no joke."

"That's the life-support device she constructed. It looks like she pilfered some hospital equipment. Keeping him at a low body temperature served to slow his metabolism. Over there is a body suspended in the process of transforming from human to vampire. Ken'ichi Amachi—an old friend of mine—is really the sixth known victim of the undocumented vampire's attacks."

"But he lived," Muraki said.

"Because Rieko, like her husband, is an excellent surgeon. After the Mitaka conference we discussed earlier, Ken'ichi was attacked by a vampire. But his wife Rieko showed up to meet him. This is only conjecture, but it's possible that even though there weren't a lot of people on the streets that night, he chose the shortest route home. Or maybe he intended to meet up with his wife for a quickie."

"But instead of his wife, he encountered a vampire."

"Probably when Rieko appeared the vampire was already in the process of drinking his blood. Ken'ichi survived. Rieko understood what had gone down and single-handedly stopped her husband's blood flow—damage control."

"Why not go to the hospital?"

"He was attacked by a vampire. If they had gone to the hospital, by law he would have been treated as a vampire. For Rieko, this would have meant losing her husband. In order to save her beloved husband, Rieko made use of our uneducated vampire. She slowed her husband's metabolism by lowering his body temperature, and while staving off his transformation gave him transfusions using the blood she extracted from the victims. By increasing the concentration of the vampire factor in his blood, she hoped to retain his personality to the greatest extent possible."

"But if that's the case, she could have procured a vampire from VLC and more easily obtained the vampire factor, right?"

"Had she done that, the vampire attack on Ken'ichi would have come to light. Rieko was afraid of this. VLC's documented vampires were no good. She needed a rogue."

"That's quite a story. To create a vampire with her husband's personality she drove a stake through the hearts of the cadavers, collected their blood, and transfused it … but is this even possible?"

"I don't know. But given that she was able to stabilize him at such a low temperature, Ken'ichi is no longer human. That's the only thing that's certain."

In place of the patrol car in which Rieko was riding there arrived two vehicles from the Metropolitan Police Department and the Ministry of Health, Labor, and Welfare. They had come to transport Ken'ichi Amachi to an appropriate facility.

"Doctor, why do you find this woman so alluring?"

Never backing down from her attack stance, even when on the defensive—that was Rieko. When she had come to Yatsuyanagi with the claim that the security system had been manipulated and their car had vanished, somewhere in his heart he had been suspicious of her story.

She had wanted to know what information the police had concerning her own crimes, and had contacted Yatsuyanagi in order to distance herself and her husband from the Kichijōji incident. He could understand this. But he wasn't in the mood to discuss it with Muraki.

"Leaving that aside, I wonder what Rieko will be charged with?"

"Surprisingly, probably something trivial. She didn't commission Kijima, so instigating a crime and compulsion don't apply. Probably she'll just be charged with luring people to a dangerous location. And though there's the matter of the car, she is the victim of grand theft auto.

"In the end, this woman probabilistically took advantage of the fact that someone else's actions were in accordance with her own desires. She took a series of gambles, and she kept winning. Whether we can call that a crime—that's above my pay grade. We could charge her with the destruction of a cadaver, but since this was done in order to save her husband's life … well, what would come of it?"

"At any rate, Rieko grew unable to keep up with this foolish behavior. That's for certain."

"Well, our rogue vampire has been disposed of, the mystery has unraveled, and these incidents are resolved. But still, collecting blood from cadavers for the sake of her husband—she's insane," said Muraki.

Yatsuyanagi turned to him and spoke.

"Is there any such thing as a sane vampiric crime?"

Jigoku by Naomi Hirahara

His son's death should have occurred shortly after his own, but Hideyoshi Osumi remained alone in his box for what seemed like hours. Days or even weeks could have transpired for all he knew. Time in Hell was funny that way.

Back on earth, when he was alive and at home, Hideyoshi could measure time by the growling of his stomach. Breakfast was usually salad with Kewpie mayonnaise; his wife insisted on vegetables for their son's health. (What good that did him.) Lunch, *teishoku* at a local eatery. And finally dinner, something traditional like *oden* with fat slices of *konnyaku* and soft balls of *satoimo,* shed of all its hairy skin.

In contrast, in Hell, Hideyoshi had completely lost his appetite. A good thing, considering there was no food there, at least in his box. Before, when he was killing the women, he never thought about an afterlife, either for his victims or himself. Reincarnation always seemed ridiculous to him. How could he be repackaged in the form of an insect or, even more ridiculous, a woman? His body—the heavy, strong hands and fingers, the rectangular face with the open forehead, his awkward toes with black and gray hair sprouting below his toenails—these were all part of his identity. To lose these physical markers would mean that he didn't exist. As it turned out, he was right. Even in Hell he still looked the same.

"Hey, are you still alone?" a voice on the other side of the cardboard box hissed.

It was a next-door neighbor, who also was an Osumi. According to this Osumi, they were all arranged alphabetically; as a result, all the Hideyoshi Osumis were to be filed together in the same box. Hideyoshi wanted to inquire to see how this Osumi may be possibly related to his family in Okayama. But the next-door neighbor didn't want to talk about his past. He did say that he had been in Hell for a very long time. Decades, in fact.

"Yes, still on my own here," Hideyoshi answered. He wasn't the type to share much about himself either. But without any kind of entertainment, Hideyoshi found that there was something satisfying about hearing his voice out loud. It was low and gravelly, a perfectly fine voice for a Japanese man in his late sixties. The noose, he thought, could have damaged his vocal chords. He had no sort of mirror to examine his neck, only the touch of the fingers on his working right hand, which revealed the evidence of loose, aging skin. There seemed to be a break in the bones underneath the skin, but he felt no pain.

Hideyoshi wondered about his son, his namesake, whom they called Yoshi. When Hideyoshi was relishing his last meal on earth—sautéed lobster with her roe inside—he had overheard the guards talking about the son's food request. Yoshi's desire was much more pedestrian. Beef curry rice with a bowlful of *rakkyo*, mini pickled onions. It was a pauper's meal. Hideyoshi, who hadn't seen his son since their sentencing seven years earlier, was both a little disgusted and charmed. His son was always satisfied with whatever was presented to him. His teachers had classified him as a bit slow, but since Yoshi was always so dutiful, they openly tolerated his academic weaknesses in the classroom. Yoshi was definitely no troublemaker.

Hideyoshi hoped Yoshi was not in pain now. Had the noose slipped? Was his death a slow one? Hideyoshi had remembered once watching an American movie, which featured actor Sean Penn, a death-row inmate who was executed at the end. His advocate, a nun, had witnessed his execution. Hideyoshi was fascinated by the scene. He had just killed his second woman, and perhaps he had a premonition that the same dismal fate would await him. But here in Japan, all hangings were conducted in secret, as if an arrow happened to pierce a certain space on a dart board one day.

"Something awful must have happened," Hideyoshi voiced his fear out loud. His son, with the same name, belonged here with him, in the same box. Could his son be in a coma, perhaps unconscious, floating in the space between earthly reality and Hell?

"Is this really Hell?" Hideyoshi wondered.

"What else could it be?" Osumi asked.

"Purgatory. Like Dante's *Inferno*."

"I didn't know that you were that well read."

Hideyoshi felt annoyed to be insulted in this way. It was true, however. Hideyoshi was not a reader in any way. It had been a guard, a Catholic, who had shared Dante's work with Hideyoshi. After reading of the nine circles of Hell, Hideyoshi had wild dreams of twirling down a giant drain of blackness, heads of red demons greeting him as he descended.

"So why are you here, anyway?" Hideyoshi asked his neighbor, who continued to ignore his questions. Instead, Osumi said, "Perhaps your son was extended mercy at the last moment. You were the mastermind behind the killings anyway, weren't you?"

Even his own lawyer didn't quite believe him, but Hideyoshi didn't intend on killing his first victim, the one whose body had been hidden below their floorboards. She, like some of the others, was young. She was about twenty, originally from the countryside. Hideyoshi ran a used furniture shop a few blocks away from Okayama station. Inherited from his mother, it was the perfect business. First of all, Hideyoshi could encounter a fresh crop of young women, newcomers to the city, on practically a daily basis. He, a native of Okayama, was the expert on the best markets for deals, the best coffee shops, the best-maintained laundromats. For fifteen captive minutes, these women's shiny faces would turn to him, open and accepting. And many times, when they ordered a large piece of furniture, they were grateful for Hideyoshi's policy to provide free shipping within a ten-kilometer radius.

The twenty-year-old woman, Chie, was the type who couldn't make up her mind.

It both infuriated Hideyoshi and excited him. "What do you think?" she'd ask him over each purchase, whether it be a skillet or an end table.

He suspected that she didn't have anyone to consult with in Okayama City. No partner, no friends, no family. This had not been the case in her past. Hideyoshi couldn't imagine this pitiful girl surviving on her own up to this point.

At the end she—well, they—decided on a *kotatsu*, a low table with a heater. You could eat at the kotatsu, use it as a desk, warm your thighs and feet. It was a piece of furniture with many uses, Hideyoshi said. The woman nodded her head as if she was trying to convince herself. "That makes sense," she declared.

Hideyoshi could have carried the kotatsu with him. But he wasn't in the mood to do that kind of labor for seven blocks. He offered to transport it in his van, free of charge. Chie bowed several times in appreciation.

It was one of those apartments where the walls were paperthin. Even though it was a cold March, sweat ran down the sides of his face as he dragged the kotatsu into the tiny six-mat room. Chie moistened a face towel with tap water, apologizing that she hadn't gotten hot water installed yet, and handed it to Hideyoshi. There was a scent on the towel, a slight perfume. He hadn't been close to such a scent in years, maybe decades. Before he knew it, he was putting his mouth over hers.

It happened so quickly Hideyoshi couldn't quite believe what happened. Chie lay limp on the floor, his fingers still around her neck. The damp face towel was on the tatami floor, a few centimeters away.

What could he do? Surely one of the neighbors had to have heard their struggle. Hideyoshi remained frozen for a minute, listening. Only a steady drip from the girl's faucet. This small apartment unit was probably full of low-level salarymen and women still hunched over their desks at their workplaces.

Think, Hideyoshi, think, he told himself. It was before five, before any neighbors would be arriving home. He quickly carried the kotatsu back to the van and then grabbed a dolly and a large flattened cardboard box.

He pulled her legs through the box and then closed both sides by folding in the flaps. After a few tries, he was able to get the box onto the dolly and quickly wheeled it into his van parked on the curb. He hadn't touched anything in the apartment aside from the girl and the towel. He shoved the towel in the glove compartment. It later became a memento of what he had done.

She had been missing for about a week when the police came to visit Hideyoshi's shop. Some neighbors had remembered seeing Hideyoshi's van in the neighborhood about the time Chie went missing.

"Let's see, Thursday. Thursday, Thursday." Hideyoshi feigned a faulty memory as he leafed through his datebook, a mess of scribbles and old receipts. He had written a receipt for Chie's purchase. "Yes, she had purchased a kotatsu. I went to deliver it but she wasn't at home."

The excuse, which he concocted on the spot, was so believable, so authentic.

"About what time was that?" the detective asked. He was in his forties, probably a seasoned veteran. Hideyoshi was more bothered by the detective's partner, a young woman in her late twenties. She was a tomboy type, her brown hair in a simple bowl cut. In fact, with her round face, she resembled a chestnut. Hideyoshi found her utterly unattractive.

"About four," he said with conviction. "And then I returned back to the store."

"When did you leave the store, Mr. Osumi?" the tomboy detective piped up.

How rude, Hideyoshi thought. *This line of questioning should be the purview of your superior. And just who do you think I am? A common laborer? I am a businessman with my own enterprise.* But he did not express any of this. Instead he said, "Hmmm. I always close at five-thirty, and then I went home to have dinner with my family. You can ask my wife."

"Surely we will," said the tomboy.

Hideyoshi wanted to slap her right then and there. But instead he just gave her a weak smile. "Of course, anytime."

They came to the house that evening. The floorboards had been reinstalled outside of their bathroom, so everything looked exactly the way it should.

The four of them sat at the dining room table by the kitchen. Atsumi wore slippers that flapped on the linoleum kitchen floor as she went back and forth to retrieve hot tea and teacups. Finally the senior detective told her they were fine and that she needed to sit down.

The tomboy detective spoke up first. "Maybe, Mr. Osumi, you could give us a moment." She gestured away from the table—so, the police wanted to question Atsumi without his presence.

Hideyoshi quickly smiled and dipped his head. "Of course," he replied. He rose and turned the corner where he stood beside the door of their first-story bathroom over the spot where Chie Toyama's body had been buried. He listened intently.

"Mrs. Osumi, can you tell us about last Thursday?"

"Well, he came as usual, around five-thirty. Maybe a little early, in fact. He ate sukiyaki that night. I always make sukiyaki on Thursdays."

"How did he seem?"

"Fine. Nothing special. Normal."

"Do you have any children, Mrs. Osumi?" the male detective then asked.

"A son."

"Just one son?"

"He's twelve. And he was there when my husband was home."

The detectives wanted to question Yoshi, but he was studying for an important test for the next day.

"I would hate to distract him in any way," Atsumi said in a quiet voice. "I'm sure that he wouldn't know of anything that could help you."

The male detective must have had children about the same age because he backed down. "Of course. If it's necessary, we will return."

That particular detective did not come back. The disappearance of young Chie Toyama confounded the police for a couple of years. She never made contact with her parents in the countryside. The local newspaper unearthed the details of her life—how she had been so mercilessly bullied by some girls at her high school that she was driven away from their quaint town after graduation. Weighed down by shame, one of these bullying girls then committed suicide, and then all interest in the missing Chie Toyama receded, as if the suicide was, in essence, penance for whatever happened to the young woman.

For several months, Hideyoshi was in a state of disbelief that he had killed someone. And after Chie's former classmate's suicide, Hideyoshi couldn't believe that he was actually going to get away with it. Every movement became intentional. Even just dragging his toothbrush against his front teeth seemed like a revolutionary action. Ironically, as a girl was now dead, Hideyoshi had never felt so alive.

Eventually, however, the mundane began to seep back into his life. More requests to pick up used furniture from retirement-age men and women, more purchases by bachelors. Hideyoshi needed to find another victim, but he knew that he had to be careful. It couldn't be an actual customer, but a window shopper who passed through all the small stores on their street. Someone with no ties to the area.

He selected the second one because of her size. She was inordinately small, maybe only four feet nine inches in height.

He was closing up the shop while she was standing there studying her phone. A map was on the screen and the image kept flickering on and off.

"Excuse me," she said to him. "I hate to bother you. But I've just moved into the neighborhood and I'm already lost. My phone seems to be malfunctioning."

Hideyoshi asked the woman for her address. He knew exactly where it was: a part of town that happened to be a web of skinny back alleys. He could have taken her but he didn't want to be seen with the woman. No, that would ruin everything.

He instead verbally told her how to get to her destination. Right, then left at the mailbox and then another right at the house with some stonework out front.

The woman giggled in embarrassment. "I can't believe that I could be so stupid."

"No," Hideyoshi said. "It's all quite understandable."

Hideyoshi took a shortcut to the woman's apartment. In spite of his directions she must have gotten lost again, because her small frame didn't appear at her door until at least fifteen minutes later.

She had barely opened her door when Hideyoshi pushed his way in behind her.

The next day the murder was on the television news. The woman's body had been found by, ironically, a deliveryman. She was discovered without her panties and skirt, although she was still wearing socks. And she had been strangled to death.

"Mah, what is the world coming to?" Atsumi commented, holding her soup bowl.

Yoshi was now fifteen and seemed mildly interested, especially with the implication that the woman could have been sexually assaulted. There would be proof, of course, but no bodily fluids. Hideyoshi made sure of that.

The newscaster mentioned that the woman, Kaneko Saijo, had been separated from her husband and had just moved into a new apartment.

"I wonder if the husband had anything to do with it?" Atsumi said in between slurps of miso soup.

Hideyoshi's eyes widened. Would other people think the same thing?

One day in Hell—actually, Hideyoshi wasn't sure if it was a day or just a moment—his box was opened. He looked up to see a person— or was it a person?—peering down at him.

She was blond like the women in his porno magazines, but only the hair was the same. The face, with its pinched nose, had an unattractive quality to it. It certainly didn't look human. She wore a tight white uniform, but even her curves seemed a bit misplaced.

Hideyoshi immediately formed a strong distaste for the woman, or whatever she was. He imagined wrapping his hands around her stringy neck, putting his thumbs against the soft spot above her clavicle.

"We don't like you talking to Mr. Osumi," the blonde said about his neighbor.

"Why?"

"It's not recommended."

"I wasn't aware of any rules. I wasn't given any when I came." He couldn't remember much about entering Hell. Only that there had been some shaking.

He tried to sneak a look beyond the uniformed creature. Rows of boxes. "How many of us are here, anyway?"

"You don't need to know that."

"I want to talk to your supervisor," he demanded.

"Suit yourself," the blonde closed the top of the box and within minutes—or was it minutes?—appeared a creature with the same pinched, beaklike nose. Instead of blond hair, however, the figure had a bald scalp with extended veins all across it.

"I want to know where my son is," Hideyoshi said. "We were to be executed by hanging on the same day. He should be here. We have the same name."

The creature wore a black suit, which again didn't seem to fit him quite right. He brought out a manila folder. "Well, let's see," he said, leafing through the papers.

"Hideyoshi Osumi," Hideyoshi repeated, in case there was some kind of bureaucratic mix-up.

"Yes, Hideyoshi Osumi. I see him now. Twenty-nine years old. Young to be executed."

What an unnecessary comment, Hideyoshi thought, but he held his tongue.

"I will look into this," the creature promised and then the box was closed again.

Yoshi was not Atsumi's biological child. He wasn't Hideyoshi's blood child, either, but they did share the same linked DNA. Yoshi was *yoshi,* an adopted child from his sister's family. She already had two sons and a girl, while Hideyoshi had none. This fourth-born would continue the Osumi lineage. Hideyoshi and Atsumi decided to call him Hideyoshi, too, although instead of kanji, they used the phonetic hiragana, Hi-de-yo-shi. His nickname, Yoshi, was an inside joke between the two. The creation of the nickname, in fact, might have been the last time they shared an authentic laugh.

Hideyoshi thought that a child would create a perfect triangle between the three members of the household, but instead Yoshi became a mama's child, a *botchan.* Mother and son stood together on one side, while Hideyoshi remained alone again on the other. And that's the way it was until the murder of the third woman.

Hideyoshi had erred in choosing her. She was physically stronger than the other two, with large shoulders and big breasts. She seemed more decisive, too. She wanted to see whether he had two more of a certain kind of chair, so insistent that she even followed him into his storage unit.

As they stood alone in a dark, dusty space, she didn't seem the least bit afraid or tentative with him. She probably thought nothing of an old man in a long-sleeved shirt and khaki pants.

It was the smell of her hair, which was long and plaited in two long braids, that first tantalized Hideyoshi. It smelled milky, like the drink Calpis. He remembered how his mother would stir in the white syrupy liquid with cold water and ice cubes during hot summer months.

The girl was examining one of the chairs when Hideyoshi fingered one of her braids. He thought that he was being discreet, but she felt his touch immediately. She turned back at him and struck his cheek. "You dirty old man!" she proclaimed. She then rushed towards the open door, but Hideyoshi grabbed her jacket, which was tied around her waist. He pulled her back and she immediately started to scream.

To stop her, Hideyoshi grabbed hold of something on one of his shelves—a faux European lamp stand. One blow with it and she fell to the ground, twisting like an injured caterpillar.

Hideyoshi tore at the woman's shirt. *How dare you slap me like that,* he thought. He held her neck as she struggled.

"Papa?" Yoshi had entered the storage unit. He was sixteen and partial to big breasts, based on his taste in semi-pornographic manga.

"Come, help hold her down." Hideyoshi commanded.

Yoshi didn't move for a second.

"Yoshi-*kun!*" Hideyoshi called out. His blood was racing. He had to have her.

After he was done with her, Hideyoshi tightened his grip around her neck until she breathed no more.

In hiding the body, Hideyoshi gave his son a series of directions. It was as if they were doing a home-improvement project together. "Yoshi-kun, get a bucket of water. Yoshi-kun, get that bag of cement mix."

Usually Yoshi had no interest in his father's business, choosing instead to stay in his room and read manga when he wasn't in school. But this, of course, was entirely different.

Hideyoshi emptied a large plastic container of various knick-knacks. "You get her legs," he instructed his son as they carried the body into the container. It was tight, but she did fit.

Yoshi helped his father mix concrete together and pour it over the body in the container. As if they were preparing a special cake with a surprise inside.

They did everything in the corner of the storage unit in order to be efficient. That way, after the concrete hardened, they could just leave the box there. In the course of five years, four concrete blocks came to occupy different corners of the storage unit. All produced by father and son.

Left alone in his box, Hideyoshi wished he could sleep. But there was no sleeping here. No possibility of escaping through dreams or nightmares.

He touched his *chinko,* but it just lay there flaccid. Nothing new. He had become impotent over the past several years. It could have been his age or just being in solitary confinement for so long. Atsumi never came to visit him, and even if she had it would have been behind glass. During his trial she dutifully came to court, sitting in the second row. Her face had taken on a strange yellowish tint, and to make it worse she sometimes even wore an ill-fitting yellow sweater. She had stopped coloring her hair and she looked old enough to be his mother, not his wife.

She came to court out of duty, nothing more, nothing less. She didn't try to divorce him, as her lifetime job was to be his wife. He wondered why she had done the things that she had, both in support of him and against him. He figured out now that she, like Yoshi, was good at following directions. Once she realized that she was the wife of a serial killer, she wore that title the best she could.

A father-son relationship was different than a husband and wife's, though, right? It was the blood, the *ki*, that was the extra connection. In spite of sexual relations, Hideyoshi and Atsumi couldn't really be one. But Yoshi, with his Osumi-ness, was a mirror, a duplicate. When Hideyoshi looked at Yoshi, he gazed at himself.

His son's absence now was acutely felt, even more than when he was incarcerated. He loved his son. Adored him. He began to cry. No tears came out of his eyes, but he cried nonetheless.

"Psssss. Hideyoshi," came the voice next to him.

Hideyoshi turned his back to the voice.

"What is causing you so much grief?"

"You are not an Osumi," Hideyoshi said. As soon as he said it out loud, he knew that it was true.

"I may not officially be an Osumi, but I work on behalf of all Osus. Osumi, Osuna—even some O'Sullivans," the voice said.

Hideyoshi considered the list of names and was confused.

"Punctuation," the voice explained. "Damn punctuation."

"What, is there some kind of union in Hell?"

"Not a union. I'm part of quality control. Making sure each newcomer is properly handled. And something obviously went wrong with you."

"I'm worried about my son. He should be here with me."

"Yes, yes," the voice said. "We are looking into that."

"What is taking so long?"

Hideyoshi's last victim was single like the others, but unbeknownst to Hideyoshi, she was a social butterfly. She had taken pictures of various tables and chairs in the store and texted those images to various friends. She wanted them to give her input, let her know which ones would work in her new apartment.

Of course, when the girl went missing, these friends immediately contacted the police. "When did you last see her?" the detectives asked.

"We were supposed to meet for dinner that Wednesday evening," the teary-eyed women reported, "but she never showed up. She did text us some photos from a used furniture shop. That's the last time we heard from her."

The detectives thus paid Hideyoshi a visit. He was surprised to see that the lead detective was the same female who had come by when Chie Toyama had disappeared. Instead of the bowl cut, her hair had grown out and was layered, wispy at the ends. He pretended that he didn't recognize her and she did the same with him. Hideyoshi considered it a very bad sign that she didn't reference their first meeting.

"Do you recognize this woman?" The detective showed a color image of a woman with caramel-colored hair. In the photo, she had bangs; they had since grown out.

"Hmmm," Hideyoshi said. "She may have come through the store. I don't believe she bought anything."

"A lot of women seem to frequent your store, Mr. Osumi," the female detective said.

"Well, of course. I sell items for the house. That would mean female customers."

Yoshi was called into the living room next. As he walked in, it was as if Hideyoshi was seeing him for the first time. Yoshi had become tall and lanky with a protruding Adam's apple and a shock of thick black hair. Before, he usually mumbled and looked down when he spoke to strangers. But that was not the case now. At age twenty-one, with four murders under his belt, he had become more confident, self-assured.

Hideyoshi went upstairs during the interview, stuck in the same bedroom as Atsumi.

"It's the same woman detective that came that day. The time when Chie Toyama went missing," Atsumi observed.

It surprised Hideyoshi that Atsumi had remembered the first victim's name.

"I didn't realize your memory was so sharp," Hideyoshi commented. He pretended to read a book on strategy related to the game of *go*.

"Surely Yoshi had nothing to do with that missing girl."

"He was only twelve," Hideyoshi commented.

"No, I mean this girl, the one the police are here about."

Hideyoshi glanced at his wife. She had certainly diminished over time. Her shoulders had become rounded and her belly slack. She had become an old woman.

"I'm sure it's nothing," Hideyoshi casually said.

"There sure has been a lot of crime here in Okayama," she stated, twisting the edge of her apron. "For being such a small town."

Atsumi at first didn't respond when the police came knocking on their bedroom door. "Mrs. Osumi," the assisting detective's voice was heard through the cheap processed wood. "You are next."

She slowly got up from the bed. Narrow wooden stairs squeaked as she made her way downstairs.

When she returned to the bedroom, she was without her apron. "They're gone," she announced and slowly prepared to go downstairs for a bath.

Hideyoshi couldn't stand it any longer. "What did they ask you?"

"The usual," she responded, choosing a clean pair of pajamas. "Except one strange question from that policewoman. She remembered that when she first came here seven years ago, she couldn't use the downstairs bathroom. She was asking why."

"What a ridiculous question." Hideyoshi felt his gut grow cold.

"You had just finished a plumbing project. I told her that you always fix things on your own."

The next day, Hideyoshi was called to the police station, and both he and the detective knew that it was only a matter of time. More police were called in and dismantled their floorboards. Only a few attempts with a shovel and the skeleton of Chie Toyama was discovered. Within the week, the furniture store and storage container had been taken over, the mysterious four concrete blocks cracked open.

Detectives found cement—the same kind of cement that had encased the four bodies—in the treads of both Hideyoshi's and Yoshi's shoes. Even more incriminating were items found in Yoshi's bedroom: a wash towel, woman's panties and flared knit skirt, all mementos that Hideyoshi had been hiding in his glove compartment. Hideyoshi had no idea when his son decided to remove the incriminating evidence from his van. And now, with the second woman's clothing discovered, the Osumis were implicated in six murders, not five.

All Yoshi had to do was to say that it had been all Hideyoshi's doing. But he refused to say anything. Hideyoshi was truly touched. He loved his son and it greatly grieved him that he really wouldn't get an opportunity to express his affection.

Hideyoshi was arrested first, but the prosecutor also wanted Yoshi's head, which he eventually got. Atsumi secured a separate attorney for Yoshi, but it didn't make any difference.

They were sentenced at the same time: death by hanging. Atsumi wanted Yoshi to appeal the sentence, but he refused. Not to be outdone by his son, Hideyoshi allowed his death sentence to stand as well.

On death row, Hideyoshi mostly spent time in solitary confinement. Other than the guards, he neither saw nor heard the voices of others. Occasionally someone would pound on the walls. He had no idea who they may be, but in his mind, he imagined it to be Yoshi. He wished that they had learned Wabun code or even the

Latin equivalent, Morse, when Yoshi was a child. With the back of his hand, he pounded the wall in increments of three. Sometimes the prisoner on the other side reciprocated. He convinced himself that the pounding was from his son, desperately trying to make a connection through concrete walls.

"So, Mr. Osumi, I regret that an error was made," the voice who claimed to be an Osumi said one day in Hell.

"What are you talking about? Is it about my son?"

"He was to be sent here. We were ready to process him. But he was recalled."

"To where?"

"It happens from time to time."

"Is he dead? Or is he somewhere else?"

The quality-control man refused to answer Hideyoshi's question. "Actually, I'm here to talk about you. You weren't fully demagnetized when you entered here."

"I don't understand."

"It's a quick procedure. We'll have to move you in your box. But it will be quick."

As the quality-control man had said, the box was pulled out and placed on something hard, almost metallic. Hideyoshi was shaken back and forth a few times—a familiar experience—and then it was over.

Before the guards took him to be hanged, they had him stand before a statue of Kannon, the goddess of mercy. In terms of religion,

Hideyoshi said that he didn't have any, but probably leaned Buddhist because he was Japanese. He refused to meet with a Buddhist priest but agreed to see the statue, which he immediately regretted.

Instead of making him calm, the statue agitated him. Kannon, with her narrow face, curved eyes, and serene expression, seemed to mock Hideyoshi.

Why did he need mercy from this woman?

They fastened a blindfold over his eyes, and instead of visualizing Yoshi, Atsumi, or his victims, he only saw that sanctimonious face of Kannon. They led him forward over something soft and carpeted. Hideyoshi could also hear the hum of instrumental music. Something with a Buddhist religious tone.

Regret, a new feeling, washed over him. He shouldn't have rejected appeals. He should have fought for his life more. He should have fought for his son.

Hideyoshi felt his legs shaking as something—the noose, of course—was placed around his neck. He could not give the guards the satisfaction of him weakening. *Those girls deserved what they got. They should have never let him in,* he told himself. But his son, his beloved son! At least they will be together in death. Even if it ended in nothingness, he would not be alone in it. That was his only consolation.

The ground then opened up and he was gone.

After the demagnetization, Hideyoshi's box was returned to its original position. His vision seemed to have improved. He could now see the gray pulp in the grain of the cardboard.

The top flipped open. It was the creature with the blond hair. "You will be alone in your box," she informed him.

"But I thought my son might be joining me soon?"

"No, we've discovered that he will not."

The cover closed and Hideyoshi could hear a male voice addressing the blonde. "That quality-control shithead. He's been on my case ever since he started. And why is this asshole asking for his son? The demagnetization should have eliminated that desire."

"He was just asking about him, not for him. It'll be fine."

"If only you had the calibrations correct in the first place."

"Oh, don't blame this on me. You're the one who said that he was sociopath. That he wouldn't have any attachments."

Their argument continued but got fainter.

"Pssss. Hideyoshi." The familiar voice from next door.

Hideyoshi was annoyed. "I thought that you had left. Don't you have any new cases to follow up on?"

"Checking in to make sure that everything is okay."

"I'm fine," he said, feeling space between his body and the box. "Never better." He didn't say anything further, and the quality-control man seemed satisfied.

"Goodbye, Hideyoshi. May you have a good stay here."

Hideyoshi grunted. He was able to extend his right elbow a little in his box. To have all this space all to himself was indeed glorious. Yes, he could easily be alone like this for a life eternal.

The Girl Who Loved Shonen Knife by Carrie Vaughn

I only want one thing in the whole world: for my band, Flying Jelly Attack, the world's greatest Shonen Knife cover band, to play at Cherry Blossom High School's Spring Dance. Two things stand in my way:

1) Lizard Blood, a Lolita death metal band, our bitter rivals
2) The end of the world

Lizard Blood isn't a real band. They only care about going viral and how many hits they get on UltraPluz. They never really learned to play their instruments. Instead, they use synthesizers plugged into programmable neuromuscular implants, upload whatever song they want to play, and play it—or "play" it, rather. They even have their implants synched so they play together—not that that really matters when it's death metal.

Lizard Blood's fake lead singer and fake lead guitarist, Yuki Niamori, is very rich—or at least her family is—and she can have anything she wants. What she wants is to be lead singer of a Lolita death metal band that will play at Cherry Blossom High School's Spring Dance.

She must be stopped.

As for the end of the world, I'm not really paying attention. It's got something to do with cyber attacks on big banks draining all the money out of their systems—not transferring it, not stealing it, just deleting it as if it never existed. The banks are shutting down and the government can't stop it. Experts are saying to change your online passwords and stuff, but that doesn't help because the hackers fix the system so it doesn't need passwords at all. Change your passwords and biometric logins all you want, doesn't matter. The hackers still delete everything you have.

It's not like I have much money anyway, since I spend everything on guitar strings and upgrading my amps. And we still have to go to school, even though half the teachers haven't shown up all week and the other half are threatening to strike if they don't get paid soon. Our parents are making us go because they think it's safe—Cherry Blossom High School's security guards are still here when the actual police have fled the city. It's all very complicated, but I'm working too hard to get the chord progression right on "Brown Mushrooms" to notice. If we don't get to play at the Spring Dance, nothing else will matter.

The big audition for who gets to play at the Spring Dance is in three days. Only two bands have signed up: Flying Jelly Attack and Lizard Blood. Attrition—we scared everybody off. Yuki possibly made threats—at least, she's made them to us.

Miki, my bass player, says our best course of action is to avoid Yuki and her girls entirely. Ru, my drummer, goes into a murderous rage whenever we even mention Yuki or Lizard Blood. She's prone to murderous rages, where all her hair stands on end and her eyes go wide and she bares her teeth like some kind of demon. Miki and I both have to hold her back to keep her from doing damage. It's this kind of thing that makes her a great drummer.

Trouble is, we can't avoid our enemy entirely when our enemy seems bent on searching us out.

There we are, just hanging out between classes—or these days, just hanging out until we find out whether we'll even be *having* classes. Miki, hair in a ponytail and her wire-rimmed glasses slipping down her nose, hunches over her deck doing something online—because she's *always* doing something online when she isn't playing—while Ru and I discuss what we should wear to the audition. Modern art mini-dresses or jeans and leather jackets? Cute or vintage rebellious? Whatever would make us the most different from Lizard Blood, is my opinion. Ripped jeans and anger.

"I don't really care, you pick," Ru says. When she isn't angry, her hair lies flat in a pixie cut. Really, I don't even know why I'm asking her—she doesn't have any fashion sense at all. Me or Miki pick out all her clothes. If we didn't have school uniforms she might not wear anything at all.

"I just want you to pick one, skirt or jeans?"

"Kit, look!" Ru points down the hallway, and I swear the lights dim and a mysterious wind begins howling past us. Even Miki looks up from her deck.

Lizard Blood appears, standing together, glaring a challenge at us: Yuki, with Azumi and Hana flanking her like acolytes. Between all of them, their poofed-out skirts fill the corridor. They have dyed their hair three different shades of pink: hot, bubblegum, and rose.

We get to our feet and it's like an Old West standoff.

"Hello, Yuki," I say. "What are you doing here? Shouldn't you be *practicing?*"

"You can't win," Yuki says. Her arms are at her sides, her hands in fists. She's wearing a black and white striped tea dress trimmed in lace and a little derby hat the size of an apple. She is above school uniforms, as she has often informed us. Just think, if she spent as much time practicing guitar as she did dressing, she could actually learn to play. "Why don't you give up?"

"We'll let the judges decide." I cross my arms. I'm not afraid of her. "It's only fair."

"I'm trying to save you the humiliation of losing."

"That's very kind of you, I'm sure."

She studies a manicured, black-painted nail. "I don't know why I bother. You're too stupid to listen to *anyone*."

At that, Ru roars and launches herself as a mad battering ram at the trio across from us. Miki and I grab her just in time, hooking our arms across her body and holding fast.

Predictably, Yuki laughs. Her henchthings start in a second later, and stop a second after she does. Throwing a last glare at us, they turn on their high-heeled patent-leather Mary Janes and march away.

"I hate her *so much!*" Ru hisses, slumping in our arms out of exhaustion.

"Our best revenge is to win the audition and play at the dance," I say. "We'll practice tonight, right after school."

"I may be late," Miki says, her expression scrunched up in apology. "I have … a *thing*."

"A thing? What *thing*?"

"Just. It's. I'll explain later."

She turns and runs, bumping up against a boy standing at the end of the corridor. It's like he just appeared. He glances briefly at Miki, then stares at us, and I wonder how long he's been standing there. Did he see the whole confrontation with Lizard Blood?

This guy, he's *cute*. He's in a pale suit with a blue shirt and a thin tie. The jacket sleeves are rolled up and his hands are in his pockets. His dark hair flops perfectly over his forehead, framing his very mysterious gray eyes.

"Who is *that*?"

"I think it's the new boy," Ru says. "Just transferred in."

I can't look away, but I have nothing to say to him. Then, with a final dismissive glance, he turns and is gone.

Seriously, this is not the time to be distracted by such things as new boys at school.

I try to find out everything I can about the New Guy, but it's not a lot. He transferred in from New Tokyo Polytechnic, but I don't know anyone from there I could ask for gossip. He's taking a normal roster of classes, but rarely speaks. Even though he's collected a gaggle of girls and a few boys following him wherever he goes, he ignores his admirers completely.

"I bet he's a secret agent," Ru says. "He's spying."

"On what?"

"I don't know. Just on something."

What can there possibly be to spy on at Cherry Blossom High School?

"Or an undercover cop, like in the movies. He's going to make a drug bust and set the whole school in an uproar."

"As long as he waits to do it after the Spring Dance."

The guy stands in the doorway of the lunch room and just … watches. I'm not thinking it's drugs because with the city falling apart and the police on strike, would they really send someone to bust drugs at a high school? This has to be bigger than that, which means he's a government agent. There's an international spy ring made up of teachers. Or a secret cavern under the school with a breeding den of giant monsters.

"I bet the school is home to a secret laboratory creating super-heroes," I say, and Miki and Ru just stare at me. I keep going. "You know, like some of our fellow students may in fact be superheroes in disguise, with strange mental and physical powers. There's a secret high-tech gymnasium under the real gymnasium where they do their training."

Miki says, "If there are secret superheroes, why don't they do something to save the city?"

That is a very good question.

Finally, school ends and we can get to work.

Despite saying she would be late, Miki's already at our practice space in a second music room behind the school auditorium's stage. She's finally put her deck away. Ru and I hurry to get our instruments and tune up. We have the space for an hour and have to make the most of it.

We've spent months working on our set: "Twist Barbie," "It's a New Find," "Banana Chips," and of course our signature "Flying Jelly Attack." This is for a dance—we have to get people dancing first thing or we're doomed. But Shonen Knife makes it easy to dance. Their music is all about dancing and being happy. How can we not win the audition, when Lizard Blood is all about death and fashion? Of course, times being what they are, maybe people are in the mood for death.

We practice and I start to feel better.

Besides the dancing and expressing happiness, another reason I started a Shonen Knife cover band is that the lyrics are pretty easy to learn.

"Naaaa na na na naaaaa na na na naaaa na na naaaa na na naaa—"

This is music in its very purest form, I think.

Everything's coming together, we're rocking, and I start to think maybe we should back off, save our strength to ensure that we don't peak before the audition. But then Miki biffs a chord. I'm about to yell, but she's staring at the door. We all look.

And there he is, studying us with this little frown and a narrowed gaze, like he's on some kind of treasure hunt. The New Guy, in his perfectly starched suit and his very cool manner. Is he following us around? What does he want with us?

"Hey!" I yell. "This is a private rehearsal, can't you read the sign?" I'd taped a handwritten sign to the outside of the door to discourage gawkers.

He glances at the sign, then back at us, and his lips press into a thin, uninterpretable line. Why doesn't he *say* something? Then I have a terrible thought: Is he spying for Lizard Blood, so they can learn our strategy for winning the audition?

Before I can yell at him again, he walks away. Only one thing to do: I unsling my guitar, gently set it down, and charge after him.

"Kit, wait!" Miki yells, as Ru shouts, "That's not a good idea!"

"I have to do something," I shout back. "He can't just lurk in doorways and get away with it!"

Miki turns panicked. "But he could be dangerous!"

He's far too handsome to be dangerous. Mysterious yes, but not dangerous. At least not a bad dangerous. Heroic dangerous, maybe. He looks like a hero.

"*Hey!*" I yell, and what do you know, he actually turns around.

"What?" he asks. His voice is soft but somehow compelling—authoritative and full of secrets. The voice totally goes with that suit.

"I want to know what you're doing here! You're not really a student, are you?"

His gaze is appraising. Smoldering, and appraising. He has better eyelashes than I do.

Finally, with a curt, dismissive nod he says, "It's best you don't know. Don't pay any attention to me. Go back to your friends." He walks on, turning the corner ahead.

When I chase him around the corner, he's gone.

Disaster.

Principal Jono is trying to cancel the band auditions for the Spring Dance. I argue with him, explaining that the auditions are a necessary distraction from the current tragic events and that hearing us perform would raise morale among the students.

"But Kit," he says sadly. He's a large, balding man with a thin comb-over and drooping face. "I don't think we'll be able to even hold the Spring Dance. Band auditions seem just a little ... pointless right now."

I declare, "What lesson are you teaching us with that kind of attitude? Are you saying we should give up? Are you telling us that perseverance in the face of adversity is not a good quality to have? Of course not! We must show that we are better than the evil that lurks in the rest of the world! Cherry Blossom High School and the Spring Dance will not be defeated!"

He relents, but I think only to make me go away.

Another reason I started a Shonen Knife cover band is the clothes. Basically, we can wear whatever we want, as long as we match. We can wear surf T-shirts or white tunics or leather jackets or bell-bottoms or miniskirts. And no matter what, we're *cute*, spreading brightly colored happiness wherever we go. Lizard Blood, with their fancy corsets and big crinolines and little bitty hats and velvet boots and too much makeup—it's like a uniform with them. Baby-doll fascists. It's sad, really.

I would spy on Lizard Blood—do they plan on playing a lot of screechy thrash or are they actually going to go with a set list that people can dance to? Because if they expect to win the audition they have to play stuff that people can dance to. Unless Yuki has paid off all the judges. This is an angle I haven't considered, and it leaves me thoughtful, because even with all the banks shut down, her family is so rich that she still has money. She keeps telling everyone she still has money, anyway.

If she's paying off judges, what can I do to compete? Nothing. Unless I can somehow expose her bribery plot. Maybe, just maybe, the New Guy is here to investigate Yuki. That would be helpful.

After the banks lost all their money, a bunch of people started looting grocery stores and things because pretty soon they wouldn't be able to buy anything. Some people tried to keep going to work and pretending everything was normal, convinced that their money would return and they'd get paid and the police would arrest all the looters and everything would be fine.

But then the water stopped. The hackers broke into the computer systems handling the city's water treatment and distribution plants and deleted the software. Water flowing through pipes stopped. No more showers, no more drinking. The hoarding of bottled water began. People fled, and the streets and trains out of the city became impassible.

Everyone says it will only be a matter of time before the hackers destroy the power grid as well. I don't think they'll go that far since they need the power grid and computer networks functional in order to do all that hacking in the first place. Nevertheless, just in case, I acquire a gas-powered electric generator for our instruments. Even if the city goes completely dark, we will still be able to audition for the Spring Dance. If I'm truly lucky, Lizard Blood will not have an electric generator, but since Yuki is rich I'm not counting on it. She has everything. If we're going to defeat her, we need to rely on our immense talent, the fact that we are good guys, and the sheer uplifting power of the music of Shonen Knife.

The dance will be in the gymnasium, the biggest room in the school, with polished wood floors, a high ceiling, and one wall full of windows looking over the city's downtown skyscrapers and monorail tracks. The monorail isn't running anymore because the hackers corrupted the system's software. A couple of trains crashed before the authorities shut it down.

Miki and Ru come with me to scout out the area where we'll be playing for auditions tomorrow. Well, Ru and I scout, and Miki sits in a corner and works on her deck: headphones on, eyes on screen like there's nothing else in the world. It's weird.

"What are you doing on your deck all day? You can't possibly have that much homework." The teachers who still bother showing up have stopped assigning homework in favor of teaching us survival techniques like starting fires, collecting dew for drinking water, and spinning wool into yarn. Who knew they're all survivalists? It's almost comforting.

"Nothing. Never mind. It's a secret."

Like that isn't suspicious.

And then when I turn around—there he is again. New Guy. Watching us from yet another doorway. *Staring*, like some creep. A very handsome creep in a nice suit, but still.

I'm about to yell, but he slips away as if he hadn't been there at all. Miki and Ru also look after him.

"That's it," I mutter.

"You said it," Ru mutters with me. Her hair starts to get messy, which means she's about to rage out.

"Don't worry. We'll find out what this is all about. I have an idea."

Here's how we set a trap for New Guy. First, we schedule another impromptu practice. Technically, we don't have the practice room reserved, but since no one else at the school is playing any music and most classes have been canceled, no one stops us. The trick is, we have to catch him as soon as he shows up. No delay, no time for him to figure out anything's wrong. Just boom, captured, and then we can shine a bright light on him and demand that he spill the beans.

But Miki isn't there. We get the practice room at the right time, have our ropes and a flashlight and everything ready to go, and she's not there. How are we going to fool New Guy into thinking this is a legitimate practice if Miki isn't here?

"This isn't going to work." Ru looks despondent.

"No, it will. The plan doesn't change."

We wait in ambush, standing on either side of the doorway, each of us holding a can of Silly String. I plug my phone into speakers and play a concert bootleg of "Redd Kross." Maybe it won't fool him—maybe he'll know it's actually Shonen Knife on a recording and not us—but I'm willing to take that risk.

We hold our breaths and wait, wait.... At our other practice, this was about the time New Guy appeared in the doorway. Sure enough, listening hard past the beat and the bass line, I hear footsteps, a careful approach of expensive loafers. Ru and I exchange a glance.

New Guy peeks in, looking confused for a moment when he doesn't see anyone. That's when we attack.

Silly String is a really good weapon because it's totally shocking and totally nonlethal. We cover him in instant rubbery spaghetti.

Futilely, he puts up his hands to fend off the swarm of plastic, but it's no good—he's covered. When he stumbles back, trying to turn and get a good look at his attackers, he trips over the rope we slung across the floor. He goes down with a crash and lies prone. We stand over him, empty cans held out like guns. Ru is growling.

"What are you *doing?*" he exclaims, picking Silly String from his face, blinking at us. His thin frown might be curled into a snarl.

"Why are you following us?" I demand. "What do you want with us? Are you spying on us for Yuki? Are you working for Lizard Blood?"

"What are you talking about?" he says with admirable calm, given that he's lying on the floor covered in yellow, orange, green, and blue Silly String. He starts to sit up. The plastic bits come off him in one giant sheet.

"Don't move!" Ru shouts. Her eyes are red and her teeth are bared like a wolf's. If she could grow fangs, she would. He doesn't move.

"It's all right," I say to her, lowering my now-empty cans of string. "I think he's safe."

He regards us both. "Where is your friend? Your bass player."

My heart gives a little jump knowing that he pays attention enough to know who plays what instrument and that he knows the difference between a bass and a guitar. Not everyone does.

"She's out. Why do you care?"

He looks at us so calmly, speaks so evenly, you'd never know he'd just been attacked with Silly String. "Because it's true. I am spying on you."

"What?!" Ru yells, and I have to grab her arm before she starts clawing at him.

"Why?" I say. "Who are you working for?"

"May I ask you a question?"

He totally isn't a student. He's not even trying to pass for one anymore, not that he ever did. He stands, scraping off the rest of the string. "Do you know what your friend Miki does on her deck all day?"

Ru and I look at each other. I say, "Homework, I think."

New Guy is very serious now. "We've traced the cyber attacks on the national banks and water system to this school. We believe one of the students here at Cherry Blossom is the hacker."

"You … you don't think it's Miki, do you? It can't possibly be Miki!"

"Why not?"

"Because she's a good guy! Because she knows all about Shonen Knife! Because I trust her!"

He presses those skeptical lips together. I almost cry.

"If you trust her, then help me clear her. Find out what she's doing with her deck. But don't tell her I'm investigating her."

"We can't spy on our friend!" Ru says. But of course, we can. We have to, and New Guy knows it.

"If you'll excuse me." He adjusts the cuffs of his jacket and leaves the room like nothing happened.

Half an hour later, Miki shows up with her bass. And her deck. Ru and I haven't had the heart to start playing without her.

"Sorry I'm late, I got held up. They're rationing water now, you know that? I'm trying to find a way to sneak bottles out of the kitchen—hey, what's wrong?"

I stare, stricken. Miki, dear sweet Miki, hacking the city infrastructure to destroy it? I don't believe it, not for a minute.

"We're depressed," Ru says, which is true enough.

"You can't be depressed, auditions are tomorrow! We have to practice!" Miki says.

I feel grim. "I think we've practiced as much as we possibly can."

"You mean—"

I nod. "We're ready. It's time to face Lizard Blood."

This is it. The most important day of my life. Will I be allowed to spread the message of true pop rock throughout the universe, or will I be defeated? I feel sick to my stomach.

We decide on wearing A-line tunics and pants in primary colors to better channel Shonen Knife, and to separate ourselves from the frilly bleakness of Lizard Blood. Sure enough, they show up in black and white with double the crinolines and corsets and curly purple wigs and giant eyelashes dashed with glitter. They carry their instruments proudly, and their neural implants gleam along their arms and foreheads. Like they think they can't lose.

All we have are calluses on our fingers.

Everyone's there. At least, everyone who is left is there: Principal Jono and the remaining survivalist teachers, clipboards in hand and pencils raised, ready to judge our worthiness to play at the Spring Dance. A crowd of students gathers in the back of the gym, thrumming with eagerness. This is going to be the fight of the century.

The stage waits, bare.

I hate this, waiting, my guitar slung over my shoulder, plinking the strings. They make weak little ringing sounds, since the instrument's not plugged in yet. It's the same sound my heart will make if it breaks, if we lose. Ru holds her fists over her eyes, like she can't even watch, her drumsticks sticking out of them like antennae.

But even right before the audition, Miki sits on the floor, working on her deck.

I glare at her. "What are you doing? You're always on your deck. I'm worried about you."

"What? Oh—it's secret. But you'll like it. I promise."

Off to the side, New Guy watches us closely. What if he's right? What if Miki is behind the destruction of the city?

What would Shonen Knife do? They would trust each other, and they would play. That's all we can do.

Principal Jono will flip a coin to see who goes first. He announces: "Flying Jelly Attack is heads, Lizard Blood is tails. Whichever side lands up will get to choose whether they go first or last."

Yuki and I stand on either side of Principal Jono, seething. Soon, it will all be over. The coin spins, glinting in the light coming in through the windows. It seems to spin forever before falling like a bullet into Principal Jono's hand. He slaps it on the back of his other hand, looks at us both, and finally reveals the outcome.

"Heads!"

I should have thought more about what would be best: play first and get it over with, play last to leave the final impression with the judges, play first to show how great we are at warming up a crowd, play last so we could respond to Lizard Blood's strategy—

Miki taps me on the shoulder. "Let Lizard Blood play first."

She seems very confident, hiding something behind her big brown eyes and glasses. Okay, then. Shonen Knife trusts each other, so I trust her.

"Lizard Blood will go first," I say and step aside.

It takes them a stupidly long amount of time to set up because they have to plug in their instruments, warm up their neural implants, synch all their systems, and I figure this will be a black mark against them because the longer they take the more restless everyone gets. But I know them, and I've heard them, and once they start playing, they'll cast some kind of weird headbanger spell that will overpower the crowd with a wall of death metal. They'll burn out everyone's hearing before we even get onstage.

But then something happens. Something *amazing*.

Yuki starts to strum a chord—that is, her uploaded programming directs her arm to play a chord. And nothing happens. Her hand goes limp and splats over the frets, and her other hand tangles in the strings instead of strumming. Azumi does a little better, getting her bass to play a couple of chords, but they're *bad* chords, out of tune and wavering. The drumsticks fall clean out of Hana's hands. When she scrambles to pick them up, she falls off her stool.

It's like they're not in control of their own bodies. It's like something has gone wrong with their neural implant programming.

I look at Miki, who nods with satisfaction. "That's what I've been doing with my deck—hacking the implant software Lizard Blood uses to play their instruments. It was tough because they had massive protections on their system. Military-grade firewalls. Best money can buy—you know Yuki. But I got through, you know?"

I stare at her with really big eyes. "You. Are. A. *Genius.*"

She's my new hero. I could kiss her, but I have to go back to watching Yuki and Lizard Blood fumble around, trying to figure out what to do with their instruments without the software to guide them.

New Guy arrives in time to hear the explanation. "Ah. That clarifies much," he says. "That only leaves one suspect in the bank-hacking case. Thank you, girls."

"What?" I blink at him.

He approaches the stage and draws a badge from his pocket. Yuki and the others finally go still.

"I am Detective Fukaya, and you, Yuki Niamori, are under arrest for destroying the city through the cybernetic network."

Well, who expected *that?*

Yuki should deny it, but she doesn't. She throws down her guitar and clenches her fists. Even Azumi and Hana look surprised, so they must not know anything about it.

At the edge of the stage, Yuki looks over us all, green eyes filled with rage.

"You think this is just an act!" she shouts. "You never respected me because you think all this is fake!" She gives her frilly skirt a tug. "It's not an act! It's *anarchy!* Yes, I destroyed the city's banking and water infrastructure! I want everything to *burn*!" She throws horns with both hands and screams, "ANARCHY!"

I have to admit, I finally sort of respect Yuki a little bit because she seems very honest about her mission.

She jumps off the stage and shoves Detective Fukaya aside. He's so surprised he doesn't go after her right away—I mean, who expects Yuki to do anything that smacks of effort? So she runs and we all think she's going to get away, but then Ru trips her. Just sticks out her foot, and Yuki goes sailing, purple curls flying and tiny hat spinning off toward the ceiling. It's great. Detective Fukaya arrests Yuki. Azumi cries while Hana leads her away, arm around her shoulders to comfort her. And that's that.

It turned out Miki had such a hard time hacking Lizard Blood's system because all of Yuki's neural interfaces and military-grade firewalls were a cover for her high-level hacking activities. Lizard Blood really was a fake band. Who knew?

So, that's how Flying Jelly Attack triumphed and won the chance to play at the Cherry Blossom High School Spring Dance. We auditioned with our signature song, "Flying Jelly Attack," and we sounded triumphant. That just goes to show that Rock and Roll Will Never Die.

Unfortunately, by the time of the Spring Dance the power had indeed gone out all over the city. But that doesn't matter because we have the generator, and we insist that the Spring Dance go on as planned for the sake of good morale. We decorate the gym and fill it with students. It seems like a miracle that everybody comes, but I know I'm right: times like these, everybody just wants to dance.

So we play for them. Outside the windows, far away in the city, mobs riot at bank headquarters and government buildings for not doing more to stop the economic collapse. A couple of skyscrapers are on fire and helicopters buzz around them, recording footage for the news. The city really is falling apart, but I don't care, because my dream has come true: my band is playing at the Spring Dance. The Cherry Blossom High School gym is the safest place in the city. Hundreds of students surge screaming at the stage, and me and my girls have our instruments plugged into amps, ready to go. I look at Miki and Ru, meet their gazes, and they nod back at me. Their hands are poised to begin. Nothing else matters.

I turn to the microphone and call, "One two three four—!"

Run! by Kaori Fujino
Translated by Jonathan Lloyd-Davies

Psychos can really leg it. You know, the ones who become bashers.

I'd never seen another basher in action, but I'd heard the story from a friend who had.

He'd seen the guy, through the window of a café on the third floor of some building, hotfooting it on the street below. He'd been going at such a pace he'd seemed to just race by.

It had been a bright afternoon.

The basher had already slipped away by the time the young woman crumpled to the ground, clutching at her shoulder. Her long hair dipped below her neckline, starting to flow, engulfing her upper arm and elbow, before it finally reached the ground.

The hair, of course, was blood.

I'm telling you, it wasn't normal, blustered my friend, who had run track and field in college.

Of course it wasn't. Of course it wasn't normal.

At that speed, the guy could have run in the nationals.

But the man they brought in had never run track and field, not even in high school. He wasn't particularly fit and, if anything, I'd say he verged on being short. He wasn't even young. In his fifties, he was divorced, isolated from his neighbors, and out of work.

I know why psychos run so incredibly fast. It's because they're running for their lives. Anyone can do it; all you need is an assassin charging in from behind. Desperate to stay alive, you push through your limits. You might not even realize what's happening. You might be convinced you're running only to hurt someone. But the truth is you hear the knife slicing the air behind your own neck—you feel its cold, keen edge.

That is why you run so incredibly fast.

The problem is that the assassin's invisible to everyone else. This means the psycho ends up taking the blame. Maybe that's only fair. There's nothing, after all, that says you have to attack someone in the middle of your escape.

Although ... the more I think about it, the more I suspect that the unseen assassin chasing the psycho is himself a psycho, pursued by his own unseen assassin. That you've got one psycho chasing another, who chases another. The pattern repeats again and again until, finally, an innocent someone who isn't a psycho, someone who just happens to be in the way, ends up footing the bill.

I know all this because I am a psycho. And because I'm the kind of guy who likes to chew on this sort of thing. Not that my way of doing things is any different from the multitude of other psychos out there. Every now and then I become a basher. I plan to keep it up, as no one's caught me yet. I'm sure they will, soon enough. I'll just keep bashing until that happens.

I don't normally use a knife.

My tools are a jar of honey and a plastic convenience-store bag. The honey is a special kind. It costs thirteen thousand yen for five hundred grams, is imported from New Zealand, and is extracted from a limited number of hives located in a specific region.

While we're talking about psychos, I personally think you've got to be a little unhinged to spend that much on honey, but my girlfriend tells me it's a bargain.

She takes it in her tea. She says drinking it is good for her skin, that it helps keep her slim, and that it keeps her looking young. She's never offered me any to try. Not that I want to. It's the weight that interests me. That and the rock-solid, sturdy jar.

My girlfriend earns more than I do, working for the kind of large corporation everyone knows the name of. According to her, her salary's going to keep on going up. She changes the design on her nails once every one or two weeks. And she's always buying new clothes. There's an amazing diversity to women's clothing. There's all kinds of tastes and styles. I'm not just talking pants and skirts. Although these—both pants and skirts—come in their own variations, from the subtle to the brash. These can be simple differences in color and design, but also differences in color and design that alter the signals describing the wearer. The signals—in a nutshell—that say whether you're orderly, provocative, juvenile, or like a doddering old lady. It's genuinely fascinating. There's more—she buys shoes, accessories, makeup. She buys underwear. All of these things come in their own vast arrays of designs. Sometimes she looks great, sometimes she looks shockingly bad. My girlfriend's got amazing latitude. When she's on form, a single look's enough to get me hard. When she misses the mark, she's awful. Can't lay a finger on her.

But she never gives up the challenge. Fashion is her hobby. It's a good hobby for a girl. I think it's cute.

It goes without saying that her insatiable pioneering extends to her hair. It gets dyed, permed, bundled, woven, hitched up, and twisted—she's a true master. Just when you think she's had it shaved like a monkey, the next time you see her it'll be long and straight and down to her waist. Yeah, she buys hoards of wigs too.

The downside is that it's impossible to find her presents. She's very selective. She passes swift but meticulous scrutiny on everything she buys. Sometimes she dresses to look like she's never even heard the word "fashion," as though she lacks even the slightest interest in clothing. That's how selective she can be. And her infatuations change with the speed of a dying man's complexion, so it's impossible to guess what she likes in any given moment.

This is why I always give her the honey. It's decided: the honey is my present. It's the one thing she is bound to appreciate. Because, as I already mentioned, it's good for her skin, it helps keep her slim, and it keeps her looking young. Plus she needs a little every day. She's always grateful when I turn up with a jar of the stuff.

"This is the best. It's like it's in tune with me. You know, a perfect fit," she says.

I like the way she describes it. It's in tune with me too.

You know, a perfect fit.

It was when I was shopping with my girlfriend, the first time I held the honey in my hand, that I heard the voice shouting *"Run!"*

It was my voice, even though I hadn't said a thing. I'd just been nodding quietly away—*uh-huh, uh-huh*—listening to my girlfriend and the shop attendant wax lyrical about the benefits of the honey. But I'd definitely heard it. My own voice, shouting *"Run!"* That was when I knew it for sure—that psychos had their own unseen psychos chasing them, that that was why they run so incredibly fast. *I was right, I was right*, I thought. I'd always wondered if that wasn't the case. I weighed the special honey in my hand. I rolled it in my palm, savoring the feel of the curved surface. *"Run!"* I shouted again into my own ear. *Sure, I'll run*, I thought. I'd finally found it. The murder weapon I'd been looking for. With the honey in hand, I would run.

It was a few days later that I started on my bashing spree, going from one criminal act to the next. My girlfriend's apartment—high salary notwithstanding—is a good twenty-five minutes on foot from the nearest train station.

"I work in the city, so I'd rather spend my private time somewhere quiet, where I can stretch out a little. Get it?" she says.

I understand where she's coming from, but I still can't believe the place she chose.

At night it's the worst place you could be. The footpath leading to her apartment is pitch black, following a factory wall, and there's a short tunnel that cuts below an overpass. There's an entrance to a shrine to keep an eye on as you walk—gaping like an open maw, the darkness heavier there than elsewhere—and you have to trail around the periphery of a barren and sinister park, which has nothing going for it bar the toilets installed slap-bang in the center. It's an ideal location for a basher. When I get the go-ahead, I tend to visit my girlfriend's apartment on a weeknight after work. I'm lucky, I guess, in that the unseen psycho behind me only closes in when the conditions are all in place for me to become a basher myself. In other words, when I happen to have a jar of the honey to give my girlfriend (not too often, at thirteen thousand yen a pop), and when there's a single person walking ahead of me. When the conditions line up like this, I hear the voice shouting "Run!"

It could be that I'm getting better at reading the signs. That something warns me, *Tonight might be the night*. Then, in subconscious preparation, I buy a jar of honey and make the arrangements to pay my girlfriend a visit.

Whatever the case, that's when it comes. "*Run!*" Frightened, I turn into a basher.

My first step is to remove the jar of special honey from the small paper bag bearing the manufacturer's logo. The latter I fold and stash in my rucksack so it doesn't get marked. In its place I take out one of the plastic convenience-store bags I keep a stock of, and slip the jar inside. Then I start running. *"Run!"* I cry into my own ear. *Right—I have to run!* The murderous knife comes veering in, towards my suit collar, the blade as broad as my arm. *"Run!"* I run incredibly fast. I'm not usually that fast a runner. No better than the next man. But everything changes when my life's on the line. Keeping up this incredible pace, I begin to swing the plastic bag in circles. The jar picks up speed, buzzing a circular orbit. My victim sees me approaching and tries to escape, but I'm faster. It goes without saying. I'm a psycho, after all.

I close the distance at a raging pace, and, with all my might, let loose the five hundred grams of honey—with the weight of the jar and the force of the acceleration—against my victim's not-so-psychotic skull. The blow is enough to knock them unconscious. By this point I no longer sense the knife behind me. I've shaken off my unseen, psychotic pursuer. *For now … this time. One more time.* Relieved, I gather my wits and shift my grip on the plastic bag. I take out the jar and position it within my palm. *This special jar of honey, how its curves cling to my hand!* I crouch next to my victim and fit the plastic bag over his head. Then, painstakingly, taking care not to spill much blood from the bag, I crack his skull from above. If I get a little messy it doesn't show on my dark suit. And my girlfriend's apartment is all mood lighting, so it's really dark and atmospheric. Once I've put the jar back inside the paper bag with the logo, I go straight over to her place.

Each time she opens the door it's like I'm seeing her for the first time. She's always fresh, like a completely different woman. You've got to appreciate the effect of pouring all that salary into dressing up. The truth, I suspect, is that she's unhappy with the way she is. That she doesn't feel in tune with herself the way she feels in tune with the honey, that she doesn't like the fit of her body. That this is why she's always on the lookout for something new. I hope she finds what she's looking for soon. I'm sure she will. The way I found the honey.

I present her with the honey and she cheerfully boils some water, making tea. She's got beer ready for me in the fridge. We clink our drinks; my can of beer with her cup of honey-infused tea. She turns pale when the news of my criminal activity shows up on the TV.

"Not again, that's near here. This is scary."

"You've got to be careful," I whisper.

"Yeah, I will. I always am," she says.

She's so cute, I end up teasing a little. "The people who do this stuff, I'll bet they're desperate too, running from their own unseen demons."

"What kind of … unseen demons?" she asks, her voice tense. She's still facing the TV. The light ridges that run along the top of her ear are on display.

I don't say, *Psychos like me.*

"Oh, I don't know … society?" I say instead. "People making unreasonable demands? Work? An inability to believe in the future of our political system?"

She doesn't turn around.

"Why don't they find a better way of doing it? There are so many different ways a person can run," she says. The tip of her ear twitches with each movement of her jaw.

Since the special honey came into my life, I've left behind no survivors. I don't discriminate. It doesn't matter whether they're male or female, adults or kids, pensioners or whatever. They all die.

I became a "professional" basher because of the special honey, which my girlfriend introduced me to, but she isn't the one to blame. I was more or less this way even before I discovered the sticky stuff. And my system hasn't really changed. I suppose I'd use all sorts of different things for the weight, but I'd always had the preference for plastic convenience-store bags. I hadn't always taken the step of killing my victims. Some would die, but the rest survived. The biggest difference was that, before the honey, I lacked the understanding I have now. I hadn't heard the warning shout of *"Run!"* and didn't really know what was going on, leading me to mistake the elation I got from barely escaping with my life for that of sexual lust; for a time I even limited my targets to high school girls. I used to struggle with the idea that I was some kind of sexual deviant, and even prayed that someone would stop me. I used to fantasize about how good it would feel if one of the high-school girls I'd marked—at the time, always the ones with chunky thighs—were to fight back and drive a sweaty palm heel into my Adam's apple, knocking me to the ground.

I don't think that way anymore. I've got the voice screaming *"Run!"* and I just do what it says. Not that running is enough by itself. That would mean having to maintain that incredible speed forever. I couldn't do that. That *would* kill me. That's why I make the blood offering. By offering a stranger's blood instead of my own, from my place at the front of the line, I can use the scent to satisfy the psycho behind me, while providing enough of a whiff to keep the psycho behind him—and the one behind him, and all of them, right up to the end of the line—temporarily at bay. These days I understand it all.

This is my way of running. What else does she think there is? I guess she's a woman, she probably just said whatever popped into her head, without thinking.

A few days later, I learned that this hadn't been the case.

That night, I heard the voice again: *"Run!"*

It's usually on edge, but it sounds more panicked than usual. *"Run!" "Run!" "Run!"* The timing's good as I'm on my way to my girlfriend's; even better, as I have a jar of the special thirteen-thousand-yen honey. All I need now is a target. I search with bloodshot eyes. *"Run!"* I start to run. I run with incredible speed. I hear the *swish swish* of the knife behind me—right behind me. It's huge. I know this even without looking back. Much larger than usual. More cleaver than knife.

With perfect timing, I find my target. A woman. No, a man. Too well-built to be a woman. No woman has shoulders so broad. I start to whirl the jar of honey in the plastic bag, fast enough to drown out the sound of the knife. The bag whistles, the jar hums. I continue to accelerate. My victim tonight is a cross-dresser. A man dressed as a woman. A cross-dresser with straight flat hair down to around the neckline, whose shoulders are packed into a light-orange jacket and too burly to be anything but a man's, who's wearing a tight yellowish skirt with high heels that match the color of the jacket. He's got nice legs, but cross-dressers usually have better legs than most of the women out there. I don't discriminate. Cross-dresser or not, they can all die. I'll put them all out of their misery.

I swing the jar, already suspended above the man's head, down. It finds nothing but air. I lose my balance and stumble forward. For a moment I'm unable to process what happened. I look ahead and see the cross-dresser storming away. The cross-dresser is escaping. *Huh …?* His speed is incredible. Is he a psycho too?

I give chase.

The cleaver slices down behind me. It feels as though it's sheared off some hair. *"Run!"* the scream ricochets through me. I'm fleeing. I'm giving chase. *Never underestimate a psycho when he's running for his life.* I start to close the distance. The cross-dresser's running barefoot now, having transferred his heels to his hands. It won't help. I'm getting closer and closer. I want to laugh out loud. The cross-dresser isn't a psycho after all, just a regular old cross-dresser. Just desperate, running as fast as he can to avoid being killed by a psycho. Everyone, crazy or not, runs faster when their life's in danger, right? That's why he was running so fast in the beginning. Yeah, well, sorry to say it, but psychos like me are in a whole different ballpark when it comes to this stuff. See, I'm closing in, within reach, right on top of him, whirling the honey so it sings in the air.

Without warning, the cross-dresser spins around. He's shorter than I am. The eyebrows are too thick, the lips too red, but he reminds me of someone. As my attention drifts to his rolling shoulders, he punches one of his shoes upward. The toes crunch into my nose, sending blood spraying everywhere. I drop the jar of honey. I can't breathe. My knees buckle and I curl inward, throwing up my hands to protect my nose. A powerful arm booms through the air. The cross-dresser drives the pointed heel of his other shoe into my right temple. It cracks my skull, snapping as it embeds itself in warm tissue.

Like all the people I've battered in the past, I hit the ground. And, like I've done so many times, the cross-dresser crouches at my side; he raises the jar of honey. But he doesn't crack my skull. He doesn't need to, I'm dead either way.

He speaks my name.

"Why?" he asks through tears.

"What …?" I just about manage. The cross-dresser isn't a cross-dresser. He's my girlfriend. "What's with those shoulders …?"

My voice is splintered, but it reaches her ears.

"They're shoulder pads! It's an eighties throwback! They're just new," she sobs, tugging off her wig. "I was late, overtime. Just hurrying to get home before you arrived …"

I open my mouth. Viscous blood spills out. There's something I need to ask her. I force my numbing tongue to move.

"Was it you? Were you the psycho chasing me?"

"What about you? Were you the guy coming after me, all this time?"

I close my eyes. The truth finally dawns. Like me, my girlfriend was pursued by her own unseen psycho, only she had her own way of running. The obsessive dressing up wasn't so she could feel in tune with herself, so she could feel at home in her own body. It was camouflage. Living in this deserted wasteland, putting on one disguise after another: it was all her way of running.

Her hands are in mine.

I'm a psycho, but I'm not the one who's chasing you. You need to keep running. Run!

My lips tremble …

Dress up! Run!

… but no words come out.

Hanami by S. J. Rozan

Every time I come to Washington it rains.

I don't know why this should be, but my father used to tell my brothers and me that there's no point in denying reality, even reality that's ridiculous. Rain fell insistently, tracing diagonal lines across the windows, as the Acela train Bill Smith and I were riding pulled into Union Station.

"It's still beautiful," Bill said. "Soggy, but at least down here it's spring."

"You don't have to try to make me feel better. I don't believe I have some paranormal effect on the weather and it rains because I'm coming. I just think I unconsciously but cleverly time my trips here to make sure to coincide with the rain."

"Not a paranormal effect on the weather, just a preternatural relationship with it? Sure, why not?"

We swung our overnight bags down and beat it to the subway. In Washington they call it the Metro and it runs on rubber wheels, and in the place we came out, Dupont Circle, it had a huge sci-fi escalator to the street. "You think we'll be on Mars when we get to the top?" I asked as the gray sky in the round opening came closer.

"I think we're already on Mars if we've really taken this case."

"We can't *not* take it. I told you, Moriko's one of my oldest friends. We were super close in high school until her family moved here her senior year. I used to date her big brother. Maybe *you* can't take it. But I have to."

"I can't take what, the fact that you used to date her older brother? Oh, you mean the case. What kind of person would leave his partner on her own with a client who thinks she's a fox? Besides, from what you say she actually is a fox, though not the kind she thinks she is."

"Hands off. That's the whole problem here—a man after her who she doesn't want."

"What makes you think she wouldn't want me?"

"Let me count the ways."

I lofted my umbrella, Bill sunk his head in his raincoat collar, and we splashed the two blocks to the row house where Moriko Ikeda lived in an apartment on the parlor floor.

As I told Bill, Moriko and I have been close since high school. We went to Townsend Harris in Flushing, Queens, which is stuffed full of brainy Asian kids but, as my brother Tim never lets me forget, isn't Stuyvesant. My four brothers and I all went to high schools you had to test into, but different ones. Tim was already at Stuyvesant when my tests came up; I didn't even fill out the application. Why? The different-schools thing hadn't applied to elementary school. I was the youngest—and a girl—and I followed my brothers all the way through Sun Yat-Sen in Chinatown. I couldn't wait to get to a school where, when anyone asked if I was related to such-and-such a kid named "Chin," I could say I wasn't, not just wish I wasn't.

Moriko and I hit it off from the beginning, even though the Chinese and Japanese kids mostly eyed each other with suspicion (and the Koreans eyed both of us that way, and the black kids eyed the Latino kids that way, and the white kids were too stunned by finding themselves in the minority to do anything but huddle together for warmth). With me and Moriko, maybe it was an opposites-attracting kind of thing. I was a short, straightforward, practical jock; she was tall, elegant, sweet, and spacey.

Never this spacey, though. She'd called yesterday to ask me to come to Washington as a last-ditch attempt to solve her problem, which was: a man had stolen her *kitsunebi*, and since she'd die without it, she had to do what he wanted so he'd give it back. Kitsunebi is the soul of a *kitsune*, a fox spirit, and in this case what the man wanted was for Moriko to marry him.

Moriko buzzed us in within seconds of my pressing her doorbell. We'd stepped into the building's small entry hall and I was folding my umbrella for stashing when she opened the glass-paneled inner door. Her eyes lit up when she saw me, and I'm sure mine did when I saw her. Bill's eyes I didn't look at because I didn't want to know.

You have to understand: Moriko is gorgeous. She's not actually super tall, maybe five-ten, but she's so slender that she gives a long-limbed, languid impression. She seems not to walk so much as flow, and the shoulder-length hair framing her narrow, high-cheekboned face is as black and glossy as her skin is pale.

Paler than usual, today. She led us into her apartment through a pair of large double doors, closed them behind her, and hugged me. "Thank you for coming, both of you. Though I'm feeling guilty about calling you. I don't know what you can possibly do. Oh, I'm sorry, that's so rude of me." She extended her hand to Bill. "Moriko Ikeda."

"Bill Smith. Don't be sorry and don't feel guilty. I haven't been to Washington in a while. Happy to come down."

"I wish I could have provided better weather."

"Don't worry about it, that's Lydia's fault."

Moriko raised her delicate eyebrows but I didn't explain. After a moment she said, "I have tea. I'll bring it right in."

While Moriko went to get the tea, Bill whispered to me, "Do kitsune control the weather?"

"No. That was human small talk."

I'm always surprised when I find myself explaining something to Bill. As he's pointed out more than once, I'm the Asian person in our relationship. But he, rumpled, antisocial, and blue-collar as he appears—though not today; today he wore a sharp navy suit with a white shirt and blue-and-silver tie—is the one with the deep background in art, music, and all kinds of culture, including Asian culture. So long before Moriko hired us, he'd heard of kitsune; but apparently he wasn't familiar with their fine points.

I was, because I'd looked them up.

For example, they're usually called "fox spirits," but that makes them sound like ghosts and they're not ghosts. They're regular foxes who've reached a great age and attained wisdom and magical powers. Like shapeshifting. Into old men, young girls, and beautiful women.

For another example, they carry their souls, their kitsunebi, outside their bodies in glowing globes of fire. In fox form, they hold the globes on their tails. When they're humans, where to keep the globes—the kitsunebi-dama—becomes problematic. And it seemed that Blake Adderly, up-and-coming young hotshot D.C. power broker, had, in the course of dating Moriko, discovered and walked off with hers.

"You don't really believe this stuff?" Bill had asked when I told him about Moriko's problem.

"Doesn't matter. She does, and I'm telling you, she'll marry this creep if we can't think of what to do about it."

I had to admit the what-to-do-about-it part kind of had me at a loss. I'd come down hoping maybe a little calm, nonchalant logic could defuse the situation, but as Moriko poured green tea into tiny porcelain cups she said, "I know you think I'm crazy."

"No, I—okay, a little," I conceded, taking the cup she handed me. "I mean, I've known you forever, and you've never—you always—"

"I like the human form. I was a fox for a long time and this is still new and fun. I'm learning a lot, too. I just never should have trusted Blake."

Leaving aside the question of why she ever *had* trusted a man named Blake, I said, "Tell us about the kitsunebi-dama. What does it look like, and how did he get it?"

"It's like a clear rock crystal globe. You can hold it in your hands." She cupped her hands together and gazed into them sadly. "If you look deep inside you can see it glow. That's my kitsunebi shining in there."

"And how did he get it?"

She looked calmly at me. "I left it unprotected while we made love."

Well, I thought, one often does leave one's soul unprotected while making love. Just, usually not on the bureau.

I decided Bill deserved extra points for not laughing, not leering, not even smiling except reassuringly.

"All right," I said. "Tell us about Blake, and tell us where to find him."

She told us, and nothing about Blake was surprising. He was an attorney, raised with a certain level of power and money, not up there in the 1 percent but somewhere around the 5 to 7. Moriko had met him at a function at the Freer-Sackler, the Asian branch of the Smithsonian, where they both, by Moriko's admission, were trolling for clients. Blake had attended his father's law school and now worked at his father's law firm, specializing in their Asian clients.

"If you can call it working," Moriko said. "His actual job seems to be lunch. And dinner. And drinks, and partying. He connects people up with other people they want to know."

Bill listened politely, sipping his green tea (which was, expectedly, excellent). His ears seemed to perk up when, in response to my question about hobbies and spare-time activities, Moriko told us Blake raced sports cars. "He has an Aston Martin. He and his friends rent tracks and all go out there and drive fast. It bores me to tears, but luckily it's a guy thing so I didn't have to go much."

"I'm sorry, Moriko, I should have asked this before," Bill said, "but what is it you do?"

"I'm a development officer at the East Asian Union. We bring artists and intellectuals from Asia to the US, and we send Americans to Asian countries, too. Cultural exchange in the name of better relations, that sort of thing. Also, if we're asked we connect Asian capital with American entrepreneurs. Occasionally the other way, but most of the capital is in Asia these days. China especially. I think that's why Blake wants to marry me."

"I thought he wanted to marry you because you're hot and he's obsessed," I said. She blushed and cast her eyes down prettily, but she didn't deny it. "There's another explanation?" I asked.

"Yes. I mean, he is obsessed. Though I think even that is more about power than lust."

"A lot of the time they're indistinguishable," said Bill.

"You're probably right. But beyond that, I have a wide network of contacts throughout Asia that could be useful to him. You know how it works there, especially in Japan, but in China and Korea, too. People I know who might not give him the time of day on their own will feel obligated to help him out if I'm his wife and I ask them to."

"Help him out to do what?"

"The one thing he's way more obsessed with than he is with me. He has this dream of opening sports car tracks all over Japan. And then, all over Asia."

After we'd pretty much run the subject of Blake into the ground—and thrown a little mud on it—I swung the conversation to more general topics. It wasn't that I particularly wanted to sit around conversing when Bill and I could be out hunting Blake down, even in the rain, but Moriko was clearly forlorn and I thought it would be good to give her a sense that life was normal and this was just another problem to be handled. I asked about her folks, who lived half the year here and half in Japan. Right now was the Japan part, and she was grateful because they didn't have to know what she'd gotten herself into. Also, of course, they didn't know she was a kitsune, and it would be hard on them to learn the truth.

"Of course," I said.

She asked after my family, and I told her my mother had recently begun to shed her dislike of my profession and insert herself into some of my cases. Because she knows my mother, that actually made Moriko laugh.

"I'm not sure having your mother work with you is a good idea," she said.

"Not to worry. She'll never embrace my way of life totally. She still can't stand Bill."

Bill nodded, as though modestly accepting a compliment.

Tentatively, I asked, "How's Tadao?" Tadao's the brother I used to date.

Moriko looked into her teacup. "I'm not sure. He's working at Georgetown, coaching mixed martial arts and judo. He says he's over that whole playing-with-fire phase."

"Do you believe him?"

"I want to. But I don't know. Once you're in with those people, do you ever get out?"

I turned to Bill. "Tadao's a jock like me, and he's a wild man. In high school that meant we'd climb up on billboards and tag them, or bodysurf at Coney Island."

"I wish I'd seen that."

"In the winter. Later, though, he started romancing the Yakuza. Everyone was worried."

"What he says," Moriko poured Bill more tea, "is that the Yakuza turned out to be an astute crowd who knew Tadao better than he knew himself. His contact toyed with him a while, then told him to go fly a kite. But I don't know. I'm afraid he's only telling me that so I won't worry."

It wasn't kite-flying weather when Bill and I left Moriko's, but all we needed to do was scurry to that whispering Metro and re-emerge at Federal Triangle, home of the white-shoe law firms. We'd called ahead for an appointment with Blake Adderly. Moriko was pretty sure he was keeping the kitsunebi-dama in his office, and whether it was there or not we needed to size up the foe. Bill had done the talking on the phone, professing himself interested in sports cars—not that much of a stretch—and as a sort of password had dropped the name, supplied by Moriko, of one of Blake's friends.

"I feel so used," Bill told me when he hung up. "You only made me make that call because I'm a guy."

"That, and because you'd know what to do if he said 'Lamborghini.'"

After IDs, photos, and name tags, we made it past the pair of guards at the security desk with its bank of closed-circuit TVs. One guard hit the button to release the turnstile and we entered an elevator that slid silently up to the seventeenth floor. Quiet appeared to be a virtue of machinery here in Washington. All the better to eavesdrop on each other?

The perfectly poised and polished person behind the sleek teak desk in the anteroom at Adderly, Bascombe, Chase murmured into her headset. In a moment a similar person came to guide us to Blake Adderly's corner office. The good news was, I spotted a solid rock crystal globe on a shelf as soon as the door opened. The bad news: it was behind locked and alarmed glass cabinet doors.

Bill's first thought had been to just buy another globe and give it to Moriko, telling her we'd managed to pull a switcheroo with the one Blake stole. After meeting her Bill could tell that was a nonstarter, though. "She'd know, wouldn't she?"

"I'm sure she would. It's bound to have some tiny chip or flaw and she'll look for that first thing."

"Or maybe it really does have her kitsunebi inside it and if we give her a phony it won't be there."

"Uh-huh. But listen, maybe we could swap a new one for the real one in Blake's office and Blake wouldn't know."

Big preppy grin folding his freckled cheeks, Blake Adderly glad-handed us to leather client chairs. Bill was all blue-suited, rep-tie friendly; I was wearing a black business suit and red blouse, pumps, had put on a touch of make-up, and was narrow-eyed and aloof. If Blake picked up on my attitude it didn't seem to faze him, although I did get the feeling he'd picked up on my legs. "So," he said, forearms on his desk. His sand-colored hair was short-top-and-sides but with a fetching unruly curl in front. I wondered how much product he had to use to make it so adorably casual. "Friends of Digger's, huh? Welcome to D.C. and our wonderful weather."

Dave "Digger" Worthington was the name we'd dropped. A car-racing pal of Blake Adderly's, he'd conveniently been trans-ferred to Geneva. We found that handy because we could be sure he and Blake wouldn't be getting together tonight for drinks after work.

"Recent acquaintances," Bill corrected with an old-boy's-club smile. "I'm Bill Smith, this is Lydia Chin." Everyone nodded hello. "I was admiring Digger's Ferrari, we traded a few war stories, and he suggested I might want to meet you."

"I thought he had the Ferrari shipped to Switzerland."

"Geneva," Bill nodded. "That's where I saw it."

"And why did Digger think we should meet? Do you race?"

"Not anymore. I did run a 911 in the ALMS for a couple of years."

"ALMS? Nice."

"Not pro. A privateer entry. Then I rolled at Lime Rock. Totaled the Porsche. Jacked up my back."

"And that was it?"

Bill shrugged. "I walked away from that one, but I could tell I was losing a step. Racing's a young man's game."

Blake grinned, accepting the credit for the accomplishment of still being young. "Then what did Digger have in mind? Not that I have any problem with chatting with you folks for a few." He looked at me, winked, and his grin expanded.

I forced myself to smile a tiny tight smile and not jump up and slap his smarmy puss.

"Well," Bill said, "Digger told us about this idea you have, about opening a series of sports car tracks in Asia. Especially Japan, I think he said?"

Blake nodded.

"Lydia and I discussed it. We represent some people who're looking for investment opportunities."

Blake sat back in his giant ergonomic leather chair. "Do you?"

"We do."

"Mind telling me who?"

Bill looked at me and I shook my head. "I'm sorry," he said. "One of the conditions of our discussions and any future relationship will have to be anonymity. You'll only deal with me and Lydia. I can tell you they're people looking for places to put a good deal of capital."

Blake looked at Bill, clearly cogitating. "Asians?"

Bill looked at me again.

I nodded.

"Yes," he said.

"Chinese?"

I shook my head.

"Sorry," Bill said. "That's as far as I can go. I can assure you the capital's liquid and available, and as long as you have a sound business plan there's no—"

My phone buzzed. I grabbed it from my bag, whispered in urgent Chinese, and put it away again. "I'm sorry." I stood. It was the first time I'd spoken, and I made sure my English was over-precise and slightly accented. "Bill, we must go. It has been a pleasure meeting you, Mr. Adderly. I am sorry to run away but an urgent matter has come up. Perhaps we can continue this conversation tomorrow? We can come to your office at 10 a.m."

I didn't speak again until we were on the sidewalk. "That was some nice ad-libbing," I told Bill. My phone, of course, hadn't rung; that had been the alarm I set before we went in.

"Oh, I could have gone on. No one even said 'Lamborghini' yet."

"So what do you think? Was that it?" The rain had retracted to a fine mist, though I had the feeling it wasn't through with us yet.

"The globe in the cabinet? I think it has to be, don't you?"

"Can you pick that lock?"

"Probably. I'd need a few minutes. But it's alarmed—did you see the wire? I don't know what we would do about that. And it would have to be during the workday. No way we can break into Adderly, Bascombe, Chase when they're closed. Not in a building that secure. Besides, law offices don't close. Some poor associate is always there being worked to death."

I thought. "Fire drill?"

"They must have a protocol. Not sure how I'd manage to get left behind. And this just occurred to me, but they might have security cameras."

"In the private offices?"

"Why not?"

"Spying on themselves?"

"They're lawyers."

Stealing the globe right out from under Blake Adderly's nose had been Plan Z anyway, even though we didn't have Plans A or B yet. We agreed to give it some thought and made our way back to Dupont Circle to check in at our bed and breakfast. We had two rooms (of course we did) in a townhouse three blocks from Moriko's apartment. My room faced the garden. A cherry tree just beginning to bloom arched gracefully over a bench in a herringbone-patterned brick yard. I'd told Bill that before we went home I wanted to make sure to go down to see the cherry blossoms along the Tidal Basin. "Even if it's pouring," I'd added, to cut off any whining about the weather, but he'd surprised me.

"Viewing cherry blossoms is a venerable Japanese tradition. *Hanami,* it's called. In the sun, in the rain, equally beautiful. You can see it in all kinds of weather in any number of woodblock prints. In fact, you can even see kitsune having hanami parties. Maybe we should take your friend Moriko down there as a celebration when we're done."

"As long as we're sure we'll have something to celebrate."

"Oh, we will," he said. "I have complete faith. You'll come up with something."

My room was supplied with a coffee maker and porcelain mugs. I took a long, hot shower, dried, and dressed. I made a cup of tea, which I drank sitting in a comfy chair at the big window, looking out on the cherry tree and the bench. The rain hadn't yet picked up again, its place held by a fine mist that blurred edges and softened colors. It was, I decided, the visual equivalent of silence. The mist grayed out nearly everything in the garden, but the brand-new cherry blossoms seemed to glow. Some things became clearer in the mist, just as some became sharper in the silence.

When my tea was gone I picked up my phone and invited Tadao to join me and Bill for dinner.

Moriko had a function to go to that evening. "Full kimono, the whole enchilada," she said. "I'm wearing that light blue one you always liked, Lydia."

"With the yellow flowers? It's beautiful. I'm glad you still wear it."

"It's my favorite. Enjoy dinner, you guys. Oh, Lydia? Don't tell Tadao about the kitsunebi, okay? He doesn't like Blake to begin with."

"Why should he?"

"No reason, but I don't want him to go off half-cocked. Or," she tilted her head in thought, "fully cocked."

"Does he know … about you?"

"That I'm a kitsune?" She smiled. "Of course. He's my brother."

And your parents are your parents, I thought, but I guess there's no arguing with a fox.

Bill and I headed through the rain to the Old Ebbitt Grill. Tadao had suggested it for dinner because he thought I needed to see old-boy, power-broking Washington.

"That's where I spent the afternoon," I'd said on the phone.

"The Old Ebbit Grill?"

"No, old-boy, power-broking Washington. Bill and I were up talking to Blake Adderly."

"Blake? Why?"

"Long story."

"To be frank, I do not like that arrogant S.O.B. I'll be happy when Moriko finally ditches him. See you at seven."

As Bill and I crossed the dining room to the table where Tadao waited for us I decided the dark wood and the marble staircase were handsome, but I wasn't sure I liked the idea of eating under the reproachful gaze of taxidermy supposedly shot by Teddy Roosevelt.

"You get used to it," Tadao said, after I voiced that opinion.

"I'm not sure I want to. And I think I'll be eating fish."

He kissed my cheek and I kissed his; then I introduced him to Bill and they shook hands quite civilly.

"God, it's been forever," Tadao said as we all sat. "You look fabulous, Lydia." He grinned at Bill. "I'm sure you do, too, though I don't have any baseline for you. So how come you guys came down? And why were you hanging out with that snake, Blake?"

"He is kind of slimy," I agreed. "Did you know he wants to open a chain of sports car tracks in Japan? From there I gather he wants to conquer all of Asia."

"I didn't know that, no. I can't say it makes me happy to hear it."

A waiter in a crisp white shirt and suspenders came to take our drink orders. While we gave them I checked Tadao out. He looked pretty good himself. He was built on a different template from his sister: stocky and muscular, square forehead and large hands. When the waiter was gone I told him, "We came here to see Moriko."

"Is she okay? Is there something she's not telling me? She seems down lately."

"She is."

"Trouble with Blake?"

"Yes."

"Well, that's encouraging. Is that why you were up seeing him?"

"Partly. I mean, I'd never met him and I wanted to check him out. As it happens Bill's interested in sports car racing, so we had something to talk to him about. I'll tell you all about it, but first, Tadao, I need to ask you something."

He raised his eyebrows, and then the lightbulb went on over his head. "You're going to ask me if I'm a Yakuza *wakagashira* yet."

A wakagashira in the Yakuza is a regional commander. "A *kobun* would be bad enough," I said. Kobun literally means 'foster child.' It's the lowest rank the Yakuza have.

"I never even made that. Relax, Lydia. Or tell Moriko to relax, if she sent you. That part of my life is done with. It was—what do the pols around here say? A youthful indiscretion. I'm lucky. If you really get in you never get out, but I wasn't allowed that deep in the first place. Just dipped my big toe, that was it. It's over with. I teach judo now. For Pete's sake, I'm on the Georgetown faculty! How cool is that?"

"Moriko didn't send us. She believes you when you say it's over. I just wanted to see for myself."

"Well," he spread his arms, "see. Peace?"

"Peace."

"So. What did you and ol' Blake have to say to each other?"

"It was mostly about cars. And the weather."

The drinks came, and the rest of the evening was spent eating oysters, crab cakes, and spicy shrimp linguine. We talked about old times, present times, youthful indiscretions, poor decisions, getting in deep, and dealing with consequences.

The next morning saw more rain, another cup of tea by the window, a lovely French toast breakfast, and the arrival of me and Bill— same suits, me a different blouse, he a different tie—at Adderly, Bascombe, Chase promptly at 10 a.m. Blake Adderly was, he claimed, delighted to see us.

Seated in Blake's office, the wet streets of Washington glistening outside his corner window, we continued our discussion.

"We've spoken to our principals," Bill said. "They've asked us to pursue your racetrack idea. They're especially interested in your plan to begin in Japan. Digger told me that's what you were thinking."

"It seemed like the best place to start. On the one hand, the

Japanese have a heavy load of complicated—actually, if you ask me, absurd—tradition weighing them down. But on the other, that's why when they cut loose, they seriously get wild." He gave us a conspiratorial grin. "I can see us really monetizing that."

One, I thought, *no one did ask you. And two, well, you're just one superior fellow, aren't you?* I smiled one of my tight, tiny smiles.

"Your business plan," Bill said. "We'd want a majority stake, of course, even if there are other investors. Seats on the board. We'd ask to be involved as you choose all the technical consultants—track designers, architects—though we expect to be able to defer to you on these decisions, as the subject-matter expert. In Japan, of course, there are all kinds of earthquake precautions that need to be taken, but I'm sure you've considered that. Not so much for the tracks, but for the grandstands and ancillary structures. The marketing is another major issue. We assume you have a strategy? Celebrity spokesperson, that sort of thing? Are there any—"

A brief commotion of raised voices made us all swing our heads to the office door. It flew open and in strode Tadao, along with a young, lean Asian guy a little shorter than he was. Both were in black suits and ties, Tadao with a bulky black leather man-bag over his shoulder. Behind them in a fluttery panic came the poised person whose job it was to not let things like this happen to Blake.

"I'm so sorry, Mr. Adderly, they just—"

"It's all right, Heather. I know this gentleman." Blake stood, smiling and extending his hand to Tadao as though these were just people coming late to our meeting. Heather withdrew in relief and confusion. I closed my mouth, which had flown open when the door had. Bill's face was wary, set and closed.

"Tadao. Nice to see you, man." Blake shook with Tadao and extended his hand to the other man. "Blake Adderly." The man ignored the extended hand but gave a short, sharp bow. Blake shrugged, pulled his hand back, and still smiling, said, "What can I do for you gents? Or is this a social visit?"

Tadao scowled. "No, it's not. Bill, Lydia." He nodded to us. "I knew you were coming here this morning. I was hoping to get here first."

"You guys all know each other?" Blake asked, smile still in place.

"We did, years ago," said Tadao.

I said, "What are you doing here?"

"This is Kenji Yokoshiro." Tadao shifted uncomfortably and didn't meet my eyes. "Yokoshiro-san is my *oyabun*."

"Tadao!" I jumped up from my chair as Yokoshiro, stone-faced, gave me and Bill the same short bow he'd bestowed on Blake. *Oyabun* is Yakuza for 'elder brother.' A kobun's boss. "You said that was over! You said it never even began!" I barely remembered to keep my accent going for Blake's sake while I yelled at him.

"Oh, Lydia, Jesus! It would've been safer for you to believe that but it's ridiculous. Once you're in, even your big toe, you never get out."

Blake was frowning, Bill was glowering, I was once again openmouthed, and Tadao looked at Yokoshiro. Yokoshiro nodded. Tadao loosened his tie, tossed it on Blake's desk, and unbuttoned his shirt. A green dragon breathing red-and-gold flames curled around the left side of his rib cage.

Yakuza tattoos are for services rendered and are strictly controlled. Eventually, an honored Yakuza soldier will be completely covered in them. Tadao seemed off to a fine start.

"Okay." Blake spoke firmly. It was his office and he was reasserting control. "Okay. Tadao, I guess you're telling us you and your buddy are gangsters. Congratulations? Is that what I'm supposed to say? Now why the hell are you here? And put your clothes back on."

Tadao glanced at Yokoshiro again, and on the oyabun's nod he buttoned his shirt and re-knotted his tie. "I used to date Lydia, long time ago. We had dinner last night. She told me about your plan to build sports car racing tracks, Blake. That's why we're here. Especially about the ones in Japan, but no, really all of them."

"You have a problem with the idea?"

"No. We want a piece of it."

"Tadao—" I began, but Bill put a hand on my arm.

"Here's the thing," Tadao said to Blake. "We have money. We have connections. We think this is a great idea."

Blake narrowed his eyes. "Who's 'we'? You and Skinny here?"

I drew in a breath, but Yokoshiro didn't react to the diss. "It might be a good idea to show a little respect," Tadao said. "Luckily for you Yokoshiro-san doesn't speak much English. By 'we,' I mean me, Yokoshiro-san and ... people above him. The rest of the family."

"Jesus. You guys talk about families, like the goombahs?"

"Our *family*," Tadao responded, "can be invaluable to you in getting this thing off the ground." He paused. "We can also get in your way."

Blake regarded him for a long moment, then sat slowly in his huge chair. He nodded, gave a slow smile. "All right. I'm willing to talk."

"Mr. Adderly," I said, trying hard to stay in the character I'd started with—no use confusing the guy—and still say what I needed to say, "you can't seriously be considering—"

"I'll call you two if I need you. Thanks for coming."

Once again, I began to say something; once again, Bill cut me off. "We'd better go," Bill said, cold eyes on Tadao. He stood. I was already standing, so the client chairs were now up for grabs.

But Tadao wasn't looking at Bill, or at me, and he made no move to sit. His eyes were on Yokoshiro, and Yokoshiro's were on the glass-doored cabinet. Without moving his gaze he whispered in Japanese to Tadao.

Tadao said, "Yokoshiro-san is asking about the globe in your cabinet."

Blake looked over his shoulder. "That? Rock crystal. As a matter of fact your sister gave it to me."

Yokoshiro whispered again.

"He'd like to see it."

Blake shrugged. "Why not?" He rummaged in his desk drawer for a key, opened the cabinet, punched a code into a discreet interior keypad, and took the globe out. I wasn't positioned well to see the code, but what did it matter now? Blake handed the globe to Yokoshiro.

Looking into the globe, the oyabun let out that Japanese guttural grunt that can mean either surprise or agreement. *"Hoh!"* He squinted and peered deeper. "Kitsunebi!"

"I—" That was me, but Blake didn't want to hear from me.

"Bill? Lydia? It's been great chatting with you. Like I said, I'll be in touch."

"No, you—" I started, but Bill put a firm hand on my elbow and guided me out the door.

Twenty minutes later Bill and I were sitting wordlessly under the awning of a sidewalk café around the corner from Adderly, Bascombe, Chase. The mist had thickened to drizzle, probably building up to the energy to actually rain. Bill was working on a second espresso and I was trying to get my oolong tea to warm me up.

"Look," Bill said.

I turned where he was pointing. Just crossing at the corner were Tadao and Yokoshiro, both in sunglasses despite the weather, both striding with that intimidating gangster roll. Neither carried an umbrella. *What do you guys plan to do,* I wondered, *if it really starts to rain?*

It seemed I was going to get a chance to ask. When they came abreast of the café they spotted us at our table.

"Well. Lydia and Bill," Tadao said. Yokoshiro bowed. "Mind if we join you?"

I looked at Bill, looked back at Tadao, and shrugged. The two men threaded their way between the tables—ours was the only one occupied—and joined us under the awning.

"Tadao—" I began, but Tadao held up his hand to stop me. I was getting mightily tired of men not letting me finish my sentences, but I shut it, to see what he was going to say.

He said nothing. He put the black leather man-bag on the table-top and drew from it a silk-wrapped object. It was round, it seemed heavy, and when he unwrapped it with a flourish I could see it was, unmistakably, the rock crystal globe.

"How about that?" he said with a smirk.

For a moment I managed to keep a straight face. Then I cracked up. "You did it! You're fabulous! You did it!"

"Well, you teed him up. All we needed to do was swing."

"Took you long enough to show up," Bill said, but he was grinning, too. "I was running out of B.S."

"You will never run out of B.S.," I said. "You didn't even get to 'Lamborghini.'" I turned to the other man. "Kenji, right? Thank you. You were so scary I believed you myself."

Kenji Yokoshiro grinned. "I had a blast," he said in perfect English. It should be perfect; Tadao had told us the young actor was from Sacramento. "Good chance to practice my gangster chops. That's why I'm studying with Tadao in the first place, so if I get any gangster roles I can do my own stunts. So this is the right thing, huh?"

"Great sentimental value to my sister," Tadao said. "Just emotional blackmail on the part of that asshat. Now she'll never have to see him again."

We all high-fived and then Kenji went in to get celebratory lattes.

"So how did this happen?" I asked.

"After we sealed the deal, I suggested to Blake that since Yokoshiro-san was so entranced with the kitsunebi-dama it might be a nice gesture to give it to him. A goodwill gift between friends.

Before he could answer I explained to Yokoshiro-san what a generous man our new business partner was. With a bow and a thank-you, the whole nine yards. Yokoshiro-san was floored and offered his gold cigarette case in exchange. Mine, I mean. Gold-plated, I mean. Anyway, Blake sort of had to give it to him, after that. Just like you said he would. Honest to God, it all went exactly like we worked it out, Lydia. You're the genius."

"I've always said that," Bill put in.

"You've always said a lot of things." I turned back to Tadao. "So you guys didn't have to improvise at all?"

"Blake doesn't have enough imagination to make that necessary," Tadao said. "One thing about the guy, he's never surprising."

"What's supposed to happen now?" I asked as Kenji returned with a tray of lattes.

"He thinks we're coming back tomorrow with one of the higher-ups. I told him to be sure to lay in a supply of good tea. I even told him where to get it. I have a friend with a tea shop. Might as well share the wealth."

"See, now, that's improvising. It's also so very you. And when you don't come back?"

"He'll call me, I guess. He has my cell number. I'll tell him, 'So sorry, our wakagashira put the kibosh on it, later, dude.' What'll he do, sue for breach of contract?"

"He'll wish he hadn't kicked us to the curb," said Bill.

"Or given away the kitsunebi-dama," I said. "Now he has no leverage to get your sister to help him, either."

"Hey," said Yokoshiro. "That thing—you don't mean you think it's really ...?"

"Depends," said Tadao. "You've met my sister. Think she's a fox?"

Yokoshiro grinned and reddened, so his opinion was clear.

We drank our lattes, we admired the globe, Tadao rewrapped it in the silk cloth, and we all got up to leave.

"I need to get home and wash off this damn stage paint," Tadao said. "It itches. Kenji, I swear I don't know how actors do it."

"Hazard of the trade."

"What are you guys going to do?" Tadao asked me.

"We'll give this back to Moriko, then we'll head home."

Moriko practically jumped up and down when I handed her the wrapped globe. As she was untying the cloth her smile lit her whole face. "This is it, I can tell without even seeing it, oh Lydia—Oh, oh, oh! Thank you, thank you!" She cupped the kitsunebi-dama in both hands and gazed into it. Looking up, she said, "You saved my life."

"No," I said. "We stopped you from wrecking it by marrying a jerk. Could you please put that thing away someplace safe?"

After lunch, a lot more thank-yous until I finally had to cut that off as embarrassing, ("And you'd better be all over your brother, too, by the way") and promises to visit more often, Bill and I left Moriko to dress for a late-afternoon function.

"Sure you don't want to come view the cherry blossoms with us?"

"I so wish I could. But I have to go to this gathering."

"What kimono are you wearing?"

"Completely different crowd, so I'm wearing the blue one again. Sort of to celebrate. Can I say thank you one more time?"

"No."

"Okay. Goodbye, and thank you."

We needed to pick up our bags at the B&B and head for the train station, but first, as afternoon gave way to evening, we went down to the Tidal Basin to view the cherry blossoms. The rain had been falling heavily while we were with Moriko, but, maybe since I'd be leaving soon, it had backed off and seemed to be giving up. By the time we reached the Tidal Basin it wasn't raining at all. The trees along the walkways were swaddled in a thick mist. It made each new set of branches a surprise and the blossoms on them seem like somebody's good idea. We strolled for a while in silence, enjoying the quiet and the softness.

"Look," I said to Bill, pointing off into the distance, "Those lights over there. What's going on?"

He peered where I pointed, and grinned. "I'll be damned. It's foxfire."

"What does that mean?"

"It's a kind of bioluminescence. Glowing fungus on dead wood in swampy soil."

"How poetic."

"But also, in Japanese art, it's what the artists show when a group of *kitsune* gather in the woods. To view the cherry blossoms or whatever. They run away if you get too close, but if you see them from a distance it'll look like that. Because they'll all be carrying their kitsunebi-dama globes on their tails."

"Now *that's* poetic. Especially given why we're here."

We stood watching the flickering lights in the distance until a movement in the mist between the cherry trees caught my eye. "Hey! It's Moriko!"

"Where?"

"Between those trees. I'd know that blue kimono anywhere. With the yellow flowers."

"I don't see her."

"Right there—No, wait, I don't anymore either." I blinked. "I lost her in the mist."

"You sure you saw her?"

"In that kimono? Definitely. I wonder where she's going? Is there someplace here in the park where her gathering could be?"

Bill didn't know, and I didn't either. But as we stared through the trees, I could have sworn I saw an isolated flicker of flame moving away into the mist. It approached the glimmering group in the distance, they gathered around it—at least, that's what it looked like—and under the cherry blossoms, the foxfire danced.

The Electric Palace by Violet LeVoit

Taro, the big boss, always has the most beautiful handkerchiefs. They really are something, silk or linen, embroidered with the letter T in Western style. That's why I was surprised to see him lay one of his best across the guillotine splicer when Goro and Oni-Chan dragged that hapless fool theater owner across the projection booth.

"I can understand a small business owner like yourself fearing the expense of insurance," said Taro in that ribbiting thunder voice of his. He is fat, big-bellied like a bullfrog, and the succulent immensity of him buttoned beneath a fine Italian shirt makes me tingle with pleasant recollection. He lights a cigarette and the *clik-fsshh* of the butane flame rides above the fool's yammering pleas like the clear peal of a temple bell, above all his stupid entreaties as they put his hand down hard on the splicer and spread his trembling fingers. I think it is so interesting how some people's hands swell like blood sausages and others turn white and clammy when gripped hard by the wrist for so long. You really cannot guess by looking at them first.

"We are only a thirty-seat theater," the fool drools. "Please, this is a family endeavor. I only want to see my children eat rice again."

Taro snorts. "If you wanted your children to eat rice, you should have paid fealty and come to me for aid." He bends over the sobbing man. "The *gaijin* occupation will feed your family, huh?" He sees me looking and darts his eyes to me, and I enjoy a moment of frisson over how my cherry lipstick and emerald silk dress are a rich distraction for him in this dull booth, with its floor-to-ceiling racks of funereal film canisters and stained cinder-block walls and the camphor stink of decaying celluloid. But the projector is oiled and immaculate. The fool is smart enough to take good care of that.

Taro gives me a measured stare, and I know him intimately enough to recognize anticipation in his expertly impassive face. He knows how I am like him, how the part of our hearts that flinches at atrocity has no electric quickness anymore, and the secret that only people like us understand: how all that death has left us austere and shining, like ivory. He loves how my face moves only when I will it to do so, and no pleasure or horror can persuade it otherwise.

For instance, I can see that the blade of the guillotine splicer is going to be dull, and won't gain enough momentum on its tiny arm to sever the top knuckle of the fool's left pinky finger, no matter how hard Goro or Oni-Chan slams it down, or how many times. And even though there's a pair of scissors on the table I make no move to suggest swapping one for the other, because I know Taro intends to make this man pay with the tools of his trade. And I'm right about the splicer, and the fool's screams rend the air—it's going to take forever—but then Oni-Chan surprises me by placing his whole weight on the blade beneath his palm and, red-faced, *ssnnnTHOK*, there's a satisfying snap, like a crisp stick yielding beneath your feet during an autumn stroll.

And as they haul the gibbering, bleeding fool down the stairs, Taro steps behind me and seizes the breasts I'm so proud of, touches under my skirt to ascertain how wet I am, betrays nothing as he pats my cheek, *pat, pat, PAT*, until it stings. "We'll burn this place down in a week," he says, licking his curious finger clean. "In the meantime, show something."

So I run my hands across the dusty stacks, looking for something complete in six reels. Not like it matters, but I have projectionist's pride. Even if this is the last theater standing in Asakusa's sixth district, even if Taro's yakuza owns the "Turkish bath" to the right and the "hostess bar" to the left, even if anyone coming in here will be looking for the cheapest, darkest space they can find on the quick, I will still show a movie the way it's supposed to be shown. My father would expect nothing less.

And I find it: something foreign, complete in six reels, the celluloid seething only slightly at the edges from nitrate decay. I heft the first pungent reel onto the projector, snapping shut the fireproof sarcophagus before threading it through the machine's metallic guts. The sprocket holes are buckled but not too damaged to catch on the teeth of the gears. I flip the switch and the metal lurches to life. The glass in the booth window is broken but the still-clinging shards don't hurt the picture quality too much. I quickly cover the lens so the audience won't see the leader: the crosshairs ending in arrow points, the fluttering numbers winking in and out, the final "3" blinking and departing. The only spectator in the audience is a bundle of old trash bunched up in one seat, but I still block the projection beam with my small hand because the leader is not meant to be seen. It is a private communiqué between film and projectionist. It is its final kiss out the door before meeting the big wide world. This is the proper way. He taught me.

The movie is a Western, cowboys shooting pistols over wide un-Japanese vistas. I hate it. It's a sound picture. I find the speaker switch. *Pow, pow.* The Victor lurches to life.

They are filtering in now, American sailors on the arms of hungry local girls. They don't care about the movie any more than I do. But I like it in here. I can pretend I am a child in Niigata again. My father's theater was magnificent: parquet ceiling, velvet curtains, the smell of incense and the fragrant taste of Sakuma Drops, sugar gemstones spilled under the seats by rapt moviegoers, rescued by my small fingers and rolled sweetly on my tongue. And the faces in the movies: suffering wives, grim samurai. The world of adults was full of roiling passions and fevers expressed quietly in tatami rooms. I was too young then to know what made the women bite their lips bitterly or duck their heads in shame. I know now.

I check the sixth reel and, sure enough, it's not rewound. I swipe the bloodied splicer to the side and spool the reels up on the rewind table. I spin the handle and remember my father in the projection booth, his small eyes peering through the window, squeezing his mouth into a stroke of ink as he twists the focus ring. *Pay attention,* he says, *soon you'll be in charge of this grand machine.* And me, small, pigtailed, cheeks pressing close to him and the hot white light, the mush-edged grey world on the screen snapping to startling clarity at my father's command: faces cut out from backgrounds like paper dolls, surfaces swimming lively with grain. The rewinding film passes between the cloth in my fingers but I don't feel it. Some part of me could still leap in delight then, before Tokyo, before men and bombs and hunger. And Taro, dark tutor. Something in my memory breaks and melts in the gate.

There's a sudden snap of sparks in the corner of my eye and I turn, hoping to watch the reel burst into an unquenchable nitrate flame. But the film is still chugging away merrily. I hear the crackle of downed wires, the burst of white smoke. A low roar of dismay wafts up from the audience, unhappy there's no cowboy gunfire to cover the sound of sucking. The Victor speaker is dead. I look out over the audience. The cowboys race around in funereal silence, their feather-light horses making no hoofbeats upon the ground, their guns emitting gentle puffs of smoke as if exhaling.

And then I hear the cultured voice wheeze up, a gentle Kyoto warble feeble with age: "Ladies and gentlemen, let us allow our orchestra to rest, so that men may continue our tale." What I thought was a bundle of trash unfolds itself out of the seat and staggers towards the stage. It's an elderly man wrapped in a brown *yukata*, tabescent chest drunkenly bare. He veers alarmingly off course into the shadowed edge of the theater, but his voice rings out clear from the dark. "Our hero!" he cries out, and blunders back into the light, saluting the cowboy. "Our hero of the Western invasion!" His pale, pockmarked flesh reflects the projector's light like the surface of the moon.

I remember: the *benshi*.

My father's theater had a benshi. He arrived on a Tuesday in a taxi, the first time I'd ever seen someone ride in one. He was ragged and elegant in his hangover. My father served him miso soup with clams and shooed me out of the projection booth and let him watch the week's movie in advance. I'd never met anyone so important that he could have a movie all to himself. I hid behind the curtains under the stage and watched him watch: whispering lines of imagined dialogue to himself, waving his hands in gentle swan wings as if to the music of an invisible symphony, nipping from a bottle under his jacket. That night he stood before a thousand patrons, bathed and shaved and sharp in a Western suit, and narrated the movie, voiced every part, colored silent scenes with his descriptions until his words bled into the audience's imagination. He would do every show, five or six times a day, Tuesday through Sunday. On Monday he would disappear, and my father would oil the projector and repair broken seats. "No one wants to see a movie without a benshi," he'd shrug.

This drunken benshi was older than the one my father hired: even from my perch in the projection room I could see his toothless mouth was a dark theater with only one ivory seat remaining. But he had the same courtly distinction, the same twinkle of conspiracy with the audience. "But what is this?" he feigned surprise as the Comanche warlord circled the wagons. "Our hero is surrounded. His bravado and arrogance have failed him. His bullying has brought just desserts. Go ahead and discharge your little weapon, bully. The ancient people outlast you."

I can't help but smile. The devil with my father's six-reel rule. I delve into the stacks again and uncover cans scrawled with names like sutras: Ozu, Mizoguchi, Naruse. I snap reels out of safety coffins and kill the cowboy monstrosity. Before the groans rise up again I've already threaded up the film I want. *Dragnet Girl.* It's only one reel, the last reel, the shootout, the rooftop escape. Tokiko, baby-faced in her smart striped dress, begging Joji to come to his senses. The benshi is tickled by my choice.

"Joji, let's give up!" he says in the moll's girlish purr. "A new life is waiting for us, right?" And then, burying his chin into his chest to growl in the voice of that callow gangster bastard breaking her heart: "You can get arrested, girl, but not me." I think about my poison-green dress and gore-red lips and how a bold girl like me in shy Niigata loved *Dragnet Girl,* how much I wanted to be Tokiko and have the world look up at me from where I'd pinned it beneath my pointed heels. I didn't know then what one must endure to be burned down into something bright, clean, shining, the white-hot atom pinprick at the start of a chain reaction that tumbles into clouds blossoming like jellyfish up into Nagasaki skies. I wear heels so I can forget what it's like to walk barefoot on rubble already sticky with other people's blood. The things I have seen … the woman I have become to wear this dress and never, ever move my face …

The benshi can see me, through the jagged window. "No regrets, my jade angel above," he cries, the clairvoyance of the drunk. "Your fortune smiles down upon me." He is sending me love letters, from one cinema lover to another. The movies made us and saved us. They are why we are still standing when nothing else stands on the scorched circle of glass, they are why we will die with our heads high in this dead, raped city, dreaming …

A beer can zings by the benshi's head. "Aw, shaddap, grandpa." A sailor staggers up out of his seat, his two girl companions reaching up to him to calm him, their slim silhouetted arms like plants straining for the sun. "And put that cowboy picture back on!"

I clench my jaw. I'll do no such thing. I reach for an empty film container to throw through the window at the gaijin when I see he's pulled a gun: skinny muzzle, a Nambu. There's better American guns afloat in Asakusa but he's so pleased with what he snatched off a Japanese casualty. His girlfriends squeal and cower. "Go ahead, Jap," he snarls, waving that corpse-stolen gun. "Keep on talking."

I grab the scissors. I wanted to stay in this projection booth until Taro burned the theater down. I know how the safety devices work: the soft-linked chains will melt and drop the metal shutters, and while the theater evacuates I alone will cremate in this coffin of dreams. But now, I have a noble death. I will die in defense of a benshi. The purity of this flutters up in me like crane wings. I tighten my grip on the scissors as I tear out of the booth and fly down the stairs. I will bury the scissors in the meat of the gaijin's back if I'm quick, I *must* be quick, I must hurt him as much as I can before he shoots me and I die here in this dying theater, I am right behind him, he does not see me, I raise the scissors, I am ready to die for black and white and dreams—

I have never heard a shot so loud. It breaks the last thing in me left to be broken.

I look up at the benshi. He doesn't know. He is in that spellbound state I have seen before, the body's grace numbness before the realization hits. He is looking at me, perplexed, as if he can't understand what has just happened. For the first time in years I can't stop the hot tears spilling down my cheeks. All my murderous rage has soured to shame. "Forgive me," I say, barely able to keep looking into his eyes, "please forgive me."

The sailor is turning slowly towards me, swinging his weapon wide. I will not allow him the satisfaction of murdering me too. I aim the scissors at my own neck, ready to—

The sailor falls at my feet.

His companions shriek. They stomp all over his corpse in their stampede out of the theater. There is a red puddle pooling over the bastard's heart. His gun is cold. The benshi is fine. His bare chest is unmarred. He is still staring at both of us, astounded. But who—

I look up. There is Tokiko, glamorous moll, standing alone fifty feet high on a dark screen, silks pressed, jaw set, pistol in her grip. The smoke from the muzzle of her gun drifts away from the screen and rises to meet the theater ceiling.

The Long-Rumored Food Crisis by Setsuko Shinoda
translated by Jim Hubbert

He was always cheerful, always hard at work, with thickly muscled, sun-bronzed arms, a man so masculine even other men fell quickly under his spell. We were both outsiders, fugitives from the big-city rat race. I wish my wife and I could've gotten to know Tetsuji Okada better, but we kept our distance.

It was my wife's idea to move to this area, thick with pension hotels, in the foothills outside the village. We managed a bakery that doubled as a café, but after two years I was already growing tired of our sham country life. Everyone, from the pension owners to the man who ran the crafts workshop, was pretending to live like Peter Mayle. The women planted herbs and berries, made jam and wreaths and vegetable-dyed cloth, and went into ecstasies organizing concerts by no-name musicians in the little local auditorium. Yet when autumn came and the tourists disappeared, many of our neighbors went back to Tokyo to make ends meet as cab drivers, factory workers, or bartenders, and routinely mocked the people of the village and their hayseed culture.

Tetsuji Okada was different. He was the only real man among us fugitives from the city. He didn't live in the alpine foothills with the rest of us. He'd settled in the flatlands where it was swelter-ing in summer and freezing in winter, built solid relationships with the locals, and managed forty acres of fields and paddies, growing rice, soybeans, and a profusion of vegetables. I was speechless with admiration.

I first encountered him in the lounge of the village hot spring. My wife and our son Hiro, almost four, had been pestering me to take them. Hiro was too excited to sit still, and we'd retired to a cor-ner of the lounge to eat our noodles, hoping to avoid bothering the locals, when Okada invited us to sit with him and his beer-drinking friends. We listened, rapt, as he talked about the joys and frustra-tions of rural life. He was a straight shooter, yet never anything but modest about his achievements.

"I gave soybeans a go last year, but I just can't get the hang of it. It's hard to match what you guys do. You've got two thousand years of experience behind you." He knew how to compliment his friends without flattering them.

The toothless old man sitting next to him shook his head. "Not at all. Your farm is outstanding. You city people are amaz-ing. You've almost got it down." He clapped Okada on the shoulder encouragingly.

"I owe it all to you." Okada's bow was modest and dignified. It did me good just to be around him.

That was how our casual friendship started. Now and then we would meet for drinks in the little eatery that served as the village pub. Sometimes he would bring us produce from his fields.

But it was around the third time we sat down for drinks that I noticed his face always took on a wild look when he got into one particular topic.

He was convinced—almost obsessed—that some kind of major food shortage was just around the corner. Whenever the subject turned to farming, his usually sunny expression changed com-pletely. A dark light seemed to shine from his haunted eyes and the words poured out of him as he condemned city people and the way they lived.

"Tetsuji would be nice to be around, except for that whole 'food crisis' thing," my wife remarked with a laugh. I chuckled too—and decided I'd keep our meetings outside the house. It would be better not to have him over. He was entitled to his own opinion, but this fixation of his seemed to border on mania. There was something unsettling about it.

True, I found his bitterness easier to understand when he told me how his decision to move to the country had prompted his wife to divorce him, take their three children and their house in southwest Tokyo, and claim half of his severance pay from the big publishing house where he had worked for twenty-three years.

"City people walk on thin ice every day," he once said. "Even after the war, when people were starving, we grew more than half the food we needed, yet look how many people died. And how much food does Japan produce now? Less than 40 percent of what we need. Remember in '72, when America stopped exporting soybeans? Now it's global warming. Soils all over the planet are being exhausted, and American grain production has to start falling sooner or later. Southeast Asia? They're paving their farmland over and industrializing as fast as they can. Doesn't matter what international treaties say. What idiot is going to export food when there's not enough at home?"

By this point, his eyes would be moist with anxiety.

"Cities are hotbeds of consumption and hedonism, but they don't create anything essential for life. One day there'll be no food in the supermarket. Nothing at the 7-Eleven. The first people to get wind of the shortage will run out and buy it all. There will be a panic. Only the ones who can pay the going rate will have food. The government won't have options. Used to be they could go around Asia with wads of money and buy whatever they wanted. That won't work next time. There won't be any countries with food to spare. They won't sell what they don't have."

"Yes, I guess Japan will be in a tough situation by the time my son's an adult."

This time I'd been in the neighborhood and dropped by to chat. We were out by his soybean field when he'd mounted his hobby-horse again, and I didn't feel like arguing with him on his own turf. I just tried to nod and be agreeable while I waited for my chance to escape.

"No." Okada gazed out over his fields and shook his head. "It's coming. Five years, ten at the most. We're on the brink. Most people are just dancing around at the edge of the abyss. They're completely oblivious."

"Uhm-hm. Your edamame are coming in well." I was desperate to change the subject.

"Edamame? Don't kid me. Are you telling me you don't know that crops like edamame and sweet corn are a criminal waste of food? Letting them mature yields far more calories. But no, people want to eat baby soybeans because they taste better. That's how people eat, without a care in the world. Same thing with corn. Cut the ears off before their time. 'Oh, it's so sweet!' Edamame, baby corn, all that crap. Won't grow it, won't eat it."

We'd reached the stage where it was best for me to just keep my mouth shut. I kept nodding and saying "Uh-hmm, uh-hmm" as I started backing away.

"In the end, there'll be no soybeans, much less any edamame. The stores will be out of rice. There won't be any food for tomorrow. And you thought they had it bad in North Korea. I guarantee you, city people will be coming out here to buy food with the money they got from selling their daughters."

"Right, selling their daughters." I started to laugh but quickly stopped myself. Okada's eyes weren't smiling.

"Listen, how about it? We're weeding the paddies tomorrow.

Why don't you come? Some friends of mine will be here from Tokyo to help out. They take the future food crisis very seriously. I've promised to share my crops with them and nobody else. They take responsibility for their own food supply by weeding the paddies and helping me plant rice. I won't sell my crops for any amount of money. But friends are different. I'll set some aside for you too."

"Thanks," was all I could say. I left without making any promises. Apparently he not only could see the future, he had disciples too. Just being around him was starting to make me nervous. I didn't feel like hanging out with a whole group of Okadas.

I got into my old Lexus and drove over the dusty roads to home. On the way I passed an unmanned produce stand, a simple wooden table with a little roof overhead for shade. Bags of vegetables, all priced at a hundred yen, were piled up to attract the tourists. I'd heard local farmers complain that the coin box never held more than 70 or 80 percent of what it was supposed to at the end of the day. Yet they still made more money this way than selling to the supermarkets.

I guess I never thought Japan's comfortable situation would last forever. Someday people would find themselves hungry once again. Still, why forgo the advantages of a free market to prepare for a day you couldn't predict with certainty? I didn't want to leave our life in this beautiful setting, selling the bread my wife baked and brewing coffee for customers, even if the tourist season only lasted for the summer months, and for the other nine months our bread went to feed factory workers.

When I got home, my wife was waiting. She was not happy.

The damn weeds again. Hashimoto's Bakery was a wooden building with a white-painted terrace out front. The terrace was surrounded by potted herbs, with zucchini, cranberries and blueberries down in front where our Afghan hound, Siesta, liked to play with Hiro. It was a peaceful, idyllic environment, but it wasn't easy to maintain. Summer was humid and the temperature got up to

30 degrees Celsius, not the ideal climate for an English garden. But I had no choice. The tourists liked it and my wife demanded it.

I went and got the sickle and a plastic bag. Of all the weeds in the yard, I hated kudzu the most. It carpeted the ground and engulfed anything vertical, from power poles to fences. It was a tenacious survivor with leaves of poisonous green and thick, sturdy stalks covered with tiny spines. No matter how much I cut it back, it always returned quickly. At the peak of summer, its sweet-smelling clusters of reddish-purple flowers hung beneath the shade of the leaves and looked rather elegant. But in the summer heat, the fragrance was oppressive, like a matron with too much perfume.

The battle began every spring. Even when I thought I had wiped it out, somehow the kudzu always came advancing back from the woods behind the house and the empty lot between us and the pension next door.

After half an hour of combat I was drenched in sweat. I noticed a customer going inside and decided to give the kudzu a rest for the day.

My hands were itching from handling the leaves and stems. I rolled up my sleeves and washed my hands in the sink behind the counter. But no matter how carefully I washed up, the spines from the stems left painful, itching welts on my hands. Okada once remarked casually that the starch in the roots was edible, but I couldn't picture digging in the dirt for a few extra calories. The kudzu was working me hard enough as it was.

August ended. The neighborhood went from bustling to sleepy, but the days were hot as ever. The owner of the pension next door went to work in a semiconductor plant. His wife took a part-time job in the restaurant near the little train station.

There was bread, but no buyers. We stopped serving coffee for the season. This was fine with my wife, who now had more time to devote to Hiro and recharge her batteries. Our contract to supply factory cafeterias with bread would start in October.

My battle with the kudzu continued.

I had just finished repainting the terrace and was hacking at the vines creeping up the awning supports when I felt the ground heave beneath me. I almost lost my footing and clung to the kudzu for support, still holding the sickle. My wife came running out of the house holding Hiro.

The shaking seemed to go on forever, though it was probably thirty or forty seconds.

By the time the tremors died away, the house was a disaster. None of the furniture was upended, but all the knickknacks were on the floor, and everything in glass on the kitchen sideboard, from soy sauce and olive oil to my bottle of twenty-year-old single malt whisky, had fallen and shattered. There was hardly anywhere to walk amid the liquid and shards of glass.

We were cleaning up gingerly, worried about aftershocks, when the announcement came over the village loudspeakers. The epicenter of the quake was in western Tokyo. Everyone was urged to take shelter in the community center. People started coming out of the pensions and the crafts workshop and gathering in the lot across the street.

Other than the potter four doors down—who was in tears because a piece he'd planned to enter in a competition had been destroyed—everyone was calm. Mainly we were concerned about the safety of family and friends in Tokyo.

"Are you going to the shelter?" I asked our neighbor.

"No. Don't see that it's necessary," he said drily. He had a point. Other than the mess, the house seemed sound, and we had water and food for a few days at least. I didn't see any sign of fire. Everything down in the village looked quiet.

We all went home to clean up. Luckily the power hadn't cut out. Things didn't seem so bad after all. I was feeling relieved when I noticed I'd left the TV on.

The announcer was saying that a major earthquake had hit western Tokyo. I noticed the station logo in the corner of the screen and cocked my head, puzzled. The station was in Osaka.

What was going on?

We were only 130 kilometers from the western edge of Tokyo. Osaka was over 400 kilometers away. Why were we getting news about Tokyo from Osaka?

The announcer said the magnitude and epicenter were unknown. The extent of the damage—unknown.

Why didn't they know more?

I quickly told my wife to fill the bathtub. I was afraid the water might go off. I had the feeling something extraordinary had just happened.

I left the TV on while my wife and I put things in order and tried to soothe my nervous son. Even two hours after the quake, the news had nothing definite to report, but the announcer had stopped urging people to remain calm and extinguish any open flame. Now she was pleading with viewers not to flee the disaster zone by car.

After we'd used up all the old newspapers and spare towels to get the floor dry, I finally had a chance to sit down and watch the news. The TV showed processions of cars snaking slowly through the streets of Tokyo. Many of the buildings were just piles of rubble and broken roof tiles. The images were being shot from a helicopter.

The announcer was practically screaming, "Please do not attempt to evacuate by car!"

Tokyo and much of the surrounding region had taken a horrendous blow from a megathrust earthquake. The announcer was hopefully vague: "So far two deaths have been confirmed. One elderly man was killed after being struck by a falling pot." The reasons for the fatalities seemed trivial; the main point was that only two people had died.

Late that night, the owner of the organic dye workshop returned from the emergency shelter. He was the only one who had left the neighborhood. He told us a few houses in the village were damaged, but there were no deaths or serious injuries. Unfortunately the water main serving the village latrines was broken and would be out of commission for some time. Even so, people were not much inconvenienced. The houses had ample garden space, and it would be easy to dig pits and rig up temporary latrines. All they had to do was cover the waste with earth and leaves.

There was still little information about the situation in Tokyo. All the footage was coming from helicopters. The whole city was without power, and the view from a helicopter over the Musashino area showed neighborhoods shrouded in darkness. Scattered pillars of fire rose into the sky, isolated islands of light.

It wasn't until the next day that images of Tokyo started coming from the ground.

Scorching foehn winds were blowing across the Kanto plain. The temperature in Hachioji reached 44 degrees. People were collecting drinking water from broken pipes. Without refrigeration, food in the stores and warehouses was spoiling fast. The announcers kept warning people to avoid consuming it.

It was around that time that the TV began to reveal devastation on a much larger scale than had been reported. Buildings had collapsed all over Tokyo and well down the coast toward Nagoya. Most roads were impassable. The number of casualties was unknown. Electric power into the disaster zone had been cut off to avoid a repeat of what happened after Kobe's earthquake, when short circuits sparked widespread fires.

Transport arteries into the zone were clogged with cars that had run out of gas or blown a tire. These abandoned vehicles were making it hard for relief crews and supplies to reach their destinations.

With indoor temperatures in the forties, many people fled outside to the shade of buildings and trees, but the heat rising from the roads and sidewalks was dropping people with heatstroke. The hospitals were overflowing with the injured, and most people suffering from the heat were getting no attention at all.

One broadcast reported—stressing that the information was unconfirmed—that cholera and other infectious diseases were breaking out in the emergency shelters.

And as always, the announcers kept telling people to stay indoors and off the roads.

Three days after the quake, things in the village seemed almost back to normal. Broken roof tiles had been cleared from the streets. Every household was well-equipped with tools, and the minor household repairs were finished. Some bathtubs had fractured, but the village hot spring was open for business.

The TV showed people trudging out of Tokyo along roads lined with destroyed buildings and tilting power poles. The national chain of command seemed to be in chaos after this shattering blow to the capital, and the disaster zone was so large that the scale of the damage was still unknown.

Waiting for relief supplies in the shelters was futile. A flow of information, food, and water had always followed big earthquakes, but not this time. Rumors of mysterious epidemics had frightened people into thinking that staying put meant death. Escape from the disaster zone looked like the best option.

Volunteers from around the country were trying to get into the zone, but the situation was so confused that relief efforts were still scattered and ineffective.

It struck me as odd, at least from watching the news, that Tokyo was no wasteland, yet more and more people were abandoning homes and apartments that seemed livable, even if they had nowhere to go. People just wanted to get away from Tokyo any way they could, even if it meant going where they had no family or friends.

I soon found out why.

Naturally, people were afraid that an aftershock might level the building in which they were staying. But more important was the stark reality that survival in a city like Tokyo was impossible without power and water.

With temperatures well into the thirties every day, asphalt and concrete became reservoirs of heat. With the refrigeration chain severed, food rotted. Urban river and ground water was mostly unfit to drink. It hit me that without constant supplies, Tokyo was as vulnerable as a biodome in the middle of the desert, or even a space station.

I was concerned about my relatives and friends in Tokyo, but I also couldn't help congratulating myself for being clever enough to move here. My wife's childlike dream of country life and her tenacity in pushing me to relocate two years ago had saved us.

I knew it was self-centered, but who wasn't feeling the same way? Other people in this district of pensions and country houses were feeling more or less the same. *I'm just glad it didn't happen to me and my family.* And we felt guilty for feeling it. It was because of this guilt—the discomfort and embarrassment that one had been spared—that whenever we ran into each other on the street, talk turned to what might be done for people in Tokyo.

The villagers and farmers in the surrounding countryside had a different reaction. Four days after the quake, when there had still been no big aftershocks and people had repaired their homes and gotten things back in order, I took my wife and son to the hot spring. The feeling of relief we had was shared by many, and the spa was packed.

After our bath, we went to the little auditorium where people were napping, or snacking while they watched the big flat-screen monitor up on the stage. The usual karaoke session by old folk who loved to sing ballads from before the war was, unsurprisingly, not in progress.

The monitor showed image after image of destruction in Tokyo. Every channel was running nonstop quake coverage. No one would watch regular programming at a time like this.

"Oh no, would you look at that!"

"That's why Tokyo's so scary."

"Ryuzo let his daughter live there. See what happens?"

"It's so sad. Ryuzo's daughter and granddaughter were killed, both of them. Their train went right off the elevated tracks. No one knows what happened to the husband."

Heat, lack of water, lack of food, cholera and dysentery from lack of sanitation. Until a few days ago, life in Tokyo had been comfortable and convenient, but the earthquake had turned its people into refugees.

Everyone sympathized with the victims in Tokyo and agonized over their situation. At the same time, the news was thrilling entertainment.

Despite the tragic images, the news emphasized that people were showing a surprising amount of patience and calm and were abiding by the law. Incidents of violence and theft were almost nonexistent, or so they said. Only later did we find out that these reports skillfully concealed the truth. The media was working hard to preserve the image of people in the zone.

As I sat with my eyes glued to the TV, someone called my name.

I turned to see Tetsuji Okada standing behind me. He must have just gotten out of the bath, because his face was flushed.

"How are you doing? Get everything cleaned up?" I asked him by way of greeting. But there was something about him that did not look normal.

"It finally came. I told you, didn't I? Tokyo's been destroyed. The hungry ghosts will be here in droves. Yes, I got everything cleaned up. My friends made it out of the city with their families. I just got a call. They're coming on foot. They've reached Kofu. People from the western suburbs keep coming in. There's water but no food, they say. A sweet bun costs five hundred yen. A bag of rice crackers is two thousand. But people in Yamanashi aren't greedy. They're dealing with half a million refugees. Kofu didn't get hit as hard as Tokyo, but it suffered. If this keeps up, they'll run out of food. And the refugees are refusing to pay. They even want priority over the locals—you know, 'because we're refugees.' Totally arrogant. They're looting convenience stores and fast-food restaurants and picking them clean. The police had to be called in."

Just then the news went from national to local. Sure enough, there was footage from Kofu. It was just as Okada said.

Refugees sitting on tatami mats in a community center, eating meals distributed by the city. Refugees receiving treatment in Kofu hospitals. The city's hot springs had stopped charging admission.

"Next time it might be our turn," a smiling spa owner told the camera. "I feel like the Buddha has rescued me from hell," said an elderly woman as she tearfully massaged her sore feet.

A miniskirted teenager in a uniform and cap was distributing value meals to refugees across the counter of a fast-food restaurant.

"This major hamburger chain has begun distributing food to disaster victims free of charge," said the announcer. But the girl behind the counter wasn't smiling. In the background I could see broken windows and a riot policeman standing behind a shield.

Okada chuckled. "The news is staged, 100 percent. Every story has a script and a director."

I disliked Okada 100 percent. He had changed from an unaffected, masculine man with a mania for one particular subject to a contemptible mocker of human misfortune.

Still, his prediction was coming true, though not for the reasons he'd expected. I could hear the agricultural cooperative broadcasting over the loudspeakers outside. The price of vegetables was skyrocketing, and the announcement was urging farmers to get their crops to distributors to keep prices from rising further.

But who would sell food at a time like this?

Millions were fleeing Tokyo. Most of the villagers, and many of us transplants, were waiting for family and friends. Food was for those who had possession of it, and for people who were close to them.

Now I knew that a food shortage didn't need some sort of global crop failure. If a major city met with disaster, if transport arteries were severed and there was no way to distribute supplies or receive them from overseas, people could easily starve.

I hurried my wife and son out to the car and drove to the agricultural cooperative to stock up on rice.

It was sold out. I drove as fast as I could to the supermarket. No rice there either. We finally found some at a specialty dealer. It was the first time I'd ever been there, and it was our last option.

But it wasn't for sale.

"Can't help you. It's already sold." The dealer wouldn't say more.

Of course we had ample supplies of wheat flour at the bakery. Unlike the people who had walked a hundred kilometers to Kofu only to find food in short supply there too, we could easily get along without rice.

As I gave up and turned to go, someone started yelling.

"You've got rice. I can see it. Can't you sell me a little?" The man was on the edge of panic. "I only need a kilo. I'll give you a thousand—no, two thousand yen."

"Can't help you." The dealer turned his back. A Jeep Cherokee with western Tokyo license plates was parked outside. A young woman sat in the front seat with a child on her lap, watching the shop with a worried look. The Jeep was scratched and muddy. Foliage was caught in the front grill guard. They must have avoided the highways by taking back roads through the mountains.

I was opening the door to my car when the man came out and approached me with a pained expression.

"I'm sorry, is there someplace around here we could buy food? We've got camping gear, we just need rice and vegetables."

I pictured them speeding in their four-wheel-drive jeep past lines of people trudging antlike along the roads, finally crashing through underbrush and fording streams to get here.

"Sorry, no idea." I avoided making eye contact. I was about to get in the car when I glanced at the Jeep and froze. There were splotches of rust red on the bumper and around the mudguards. It looked like they'd hit someone.

I swung round and stared at the stranger. He was an ordinary-looking man in his mid-thirties, wearing a white polo shirt. Just a middle-class consumer buying a piece of the outdoor life with an expensive off-road vehicle. I wondered what kind of hell he'd witnessed and what crimes he'd committed to get here.

The child in the car smiled at me.

On the way home, I passed a few more off-road vehicles with Tokyo license plates: Hachioji, Nerima, Shinagawa. They'd made it to safety ahead of the walkers and were racing around trying to secure food for themselves.

The same scenes kept playing out in shops and along the roadside: people pleading to buy food and being refused. I stopped to watch one exchange at the edge of an irrigation ditch.

"You've got lots of food. We drove a hundred and fifty kilometers to get away from Tokyo. We've been through a terrible experience. Can't you give us one ear of corn?"

Another car pulled up. People got out and joined in badgering the farmer. "Don't you have any human feelings at all?"

The sunburned old man just glared at them. Finally he turned his back, muttered "Go away," and returned to pulling weeds at the edge of the ditch.

A bit farther down the road, the same thing was happening at Okada's farm.

"Go away. I've got no rice or beans or corn for you. I don't care how much money you throw at me. You never had to come to a place like this, did you? You could go to 7-Eleven and buy what you needed, twenty-four hours a day. Convenience stores were made for people like you. You don't belong here. Nothing at the store? Then sit and wait till the food comes. They have deliveries all the time. Isn't that how the system works?"

He laughed in their faces. I'd never seen him so ecstatic.

The whole thing was nauseating. I started to drive off, but Okada waved me over. I stopped and leaned out the window. He leaned in and whispered to me.

"It looks like there's no food to be had, pretty much anywhere. The population of Kofu and Takasaki has quadrupled. The refugees are pretty much eating their way through everything."

"Aren't any supplies coming in?"

"The government's paralyzed. Food can't get through from Osaka because the roads are destroyed, or full of people trying to get out. Supplies from outside Japan are coming soon, but it could be months before people can put the food in their mouths. By then they'll be starving."

His expression had changed completely. It was warm and friendly. "If you run out of food, just let me know. I don't have much, but you're a friend."

"Thank you." I couldn't think of anything else to say. I was disgusted and drove away quickly.

Toward evening a Mercedes stopped in front of the bakery. Soon there was a hesitant knock at the door. A women in her twenties with expensively styled hair was standing there with two small children. She held out a Thermos and asked for water.

I asked where she had come from. She told me she lived in Kofu and had fled her apartment. I was surprised; Kofu wasn't in the disaster zone. Her husband had been in Tokyo on business, and after waiting five days she had finally run out of food. By then the stores were empty.

She thought she might find someone who would sell her food if she drove west. And so she had finally ended up all the way out here.

"But you must've had something in the house. No rice? No instant noodles?"

She shook her head. There was a convenience store on the first floor of her building. The only thing she had ever bothered to stock up on was snacks for the kids.

She didn't ask me to bake for her. Her pleas for food must have been refused tens, maybe hundreds of times already. When I handed her the Thermos full of water, she thanked me and turned to go.

"You can rest here for a moment, if you want." I pointed to the coffee area.

My wife poked me in the back.

"Don't. She'll never leave. And there'll be more like her. You can't make a habit of inviting strangers into the house."

My wife, who a few days ago was wallowing in the world of Kenji Miyazawa and Peter Mayle, had suddenly become a flinty realist. I was appalled.

The woman sat her children down under the big larch tree in the front yard. They shared the water and started munching on little cookies.

As I looked closer, I doubted my eyes. The "cookies" were dog kibble. It must have been the only thing they could find in the stores after five days.

I hurried back into the shop. Two of my wife's butter rolls were left over from yesterday's batch. She was preoccupied helping our son change his sweaty T-shirt. I grabbed the rolls, went into the garden and pressed them into the woman's hand.

She looked like she was going to cry. "I'm so sorry," she said, and drew a thousand-yen bill from her purse.

"You don't need to pay me."

"You're so kind. At least some people are still human."

I went inside. My wife stood by the window, staring out coldly. "Next it'll be some old man or woman. You'll feed them too, I suppose."

I didn't answer. If none of this had happened, I never would've discovered what my wife was really like. I could have gone on loving her in blissful ignorance.

The next morning the woman and her children were gone. They had probably headed for Nagano in search of food. The village was filling up with people. Every household seemed to be sheltering family and friends who had survived the trek from Tokyo. There were many others with nowhere to stay.

For miles around, in fields or on farmhouse doorsteps, refugees were flashing wads of cash and still being turned away. Strangers were gradually taking over the village, squatting in the grounds of the village shrine, sheltering in the co-op warehouse, or commandeering space at the village hot spring.

Three of Okada's friends finally arrived too. He'd told me he was expecting to shelter twenty or so people from eight households, assuming they all made it through.

True to his word, he had a sack of soybeans ready when I dropped by.

"It's nothing much. I'm still an apprentice farmer," he said awkwardly as he gave it to me. I felt abashed and grateful. My family had nothing but bread to eat.

"Three women came this morning. They must've been in their thirties. Wanted me to sell them some corn. They offered to trade me a necklace and a bag, some fashion-house brand. Of course I said no. Finally one of them actually said 'How about me?' I almost told her to go look in a mirror, but then I felt sorry for them. So

I took all three of their designer bags and gave them some rice."

I was relieved to hear this. Okada actually had some compassion after all.

"But I didn't give them anything to put it in. I told them to hold out their hands, and I filled them with rice. You should've seen them panic. Finally they had to put it on the ground, take off their tops, pick up every grain and wrap them up. Then they went off in their bras. I don't know how they planned to cook that rice, but I wish you could've seen them down on the ground, picking it up with their tits spilling out."

"Take it." I thrust the bag of beans at him. I felt like a coward for even thinking about depending on a man like him for food.

"Whaat?" He gaped with surprise. "What's wrong? What did I say?"

"I'll starve before I take food from you."

Before he could answer, we heard the roar of a car revving its motor. We both looked around, but the road was empty.

It took a few seconds to realize that the noise was coming from Okada's field, beyond the tall corn. There was a sound of crashing stalks before the huge grill guard of an SUV heaved into view and stopped. I turned instinctively and ran.

"You idiots! What are you doing?" Okada shouted.

The car spun its tires against the fallen corn and lurched toward him. The grill guard struck him with a sickening sound. His body vaulted up onto the hood and over the roof, corkscrewed through the air and plunged headfirst into the tomato patch.

I screamed and covered my face. Okada was tough. He groaned and tried to rise up.

The SUV backed up. Trembling like a fool, I half-hid behind a tree and tried to memorize the license number, thinking they were going to run. But the car made straight for Okada. Its huge tires threw up sprays of soft black earth, crushing the eggplants and tomatoes and pumpkins as it rolled over him and backed up again, spattered with tomatoes and something else that was a deeper red.

Okada's body was half-entombed in the dirt, but he was still groaning.

The car stopped. Four young men in suits leaped out. They started ripping ears of corn clumsily off the nearest stalks and pitching them into the back of the car.

One of Okada's friends came running out of the house. The men jumped in the car, gunned it again and went for him. I heard the man scream as he somersaulted through the air and landed in an irrigation ditch. After that he didn't move.

Their next move was calm and deliberate. They drove across the field to Okada's storage shed, removed all the rice, soybeans, and whatever else they could lay their hands on, loaded it quickly into the car, and drove off. It was all over in a few minutes.

They probably hadn't had a plan. At first they must have tried to buy food, but after failing too many times, they'd decided to use their car as a weapon. At first they were only after food that was ready to be harvested, but after killing one person, killing the next one who tried to interfere was easy. After that they'd have no qualms about stealing anything they could.

But at what price? Okada's lifeless body lay amid the flattened remains of his garden. What had he died for? His unshakable faith in the coming food crisis had found its ultimate vindication, but his beloved crops—for which he had given up his family, his Tokyo home, his social standing, and nearly all his money—had been ground into the dirt, and he had been robbed not only of them, but of his life.

I retrieved Okada's final gift of soybeans and raced to the police box, five minutes away. The little hut was locked and dark. In the last few days the village seemed to have filled with strangers. With trouble breaking out all over, I could hardly expect to find the officer relaxing in his chair. No, there was more than trouble. We were descending into lawlessness. The police, the armed forces, the government, they were all floundering. Japan's command and control systems had broken down completely.

The soybeans were missing when I got back to the car. I'd been in such a hurry to find a policeman, I'd left the key in the ignition. The car was untouched; the bag in the front seat was the only thing missing. I clucked my tongue in frustration and turned toward home, feeling helpless.

As I emerged from the village I almost ran over a young man in a T-shirt who sprinted in front of me. I slammed on the brakes and saw a farmer in hot pursuit, brandishing a hoe. The youth was clutching an entire soybean plant. The farmer caught up to him and started beating him with the hoe.

When I arrived home, the metal shutters were down. I'd never closed them before, even outside business hours. I went through the back and found my wife clutching Hiro. She was nearly apoplectic.

"Somebody tried to get in here. They heard you were giving out bread." She glared at me with moist eyes that flashed with panic and fear and anger. "You knew this would happen if you helped one of them."

"What happened?"

My wife drew our Afghan hound close and stroked his long, slender neck.

"Siesta is a better protector than you are." She showed me the pot on the stove. It was filled with soup and flour dumplings. "This is dinner. I can't bake anymore, they'll smell it. I don't want those people to come back."

I couldn't ignore the sense of dread rising in the back of my mind. Another incident like this and we might have to flee. But we had nowhere to go. If we left, we would be refugees too. We had enough food to survive for the time being, but we'd be very vulnerable if we couldn't use the car. All this time I'd been thinking about food without realizing that our local filling station might run out of gas at any time.

I rushed back to the car. I had to get the tank filled.

On the way, I passed a family squatting by their car at the edge of a drainage ditch, peering at the tires. They would have driven over rubble and debris to get here, and even the toughest all-terrain tire is not immune to punctures, but all four of their tires were blown.

When I got down out of the foothills, I saw a farmer in a broad-brimmed straw hat by the roadside, biting her lower lip. The black earth of the field behind her was crisscrossed with tire trails. Her vegetables had been pulled out by the roots.

I saw the same thing in other fields. Okada had warned everyone that a food crisis was coming, but he thought the cities would be vulnerable, that people with farmland in the countryside would be safe. I sighed.

City people would sell their daughters to buy food. That's what Okada said. But while the cities were vulnerable, city people were not. They had weaponized their motor vehicles. Okada had assumed that people with land, people growing food, would be in a strong position at a time like this, but he was wrong. The winners were not the people who grew food, but those who used force.

I saw another disabled vehicle beside the main road, then a line of them with flat tires. They all had Tokyo plates.

Finally I figured out what was happening. A group of village men blocked the road ahead, armed with knives and pruning shears. One of them ran toward me, but another was already calling to him.

"Calm down! That's Mr. Hashimoto, from the bakery."

My Lexus still had its Tokyo plates. A man I'd never seen before, wearing fire brigade gear, strolled up to my window.

"We're out here hunting cars. Kazuo's son, old Mrs. Yamashiro, Ryuzo's grandson, all of them, run down in the fields by these damn cars. They boom right across the fields with their four-wheel drive, steal our crops and run away. Don't bother with 110. Help never arrives."

What happened to Okada was happening at other farms, but the police didn't have the manpower to deal with hit-and-run incidents. Many refugees had probably run someone down on the way here. Law and order had broken down everywhere. Now the village men were defending themselves against the only weapons the city people had.

The firefighter waved me through and I headed toward the gas station. I was too late. The part-timer manning the pumps dismissed me with a wave. "All out."

A broken-down light truck pulled in after me. "Round the back," the boy told the driver. They had gas after all. They just weren't selling it to outsiders.

"Listen, I live here. I run the bakery." I was starting to lose my temper.

"Sorry, I can only sell to people with local plates." He hurried toward the back of the gas station.

"Hey, I'm a legal resident. I pay property taxes. I'm not a refugee!" I yelled after him, but he ignored me. I gave up and pulled back out into the road. Things couldn't go on like this for much longer. Once the situation in Tokyo was under control, this lawlessness would end and things would return to normal. They had to.

The thought helped me calm down.

Nearing home, I sensed something was different. As I passed

the pension two doors down from my house, I saw that the white paint was scorched black. It looked like arson. I pulled up at the house with a sense of dread and hurried through the backdoor into the kitchen.

I gasped. Tufts of Siesta's hair were scattered all over the room.

"Siesta!"

I called my beloved dog, but there was no sign of that long, joyous face. Alarmed, I called his name again. An answer came from behind our upstairs bedroom door. It was my wife.

"Siesta's gone." She came down holding Hiro. Her lips were bloodless and trembling.

"They took him. Goddamn it, I swear I'll kill them. They waited for you to leave. They stole all the flour, forty kilos, and took all the food in the house. Siesta went after them. They had metal bats. They beat him senseless and dragged him off, laughing. 'Looks like meat's on the menu,' one of them said."

My knees nearly buckled. I barely had the strength to ask the next question.

"Did they hurt you?"

"What's that supposed to mean?" Her tone was sharp and incredulous.

All I could do was mumble something unintelligible. She started screaming at me.

"What are you thinking? People don't want sex when they're starving. There was a woman, a young woman wearing sandals. She beat Siesta with a bat. She called to him. 'Here boy, nice dog.' Then *wham*, she hit him. I'm going to find that bitch and kill her."

"Please don't say that. You can't say that."

I collapsed to my knees, surrounded by hanks of golden fur, and held my head in my hands. When I saw the first footage of the quake, I thought we'd dodged a bullet. If people from Tokyo made their way here, I was ready to extend a hand and do whatever I could.

Everything was going wrong. If the quake had affected a smaller area, the refugees wouldn't have come. If only a dozen or so had shown up, the village would probably have come together to help them.

By evening, the empty lot across the street was filled with tents. My wife peered out from the cracks in the metal shutters, muttering about murder and mayhem. I had to force her to sit down and try to be calm.

There was a commotion outside, then someone pounding on the shutters.

"Help! We need help out here. People are hurt. They need water."

I didn't move and didn't answer. Neither did my wife. My son stared at us. He seemed baffled. "Aren't you going to help them?"

"Please!" The voice came again. "They're bleeding terribly. Please help." Whoever it was sounded genuinely panicked. My wife smiled thinly.

"What should we do?" I whispered.

"It's not our problem. Our problem is, we've *got nothing to eat*."

She was right. Yet once the situation was under control, we'd get along somehow. Vehicles could reach us from Nagano, to the west. At least they could bring in enough to supply the village. Relief supplies from other countries had to be coming. Even now, I couldn't see things any other way.

"Go get something," said my wife.

"What?"

"Go to the village and get us something."

"Nobody's going to give me anything."

"You're a local. You live here."

"Here. Not in the village. We're outsiders."

There was another loud bang on the shutters.

"Please, they're going to die! We need medicine and bandages."

These people were not our enemies. They were city people like us. They were victims of a terrible disaster. I ignored my wife and reached for the first aid kit.

"Fool." She sounded like she'd given up on me once and for all.

I went outside. A crowd of refugees was milling around in the darkness. In the middle of the crowd I could make out bodies on the ground. There were six of them, four men and two women, all covered with blood. One man's shirt was pulled up around his neck. His intestines spilled from a wound in his abdomen. One woman had a sucking chest wound and was struggling to breathe. The air wheezed from the hole in her breast.

"What happened here?" I held out the first aid kit to one of the refugees. All it contained was a few Band-Aids and some iodine, useless for injuries like these.

"They attacked us when we tried to take a shortcut across a field."

That was probably a lie. They hadn't cut across the field. They'd been stealing.

The woman with the chest wound shuddered violently and breathed her last as we stood there watching helplessly. The same thing would probably happen to the rest of them before first light.

But I had a far bigger problem. When the sun rose, my family would have nothing to eat.

Next morning, my son wore himself out looking all over our little home for Siesta. If I tried to step outside, he whimpered fearfully. My wife stood in the empty kitchen, staring into space with an irritated look. Finally she took a carving knife from the drawer.

"What are you doing?"

"I'm going to find a farmer and get some food."

"Are you crazy?" I tried to take the knife away from her.

"Let me go. I won't threaten anyone. It's for protection. Who knows what they'll do to me if I'm carrying food?"

I sighed. It was true. Things really were that bad.

"Don't worry, I'll go." I grabbed the cars keys and went outside.

A middle-aged man with thinning hair walked up to me as I was getting in the car.

"Thank you for last night." He bowed politely.

"What happened?"

"They didn't make it. But at least you tried to help. We won't forget it."

Even in the midst of tragedy, some people were still human. Not demons who would take someone's beloved dog, beat him to death, and eat him.

As I drove toward the village, wondering where I might find a farmer willing to sell me some food, I noticed a man standing at the edge of a field under the blazing sun. He was holding a sharpened spear fashioned from a length of bamboo.

My jaw dropped as I got closer. It was the potter who lived down the street. I was careful to avoid his eyes as I passed. Farther down the road was the home of a farmer I'd met once or twice. I pulled up in front of his garden.

A voice called from somewhere in the corn. "Oh, it's the baker."

"Excuse me. Might I possibly buy food from you? Some people forced their way into my house and made off with everything we had. They even took our dog. If you could spare us a little, just enough for my son. I'll pay you generously, of course." I kept bowing obsequiously as the farmer came closer.

"No, no, that's not necessary." Always gentle and taciturn, he seemed to be groping for words. "I don't need money, but a favor if you could. I need you to stand guard. I'll make it worth your while." He glanced at something on the ground near my feet.

A bamboo spear. I remembered the woman from the night before and shuddered. This was just the kind of weapon that could have dealt someone a wound like hers.

"The fire brigade and some boys from the youth association got together and whipped up three hundred of them. We can't work the fields with people trying to run us down or sneak up and whack us over the head. If we don't stand our ground, they'll pull the crops up, no matter if they're not ready to harvest. I can't see stabbing anyone, even in self-defense. Throttling chickens is bad enough. Can't work, either, with one of these in my hand."

"What would I do with it?" I squatted and picked up the spear.

"I'm not saying you have to use it. Just stand guard with it. They're sure to stay away. Then me and the missus can work without worrying. The pumpkins and eggplant are going to rot if we don't get them in."

"Kind of like a scarecrow."

"Something like that." The farmer smiled.

I accepted the primitive weapon and took up a position at the edge of the field. I had discovered the truth: no one was going to sell me an ear of corn, no matter what I offered.

I looked down the road and saw another man with a spear coming toward me. It was the owner of Le Lagon, a small hotel in our neighborhood. He looked like a proper mercenary with his camo shirt. When he saw me, he acknowledged our shared mission with a bow.

"Things are bad, aren't they?" I said by way of reply. I looked closer at his shirt. My throat tightened. The camo pattern was spattered with blood.

"What happened? Are you all right?"

He thrust his chin out proudly and smiled.

"I got a young one. An old lady surprised him trying to steal her potatoes. He slugged her and ran off. When I yelled at him to stop, he pulled a knife on me. I had to run him through."

He stood legs apart, spear planted on end in the road, chest thrown out like some old samurai. I was speechless. All I could do was gape at him.

"Let me tell you something, Hashimoto. There's no shame in living like a mouse. A man can stand behind a counter and kiss the customer's ass. 'Very sorry, it won't happen again.' 'Yes, I'll do exactly as you say.' That's life. But to defend your wife and children, you do whatever it takes."

I spent the rest of the day by the road, holding my spear while the sun roasted the top of my head. Luckily I didn't have to use my weapon, and as the light was fading, a few young men from the fire brigade arrived to take over for the night.

The farmer gave me two rice balls, some pickled eggplant, and an ear of boiled corn.

When I got home and told my wife what I'd been doing, and showed her what I'd earned for it, she smiled gently for the first time in days.

"You stood guard. Good for you. Be careful, though. You can't just stand around with a spear. You have to know how to use it."

My heart froze. My wife woke our son up and fed him steamed corn and a rice ball. I let the food sit. I didn't feel like eating. She pushed the rest toward me.

"Come on, eat up. You'll need your strength when the time comes. Don't worry about me, I don't need it." She smiled affectionately.

Morning came sunny and cloudless again. The sky had the deep blue of autumn, but the sun had lost none of the heat of summer. I idly pictured a helicopter passing overhead, parachuting big packages of food and medicine. Sure enough, soon after that a helicopter did pass by, but it dropped no packages. It was heading straight for the shattered metropolis. It wouldn't be dropping supplies there, either. It was a broadcast helicopter, on its way to capture scenes of starvation and violence for the titillation of people watching safely at home.

I still couldn't grasp what was happening. Even if there was no relief from abroad, people wouldn't have to risk their lives to steal food if the rest of the country pitched in to gather supplies and distribute them equally. It wasn't as if Japan was facing a food shortage like the one Okada always warned us about.

The little tent village in front of our house was gone. Probably they had given up trying to survive here and had pushed on toward Nagano. But people kept trudging in from the direction of Kofu.

The news showed rescue teams reaching emergency shelters on the outskirts of Tokyo. Now the death toll was five thousand. That didn't mean five thousand had died, it was just the number confirmed. There was nothing said about the breakdown of order and the shortage of food.

I set out for another day of security duty. When I reached my post and got out of the car, I heard a strange, high-pitched mewling that sounded like an animal in distress. Late at night, when footsteps sounded on the road outside our house, Siesta had often whimpered like this.

The sound seemed to be coming from a cabbage patch by the road. I crept closer. Someone, probably the fire brigade, had dug a deep pit a few feet off the road. I peered over the edge. A man and a woman, clad in blood-soaked T-shirts and jeans, lay at the bottom. They were impaled on sharpened bamboo stakes.

A booby trap. Who could have done such a thing? A pit of sharpened stakes in the middle of a cabbage patch?

"What now?"

"Nothing. They're done for."

I turned to see two fellow guardsmen from the neighborhood, standing in the road behind me.

"I don't have to listen to this noise. Let's get on with it." One of them was the owner of the pension that had been torched. He picked up a shovel and started slinging dirt into the pit.

"Not on my property!" The farmer's wife came out of the house, yelling and distraught. "Get rid of them somewhere."

"No way I'm going to touch those things," said the other mercenary.

"You think I want to?"

The farmer's wife chanted a Buddhist prayer as they busily filled the pit with dirt. The mewling sounds eventually ceased.

"Maybe we should put up signs warning people about the pits," said the pension owner with a wry chuckle.

"Yeah. If they ignore them it's not our fault."

That afternoon I brandished my spear for the first time. A family came up the road from the direction of Kofu and began badgering the farmer's wife to sell them food. They looked like they hadn't eaten in several days. The woman refused the man's repeated demands, and he was about to use his fists on her and her elderly father-in-law when I stepped in with my spear. To my relief, the family turned heel and left immediately. Carrying a weapon didn't make me feel safer. Just threatening someone with it, much less having to use it, is terribly stressful for a normal person.

I drew night duty the next day. For the first time I used my weapon. A refugee pulled a knife on me, and I gave him a spear thrust. It certainly had an effect. I wondered what would happen to the man as he staggered off, still clutching a whole stalk of corn. I let him go. I was too terrified by what I'd done, and too conscience-stricken, to move.

When dawn came, the farmer paid me with a rice ball, some pickled eggplant, and a small portion of cooked soybeans. I returned home, gave the food to my wife, and went to bed immediately. I was due back on duty in the afternoon, but I stayed in bed.

At first my wife worried that I was ill, but when she realized I was afraid to go back, she stared down at me with contempt.

"You're completely irresponsible. You can lie there without a care in the world while your family starves. If you don't care about me, fine, but what about Hiro?"

I shook my head. "Don't say that!"

She started in on me then, screaming like she did before. I couldn't handle it; I got up and slapped her. She stared at me for a few seconds, dazed, and turned and ran downstairs. Seconds later she came pounding back. When I spun round to face her, she gave me a crack on the head. She was wielding a rolling pin. She bounced it off my skull a second time.

"Weakling! You can't kill a stranger, but you can kill me and Hiro?!"

I covered my head with my hands and ran downstairs onto the terrace. The picnic table and chairs where we used to enjoy family barbecues were still there. Thick strands of that hated kudzu plant were twining up their legs.

Kudzu. That was it. Okada had said you could extract starch from the roots. The refugees who risked their lives to steal crops didn't know it. I looked out from the veranda. Now everything seemed to be blanketed in a sea of vivid green. I raced to grab the shovel and started digging as fast as I could. The thick white roots dove deep into the soil. Ecstatic, I brought a bundle of roots into the kitchen, washed them, pureed them in the blender with water, and filtered the milky liquid. Heated on the stove, the result was a thick, translucent starch with a unique sweetness, like arrowroot.

My son loved it. My wife did, too, and smiled, a smile I'd given up hope of ever seeing again.

"I hope you don't expect us to survive on this morning, noon and night."

"Come on, things won't be like this forever."

"Then how long do we have to wait? When and how is someone going to help us?"

My wife took over for me that night. I stayed up till morning holding our son, who fell asleep crying for his mother.

She returned next morning laden with an astonishing amount of rice and worm-eaten beans and corn. To me, her youthful face was all the more attractive when she was angry. I wouldn't have been the only one who thought so. I had an idea I knew what she'd done to earn this much food.

As a last resort, women have something they can always sell.

I felt a mixture of anger, sadness, and resignation as she stripped off her black T-shirt, threw it on the floor and went upstairs. But when I tossed it dejectedly into the washing machine and started the water, I froze with disbelief. The water was stained bright red. What I'd thought was sweat was something else entirely.

My wife wasn't hurt. The blood was someone else's. She'd earned the food, but not the way I imagined. I wasn't sure which was worse.

I went quietly upstairs. She was already asleep, cradling Hiro. Her breathing was deep and powerful, like a lioness after the kill.

That was four days ago. Since then, my wife has stood guard over the fields eight hours a day. Things are getting better all the time. Today, for the first time, a truck arrived from Nagano and distributed toilet paper, vacuum-packed rice, and canned food. But the supplies were strictly for the refugees. The locals were told to rely on their own resources. For the transplants in the pension district, there was nothing. Well, at least things haven't settled down yet. Standing guard is the only way we can earn our food.

Yesterday my wife came home looking overjoyed. She had found the woman who murdered Siesta, and beaten her legs with a club until the woman was unable to stand.

I'm beginning to notice an unmistakable look of pride in the faces of the farmers. It's the mercenaries, with no farming skills, who are bathing in blood to protect them, and being fed by them.

Okada was right. The farmers have the upper hand after all.

The rumor now is that people from Tokyo are bringing disease with them. The news was reporting it too, until two days ago, but then suddenly stopped talking about it. It's a taboo subject, like the breakdown of public order.

But things can't go on like this indefinitely. In a week everything will be better. I'm sure of it.

I'll be digging kudzu roots again today. I never touch the rice and corn and beans my wife brings home. Surviving on kudzu starch alone is the only thing I can do to preserve my self-respect as a human being. But I'm dizzy all the time. The diarrhea is terrible. I keep getting these bruises, I don't know why. Maybe it's one of those diseases people are talking about.

Still, I believe things will get better. Very soon, now. After all, this isn't a real food shortage.

Three Cups of Tea by Jeff Somers

"Hideki didn't speak any English," Spense said laboriously as they made their way up the narrow, poorly lit stairs. "Didn't care to. So I took him under the wing, so to speak. Helped him make his way."

Philip K. Marks tried to control his breathing as they tackled the third flight of stairs, but he was feeling his age. And weight. He contemplated the unfairness of things: having forgotten half his life for reasons he had also forgotten, he'd had the usual middle-aged epiphany and gone sober, started walking. And still he huffed and puffed up the stairs, and he wondered why all of his acquaintances lived in walk-ups. And then he wondered how one upgraded his acquaintances to people who lived in buildings with elevators.

"How'd you communicate?" Marks said, careful to mask his shortness of breath.

Spencer rolled his broad shoulders. He was a tall, dark-skinned man in well-used, oily overalls, rail thin except in the belly, where what appeared to be a swallowed basketball ballooned the front of his clothes. "We said a lot just bein' in a room, you know? Ain't that hard."

The fifth floor was a long time coming between Spense's arthritic knees and Marks's labored breathing. When it took Spencer a few moments of struggle to unlock the door to apartment 5B in the dark, stifling hallway, Marks was grateful for the opportunity to collect himself.

The apartment was a five-room railroad. The door opened into the kitchen, which was a large room with very few cabinets and little counter space, dominated by a grease-encrusted old behemoth of a stove, a gas-on-gas model that was also the heat source for the apartment. A water heater had been wedged into the space between the refrigerator and the stove, and a large wooden table filled the center of the room. The walls were an unfortunate shade of yellow, the floor was thick vinyl tile in a shade of holiday green, and Marks found he couldn't look at both simultaneously without getting queasy. The rest of the apartment, three rooms like a wide corridor leading into darkness, somewhere in the gloom past the stove.

At first Marks thought two people were seated at the table. One was an elderly Japanese man with long silver-black hair, dressed in blue boxer shorts, black socks, and a white sleeveless undershirt. A teacup sat in front of him, a spoon neatly on a folded napkin next to it. There was a slip of paper on the other side of the cup, characters written on it—Japanese or Chinese or something, Marks assumed—in a firm, steady hand.

The other at first appeared to be a young woman in lingerie, but she was unmoving, staring blankly, her hands palms down on the table.

"Jesus," Marks said, frowning and hunching down a little to get a lower angle. "Is that a mannequin?"

"Doll," Spencer said, his voice suddenly darker and choked. "Sex doll. They call 'em Dutch Wives."

Marks stared at the doll. It was the most realistic sex doll he'd ever seen or imagined. Even the eyes looked right, at first. Staring at them he was filled with a sense of dread, a panic welling up from his belly, making his bowels squirm. But out of the corner of his eye she looked like a beautiful woman wearing a teddy and thong, her hair mussed, her makeup perfect. The face had a vaguely Asian cast to it, and the figure, beneath the wrinkled and stretched lingerie, was flat and childlike with only the barest hint of maturity.

Marks looked at the man, then turned his head slightly, keeping his eyes on him. "He's dead."

"Yup. Murdered. Poison, I think."

Marks pursed his lips and then turned to face the taller man. "Spense, you call the cops?"

"Not yet."

Marks waited a beat, raising his eyebrows. A sense of fatigue ballooned inside him. He knew where this was going, because it was a one-act play he'd performed over and over again. When Spencer didn't nail his line, Marks sighed. "Why not, Spense?"

Spencer grimaced. "They won't believe me. They'll rule this a goddamn suicide. That's why I called you, Philly. We go back, I know you've been in some weird shit. I know you take that weird shit serious. I know you'll hear me when I say, Mr. Aoki? He was murdered." Without turning to look, he thrust one long arm at the doll. "By *her*."

Marks followed his arm with his eyes and stared at the doll. The sense of dread returned, but he wasn't sure if it was the doll, or his growing sense that he was pushing fifty and still walking up the steps of ancient tenements that smelled like boiled cabbage and cumin, still being shown things he didn't want to see, still wondering if sobriety was worth it, because not drinking hadn't exactly transformed him into a prosperous, celebrated figure.

Just as he was about to turn away, say something biting to his old acquaintance, he paused. The dread had clarified, and he knew without doubt it *was* the doll.

It wasn't the dead-eyed stare, though he couldn't imagine sweating and grunting over that face, looking into that empty abyss where eyes should have been. It wasn't the near-perfect skin, it's near-perfection somehow worse than complete failure. It wasn't the unmoving stiffness of the pose, without the telltale humanity of trembles and shivers and twitches. It wasn't the way the clothes hung off the frame without movement or animation.

It was the expression on its face. On *her* face.

There was no expression. He knew that. The doll's face was slack and inscrutable, the mouth slightly open, eyes at half-mast. If anything, it was an approximation of lust—the parted lips, the sleepy eyes. The face stayed with him, though, and even as he struggled down the stairs, Spense calling the police as they escaped, his rough, deep voice guiding Marks through the orange-tinged gloom of the stairwell, he could see it in his mind. The expression was blank. Nothing. And yet it was *hungry*. Marks couldn't explain it, but he made his way through life being unable to explain things. It was simultaneously his comfort zone and torture.

As they emerged into the fresher air of Jersey City, Spense snapped his ancient phone shut. "Cops on their way," he said. "You wanna hang at the diner and I'll swing by when they're done?"

Marks nodded. He wanted four fingers of Four Roses, with a sweating bottle of beer for company, and that meant he would spend the afternoon drinking coffee refills until he turned yellow and died. "Why'd you call me, Spense? I don't write about this shit anymore. Or about any shit."

Spencer shrugged. "You look into things, right? That's how you pay the rent, right?"

Marks considered the various definitions of *pay* and *rent*. Finally he nodded. "Sure."

Spencer pulled his shoulders back and opened his eyes wide. "There you go. I want you to look into it. Cops sure won't."

It had all circled back to grade-school math. Although, like many other things—most other things, if he was being honest—he'd forgotten grade-school math almost entirely. The experience of it, not the actual knowledge. He could add and subtract and was aware that someone had taught him how—but he couldn't remember who that had been or what it had been like.

Those skills, however acquired, defined him now. A decade since he'd held a salaried job, he survived on small math problems.

A cup of coffee in the morning, light and sweet for the extra calories and energy: One dollar at a cart on the street. It tasted terrible. Seven dollars a week.

Office space in the communal building where you were supposed to be out by nine and stay away over the weekends, but where he'd been sleeping without incident: Fifteen dollars a week, three bucks a day.

The phone in his pocket, elderly and underpowered: Ten dollars a month, thirty cents a day, and you couldn't send email or browse the Web on it.

Lunch and dinner (never breakfast): Five dollars a day. He'd lost seventeen pounds in six months.

Incidentals, the stuff you never expected to have to pony up for, surprising you: Three bucks a day, give or take.

His whole life: Twelve dollars a day. Three-sixty a month, forty-three hundred a year. Small math.

Coffee at the VIP diner cost a dollar-fifty, but refills were free so he argued to himself that he could average it down to something reasonable. By the time Spencer walked in, looking sweaty and tired, Marks was on cup number three and feeling good about his chances of getting Spencer to buy him lunch.

The VIP had been remodeled a few years before, miraculously looking worse after all the work. Gone were the workmanlike Formica and vinyl booths, in were faux granite and scratchy fabric that reminded everyone of the seats on a municipal bus. Gone were the ancient but beloved dime-a-play jukeboxes at the tables, in was an unwelcome extra three pages of menu offering all the sorts of dishes no one in their right mind ever ordered at a diner. Gone was the word *diner,* in was the word *restaurant.*

Spencer slid into the booth and wiped his brow with one hand. "Fucking cops, man," he said, looking around. "Don't wanna do nothing, but like to act like they know all about you and are letting you slide outta the goodness of their hearts."

"You tell 'em about the doll?"

Spencer flicked his yellowed eyes at Marks, looking out from under his brow. "What, I'm an idiot? I tell *you* that shit because I know you. You're open-minded."

Marks nodded. Open-minded, he'd found, usually meant *fucking crazy* right up until they needed his help on something. "So, tell me."

Spencer settled himself. "Hideki moved into the place, what, eight, nine years ago? I don't know shit about the man. Like I said, no English. And I got no Japanese. He kept to himself, didn't make any noise, but people started complaining." He looked at Marks and leaned in. "Not really because the man done anything wrong, you see, but because they didn't like him. Because he didn't talk. Because he never smiled." He waved a hand between them and leaned back—looking, Marks thought, like a man who'd been tired since the day he'd been born. "These fucking people. Same folks who call me when their heat don't work, all piss and vinegar, same folks don't tip me come Christmas. Shit." He blew his breath out and shook his head as the waitress arrived and slid a coffee cup in front of him. He watched her pour coffee and then waved her off.

"So I went up there, knocked on his door, tried to explain to him that the tide was rising against him, you know? And the man made me tea." He snorted. "I'm standing there, being an idiot, talking loud and slow like that's gonna make the man understand me, and he's puttering around in his bathrobe and then all of a sudden he brings me a cup of tea. Was good, too. Light. Orangey."

Marks sipped his coffee. He hated tea. Always tasted like water to him. Water with a defect.

"I don't know how we became friends. Friends gotta be able to talk, right? I came up for tea. We listened to music. I brought up some of my own, he'd put it on. Sometimes we drank booze, got a little high. Not one word understood between us." Spencer smiled slightly, studying the light in the windows of the diner. "Not one word." He looked at Marks and sobered. "One night, I stop up, there's a box in the hall, all this foam wrapping and plastic, and I go in, and there it is: The doll. Hideki's Dutch Wife."

For a moment, Marks saw the eyes: Perfect and empty.

"What can you do? Man marries a doll. I didn't say anything. Or do anything. He started dressing her up. Bought nice things, expensive things. Started putting a cup of tea out for her."

Marks studied the coffee cup up close as if it was fascinating. "He, uh, *sleep* with her?"

Spencer snorted. "I don't know the man fucked the doll, Phil. You spend ten grand on a sex doll and not fuck it?"

Marks tipped his cup towards him. "You're pretty sure it killed the old man, though," he said. "Despite being a doll."

Spencer didn't say anything for a moment. He sat looking out the window, chewing his thumb. "Just look into it, okay, Phil? All I'm asking. Call me crazy, you want. Hideki deserved better. I was his only person, you know? Maybe he got family back home, I don't know. I do know they never once looked for him, reached out. All Hideki had was me. Just look into it. I'll pay your fee."

Marks nodded. "And I'll let you."

Marks leaned against the warm chassis of the car and fished another nut from the plastic bag. Honey-roasted peanuts, one dollar from a vending machine that looked like it had last been serviced in a previous decade. They tasted like corn syrup and salt and made him sick, but he figured he needed every empty calorie he could get.

Across from him, a dark green metal door opened, and a uniformed police officer exited—fat, edging towards middle-aged, and wearing his uniform like it had been found, mysterious, in his closet that morning. He walked furiously up to Marks and handed him a bundle of files wrapped in several thick rubber bands. "We square?"

Marks glanced at the files as he stuffed the bag of nuts into his jacket pocket. "One more thing: The doll. I'm gonna need it."

The officer's eyes bulged. "The *doll*?"

Marks shrugged. "No one's gonna miss it."

The officer pulled one large hand down his face and left it covering his mouth for a moment. "Shit, Phil, I know I … I mean, the official ruling's a suicide and there's no family, but shit, that's in the lockup, you know?"

Marks nodded. "I told you it would be a *big* favor."

The policeman nodded, slumping. "All right. I'll call you." He started to turn, then stopped. "The *doll*, Phil?"

Marks sighed, extracting the bag of nuts from his pocket. "Christ, Stan, I'm not going to fuck the doll."

Marks drove to the Starlight Motel and paid forty-one dollars for a room, using the wrinkled and worn fives and singles Spencer had given him. It felt like a huge expenditure, all for a room that had been theoretically cleaned, hot water, and that exotic feeling of a private space sealed to the elements. He stood in the doorway for a moment, rain crashing down outside, and tried to remember how he'd gotten here. The series of decisions, the flowchart of his existence. It was vague, as it had been as long as he could remember. He assumed he'd been clear at some point, but there was a ... live wire in his memory. When he touched it, he jumped back, and when he came to he'd lost another five seconds.

The room was larger than he'd expected. It had a living area with a couch and a table and a TV, a small desk area, and the bed. A thin-looking door hung half-open in shadow, the bathroom. The room smelled strongly of disinfectant. He wasn't sure if this was encouraging or discouraging.

Turning, he picked up one end of the duffel bag and dragged it into the room, kicking the door shut behind him. He unzipped it, pulled the doll from it, and set it on the small couch, its upholstery orange and angry-looking.

The doll looked awkward, the limbs jutting out stiffly, and he had to resist the urge to arrange it, to make it more comfortable-looking. He didn't like looking at it, and turned to inspect the rest of the room. He didn't like looking at *that,* either. Green carpet, heavy, oily-looking bedspreads in floral patterns that almost, but not really, matched the walls and carpet, an ancient television on top of a pressed-wood dresser he never wanted to touch. He had an idea that if he pulled open a drawer, bats would fly out, or roaches, or bedbugs, a torrent of wriggling bodies that would envelop him and consume him.

He turned and dragged the blond wood chair from the desk

and sat down, crossing his legs and folding his hands in his lap. He stared at the doll. The easiest way to earn his fee from Spencer was to simply demonstrate that the doll was just the most creepily realistic sex doll he'd ever seen.

It did look realistic. The skin, the hair, the teeth hinting out from the slack, half-open mouth. The eyes, blank and dead but with a believable shine to them. The eyelashes, delicate, soft. He could imagine, in low light and from the right angle, mistaking her for a zoned-out girl just sitting in a room, staring at nothing. And he could imagine, every year, the lighting getting a little higher and the angle getting less severe, until one day in broad daylight you'd walk by this doll and fall in love.

He startled. The light in the room had changed, and he pulled his phone from his pocket. Two hours had passed. His head ached. Sleep came easy for him, these days, but he never felt rested. He woke up with headaches, all the time. He stood up and staggered, his legs asleep and filled with needles. He stretched them out, walking around the room turning on all the lamps, suffusing it in a weak orange light that felt cold and useless. He wanted a drink and a cigarette and stood in the middle of the room, frozen and afraid to move.

The doll hadn't changed expression or position, but he was aware of it. As if it was putting out a specific signal that he could feel.

He leaned over it and then crouched down, getting close to its cold, elastic skin. He smelled it—perfume. Light and fruity, citrus.

Something suddenly *clicked* inside the doll's mouth, and Marks leaped back, almost tripping over his own feet. Heart pounding with giddy, ridiculous reaction, he knelt down and shuffled on his knees back to the doll. He pinched its mouth between two fingers—the lips parting in a terrible, realistic way—and forced it open.

Inside, on the pink, gleaming tongue, was a tiny turtle. As Marks stared at it in surprise, it slowly, calmly pulled its head back inside its shell.

Marks stood up with popping joints and shaking hands, adrenaline burning off as the silence and thick air of the room crowded in again. Pushing a hand through his hair, he turned and picked up the files, carrying them to the desk area and sitting down. Turning on the lamp, he began flipping through them.

Crime scene photos. Coroner's report. Incident form—no mention of a turtle, which didn't surprise him. Thinking it a clear-cut case of suicide, there would be few volunteers to explore the cavities of an old man's Japanese sex doll.

There were copies of the document Aoki had tucked into the waistband of his boxer shorts: A short, concise will, leaving his only sizable asset—the doll—to Spencer. Marks looked up at the mirror over the desk for a moment, chewing his lip, staring at but not really seeing himself.

Looking back down, he found the photos of the scrap of paper and stared at it, the characters meaningless to him. He folded the photo once, crisply, and slid it into his breast pocket. He turned and stared at the doll. It gave every impression of waiting patiently for the television to be switched on, its mouth still slightly open.

"*Kotodama*," the fleshy man in the old sweater said. His hair was in retreat from his face, and the top of his head had been burned pink, peeling eternally. The sweater was shapeless and thin, fraying and stained. Under it he wore a similarly elderly and disreputable button-down white shirt and a pair of soft-looking tan trousers. He wore thin, delicate round glasses that he pushed up the bridge of his nose every few minutes. "Japanese, literally 'spirit of language.' If you were an asshole, you could call it a magic spell."

He slid the photo of the note along the worn wooden bar and picked up a tumbler of whiskey, but didn't sip it.

"We both know I'm an asshole, Ivan," Marks said, tapping one finger on the photo while he looked at the collection of amber bottles on the shelf. "What does the note say?"

"Oh, you're an asshole, all right. No, *How are you, Ivan?* No, *How's the research coming for the book?*" Ivan leaned back in his chair and sighed. "It's a request for immortality, essentially. If, as I said, we were *both* assholes and were going to regard this as some sort of spell, that would be the desired effect."

"What about the turtle?"

Ivan looked up at the ceiling of the bar, which was rusting old tin in an elaborate design. "If we're going with my bullshit immortality interpretation, it might be a way of anchoring the spirit. The *minogame* in Japanese legend is a turtle that's so old it has seaweed growing on its shell like moss. If I were, say, doubling down on being an asshole, that's what I'd say."

He set his glass on the bar and adjusted his glasses. "Phil, you called me here to not have a drink with me and ask me about bizarre Japanese love notes?"

"You'd call it a love note?"

"If I wasn't an asshole, yes."

Marks chewed his lip.

In the hotel, Marks had a moment of thinking the doll had moved. Its position seemed subtly changed, as if it had heard him coming and rushed to settle back on the couch. He stood for a moment in the doorway, smelling the stuffy air. It was the scent of burned fabric and cleaning supplies that had made him nervous before.

He shut the door gently behind him and walked carefully towards the doll. He sat on the small wooden coffee table in front of the couch, the doll's face right there in front of him. He forced himself to look into the perfect, lifeless eyes. He held the position for a minute or so, studying the face, the eyes.

"Your problem," he said suddenly. "Is you got no backup. No exit strategy. Big mistake. We're all afraid. Of the nothing, of the unknown. Even me, and half my fucking *life* is unknown. But I still got options, and that's the key."

Then he stood up.

"Sorry," he said as he reached for the duffel bag. "But it's back in the bag for a while."

Spencer opened the door about two inches and peered into the gloomy hallway. Marks noted the fourth floor smelled like cabbage and cumin too. The door opened wider.

"Phil?"

Marks shifted the weight of the duffel bag on his shoulder. "Got a moment?"

Spencer glanced at the duffel, then stepped back, pulling the door open with him. "Sure, Phil, sure."

Marks walked into the kitchen. The apartment, directly below Aoki's, had the same layout—the big, empty kitchen and the tight corridor of rooms heading back into orange lamplight. He set the duffel on the floor and knelt, knees cracking. Spencer watched silently as Marks pulled the doll from the bag and set it on one of the old wooden chairs. He breathed heavily as he crouched, arranging her: feet on the floor, arms on the table, hands folded, face relaxed and with the hint of a smile. When Marks stood up, he was flushed and sweating. "Spense, there's no murder here."

"All right, Phil," Spencer said. "What's this?"

Marks pulled the folded file from his jacket and handed it to Spencer. "Your friend, Aoki, left you the doll in his will."

"That fucking thing—"

"Did not kill Mr. Aoki," Marks said.

Spencer flipped the file shut and stared down at it for a moment. He swallowed and looked up at the doll, sharply. "Me and Dek," he said, then stopped and looked down at the floor. "You get older, Phil, you don't have friends like you used to. People fade away."

Marks nodded, leaning back against the front door. "I'm fading away myself."

Spencer kept talking as if Marks hadn't responded. "I can't explain what … I just … miss the guy. In a way, you know, I ain't never missed anyone." He snorted. "And we never spoke one word to each other we understood."

Marks nodded. "You meant a lot to each other," he said slowly. Then he shrugged. "That's why he wanted this."

Spencer frowned and flipped open the file. The photo of the will was on top. His frown deepened. "Shit, Phil, there's procedures—"

"Spense, no one's gonna follow up on this one. Your pal didn't have family, you were his only friend. Even if PD notices this shit missing, none of them are going to blow a weak fart in the effort to track it down." He took a deep, unsteady breath, feeling old. "Your friend wanted this. He went through some trouble to make this happen. He's yours."

Spencer stared at the doll. Marks waited a moment, and then gathered himself, standing up and shrugging his jacket into better position. "All right. I'll leave you alone." He turned for the door.

"Jesus, Phil," Spencer said. "What am I supposed to do here?"

Marks turned halfway and looked at the doll and then back to Spense. "I don't know. Make him a cup of tea, huh?"

Out on the street, Marks paused and stood on the sidewalk, feeling the chill in the air through his jacket. He considered his options, which were simultaneously infinite and desolate, and clutched the lapels of his jacket close together to protect his chest. He considered having no place to go and no one to go to. He started walking.

Out of Balance by Chet Williamson

Toshiro Takeda sighed and took another bite of his ham and egg donut, washing it down with coffee far better than that in the hot cans of Boss Coffee in the vending machine outside his front door. The Mister Donut coffee was more expensive, 250 yen, but you got all the refills you wanted, and Takeda could easily afford it, regardless of how he lived. He signaled the young man in the Mister Donut uniform, who placed an automatic smile on his face, brought the carafe of black coffee and filled the cup once more as Takeda tightly nodded his thanks.

When the young man went away, Takeda popped the last bite of donut into his mouth and washed it down with the hot coffee, then looked out the second floor window of the shop at the large utility pole, a pole girded with so many cable brackets that its wood was nearly invisible. Over thirty separate lines gripped the pole: electricity, telephone, television, all the wire-transmitted units of energy and data that kept Jujo and Tokyo and Japan connected.

For many years, from the day he started school until the day he walked away from his salaryman job, his wife, and his children, Toshiro Takeda had been as connected to life as the cables on that pole. But on his thirty-fifth birthday he had broken that connection, and for the last fifteen years he had lived in the shadows of Japan's cities, making his living by making others die.

Today would be, like so many days following a job, one of leisure. He had made one and a half million yen plus expenses from the killing in Fukuoka, which had taken him three weeks to plan and carry out—one or two weeks longer than usual, so he was behind for the year.

He tried to schedule a minimum of six jobs annually, and no more than nine, charging between one and a half and two and a half million yen for each—the billing dependent upon the financial status of the client, but averaging two million yen per hit. Six jobs gave him an average annual income of twelve million yen, while the maximum of nine provided eighteen million. It was not a huge sum, but even the minimum was far more than he had made at his previous work.

For the first three years after leaving his wife, he had sent her biannual payments of 200,000 yen in cash, with no message or return address. When she divorced him and remarried, he ceased the payments, not from spite but from the practical consideration that she would no longer need them. He had not felt any emotion toward her for a long time. The money had been for his children.

When he dreamed at night, he often dreamed of the family he had left behind. His wife and his son and his daughter never aged in the dreams. They were always as they were when he had left.

The dreams were peaceful, of family life. He would be sitting in a chair in the center room, after the evening meal was finished. The television might be on, the children in front of it. His wife was in the kitchen, washing the dishes and putting things away. He would be watching the television or reading a magazine or newspaper. When he awoke, he could remember the scene and the sense of calm, but never what he had been reading or what had been on the television.

After such dreams, he felt sad but also grateful at being given the opportunity to return to those days, just as he felt grateful when he dreamed of his father, who had died several years before Takeda had left his family. Takeda had never hated his family. He had merely found himself unable to continue being a part of it. He could not remember loving his wife, or even his children, though he dimly recalled feeling affection, and a father's pride in the children's successes, as well as concern for their health and their own feelings.

Shortly after he had left them, however, he began to realize that this pride was not in his offspring but in himself, since he had created these children, and that their triumphs were due to his own influences. His efforts to keep them healthy and contented had also been born of self-interest, since their ill health and discontent would have negatively affected the quality of his own life. It had taken Takeda thirty-five years to know that his life was better led without responsibility. Man was ego, which was poorly served by serving others.

He firmly believed the persistent demands of ego to be the source of all evil, for he had been taught as much since childhood, but he also believed that his own ego was his master, and that he had done what he had because of it. Still, the dreams were pleasant, giving him the sense of family life without the responsibilities that accompanied it, the very things from which he had fled.

When Takeda had come to Tokyo from Kobe, he had no idea what it was he wanted to do or how to go about doing it. He had taken enough of his savings to see him through for several months, but when that time was up he would have to find employment somewhere, and when he did he would have to give his employer information. If that information were truthful, his wife could trace him. So Takeda had gone into the floating world, the nightless castle, the substratum in which one could be free of the restraints found in the rest of Japanese society.

For several days he had wandered the city, until his senses drew him to Ikebukuro, with its rough, working-class spirit. On its edges he found that for which he had been seeking, a place in which he could find outlawry if he looked carefully—and the more carefully he looked, the more he saw. He was a man who had stumbled into a new world filled with monsters, but who was happy to have found them, for their existence implied that he could become one himself, and that was what he most desired. He wished for freedom, and at that point in his life freedom was most easily equated with anarchy and lawlessness.

He had already stepped outside of the law and reneged on its debts when he left his family, and to cross the border into criminality seemed the next logical step. Besides, from a purely practical standpoint, it was the only way he could see to make any money. His steps to becoming a professional killer had been nearly accidental: a favor done for a new friend, the realization that he could kill without compunction, the acceptance that he was deadly. It helped that Takeda did not believe in ghosts, nor did he believe in any aura of death about him through which people could sense his occupation. Within him, however, he carried something that he did not think would allow him to relate to those outside his extremely limited sphere. Even if he wanted to, the dead would not permit it.

They were with him in some way, all of those whom he had killed, not as ghosts nor even as clinging spirits of his own imagination, but as past realities and present memories. Sometimes he would recall the expressions on their faces in the moment of knowing, as he came up to them, and they realized that the flat-faced, seemingly emotionless man before them was ending for them all that they had ever known and would ever be, and those moments were as close as Takeda had ever come to true understanding.

It is always this way, their faces seemed to say, even in the midst of their terror and fear. And when his hands moved and their bodies fell, the knowledge also flowed through him: *It is always this way.* He would not have known had it not been for them, and he was grateful, and carried them with him to show his thankfulness. It was not knowledge that could be shared by the living.

After a day of idle strolling, Takeda went back to his room, where he soaked in the tub for twenty minutes. Afterward, he tried to listen to some music, but he found his attention wavering, so he turned it off and picked up his novel. Words could not be read without concentration. After several chapters he grew tired, turned off the light, and lay back to sleep.

Even the night after a job, Takeda never had any trouble getting to sleep. Tonight, however, he lay awake in the dark, his eyes open, noticing the texture of the blackness, and how there was enough light outside, even though his window looked out on nothing but the space of a meter and a wall beyond, to allow thin strands to edge his curtain.

He watched the dim lines of light, and made himself think about a beautiful but sad-faced woman he had seen on the train that day. Sometimes when he thought about something before he went to sleep, he would dream about it, and he thought that a dream of her would be interesting. At last he slept, but the only dream that he remembered was one that he had just before awakening.

He was sitting at the kitchen table of his old house. His wife was working at the sink, and the children were playing on the floor of the next room. Before him on the table was a plate. On the plate, partly wrapped in a black casing, was a partially eaten block of cheese, perhaps cheddar, its color a vivid orange-yellow. Takeda was holding a knife, and he raised the knife to cut off a portion of the cheese, but as he started to do so, he noticed that the surface of the cheese was discolored in various places by black specks.

They were not the blue-green threads found in aged cheeses like Roquefort, but seemed instead to be areas of black rot, and he picked at several with the tip of the knife, carefully excising them and wiping them on the edge of the plate. After doing this several times, he realized that the cheese was so filled with these black spots that removing them all would be impossible. He looked more closely to determine what they were, and saw that the large black spots and smaller flecks moved, not falling off the surface, but traveling upwards as well, and when he carefully examined one particular speck, he saw that it was in the shape of a thin, segmented worm with millipede-like legs.

The cheese is bad, he said to his wife, and then he observed that the aluminum foil on which the block of cheese sat was not large enough to wrap it fully, and he felt annoyance at his wife that she had been so careless as to let these insects get into the cheese. If it had been tightly wrapped, it would not have happened.

With that thought he awoke, and when he realized that it had been a dream, he closed his eyes again, impressed as always by the sense of reality it had carried, and the absurd, illogical novelty that only dreams gave to life. He frequently did this upon awakening from a dream, and was often able to fall asleep again and reenter the same one. Now, however, he was awake, and though he lay there and remembered the color and texture of the cheese, and the tactile sensation of his knife picking away the black specks, he did not fall asleep again. It was not a dream he wished to resume. The light around the edges of the curtain had brightened, and when he looked at the clock it read 7:43.

He lay there for a few more minutes, thinking of how odd the dream had been, how unlike the others that he had had of his previous home life. Before, they had always been sedate, with nothing to mar the tranquil surface, and now there had come this dream of a cheese teeming with black bugs, and the thought made the night-taste in his mouth all the worse, until he got up and brushed his teeth.

Takeda made a small breakfast of cereal and milk, then sat and listened to a number of jazz CDs he had bought the previous week. At noon, he dressed in his suit and went out. He took the train to

Shibuya, where he had lunch, and then browsed Tower Records again.

He was in the book department, looking for new volumes on jazz, when he saw a salaryman in his early forties in the next aisle. The man was looking at him intently, and when Takeda returned his gaze, the man bowed quickly, as though apologizing for his close scrutiny. Then the man licked his lips quickly and said, as lightly as a breath, *Takeda-san?*

Takeda had not heard anyone speak his true name for fifteen years, and it seemed as though the floor had dropped from beneath him. Suddenly he felt the truth of the old saying that naming something gave one power over it. Despite his shock, he managed a quizzical look and shook his head in denial. As he did so, he recognized the man. His name was Suyama, and he had come to work for Takeda's company a month before Takeda had disappeared from Kobe. By that time, Takeda had been uncommunicative, barely speaking to anyone, but he had spoken once to Suyama over drinks after work.

After-work drinking was more ceremonial than an actual release. It gave people the chance to behave more drunkenly than they really were, and express some opinions that they might otherwise keep to themselves. The next day they could always apologize and say that they didn't remember a thing when they truly did. By that last month, Takeda had nearly given up drinking, feeling that his problems were too serious to be further muddled with alcohol. He nursed a drink for an hour or more, observing the others, speaking only when spoken to, allowing his bitterness and disgust for his colleagues to grow.

Suyama, however, he had pitied rather than despised. In the young man he had seen himself ten years earlier. The others were already lost, but there still might be hope for Suyama.

Takeda always remained late on drinking nights, since it was easier to remain in a place that only repulsed him rather than to go home to a place that was such a major part of an intolerable life. It was nothing that his wife or children said or did to make it so. It was what he had become that did that.

So it was that one night, two weeks before he changed his life, Takeda found himself alone in a bar with Suyama. The others had gone home, laughing with drunkenness, some of it real, some a pretense, and Takeda, his second glass of Kirin still half full, sat across from the young man. Suyama had not yet learned the tricks, and his face was reddened with too many drinks, most of which had been bought for him by his elders, and which he had not yet learned to gracefully evade.

You are drunk, Takeda had said to him, trying to keep judgment out of his voice.

I am. Suyama giggled. He sounded, Takeda thought, like a girl.

And how drunk are you?

I am ... very drunk, I believe.

Takeda watched him for a minute. Suyama wore an empty smile, his lips pulled over his slightly crooked teeth as though he was not too drunk to be self-conscious about them. *Not all that drunk,* Takeda said. He leaned forward over the table that was damp with spilled beer and rank with filled ashtrays. The stench from it made Takeda take shallow breaths. *Are you too drunk to learn something?*

Suyama looked at him, his eyes blinking, then snorted a laugh, as though the concept of learning something in his condition was so absurd as to be funny. Takeda sat back and sighed in disgust, looking at the ceiling.

No, no! Suyama said. *I can ... I can learn, really. I am sorry, I'm just so drunk ...*

Takeda looked at Suyama without moving his head, then said something so quietly that Suyama frowned and leaned forward.

What? What did you say?

Takeda repeated himself. *I said get out now.*

Get out? Of here?

Takeda looked around the bar, then back at Suyama, and made a broad, all-encompassing gesture. *Of here,* he said, heavily stressing the last word.

I don't … understand. I am so drunk …

I mean get out of here. Get out of all of it. Don't do this. Don't make my mistake. You still have time.

Suyama's expression changed in a way that told Takeda that he was sober enough to understand. *Why?* The young man said.

Takeda shook his head slowly. There was no way he could explain. He wasn't sure if he understood himself. He could say that this life was empty, but it wasn't, not always. He could say that it would drain away Suyama's spirit, but Takeda's was still strong, strong enough to rebel. There was only one word that fit, and he finally spoke it:

Duhkha.

Takeda could tell that Suyama knew the term, as anyone who had even rudimentarily studied Buddhism would. The word was Sanskrit, meaning suffering—or, more specifically, a wheel out of balance.

Duhkha, Suyama repeated, and Takeda nodded. Suyama made the same wide gesture that Takeda had made only a moment earlier, then smiled and shrugged. *Duhkha,* he said again, telling Takeda as eloquently as a drunken man could that he already knew, young as he was, that this was the way of things.

Takeda had stood up then, and bowed, respecting Suyama's perception, but knowing also that the young man was a fool, perhaps the greatest fool, since he already understood what had taken Takeda too long to learn, and chose to do nothing.

The next day, Suyama had come to Takeda's cubicle and apologized, saying that he had been very drunk, and that he hoped he had said nothing that Takeda had found offensive. *Not at all,* Takeda had replied, and added that, on the contrary, he recalled only a delightful and stimulating conversation. Suyama had smiled uneasily, bowed, thanked Takeda, and left. Takeda never spoke to him again. Ten days later, Takeda had vanished from Kobe, from his work and from his family.

Now, fifteen years later, there was Suyama, standing and holding a coffee table book on baseball, looking at Takeda with an awkward mixture of emotions that encompassed embarrassment, expectation, and suspicion. He recognized Takeda despite the fact that he no longer wore the thin moustache he had had at the time he met Suyama, and his hair was styled differently as well. Takeda had even had some plastic surgery in order to change his appearance after completing his first job. It had changed the shape of his jawline and had straightened his once slightly crooked nose, but Suyama had seen past the illusions of the blade and the passage of years.

No? Suyama asked.

I'm sorry, said Takeda, *but I don't know what you mean.*

I must apologize. You look like someone I knew a long time ago. A man named Takeda.

I don't know anyone by that name.

The resemblance is very close, but now I see my mistake. I beg your pardon.

That's quite all right, Takeda said, and turned back to the books through which he had been browsing, although the titles were not registering on his whirling mind. He wanted nothing more than to leave immediately. He could feel the man's gaze still upon him, and was nearly as offended by Suyama's rudeness as he was alarmed by his recognition of him. Had the man no sense of protocol or manners?

Takeda was tempted to look up and stare right back at the man, but further direct contact might only add to Suyama's suspicions. One can change a chin or a nose, but the eyes remain the same, and Suyama might remember the piercing look that Takeda had given him years before. Had he made such an impression on the man,

Takeda wondered, that he still recalled Takeda so accurately after only one true conversation so long before?

Takeda crouched and drew a volume from the bottom shelf, hiding himself from his observer. His weight on his ankles, Takeda felt his stomach cramping, and he shifted to reduce the pressure in his bowels, causing a bit of gas to escape involuntarily. Though the emission was silent, Takeda was still embarrassed and angry at himself. He was acting like a caught child, wetting himself at the fear of unknown consequences.

He pushed back his anger and alarm, replaced the book he held, chose one that he thought he would actually want to read, and stood up. While watching Suyama only peripherally, Takeda crossed the room to the cashier and paid for his book. Then he walked to the escalator and went down several levels to the street.

There were many ways of looking behind oneself without obviously doing so, but Takeda did not look back, even surreptitiously, until he had traversed several blocks. He did not do so because he did not want to see Suyama following him, because he did not know what he would do if he did. At last, however, in the middle of a crowded street, Takeda stopped and turned around. He looked behind him, and across the street. There were hundreds of people in view, but Suyama was not one of them.

Relieved, he slowed from the steady pace he had held, not fast enough to look as though he wished to outdistance anyone, nor slow enough to invite a pursuer to catch up. It had been a guiltless, easy stride that he had intentionally chosen, and he felt foolish that he had had to choose at all concerning what should be such a spontaneous activity.

Slowly the sick feeling started to leave Takeda, and the sweat dried on his forehead. The memory of the sweat and the sickness, however, remained with him, and he wondered about the very core of himself. It was not the first time that he had been in danger of being discovered, but it was the first time, at least to his knowledge, that he had encountered anyone from his past who had recognized him.

There had been several times in the last fifteen years when, moving through the cities of Japan, Takeda had seen people he recognized from his previous life. When such a thing occurred, he turned the other way so that they would not see him. Once, in Hiroshima, he had seen a grocer of whom he and his wife had been customers in Kobe, and another time in Tokyo he had seen a woman who had been a secretary in his office. Neither of them had noticed him. A few years before, another former coworker had looked directly at Takeda without recognition in the Yokohama Joypolis.

Takeda would never accept a job in Kobe, and had not been there since he had left. There were too many people there who might recognize him as the man who had walked out on his job, his wife, his children, and never returned. Besides, there was no need to go to Kobe. People wanted killing everywhere.

All right, he thought, so someone did recognize him, but he had bluffed it out, and in all likelihood Suyama thought he had been mistaken. Even if he had not, even if he was convinced that the man he had seen was Takeda, he would certainly do nothing about it. As far as he knew, Takeda had vanished to begin a new life. He had not tried to make his disappearance look like a suicide; he had simply walked away, so what business was it of Suyama's? It was not worth another thought.

Despite his conclusions, Takeda thought about Suyama for the rest of the day, seeing the man's knowing expression every few minutes. The thoughts dulled his enjoyment of the film he viewed, the book he read, the music he listened to, and when he lay down to go to sleep, the harder he tried not to think of Suyama, the more he saw his face. Takeda awoke several times in the night from troubled dreams. He could not recall specifically what they were about, but there remained a sense of having been discovered, and he suspected that they had been about Suyama.

He recalled only one dream. It seemed to him that in the middle of the night he got up to go to the bathroom, doing so in the dark. But when he realized that he was in his house back in Kobe, Takeda knew that it must be a dream. When he came out of the bathroom, his wife was standing in her nightdress in the hall, and he had to walk around her to get back to the bedroom. No sooner had he made his way past her than she was there again, standing in front of the bedroom door, so that he had to edge past her once more. When he entered their bedroom, she was standing precisely at the foot of the bed, where he needed to go in order to get to his side. Once more he pressed past her, only to see her again, now standing by the bedside, leaving him no room to go past. He stood there looking at her looking at him, unable to move any farther, until he awoke.

Takeda relaxed during the morning, and went out in the afternoon to buy groceries and toiletries. By the time his shopping was completed, a cold rain had begun to fall, and he headed back home.

He took off his jacket, loosened his tie, and sat and relaxed over a pot of green tea, contented to be warm and snug inside his small warren. He turned on the television and watched a game show, then the news. By seven o'clock he was hungry, and decided to go out and get an omelet at a small restaurant several blocks away. He put on his suit jacket and topcoat, and left his apartment.

He had not gone a block before he was aware that someone was following him. He continued to walk through the streets crowded with people coming home from their jobs or from shopping, but paused briefly at a store window angled enough to allow him to see behind him. Among the many pedestrians was one who slowed significantly when Takeda stopped, and although Takeda could not see the man's face clearly in the warped reflection, for some reason the figure seemed familiar, and Takeda thought perhaps that it reminded him of a man he had himself tailed many years earlier, a man he had followed a long way before killing.

Whoever he was, if he was following Takeda, then Takeda would have to deal with him. It meant doing things correctly, and with no possibility of failure, so he thought quickly and calmly.

He was in Higashi-Jujo, walking north, and thought of the warehouse in Akabane-Minami. It would take a half hour to get there.

He walked slowly, never looking back, only ascertaining his follower's presence through reflections or peripherally as he glanced in shop windows. The man was hanging far back, which suited Takeda fine. He didn't want a confrontation on the street with other people around, and apparently his follower didn't either. They would both have to be patient.

The crowd began to thin the nearer Takeda drew to the warehouse. He thought the man might confront him, but he still hung back in spite of the ever-dissipating cloud of witnesses. Apparently the man only wanted Takeda when he was all alone.

They moved away from the shopping area with its stores and cafés and into a more industrial part of the ward, with small machine shops and warehouses side by side. Here the street layout grew more chaotic, with numerous turns, dead ends, and blind alleys that made it difficult for Takeda to allow his stalker to keep up with him without losing him completely.

Indeed, he noticed that the man had increased his pace and was closing the gap between them. Takeda picked up speed again, not wanting the man to catch up with him yet. Then he saw the warehouse ahead. It was a two-story building between a larger warehouse and what looked like a small abandoned factory.

Takeda took the few steps up onto the truck dock and walked toward the door next to the roll-up loading gate. Takeda quickly unlocked the door and walked in, leaving it open behind him. The warehouse was nearly full, but there was an open aisle through the clutter, and Takeda followed it, walking more slowly now, but still not looking back. He felt tension press across his shoulders, and steeled himself, fearing the impact of a bullet in his back. He rounded a corner where he would be hidden from his pursuer, and stopped.

Takeda reached into his pants pocket and brought out a lock-back knife with a four-inch blade, which he quietly opened. The thought occurred to him that perhaps he was wrong, romanticizing again, and that the man was simply a mugger, following an older salaryman to a lonely place where he could be victimized, but the next words he heard put that theory in its grave.

I've been looking for you.

In spite of himself, Takeda trembled at the words.

I've been looking for you for a long time.

And, for a moment, the man coming down the corridor was indeed the man he had killed years before, a ghost come back from the dead to find his murderer and wreak revenge, and though Takeda knew that such things were not possible even in this land of ghosts, he felt panic grip his chest, but told himself that it was not a ghost, but a hunter, a man who had come to either kill or capture him.

When the footsteps grew so loud he knew the man was around the corner, Takeda surged out toward the man, who recoiled in surprise, but Takeda was too fast, stepping into him, right hand low, legs driving his trunk, trunk driving his arm as it rose seeking the man's midsection, and passing into it as smoothly as in a dream, where all movement cuts through that combination of air and water, a sensation which can never be attained in the waking world. The knife tore up and across and out again, and Takeda heard the breath leave the man as his life, heard the blood patter onto the concrete floor of the warehouse, and something heavier and sodden follow a moment later. The man fell to knees incapable of holding him, and then forward onto his face and his open wound.

Takeda had stepped back as soon as he had withdrawn the knife, but the man's face hit the concrete right at his feet. He heard the crack of the nose breaking, and saw blood, black in the dim light, flow from beneath the face as greater amounts pooled about the opened stomach, and the hands and feet twitched.

At last they slowed, and Takeda knelt carefully so as not to get any blood on him, gripped the man's right shoulder, and pushed him over onto his back. He looked at the opened bowels, then at the man's face.

Remarkably, he was still alive. Takeda could see who he was now. It was not the man whom he had killed all those years before.

It was Suyama, whom he had seen the day before, when he was shopping for books. Suyama, who had recognized him. Suyama, who had found him again and followed him.

Suyama's eyelids fluttered and his mouth was open wide and moving. Blood from the broken nose was running down over the upper lip and into the mouth, and it made the man's breath bubble as he tried to keep breathing. It seemed as though he was trying to say something, but could not force out the words. Takeda looked at him intently, as though willing him to speak, and he did.

I only ... wanted to ... thank you. The words were wet and muddy, but Takeda thought he understood them. Suyama coughed and blood came out, and he managed to say one word more.

Duhkha ...

Takeda's heart felt as though it were made of stone, and his flesh of glass. He hardly dared breathe, nor even think, lest he shatter, and the only sound in the world had become the racing breath of the man lying on the concrete. After an incalculable time, that breath caught, rattled, and stopped. The eyes were open, but saw nothing.

Takeda looked at the dead face for a long time. Then he knelt and wiped the knife on the legs of Suyama's trousers, folded it, and slipped it back into his pocket. He pushed up his sleeves and reached beneath Suyama's hip, sodden with blood, and withdrew the wallet from the left hip pocket. It was still dry. He stood and opened it, looking for an answer.

He hoped for compassion, mercy, relief, but the first thing he saw was a photo ID in a clear plastic sleeve. It identified the man on the floor as Detective Hideo Suyama of the Tokyo Metropolitan Police.

The warehouse seemed to spin for a moment, and Takeda staggered dizzily, then regained his footing. It seemed a rift had opened between his world and another of which he had never known, and he realized that his life had irrevocably changed, due to the presence of the man at his feet, a man who had wanted to thank him for his warning, a man who had heeded that warning, and had chosen to put his wheel into balance as best he could, and found his calling.

Takeda wept for having killed without purpose for the first time. Then he did what needed to be done, and went back into the world, with a new and damning memory.

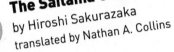

The Saitama Chain Saw Massacre
by Hiroshi Sakurazaka
translated by Nathan A. Collins

1.

I love Takumi.

I love Takumi.

I love Takumi.

I love Takumi more than anyone. I love Takumi so much I could die. I love him more than anyone in the whole world.

But Takumi chose her over me.

I hate, hate, hate her.

I'll never forget the look in her eyes that day. Takumi never saw me, but I saw her glance. She looked at me like I was some pitiful sewer rat crawling out from a drainpipe to find itself on a subway platform.

I won't forgive her. I won't forgive her. I won't forgive her. How dare she touch and cling so to my Takumi. I'll never forgive her.

For two days I cried, and then I made up my mind. It ends today. I will settle things, my way, with the boy who threw me away and chose her. I can't do it with words; I'm not a good speaker, and can't express my true feelings. Besides, even now that we're lovers, I still get nervous every time I see him.

Except that's not true.

We're not lovers anymore.

As painfully sad a truth as that is.

Anyway, I came to school today to express objection in the most extreme way I can.

Sever the telephone line, check.

Sever the coaxial cable line, check.

Destroy the cellular broadcast towers, check.

With my preparations complete, I stand before the school gates. I fill my lungs with the damp morning air.

If I were to stop now, my actions would only be petty offenses, maybe even chalked up to teenage pranks. After all, I've never acted out before. I can still turn back and make it as if I never intended any more. Were I able to forget about Takumi, go home, and bury myself within my bedsheets, nothing would come of this.

But …

My mind is made up.

I will kill him, and I will die.

2.

But let's go back three days to when a new girl transferred to my school.

It happened just before morning homeroom. Our teacher came in just like usual. And as usual our jeering rattled the blackboard, but not him, and he stood at his lectern and called roll with his usual glower.

Then he said, "Ah, I know this is sudden, but we have a new transfer student."

As usual, I was seated at my desk beside the window, absorbed in a paperback I was reading half-hidden behind the curtain. Sorry, but the story was just too interesting for me to pay attention to some new girl. I noticed her enough to think *She's prettier than me*, but that was just about the beginning and end of my impression of her. Takumi, sitting diagonally across from me, was showing about 30 percent more interest than I had, but when our eyes met he gave me a grin.

As for my introduction, my name is Fumio Kirisaki. I'm an only daughter coming from a line of lumber brokers stretching back to the nineteenth century. My grandfather on my mother's side was an American. He left Texas for Japan in some weird search for this leather something-or-other. He fell in love with my grandmother at first sight, married into her family, and was buried in this foreign, eastern land.

I'm one-fourth Caucasian, but as far as being graced with beauty and proportions unattainable by someone purely Japanese, I wasn't. Not in the slightest. Here I am in high school, still short and flat-chested. All I inherited from my big, tall grandfather was the color of his eyes. If you were to look closely, in the brightest sunlight of a midsummer's day, you'd notice their light steel-blue color, but most times they come across as two concentric circles of smeary black ink. No, my ink-wash eyes only lessen my already unremarkable looks. That's why I wear glasses even though my 20/28 vision means I don't need them. If my grandfather was going to give me anything in his DNA, why couldn't it have been a body with the grandeur and beauty of the Rocky Mountains and the Grand Canyon? But such is the hand that life dealt me.

The new girl gave her simple introduction, then walked past me to a desk somehow already waiting for her in the back row. A slash of morning sunshine cast half of her desk in glaring light, while a number of dust motes floated in the corn-silk rays.

The girl looked at me with a hint of a smile. She was pretty enough, but something about her smiling face was inorganic. She wasn't plain-looking by any measure—it was more like one thousand parts from one thousand beautiful faces had been reassembled into one indistinctive whole. I returned to the world within my novel.

In the break after first hour, the other students swarmed around the new girl. I didn't join them. I wasn't interested in her, nor was I friends with any of the students surrounding her. Besides, I had promised to eat lunch with Takumi, and I needed to finish reading my paperback while I had the chance. It was a funny story about a kooky transfer student stirring up trouble at her new school. As I turned the pages, I thought about how I liked fictional stories because things could happen in their pages that couldn't in real life.

But I was about to find out that real-life transfer students cause trouble too.

When the lunch break came, I witnessed something I couldn't believe.

I was bringing lunch to Takumi at our meeting place behind the school. The sky held more clouds than blue, but I was walking fairly upbeat. Despite being in the same class, we always left separately; leaving as a conspicuous couple would have been far too embarrassing.

But on this particular day, Takumi wasn't alone beneath our tree. Someone else was with him—someone who wasn't me—in our secluded spot in back of the school. He had once told me, "It's the perfect place for us to eat in private."

They were in each other's embrace, Takumi and that transfer girl. His arms pulled her closer. I blinked and I blinked again, but the vision before me remained unchanged. His eyes were fixed on her, never even turning my way.

I tried to call out his name, but nothing beyond that initial "T" ever escaped my throat.

Instead, what spoke for me was the loud, harsh clattering of the bento box lunches, which I'd woken up early to make, tumbling to the ground. But even then, Takumi's gaze remained on the new girl. No part of my existence reached his awareness, not my voice, nor any sound I made, nor my puny little figure.

The girl sent me a glance from the corner of her eye and waved me away as if I were a stray cat. I scooped up the bento boxes and left the couple behind the school.

For the rest of the break, I sat on the concrete of a disused entryway, the typically cold surface warmed by my body. Oil leaked from the bento boxes, staining the polka-dot cloth into a dull brown.

I took out my cell phone and texted Takumi.

He didn't reply. No matter how many messages I sent him, he never replied. My texts transformed into radio waves that raced across the ether and through the relay tower to finally reach Takumi's side. Maybe my words, broken down into emotionless signals, hadn't been able to deliver him my true feelings.

"You there," an officious female voice said. "Keep your phone turned off until the end of the school day."

I looked up at the intruder. Everything about her, from her clothes to her features, was by the book. Her armband, denoting her as a member of the student disciplinary committee, caught the light.

"Go away," I said.

"Texting during class time is against school rules."

"Shut up! Go away!"

I hurled the bento box bundle at her. It grazed her before loudly crashing to the floor. The cloth split open, and the plastic boxes burst, their contents—slightly charred eggs and sausages cut to look like octopuses—bursting across the concrete.

She gave me a look of disgust, then walked away. I was alone again.

Takumi had told me he fell in love with me at first sight, just as I loved him from the very start. We became lovers after what felt like an excruciating wait, but our breakup came without warning.

I'm not particularly pretty, and I don't have proportions worthy of bragging; neither was I given a personality to make up for it. The singular miracle in my life was the deep love Takumi and I shared.

But now the arrival of one girl has plunged me headfirst into the abyss.

What point is there to my life without Takumi, my only sunlight?

3.

But even I have someone—one, and only one—whom I can call a friend.

Kaoruko Odagiri is quiet, tall, with a delicacy belying her well-placed curves and an ever-present elegance that readily conjures the image of her wearing a long skirt trimmed with lace as she plays the piano on a weekend afternoon.

Kaoruko had been the one to approach me. After all, someone as shy and ill-spoken as me would never be so bold as to talk to anyone who was, aside from being assigned to the same classroom, a complete stranger.

She had come to me when I was reading as I always do, half hidden behind the curtain. The paperback was one of those "boy love" books, and I was just getting to the big love scene between the leading man and the man in the part of the heroine, but Kaoruko's soprano voice coming from above me would have been a surprise regardless of the contents of my book.

"You're a reader," Kaoruko said.

I answered with an uneasy nod.

"Does the human mind store knowledge in a textual form?" she asked, whether to herself or to me, I couldn't tell. "Or is it all sound and vision? Or something entirely else?"

Her words were incomprehensible to me. My thoughts were wholly occupied with figuring out how to get my book back into my bag without her asking what it was about. Even had she already gotten a glance at its pages, she surely wouldn't have realized what it was that I was reading, but I felt the same sort of embarrassment as if a boy had caught me changing clothes.

"You don't have to be so nervous," she said. "There's nothing unusual about a girl in high school reading a romance novel … even if it were, say, homoerotic fiction."

"What?"

"I can't stand saccharine love stories. They lack realism."

My mouth dropped open, and I looked up at her.

"Not that I particularly read much in the first place," she said. "I find it so dreadfully inefficient, having to turn one's knowledge into words in order to transmit it to a third party. If you could open up a human mind, you would find no words there."

"But," I stammered, "without words, humanity never would have evolved from lower animals, don't you think?"

"True. Just as land-dwelling creatures would never have arisen without first going through gill breathers, words were likely a necessary protocol in the process of human evolution. But that doesn't mean they'll remain necessary forever. We don't have gills, after all."

"I … I suppose."

"If we could form a direct connection between one mind and another, letters and words would become obsolete."

"But how," I asked, pausing to gather the courage, "do you know about my book?"

She said, "I know everything about you."

"How?" I managed to squeak out, my voice catching in my throat. I could feel my hands becoming sticky with sweat.

With a grin, Kaoruko answered, "Because we've known each other since long before we were born."

I'll summarize her story.

Supposedly, we're the reincarnations of two knights from a tiny European kingdom whose name has been lost to history.

Kaoruko was a descendant of royal blood and a knight with a promising future, while I was a common soldier of mixed foreign blood. Kaoruko was of higher standing, but my skill with a sword was formidable, enough so that my name was known among neighboring kingdoms. Indifferent to our disparities in birth and upbringing, Kaoruko and I fought shoulder-to-shoulder on the battlefield and became the two greatest knights in the royal army. The people waved flags with our heraldry as they prayed for our victory. Opposing armies began to take flight at our very sight. Until a foul betrayal led to our execution, we fought ever to-gether, sharing in our laughter and sometimes in commiseration. With our heads on the axmen's blocks, we vowed to reunite in the next life.

Her story was too much to believe all at once. Ugh, I thought, why did she have to come over to me? Sure, I read at least three hundred books a year, and my mind half-resides within their fic-tional worlds, but I've always felt that enables me to be, if anything, more of a realist.

But I've never been able to express those thoughts to her, being as bad at talking as I am. Slowly but surely, she wore down my skep-ticism, until I found myself going along with her fancies.

For example: Kaoruko hears voices she calls the "voices from above." When I asked her what she meant by "above," she simply said, "I hear them coming from above me, so they're the voices from above."

If she had told me it was a higher spirit or an alien or her future self, I don't think I would have been friends with her. But she didn't know the true nature of the voice, and told me so honestly.

I teased her by pointing out that her head might be picking up on random chatter from some local pirate radio station. Straight-faced, she responded that she couldn't discard that possibility. After that, we obsessively checked every possible signal, from FM stations and amateur radio (the obvious places to start) to police scanners, truckers' CB radio, and even North Korean numbers stations. But none of these signals matched the voices directing Kaoruko from above.

Everything the voices have told her has come true, whether it was the car accident that would befall the head teacher of C Class, or what would be on our math test, or the whereabouts of Sakagami's missing gym clothes.

Anyway, that was how our friendship began.

And everything was going all right until that girl came to our school.

When I told Kaoruko about Takumi and the new girl, my friend stated matter-of-factly, "Takumi is being targeted by aliens."

"Aliens?" I asked.

"Yes. Aliens."

You've probably heard of the butterfly effect. A butterfly flaps its wings in Beijing, and a hurricane arrives in New York. It's all based on some theory that I might understand if I were more into science than literature.

According to Kaoruko, galactic science has progressed far enough to be able to see through the chaos and predict the future. For each future, certain starting conditions become crucial, and Takumi plays the role of one such condition. Supposedly, Takumi's fate plays a decisive role in the outcome of a galactic war. Aware of this fact, aliens have come to secure their so-called "butterfly from the galactic frontier." And now, Kaoruko told me, I've gotten caught up among the events.

I knew she was saying all this to make me feel better. Regardless, I argued with her.

"I can't accept that," I said.

From Kaoruko's expression, I might as well have denied that one plus one equals two. "Why not?" she asked.

"I just can't."

"You can believe in reincarnation, but not aliens?"

"That's not what I mean," I said. "I can't accept it, period. End of discussion."

"I'm telling you, Takumi is under her control."

"Please, just drop it!"

She gave me a look I've never seen before, like she had accidentally touched a searing-hot metal plate.

It wasn't that I didn't believe her. I don't hate science fiction. In fact, I wanted to believe her. She would never lie, and she always looks out for me. We're true friends who share a soul-bond.

But I couldn't allow myself to deny the truth that Takumi had dumped me. Whether or not that was actually true mattered less. It was a problem of self-respect. Between choosing to believe in my one and only friend, or in the "truth" that my boyfriend had dumped me, I chose the latter. That's the kind of girl I am.

The following day, I tried to apologize to Kaoruko for dismissing what she had to say.

But she no longer had any words for me. She ignored me, her manner that of a complete stranger. Takumi did it too. He ignored me the same as if I were some part-time worker distributing tissue-pack advertisements outside the train station and he was just trying to walk by. He didn't respond to my texts, either. Nor, of course, would he answer my calls. I was all alone.

I left school after second period that day.

The following day, I skipped entirely.

Then, wiping my tears, I withdrew my chain saw from its resting place at the back of the storeroom.

It was a birthday present from my departed grandfather.

4.

The next morning, I went to school, bringing with me my grandfather's present, polished to a shine.

I'd already cut the cord to the receiver of the public phone at the convenience store nearest the school. I also destroyed the nearby cellular broadcast towers. My preparations should buy me some small amount of time before the police would be contacted, whether someone runs far enough to get a signal or finds some house with an open door. Once notified, the police should take another five minutes or so to arrive. By my worst estimate, I'll have roughly twenty minutes starting from the first casualty. A mere twenty minutes to finish everything I must do.

I pressed the button on the stopwatch I'd prepared. The numbers on the digital display began counting down this most special time for Takumi and me. I tucked the watch, and those precious, precious numbers, into my skirt pocket. Those numbers are for him and me alone. I won't show them to anyone else.

Cradling my chain saw, I stood before the school gates, my feet planted firmly. I pushed on the hand guard and activated the chain brake. I engaged the choke's lock-out switch and pulled the starter rope, first slowly, then, when I felt resistance, I gave it more force, and then—

With a great noise, the chain saw's engine began to breathe. It seemed to like the clear morning air. The machine let out a bestial roar as it greedily burned its fuel. I released the choke, switched the control lever to idle, then squeezed the throttle trigger.

"You there!" a voice shouted. "Kirisaki! What do you think you're bringing into school? Hey, I'm talking to you—"

It was one of the teachers. He scowled at me, still yelling, but it was all drowned out in my chain saw's roar. Fourteen summer cicadas could be perched at my neck, and they'd still be quiet compared to my machine's fury.

Releasing the brake, I swung my chain saw. At the impact, a light jolt traveled up my arm, and the teacher's head, high above me to begin with, went flying even higher, tracing an arc some three meters up in the sky before thudding against the schoolyard gravel, bouncing a couple times before it came to a stop. A fountain of dark red blood sprayed from his stump of a neck, sent there by a heart unaware that his head was long gone, and the fluid began adding black to the red of his shirt.

Some of the blood cascade landed on me, imparting my school blouse with its deep crimson color and iron smell. I'd hoped Takumi's blood would be the first to fall on me, but oh well. You start swinging a chain saw around and I suppose this is what happens. By the time I reach him, I'm sure my pure white uniform will be red all the way through.

Cradling my growling chain saw, I ran across the schoolyard and arrived at the front of the building.

Our classroom is the farthest on the third floor. There is one more room behind ours, but everyone's having fewer children, and that means fewer students, so that room is going unused. At our school, students graduate down a floor each year. Those on their third and final year get the ground floor, but luckily for me, they must have been too stressed out by their college entrance exams to have noticed anything amiss.

The building had a side stairwell for emergencies, but I snuck in last night and jammed the locks on every floor with superglue. If Takumi tried to leave, he'd have no choice but to take the central staircase, which was right where I was headed.

Knowing I'd only have one chance at this, I called Takumi's mother this morning to check that he'd come to school. He's a diligent student like that. I bet he's sitting at his desk now waiting for the chime to announce the beginning of class. He has nowhere to run except right past me.

I'd be seeing him soon.

The thought sent my heart racing with elation.

A boy was standing at his shoe locker, in the process of switching out his outdoor shoes for indoor slippers, when he noticed me and said, "What the hell are you doing?"

He's one of my classmates, although I don't remember his name. Even though we're in the same class, he never said a word to me before now. His eyes locked on to my chain saw.

You never speak to me, I thought, so don't butt in now.

I swung my chain saw upward. With a roar, its sharp teeth tore through the side of his waist, severing his torso along a diagonal line that reminded me of sashes worn by the anchors in our school relay races. From the force of my swing, the portion with his head and one arm sailed upward and got snagged on the very top of the lockers, where it dangled in a limp, beckoning wave. His lower half twitched before collapsing to rest on his knees. The angled cut revealed his gray lungs, white bones, and pink heart.

When my grandfather taught me how to wield a chain saw, he told me that the fighting style was developed by lumberjacks near the end of the American Civil War in hopes of staving off the Union advance. As simple men lacking rifles or cannons, they utilized the familiar tools of their profession to wage guerrilla warfare within the thick woodlands. These rough woodsmen had created their own martial art, and much like the slaves in Brazil and their capoeira, the men took great pride in it. Not that I know a thing about capoeira.

I do know for a fact that the lumberjack trade had boomed in Texas, until the twentieth century and its oil fields came along. I'm not so sure about chain saws being invented in time for the Civil War, but on the other hand, my Texan grandfather could masterfully wield three chain saws simultaneously, so who knows. Maybe chain saws were around back then, if only in America.

Without changing my shoes, I stepped up into the school proper and began climbing the central stairs. At the first landing, I opened the window, bringing into the school fresh air free of the scent of blood.

I didn't see anyone in the yard below.

My chain saw's battle song resounded through the hallways, echoing off the walls. Butchered corpses lay in the front gate and entryway. Despite all that, had none of the students on the first floor noticed? Or had they decided that someone waving a chain saw through the school wasn't any of their concern? The indifference of the latter seemed extreme, even for high schoolers. Well, it was working out fine for me.

I don't want to place the blame for this massacre on anyone. Neither Takumi nor Kaoruko are at fault. This decision was my own. I'm not sure I carry any blood or tears within me. I'm a cold-blooded girl; of course Takumi would dump me, and of course Kaoruko would ignore me. The only blood I have is the stuff dripping from the stainless steel teeth of my chain saw.

I had believed Kaoruko's talk of reincarnation not because I needed a friend, but rather because she was my first friend.

But that's all over now.

I'm without my love and without my best friend.

The class bell rang.

Carrying my bloodied chain saw, I climbed another step.

5.

At the second floor, a male and female pair blocked my path.

The girl was the disciplinary committee student I encountered in the entryway three days ago. The boy looked fit, like he did judo or something. If we were to take a measure, I wouldn't be surprised if he had three times the muscle mass I do. The committee girl brought him along like her guard dog.

Angling her armband so I could see it, she announced, "You there. Wearing your shoes inside the main building is against school rules."

I had some trouble hearing her over my chain saw's echoing rumble. Its steel teeth were still dripping blood.

Having stepped in the pool made by my now-former classmate, the sticky mess was clinging to the bottom of my shoes, leaving black-red graffiti behind every footstep. So, yes, I was wearing outside shoes, and that was against school rules. But didn't she have more important things to point out? I guess the student handbook doesn't explicitly forbid bringing a chain saw into the school, nor is there any rule against decapitating fellow students.

What was this, some sort of sick joke?

Thinking objectively, my entire existence this moment was some kind of sick joke, but somehow her reaction was on a whole other level of messed up. On a basic level, I'm actually impressed. I'd thought that only in a manga would a morals committee student care enough about her duty to confront a person swinging about a chain saw.

Up until now, I'd been so obsessed with Takumi that I'd never realized I attend what's kind of an interesting school. Too bad I only noticed it once I'd already begun wreaking havoc with a chain saw. Maybe only in this most extreme of circumstances is it possible to notice the beauty in the world around me.

But anyway. I had little time. Anyone standing in my way must be removed.

The committee girl said something else, but her voice was drowned out by engine noise, and I couldn't make out her words. Her guard dog, ferocious, stepped toward me. I swung my chain saw.

The blades sank into his shoulder, the saw grinding and jolting as it cleaved through his collarbone, spine, and ribs, splitting him into two pieces. He was sturdily built, and big-boned, and slicing through him was fairly tough. Maybe he drank his milk every day. His lower half, dead and disconnected, relentlessly continued its charge, knocking me flat at the very top of the stairs. I choked on the 98.6 degree heat emanating from the cross-section cut of his corpse.

The girl ran toward me. With a flash of my chain saw, I severed her legs. Everything from her knees down remained on the second floor, while the rest of her, blood spraying, tumbled past me, her skull jolting and bouncing down the steps.

I stood up.

Now I was covered in even more blood. I took out a handkerchief to wipe the specks from my glasses, but the gore had seeped into my pocket and stained the handkerchief bright red, so I used the hem of my skirt instead.

I wanted as few people as possible to meet their ends as a future source of rust on my chain saw. If they valued their lives, I hoped they'd remain in their classrooms until I reached Takumi. For Takumi and me to die in this sudden, unhappy ending was already two lives too many.

But my wish went unfulfilled. While my attention was elsewhere, easily one class's worth of students had filled the stairway above. Everyone from the second floor up had no other route of escape. The students stared at me in silence. Or they could have been talking among themselves, with nothing reaching my ears. My chain saw's battle cry swallowed all other sound. Slowly I scanned my surroundings.

If they wanted to go around me—keeping their distance, of course—I'd make no move against them. My goal was to kill Takumi; everyone else was nothing more than obtrusive white noise. The actions taken by the morals committee girl left her lower legs on the second floor and the rest of her down the stairs. These students could take that result as a warning or as a declaration of war. It was all up to them. Keeping a watchful measure of the distance between the group and myself, I advanced.

"Do it now!" a boy shouted. "Crush her!"

Had they lost all reason, feeling that there's no escape? Packed in that swarm, did they feel safe from my spinning blades? Did they think me a short, bespectacled girl who would be easily defeated? Fine then. I'd play their game. I raised my chain saw.

The gleaming steel entered the crowd of uniforms. Bits of heads and arms caught in the whirling teeth and sailed through the air, smacking into the walls, leaving bright red brushstroke smears against the surface. Intestines spilled from cut-open stomachs and slithered to the floor. The motor roared. Within this blood-mist sauna, I placed each step carefully so as not to tread on any viscera that might cause me to slip. All who approached got carved up by my chain saw.

The machine is built to fell trees of thick and hard wood. It weighs nearly eighteen pounds. The guide bar for the rotating chain is thirty inches long, which is longer than my arm. Frankly, it's all more than a girl should handle, but when I swing it, all that weight makes for tremendous power. It rips and tears through anything it meets, whether flesh, bone, or even an entire wall if I were to strike at one. It's as my American grandfather always said: in the end, victory goes to the one with the most power.

I was cutting my eighth opponent when the ninth slipped in the blood. As he fell toward me, I kicked his head back up, then lopped it off with my chain saw. The linoleum floor was super slick from all the gore, and those school slippers have hardly any grip. That's why I chose shoes with good traction.

Another boy said, "Chain saws are vulnerable in close quarters! Get in there!"

He was right, at least in immediate range. Chain saws aren't all blade, but require the bulk of a handle and a drive mechanism to function. In that way, they're probably weaker than spears or swords, and possibly even handguns. The second any of them grapples me, I'm finished. When I kicked my falling enemy's head, it was a split-second action to give myself distance; if whoever shouted had the insight to see that move for what it was, he deserved respect.

Four students, boys and girls alike, rushed me.

But I came from a line of chain saw wielders going back a hundred and forty years. No martial art lasts a century without addressing its weaknesses.

I locked the throttle into place and swung the chain saw over my upper arm, twirling the deadly machine tightly around my body like a pair of nunchucks. It's a dangerous technique, as the rapidly spinning teeth pass perilously close to the arteries in my neck. When I first started practicing the maneuver, it was of course with the chain saw switched off, but mistakes still resulted in shredded skin and blood everywhere.

The chain saw ran freely across my body in every which way. Over my shoulders, then across my back, then around my waist, roaring all the way. No other weapon can do the same. Only a chain saw, hurling aside anything it touches, can perform this, my chain saw dance. Against these pitiful sheep in school uniforms, the steel teeth carved up hands, sliced away shoulders, and scraped off faces. My foes scattered in little bits and pieces.

In a flash, I realized that I'd been prioritizing cutting down the girls before the boys. I wondered if it was out of jealousy. The thought brought me a wry smile, tightening my eyes behind their blood-misted glasses.

I don't want to carry dark thoughts about how that girl stole Takumi from me. Takumi isn't an object. He's his own person, and he chose her over me. If he were some mere object to be stolen, then his declaration of love for me would lose all value.

It's a painful truth, but the first boy I fell in love with had fallen in love with her, and not me. Our love ended in a fleeting moment. Nothing remains to be told in the story of my life but a tragic ending. Did I pick the wrong branching path somewhere along the way, or was this always my fate?

I will kill Takumi and I will die. I will bring an end to this story gone wrong; my chain saw will tear out the final scenes from the book titled *Fumio Kirisaki*. I have absolutely no intention of idling by, listlessly turning the remaining pages of a life without him.

I imagined him seeing me there with my chain saw, and I pictured him crying and throwing his arms around me, saying, *It isn't true It's all a misunderstanding You're imagining it I'm sure of it now Fumio I love you I love you more than anyone I love you so much I could die I love you more than anything in the world I'm sorry I hurt you I won't leave you again.*

But no ... Takumi would never be so false. I know that better than anyone. If I didn't, I never would have retrieved the dusty chain saw from the storeroom.

I've lost count of how many people I've killed now.

Takumi, Takumi, Takumi.

Each swing of my chain saw carries his name in refrain.

My back ached. My arms and shoulders were heavy. I felt like I'd killed half the school, down to the teachers who'd blundered by on their way to their classes. Reinforcements kept streaming in from the third floor, and even from classrooms on the second and first floors, all of them trying to keep me from Takumi. But why?

I was used to the smell of the blood and the noise of my motor now. The linoleum floor was a crimson sea, with blood leaking from corpses and oozing down the stairs. Limbs and gore were piled along the edges of the hall, and everything glistened in more shades of red than I ever thought could exist. Light caught the mountain of bodies, flickering across their wetness like an old, noisy TV screen. But none of this got to me. My hands were full with my enemies who yet lived.

I kept swinging.

Come tomorrow, the newspapers would report the exact number of victims. They'll all have articles about the girl from somewhere in Saitama Prefecture, who went to school with a chain saw and slaughtered her classmates before killing herself by removing her own head. Not that I'd be around to read them.

But if I stay calm and think about it rationally, I've probably not killed all that many. In all the excitement and stress, I likely overestimated my actions. If I'd truly murdered half of the students, then the riot police would have already rushed in with knockout gas.

I took out my stopwatch.

The LCD screen was cracked. The numbers so precious for

Takumi and me were gone. I pressed the buttons again and again, but the watch was dead. It must have happened when that guard dog tackled me.

Now I wasn't able to know how much time was left. I felt like our special time had been crushed under a bootheel, and it was an awful feeling.

But there's nothing to be done about it. I'm almost to him now. He can't be more than twenty yards away. Even if the police cars were to pull up to the school gate this very moment, and the cops came running as fast as they can, I'd still reach Takumi first.

Listen up, all of you, and get out of my way or I'll cut you down.

Chain saw in hand, I proceeded down the hall.

Ahead of me stood only one girl.

My best friend, Kaoruko Odagiri.

6.

Kaoruko stood in the middle of the hallway, resting her backside (not large or small but ladylike, as is the rest of her) on the edge of a student desk. The elegant fall of her skirt made the plain desk seem an antique brought over from an old European castle. Her long, delicate hair gently billowed in the cool morning breeze blowing in through an open window.

Meanwhile, my uniform was covered in blood. My once navy skirt was soaked to a deep purple. My hair was caked stiff, and my bangs stuck to my forehead as if glued there. Dangling from my reddened arms was a chain saw encrusted with ichor and flesh and fatty bits.

Whatever she may have thought of me now, I still considered her my friend. I didn't care if the feeling wasn't mutual. Even though a fight split us apart, she was still the first person who got a shy girl like me to open up. We still shared the bond from our previous lives. Even now, she was important to me.

I couldn't tell if she knew how I felt. She looked at me as if nothing ever happened between us. Maybe she intended to talk me into stopping this senseless slaughter. No matter how much I were to wash my hands now, the stench of blood would never come clean. But Kaoruko wasn't like other people. Maybe she believed I could still redeem myself.

I didn't want to take her life. I didn't want to include her among the countless bodies piled in my wake.

The world diverged into two parts centered on me in this moment.

Ahead of me waited the end of the road.

Behind me lay a sea of blood.

I hoped Kaoruko would remain in the classroom until I'd reached Takumi. If she'd never strayed from the safety I'd intended for her, she wouldn't have to die.

I put the brake to the chain saw for the first time since this started, then I returned the control lever to neutral. The machine rumbled in protest as the chain stopped its rotation.

I could hear the noise of the city coming to life outside the open window. Was that a sparrow singing, or maybe a bulbul? A truck slowly passed the school grounds, its loudspeaker advertising recycling services for electronics and appliances. I clenched and unclenched my fingers to work out the stiffness. I could hear my knuckles creak.

Then Kaoruko said, "That all was a little over the top, don't you think?"

I nodded.

"You'll have to wash your hair more than once or twice to get all that out," she said. "Dried blood is nasty stuff, so you should hurry up and get a shower. You have such nice hair—I wish you'd take better care of it."

"Who gives a damn about my hair?"

"I don't know why you keep talking like that when you're so cute. It's a bad habit."

"I do it because unlike you, Kaoruko, I'm not cute," I said.

She puffs out her cheeks in mock irritation. "People stopped calling me cute after grade school. Ever since I sprung up like a bamboo tree, even my family stopped saying that."

Not knowing what to say to that, I waited for her to continue.

"The taller I grow, the harder everything gets." Kaoruko grinned, and said, "I wish we could add our heights together and each take half."

I tightened my fist around the chain saw's handle, the machine vibrating with a low rumble, and forced out the words "Move, Kaoruko."

"You know," she said, "I always thought that when a soul reincarnates, it's only imprinted with its previous bonds. But now I'm thinking I was wrong. Even in this life, you're still an expert warrior. I never expected that."

"Step aside."

"I wonder if I'd be a good fighter too. I know that when we got put on the same volleyball team, we got trounced. I never imagined you were hiding such talent."

"Get out of my way. I'm begging you, please!"

A nasty smile came to her well-bred countenance. "Now, now, now. Don't tell me you're tired of sharing our bond."

"N-no, it's not like that."

Then Kaoruko said, "You've made it all this way, but I'm sorry to tell you that Takumi isn't here."

"You lie!"

"He went down the emergency stairs with several of the others. I stayed behind to tell you."

I stared into her eyes. Unwavering, they stared back at me.

There had always been only one rule between us.

Kaoruko never told me a lie, no matter how inconsequential. In exchange, I always believed what she said, no matter how preposterous. When we formed what was for both of us our first friendship, that was the one and only rule we resolved.

I believed her story about the mysterious creature that appeared in the Ayase River. I believed her story about the strange caped figure who appeared in the girl's restroom. I even believed her about the underground dwellers who ride white alligators.

But then I broke our rule. Rather than believe Kaoruko when she told me that aliens were controlling Takumi, I chose to face off against the new girl. And here we are now, with Kaoruko telling me such a blatant lie.

I made perfectly sure that those metal escape doors couldn't open without destroying the hinges first. I could see the door directly behind Kaoruko, and it was closed tight and entirely unharmed.

So this is what heartbreak feels like, to be utterly gutted. As I stood there covered in blood, the cold breeze passed straight through me.

This too must be fate. Must those who chose the path of Asura inevitably war against their friends? But now I understood that I would never reach Takumi's side without climbing over my best and only friend's corpse. Her luck ran out when she became friends with a girl like me. The only way to honor our friendship was to follow her to the depths of hell.

I squeezed the throttle. The control switch automatically flipped from neutral to idle. Reading my thoughts, the chain saw eagerly roused, raising a battle cry that rattled the heavy window glass.

"I'll take care of everything," Kaoruko said. "It'll all work out. I can get you and Takumi back together again—"

I released the brake and swung the chain saw.

Her neck was as slender as the rest of her, and the blades, whirling at high speed, removed her head with ease. I didn't even feel the difference between the teeth passing through her flesh and it grinding through her bones. A deep sadness filled me as I thought of how the chain saw roared as it pushed to grind that committee busybody's attack dog judoka into two parts, and yet it sliced through my dear, dear friend in an instant.

My best friend's blood geysered from her neck and showered my body.

"Kaoruko, I'm ..." I said, but I held the rest back. I wasn't sure if I should be directing the apology to her severed head or the rest of her fallen body.

But no. I won't apologize. I decided I would crush any who stand in my way, whether it's my best friend or even my parents. To weaken my resolve would disrespect everyone I've killed.

When I turned on my chain saw, whatever human there was in me switched off. Now I was a walking corpse. I will kill Takumi, and I will die. It is that sole purpose that moves this zombie.

The chain saw is all of me; it is my whole existence. My chain saw is, therefore I am. If each person is born with a single purpose, then mine is to kill.

But I make myself one promise.

If, as Kaoruko told me, another life awaits me, then I will be her friend once more, and I'll strive not to choose the wrong path again.

7.

The classroom was nearly empty. The desks and chairs were put away as if for the big cleaning day at the end of the school year. The forty students of the class were gone. Maybe I'd already killed them all.

In the center of this cavernous space sat a single chair at a single desk, and in that chair was Takumi. The transfer girl stood behind him, cradling her arms around his neck, just like she had been when I went to bring him his bento box lunch.

Takumi had his notebook open, and was jotting down notes

from a blank chalkboard. My chain saw's clamor was keeping cats on the other side of the schoolyard from napping, but Takumi didn't seem to notice the sound.

My hands tightened around the grip until my fingers turned white. I stepped into the room.

Raising my voice above the machine roar, I said, "Get away from him."

"And if I do, what then?" she said.

"I'll kill Takumi."

"And if I don't?"

"I'll kill you."

The girl gave me an exasperated shrug. "I never expected to encounter such resistance to altering the delicate state of this start-ing condition. This is the price I pay for underestimating you as a mere native of an undeveloped planet."

"I don't know what you're talking about," I said.

"We weren't supposed to be enemies, you and I. I'm protecting your beloved man from assassins. But by being constantly at his side, you'd get in my way."

"Are you moving, or aren't you? Choose."

I readied my chain saw, holding it level. The teeth rotated around the guide bar as rapidly as my heart was beating.

"Fine," she said, her expression mocking me. It's that same look from before, the one for the pitiful sewer rat that had come crawl-ing out from a drainpipe to find itself on a subway platform. Blood rushed hotly up the base of my neck.

"Go on," she said. "Do it if you can."

She put her hands on Takumi's waist, stood up, and thrust him at my chain saw. It happened in a flash. Propelled by her force, he staggered limply toward the blades. I looked to the steel teeth as they raced down the guide bar at forty-five miles per hour, their metal flashing as they caught the light, and I looked to Takumi's face and its sleepwalker's expression, and …

I can kill him right now.

Reflexively, I pulled back the chain saw.

The sharp metal grazed his shirt and left a tiny scratch in his skin. Dark red blood splashed from the tear. Most of it hit the linoleum floor, but a single drop landed on my clothing. This one single drop seemed more tragic than the sea of the stuff I'd already spilled. But with my uniform thoroughly soaked red, I couldn't determine where his went, and something about that was utterly heartbreaking.

Takumi passed me and fell limply to the floor.

My hands trembled. I'd come all this way only to hesitate in killing him. After piling up all those dead bodies, I flinched at adding just one more. It was my purpose, my only purpose, that led me here, but I didn't do it. How weak does that make me?

I looked down at Takumi and asked, "Don't you have anything to say?"

He seemed a little confused. Lying on his side, he looked around the room, then finally up at me and my chain saw.

"I don't really know what's going on," he said, "but if it's your choice to kill me, that's good enough for me."

There was trust in his eyes. Not fright or dread, nor a hint of despair. He looked at me with unwavering trust.

And now, in this moment, I knew.

I couldn't kill him.

I could carve up every human being on the face of this earth, but not Takumi. I can't take his life. Takumi, my love, my love, I want you to live forever, even if I'm gone, even if you don't love me, even if you give that smile to another woman.

My head drooped.

"I'm sorry," I said, the words coming out on their own.

And I told myself I wouldn't apologize. There's something terribly wrong about refusing to apologize to the people I kill, and apologizing to the one I let live. But I really was sorry. If Takumi had never met me, he might have had a happy life, found a wife with perfect teeth, and been surrounded by disgustingly happy and cute children.

Because of me, his life was strewn with corpses. And yet I still couldn't kill him. I'd caused all this mayhem only to abandon him in the absolute worst place and in the absolute worst way.

And she was just standing there with that calculated smile, watching us.

She knew. She knew I couldn't kill Takumi. She pushed Takumi at me fully aware that I would pull back the chain saw. Tears streaming, I readied my weapon and said to her, "You, I'll kill."

I didn't care how much he'd hate me for it. I could never forgive a girl who would push him into a chain saw. A girl like that had no right to love him.

She said, "I'd much rather you were the one to die."

Takami called my name, but I told him to stay back.

"Die!" the girl cried, rushing toward me.

I swung my chain saw up.

Sparks flew, accompanied by a harsh metallic noise, like train wheels screeching against the tracks during an emergency stop. The girl deflected my chain saw with something like a metal pipe. I didn't know where in that school uniform she had been hiding it, but I guess the kind of girl it takes to draw Takumi's attention would be full of surprises.

Our weapons clashed two times, then a third. She seemed to know how to fight. Her footwork and stance were masterful.

But the advantage remained mine. No weapon exists on this earth superior to the chain saw. Its stainless steel teeth shred anything at the slightest touch. My opponent had to put force behind every thrust and slash, but all I had to do was make contact. A chain saw in skilled hands will overpower anything else in a close fight.

If she had really wanted to kill me, she should have blown up the entire school with a missile. She wouldn't even need to be an alien or anything so wild to pull it off. The American and Japanese militaries have missiles; even terrorists have them. There are things of this world that she could use to take me down.

At least that way, Takumi and I would have died together. But no, she had to do it this way, and now she was going to regret it.

I pressed her with blows from above, from the side, from below, and followed with a flip. I swung the chain saw up in an arc and again we clashed among the flying sparks. Each time we met, I pushed her back a little farther.

I nearly had her cornered against the wall.

"With this body," she said, "our abilities are too mismatched."

"What are you going to do about it?"

"I'll become you. If I had done that at the beginning, there wouldn't have been any trouble. Not with you, and not with him."

Her shape began to change.

Her chest, rather large for high school, shrank, and her arms and legs shortened. Her spotless uniform became as blood-soaked as mine. Within ten seconds, this girl was a perfect replica of one Fumio Kirisaki, her too-pale ink-wash eyes staring back at me.

I froze in astonishment as the girl with my face extended her hand to me. Her fingertips caught the temples of my glasses, and she flung the bloodied things to the floor, where Takumi picked them up. The girl reached into some other space and retrieved a chain saw identical to mine.

Takumi looked up at us.

But we were both covered in blood, we both had the same face, and we both were sans glasses. Takumi didn't seem to know to which of us he should return the pair.

The me who wasn't me pulled on the starter rope and brought her chain saw to life, performing the operation with a skilled hand. Our two metal beasts roared. The classroom floor shuddered under the overwhelming noise.

The imposter said, "Now you die," and swung her chain saw.

I immediately dodged back.

A battle between chain saw duelists is unlike any other. Whenever the guide bar's tip strikes or catches on something solid, the chain saw's force causes a kickback, suddenly turning the sharp cutting blades against their wielder. On the other hand, if the guide bar is struck from below, the chain saw kicks forward. The high-speed metal teeth are the chain saw's greatest strength and simultaneously its greatest weakness; the key to victory lies in making contact where you expect to and where your opponent does not, thereby sending her off balance.

We swung our chain saws, pulling back the strikes just before the blades met. A single careless connection equals defeat. A single, fleeting lapse of concentration will not be pardoned.

Clang. Clang.

Sparks flew.

Her technique was expert. She was as good as me—or rather, exactly the same. She feinted from the upper right, only to switch into a horizontal spinning strike. It's a move I came up with on my own. She's not only a copy of my outer appearance, but everything inside as well.

Our skills were matched. Our bodies, matched. Our chain saws, matched. But I'd come from fighting my way through the school in a bloody battle. I'm merely a teenager, and I was at the limits of my stamina. The eighteen pounds of my chain saw grew heavy. My muscles ached and protested, and every joint in my body creaked. My lungs thirsted for oxygen, and my heart was about to explode.

But the enemy I faced was as fresh as a boxer who's just heard the opening bell.

Her attacks began to surpass mine. My tired muscles responded just a little more slowly, and she steadily pressed me into an increasingly disadvantageous position. My feet moved ever backward, never forward. Once she got me against the wall, I'd be finished. I no longer had the strength to repel a fatal blow.

Desperately my mind worked.

She was different than me. She must be.

She had my power and my knowledge, but what did I have that she didn't?

And in that moment, I saw Takumi.

Takumi stood, unmoving, in the same place he had fallen. The gash in his arm was painful to see. Surely by now he'd realized this girl's true nature. She was no transfer student or anything like that, but something unknown. A thing that stole my body. But he wouldn't be able to tell which was the real me by looks alone.

She was using Takumi, and nothing more. But I trusted in him. She and I both needed him, but I loved him. I could accept death if it were him killing me and not her.

An idea came to me.

I edged away from her, then broke into a sprint, putting Takumi between us. She and I circled clockwise around him. But this clock had no hour and minute hands; our chain saws were exactly the same length.

"Takumi!" I shouted, and he turned to me. "Don't move a single step."

If he dodged, I would lose.

I shifted from my circling pattern and ran toward her in a straight line. Takumi was between us. I saw the trust in his eyes. I swung the chain saw in an arc that would cut him clear in two, from between his legs straight up to the top of his head. From here, she couldn't see my chain saw. The metal teeth growled, almost upon Takumi now.

She was already reacting, moving to intercept my attack. As I came around Takumi's left, her weapon bore down at me, dead on target. With my heavy chain saw, I could never hope to dodge. The gleaming blades passed over my right arm, aiming to knock my weapon aside before she would deliver the killing blow.

But my chain saw wasn't there. Her blades made a jingling sound as they caught the fabric of my collar.

I appeared,

from Takumi's left,

and my chain saw appeared,

from Takumi's right,

coming for her.

I slid my chain saw along Takumi's body. The metal beast, drooling oil, pivoted around him in a mad dash to exactly where I wanted it to be.

Takumi didn't move, and nothing ever made me happier. He didn't flinch from those deadly blades. Had he moved one iota, the chain saw could have flown anywhere.

I extended my right arm. I didn't have to look where to reach. The chain saw's grip landed in my hand. Welcome home.

Her face distorted in astonishment. Mine was smirking.

"Wait!" she cried. "You've got it all wro—"

Too late.

Die.

The rotating blades dug into skin the same as my own. The hooklike teeth spaced every three-eighths of an inch tore her clothes, shredded her skin, carved her flesh, shattered her bones, drove all the way through and split her in two. Her face, identical to mine, stared back at me, her mouth in the shape of a scream and her eyes bulging.

That's right, I thought. You're the only person I could never forgive.

Before she fell, I pivoted my chain saw and matched the vertical cut with a horizontal one, splitting her into four pieces. The two top parts went flying, creating a starburst organ splatter on the wall. Her two legs wobbled, then fell in different directions. Amid the thick, bloody mist, I took in a deep breath and blacked out.

8.

I woke up on the floor. Faces I recognize were looking down at me with concern. I scanned the crowd for Takumi, but he was not among them.

So this is Hell, my mind told me through an exhausted haze. I wasn't sure why all the classmates I'd killed were down here with me, but they each must have done something that sent them to hell. As long as Takumi hadn't been brought here with me, I didn't care if I was dropped into a pool of blood or thrown onto a mountain of thorns.

"Are you all right?" asked the teacher whose head I had lopped off first.

For a moment, I didn't know what to say, but then I answered, "Yes."

"Well done. We all owe you."

He thanked me? Had I heard him wrong? Not, "You killed me, you piece of shit," but, "Well done?" I suppose I did well by some measure, but those aren't words that should be coming from a teacher I brutally murdered. What's going on here?

I sat up and found that I was in the classroom. The desks were all cleared away, as they were when I killed the girl who had appropriated my body, and my classmates were all standing around.

I asked, "What happened to Takumi?"

One student pointed to a hole in the wall that looked like it had been punched out with a cookie cutter.

The hole offered a dazzlingly bright view of the outside. The punched-out concrete rested at an incline, along which blood droplets formed a dotted trail down toward the schoolyard's center.

In the yard was a deep impression left where some massive object must have been only moments ago. I looked to the sky, and just barely caught a glimmer of light. In the blink of an eye, the thing vanished, not even leaving a contrail behind.

I touched my hands together. There was no blood on my skin. I felt around my face next. My hair was where I had left it after my morning routine. Even my bangs were in place, although I might have missed a few kinks from when I woke up. My blouse was clean and white, but my glasses were gone.

The only spot on my white top was a single red speck.

Somehow I knew it was Takumi's blood. It was the first real, actual blood absorbed by the cloth.

Slowly, I figured out what had happened. This wasn't hell. It was the real world. The classmates I thought I'd killed were really alive, and Takumi was really gone.

Did that mean that the battles were all an illusion?

Were they all delusions of a jilted mind?

Was Takumi fleeing somewhere right now on his own two legs, while my classmates desperately attempted to pacify the deranged girl who ran into school with a chain saw?

I charged in fueled by a once-in-a-lifetime conviction, slaughtered my classmates, and confirmed Takumi's love for me … but in the end, could it all have been fantasy?

I can't deny the possibility. Along the way, I saw many extraordinary things. I wish I could have stated with confidence that my mind was in perfect health, but I couldn't. Even that hole in the wall could have been the product of a deranged mind and a chain saw.

My eyes searched for Kaoruko. She'd have the answers I need. She wouldn't lie to me. She has always told me the truth, with every single word an honest one. That included what she said about Takumi. I don't think that will have changed.

But when I found her, she said, "I'm sorry. I don't know."

She told me that her memory of the past few days was a jumble. She, along with the other teachers and students, had been trapped in a mysterious space in the empty adjacent classroom ever since that transfer student came.

I had killed their doppelgängers, which is why all the corpses vanished. After losing to me, the girl made a change of plans and fled, taking Takumi.

When I admitted to Kaoruko that I had killed her, she said, "That's okay. I don't mind it from you."

Without another word, I stood and picked up my chain saw from the floor beside me. The eighteen pounds of machine weighed heavily on my exhausted muscles.

All Kaoruko asked was: "Are you going?"

I nod.

She's my best friend. My companion from another incarnation. With my chain saw, I killed something that seemed to be her, and yet she still cares for me. I treasured her friendship like none other. I sensed that she'd be with me in the next life too, where she'll find me alone and call me her friend.

But she was not Takumi.

She was not the one I love.

I didn't give a damn about any galactic war or frontier butterflies or whatever. It's not that I didn't believe what Kaoruko told me. I just didn't care. I didn't care about any of it. This could all be an illusion as far as I was concerned. None of it had anything to do with Takumi and me.

What do I care if some missile is screaming its way toward ten billion people from somewhere out in space, or if the Earth and humankind are on the brink of disaster? If they're going to die out they can go ahead and do it. A world without Takumi at my side is a world not worth existing. I'd rather, much rather, have some planet destroyer come flying from the edge of the universe to blow him and me into smithereens. At least that way I'd be saved the trouble of carving my path through any and all who would try to keep me from him.

With the chain saw my grandfather gave me, I'd cut through a line no student, no girl, and no human should ever cross. Even if everything I'd done was an illusion, I can't take my actions back. I can't deceive myself.

It's time for me to step outside. My journey begins not from the front entrance with its proper door, but through a hole cut in the wall. I will follow my missing Takumi anywhere, no matter how far.

The sea of blood awaits me. I will bring him back, or I will die trying. A game of chicken without a target in sight awaits me, but my hand is already pulling at the starter rope.

The only reality for me is my solid, hefty chain saw.

Squeezing the grip tight, I take my first, firm footstep toward whatever world holds my beloved Takumi.

CONTRIBUTORS

RAY BANKS is the author of ten novels, including the Cal Innes quartet and, most recently, *Angels of the North*. He lives in Edinburgh and online at www.thesaturdayboy.com.

LIBBY CUDMORE is the author of *The Big Rewind*. Her short stories have appeared in *The Big Click, Stoneslide Corrective, Big Lucks,* and *PANK.* She blogs at www.libbycudmore.com, and tweets frequently @libbycudmore.

BRIAN EVENSON is the author of a dozen books of fiction, most recently the story collection *Windeye* and the novel *Immobility*, both of which were finalists for the Shirley Jackson Award. His novel *Last Days* won the American Library Association's award for Best Horror Novel of 2009. His novel *The Open Curtain* was a finalist for an Edgar Allan Poe Award and an International Horror Guild Award. Other books include *The Wavering Knife* (IHG Award for best story collection), *Dark Property,* and *Altmann's Tongue.* His work has been translated into French, Italian, Spanish, Japanese and Slovenian. He lives in Valencia, California, where he teaches at CalArts.

JYOUJI HAYASHI was born in Hokkaido in 1962. After working as a clinical laboratory technician, he debuted as a writer in 1995 with his cowritten *Dai Nihon Teikoku Oushu Dengeki Sakusen.* His popularity grew with the *Shonetsu no Hatou* series and the *Heitai Gensui Oushu Senki* series—both military fiction backed by real historical perspectives. Beginning in 2000, he consecutively released *Kioku Osen, Shinryakusha no Heiwa,* and *Ankoku Taiyo no Mezame,* stories that combine scientific speculation and sociological investigations. He continues to write and act as a flag bearer for a new generation of hard SF. The first book of his science fiction AADD series, *Ouroboros Wave,* was translated into English by Haikasoru in 2010.

Born in Pasadena, California, **NAOMI HIRAHARA** is an award-winning author of two mystery series. The third in her Mas Arai mysteries, *Snakeskin Shamisen,* won the Edgar Award for Best Paperback Original in 2007. *Murder on Bamboo Lane,* the first in her Officer Ellie Rush series, received the T. Jefferson Parker Mystery Award in 2014. Her books have been published in Japanese, Korean and French. A former editor of *The Rafu Shimpo* newspaper in Los Angeles, she has written nonfiction books and novels for middle-grade readers. Her short stories have also been featured in *Los Angeles Noir* and *Los Angeles Noir: The Classics.* She earned her bachelor's degree from Stanford University in international relations and attended the Inter-University Center for Japanese Language Studies in Tokyo.

YUMEAKI HIRAYAMA is Japanese mystery and horror author. He debuted as a novelist with the psychological thriller *Sinker—Shizumu mono* in 1996. In 2006 he won the Mystery Writers of Japan Award for short fiction with "Monologue of a Universal Transverse Mercator Projection," and his collection of the same title took the first place in the 2007 *Kono mystery ga sugoi* (This Mystery is Great) ranking. His other works include *Diner* and *Hitogoto* (Somebody Else's Problem).

KAORI FUJINO was born and resides in Kyoto. She won the Bungakukai Prize for New Writers with "Iyashii tori" ("A Greedy Bird") in 2006 and published her first short story collection of the same title in 2008. Her 2009 short story "Ikenie" ("Sacrifice") was a finalist for Akutagawa Prize; she took home the Akutagawa for her novella "Tsume to mé" (Nails and Eyes) in 2013. Her recent collections include *Ohanashi shiteko chan* and *A Final Girl.*

VIOLET LEVOIT is the author of *I Am Genghis Cum* and *I'll Fuck Anything That Moves and Stephen Hawking,* both of Fungasm Press. She is also a film writer whose reviews and essays have appeared in the *Baltimore City Paper,* PressPlay.com, TurnerClassicMovies.com,

Bright Lights Film Journal, FilmThreat.com and AllMovie.com, as well as the anthology *Defining Moments in Movies* (Cassell Illustrated).

YUSUKE MIYAUCHI was born in Tokyo in 1979, and grew up in New York from childhood till the age of twelve. In 2010, he won the Sogen SF Short Story Award with his debut fiction "Banjo no yoru" ("Dark Beyond the Weiqi"). His first collection, of the same title, was nominated to the Naoki Prize and won Japan SF Taisho Award in 2012. His second collection, *Johannesburg no tenshi tachi* (City in Plague Time), was also nominated for the Naoki in 2013; he took home another Japan SF Taisho Award (special award) in 2013. In 2015, he published his first full-length novel, *Exodus shokougun* (Exodus Syndrome).

S.J. ROZAN has won multiple awards, including the Edgar, Shamus, Anthony, Nero, Macavity, and Japanese Maltese Falcon. She's published thirteen books and fifty short stories under her own name and two novels with Carlos Dews as the writing team of Sam Cabot. S.J. was born in the Bronx and lives in lower Manhattan. Her newest book is Sam Cabot's *Skin of the Wolf*.

HIROSHI SAKURAZAKA was born in 1970 in Tokyo. After a career in information technology, he published his first novel, *Modern Magic Made Simple*. The first novel was quite successful and is now an ongoing series of seven volumes. It has also been adapted as a manga, in 2008, and as a televised anime series in 2009. He published *All You Need Is Kill* in 2004, earning a Seiun Award nomination for best science fiction novel, and forming the basis for the international box office smash *Edge of Tomorrow*. His 2004 short story "The Saitama Chain Saw Massacre" won the 16th *SF Magazine* Reader's Award. His other novels include *Characters* (co-written with Hiroki Azuma) and *Slum Online*, released in English in 2010 by Haikasoru. Sakurazaka's short fiction has also appeared in the English-language anthology *Press Start to Play*.

SETSUKO SHINODA is one of most popular cross-genre fiction authors in Japan. Her work includes science fiction, horror, mystery, and literary fantasy. Since her debut in 1990, she has published over fifty books and won many important literary awards such as the Yamamoto Shugoro Prize for *Gosaintan: Kamino za* (Gosaintan: Seat of the Gods), the Naoki Prize for *Onna tachi no Jihado* (Women's Jihad) and the Shibata Renzabro Award for *Kaso Girei* (False Rites). Her work is acclaimed for its focus on cotemporary social issues and rigorous research. Her recent works include *Black Box* and *Indo-Crystal*.

JEFF SOMERS began writing by court order as an attempt to steer his creative impulses away from engineering genetic grotesqueries. His feeble memory makes every day a joyous adventure of discovery and adventure even as it destroys personal relationships, and his weakness for adorable furry creatures leaves him with many cats. He has published nine novels, including the Avery Cates series of science fiction novels, the darkly hilarious crime novel *Chum,* and most recently a tale of blood magic and short cons, *We Are Not Good People*. He has published over thirty short stories, including "Ringing the Changes," which was included in *Best American Mystery Stories 2006*, and "Sift, Almost Invisible, Through," which appeared in the anthology *Crimes by Moonlight* edited by Charlaine Harris. He has also published the zine *The Inner Swine* since 1995, but the less said about that, the better. He lives in Hoboken with his wife, The Duchess, and their cats. He considers pants to always be optional.

GENEVIEVE VALENTINE is the author of *Mechanique: A Tale of the Circus Tresaulti*, *The Girls at the Kingfisher Club*, *Dream Houses*, and *Persona*. Her short fiction has appeared in *Clarkesworld*, *Strange Horizons*, *Journal of Mythic Arts*, and others, and the anthologies *Federations*, *Teeth*, *Fearsome Magics*, and more; several have appeared in Best of the Year anthologies. Her nonfiction and reviews can be found at NPR.org, AV Club, *The Dissolve*, and *The New York Times*. She's currently the writer of DC's *Catwoman*.

CARRIE VAUGHN is the author of the *New York Times* best-selling series of novels about a werewolf named Kitty, the fourteenth installment of which is *Kitty Saves the World*. She's written several other contemporary fantasy and young adult novels, as well as upwards of eighty short stories. She's a contributor to the Wild Cards series of shared-world superhero books edited by George R. R. Martin and a graduate of the Odyssey Fantasy Writing Workshop. An Air Force brat, she survived her nomadic childhood and managed to put down roots in Boulder, Colorado. Visit her at www. carrievaughn.com.

CHET WILLIAMSON has written in the fields of horror, science fiction, and suspense since 1981. Among his many novels are *Second Chance, Hunters, Defenders of the Faith, Ash Wednesday, Reign,* and *Dreamthorp. The Night Listener and Others, A Little Blue Book of Bibliomancy* (both story collections), and *Psycho: Sanitarium,* an authorized sequel to Robert Bloch's *Psycho*, appeared in 2016. Over a hundred of his short stories have appeared in such magazines as *The New Yorker, Playboy, Esquire, The Magazine of Fantasy and Science Fiction,* and many other magazines and anthologies. He has won the International Horror Guild Award, and has been shortlisted twice for the World Fantasy Award, six times for the Bram Stoker Award, and once for the Edgar Award. A stage and film actor (his most recent appearance is in Joe R. Lansdale's film *Christmas with the Dead*), he has recorded over forty unabridged audiobooks, both of his own work and that of many other writers. Follow him on Twitter @chetwill or at www.chetwilliamson.com.

HAIKASORU
THE FUTURE IS JAPANESE

GREAT ANTHOLOGIES FEATURING SHORT WORK FROM AND ABOUT JAPAN

THE FUTURE IS JAPANESE

A web browser that threatens to conquer the world. The longest, loneliest railroad on Earth. A North Korean nuke hitting Tokyo, a hollow asteroid full of automated rice paddies, and a specialist in breaking up "virtual" marriages. And yes, giant robots. These thirteen stories from and about the Land of the Rising Sun run the gamut from fantasy to cyberpunk, and will leave you knowing that the future is Japanese. Featuring the Hugo Award-winning short story "Mono No Aware" by Ken Liu!

Pat Cadigan	David Moles	Rachel Swirsky
Toh EnJoe	Issui Ogawa	TOBI Hirotaka
Project Itoh	Felicity Savage	Catherynne M. Valente
Hideyuki Kikuchi	Ekaterina Sedia	
Ken Liu	Bruce Sterling	

THE BATTLE ROYALE SLAM BOOK

Koushun Takami's *Battle Royale* is an international best seller, the basis of the cult film, and the inspiration for a popular manga. And fifteen years after its initial release, *Battle Royale* remains a controversial pop culture phenomenon.

Join *New York Times* best-selling author John Skipp, *Batman* screenwriter Sam Hamm, Philip K. Dick Award-winning novelist Toh EnJoe, and an array of writers, scholars, and fans in discussing girl power, firepower, professional wrestling, bad movies, the survival chances of Hollywood's leading teen icons in a battle royale, and so much more!

PHANTASM JAPAN

The secret history of the most famous secret agent in the world. A bunny costume that reveals the truth in our souls. The unsettling notion that Japan itself may be a dream. The tastiest meal you'll never have, a fedora-wearing neckbeard's deadly date with a yokai, and the worst work shift anyone—human or not—has ever lived through. Welcome to *Phantasm Japan*.

Nadia Bulkin	Alex Dally MacFarlane	Benjanun
Gary A. Braunbeck	James A. Moore	Sriduangkaew
Quentin S. Crisp	Zachary Mason	Seia Tanabe
Project Itoh	Miyuki Miyabe	Joseph Tomaras
Yusaku Kitano	Lauren Naturale	Dempow Torishima
Jacqueline Koyanagi	Tim Pratt	Sayuri Ueda

VISIT US AT WWW.HAIKASORU.COM